P9-DDZ-208

FEMLANDIA

FEMLANDIA

CHRISTINA DALCHER

THORNDIKE PRESS
A part of Gale, a Cengage Company

This is a work of fiction. Names, characters, places, and incidents either are the product of the author's imagination or are used fictitiously, and any resemblance to actual persons, living or dead, business establishments, events, or locales is entirely coincidental.

Thorndike Press® Large Print Core.
The text of this Large Print edition is unabridged.
Other aspects of the book may vary from the original edition.
Set in 16 pt. Plantin.

LIBRARY OF CONGRESS CIP DATA ON FILE.
CATALOGUING IN PUBLICATION FOR THIS BOOK
IS AVAILABLE FROM THE LIBRARY OF CONGRESS.

ISBN-13: 978-1-4328-9214-2 (hardcover alk. paper)

Published in 2021 by arrangement with Berkley, an imprint of Penguin Publishing Group, a division of Penguin Random House LLC.

Printed in Mexico
Print Number: 01 Print Year: 2022

To Bruce and Luis and
Alfred and Pedro . . .
and all the men I've loved before.

i'm not a cute misandrist. i don't have a fridge magnet that says, "boys are stupid, throw rocks at them." my loathing cannot be contained by a fridge magnet.

— Samantha Allen

You could see the little girls, fat with complacency and conceit while the little boys sat there crumpled, apologising for their existence, thinking this was going to be the pattern of their lives.

— Doris Lessing

All movements go too far.

— Bertrand Russell

#KillAllMen

— Twitter

WOMYN-ORIENTED
SELF-SUFFICIENT
COOPERATIVE
SAFE
ACCEPTING
NATURAL
FREE

This is the Femlandia creed.

Established in the last century by notable feminist Win Somers, our communities are havens for sisters looking for something different. A world without men. A world without worry. A world where womyn live together in peace and solitude.

If our world sounds like utopia, consider joining us. We will welcome you with open arms.

Yours in sisterhood,
Jennifer Jones
Cofounder

ONE

Two men and a truck are all it takes to finish us. The last of our furniture disappears out the front door and into the dark cavern of the bailiff's trailer. It's my bed, the one I shared with Nick for almost twenty years, a queen-sized mattress now in the hands of two burly men with tattoos and ponytails. They curse for the fifth time on this early-May morning and push the pillow-topped Tempur-Pedic slab into the last remaining space while Emma and I watch from the porch.

Mattresses are so stable when they're horizontal, much less so when you tip them on end. They flop and bend; they want to curl in on themselves. Maybe that's a metaphor I should remember. Maybe mattresses are like marriages. Or husbands.

Emma shudders as she watches the truck's rear doors slam shut, severing us from everything we own. "It's really gone, isn't it?" she says. I don't know whether she's talking about our stuff, the house, or the world outside. In any case, she's right. Sixteen years old is old enough to know.

"Yeah. All gone to shit." I pull her close and sip the last of my instant coffee, cold now. No microwave to heat it up. I could probably put the mug in the oven. By some miracle, the gas is still on, but I don't know whether it will be tomorrow.

No money changes hands before the men drive off. This move isn't on me; it's on the bank. Or the IRS. Or the credit card companies. Anyway on someone, somewhere, who still has a pot to piss in.

They even took our kitchen pots and pans, a full set of All-Clad stainless. "Restaurant quality," Nick had said when he brought the box home on our last anniversary. "Nothing but the best for my girl." One of the moving men hefted a paella pan and made a comment when he thought I couldn't hear. The boxes with the All-Clad went into the truck's cab.

We should hit the road soon, Emma and I, to get a start before the crowds turn our local Safeway into a kind of organized human zoo. If the past two weeks are anything to go by, the lines will already stretch a block by noon. The pushing and shoving and crying of *I was here first* will have started by eight in the morning. While I get two backpacks from the hall closet, I run through a list of where we might head next.

The front seat of my Mazda roadster would have been all right, uncomfortable as it sounds. Cramped and sticky, but all right. Someone came for it a week ago, minutes after our mobile phones made their last calls and texts. So the car won't do. With gas at twenty bucks a gallon — and that was last week when the pumps were still flowing — the Mazda wasn't really a car anymore, only a couple of leather seats on wheels, a static jumble of metal and wires that wasn't going anywhere. It was a car in name but not in function, like a clock with all the right parts that no longer tells time. Which is fine, I guess, since I have no idea where there is to go.

One of those last calls I made was to our local YMCA. We'd been members since Emma was born so she could use the pool. Sixteen years of seventy-five dollars a month should have been worth something — a cot or a yoga mat in the corner of the Pilates room. Use of the showers and towels, the same ones Beatrice, the massage therapist, used to drape carefully over my limbs when she worked on me.

Nobody answered the Y's phone, so I tried Emma's high school. Then the local shelter. Then the zoo as a last resort.

The zoo.

It sounds worse than it is. There were a few rooms there, emergency pit stops for veterinarians who needed to monitor the primate house. They had beds and bathrooms and functional kitchenettes. And that holy of holies — air-conditioning.

Again, no answer.

Robert picked up on his cell, though. He sounded tired when he told me they were down to a skeleton operation, enough to oversee the animal transfers to another state before the feed ran out and the prize fauna resorted to cannibalism.

"How's Bunny?" I asked.

"He's okay. All the primates are confused but okay. Look, Miranda, I'm up to my ears here in paperwork."

At least you still have a job, I thought.

"Any chance I can have one of the spare rooms next week? Just for a few nights. They're coming for the furniture on Wednesday." I hated the desperation in my voice. I hated it more because I already knew the answer.

"Miranda, we might not be here next week."

And he was right. The zoos, like the schools and the YMCAs and the shelters and everything else that depended on public funding, were on what the bastards in Washington were calling "temporary hiatus." They still are.

This isn't the way I expected to spend my forty-first birthday, wondering what Emma and I will do from one day to the next, coming inches closer to painting a sign that says *Will work for food.*

When I think of last year, of Nick bringing me breakfast in bed and showering me with two dozen yellow roses, I die a little on the inside. The flowers were a teaser; my real present wasn't the roses or the new KitchenAid stand mixer in ruby red or the iPhone XX. No, Nick went all out for the big four-oh and bought me a Porsche cabriolet.

"You deserve it, Miranda," he told me after he led me out the back door. What he didn't tell me was that he'd siphoned the last of our liquid cash to make the down payment. Plus, Nick did a few other shitty things behind my back, like remortgaging the house. Twice.

I don't know how many days it will be before the bank takes the house and we end up on the road, me and my gal.

Nick took a different road, one that ended on the last day of April when he set off for the North Carolina Smokies in his car, texted me an "I'm so sorry, babe," and drove the Maserati coupe off the side of a mountain. It couldn't have been fun for him, but I have a hard time feeling sympathy for a man who saw an easy way out and took it, leaving us with no car, no furniture, and no cash. I went to identify the body when I still had the Porsche, scraping together the last of my crappy severance pay to fill its tank with gasoline. There was barely enough for the trip out and back after the gas prices tripled. Airfare would have been more affordable — if we were talking about airfare a year ago or my bank account a few months back, but we're not. We're talking about now.

When I got to Asheville, I had to sign a form releasing Nick's car to the insurance company. The good news was that his Maserati was paid off. The bad news is that we're still waiting for the insurance to pay up.

I'm so sorry, babe.

As if that could fix things. As if that could undo the damage.

"Fucking men," I say, staring out into the street as the truck drives away with my life inside of it.

"Fucking men," Emma says.

I don't bother correcting her. Sometimes you need a little trash mouth. Sometimes the situation calls for it.

I could kill every single one of them, starting with Nick, continuing with Robert, and ending with the tattooed assholes who stole my kitchen pots.

Two

Nick used to say that when humans get into deep shit, when the pain becomes so bright it burns, when every last part of everything seems to worsen with each second, people want their mothers.

Am I one of those people?

Yes and no, and no and yes. And somewhere in between. I wish I had a mother right now, or at least some motherly construct, a woman to lean on. A lap or a shoulder. Hands to brush the hair from my eyes and tell me it will all be okay. I'm tempted to squeeze Emma close to me, but it's too hot for hugging, as if Mother Nature herself is against even this small intimacy.

Emma is plugged into her iPhone as I count out the last of our cash. I sold my XX version the day our accounts were canceled — it was a smart move, and it's kept food in the house. But I couldn't take Emma's, not once I suspected how deep this rabbit hole was going, and I counted on hocking my engagement ring. Unfortunately, I counted a little too long — by the time I worked up the courage to ask for a quote, no one had any cash left. As she bobs her head along to her music and wanders from room to room around the house, her shoulders a little straighter without the heavy pack she'll be carrying when we return, I follow her. But only in body. In mind, I'm moving backward.

To the day I married Nick Reynolds. Or Nick the Dick, as my mother called him when she was in a good mood.

Mom didn't come to the service, a ten-minute exchange of words in the circuit court with Nick in a black leather bomber jacket and black jeans, a dot-com entrepreneur's version of a suit. The clerk stood behind a lectern as she recited and called out "Next!" before Nick had a chance to kiss me. So I guess Mom didn't miss much.

"So you did it, Miranda," Sal Rubio whispered when she signed her name on the forms next to Nick's brother Pete's scrawl. "You married the bad boy."

"I guess she did," Nick said, curling an arm around my waist. "And this bad boy's gonna take care of her until the day she dies." He planted a kiss on me outside the courthouse. "Who's coming for drinks? On me."

Sal tagged along, mostly, I think, because she felt sorry for me. She sure as shit didn't feel anything for Nick. Two minutes after we got to the bar, Pete started putting the moves on her.

"I'm immune, honey," Sal said, and dragged me off to the ladies' room, that sanctuary for all things girl talk since we were in the first grade. "You happy, girl?"

"I'd be happier if my mother had showed up."

"You know what I mean." Sal puckered up in front of the mirror and ran a glossy red gash across her lips. It was her trademark color. The only problem with it was that the lipstick, combined with the gold band on her left fourth, acted like a magnet for any man on the lookout for a no-strings-attached fling. You could say it was counterproductive. "Me, I wouldn't trust a man as far as I could throw him. Just don't let him run everything, okay?"

I promised, and Sal kissed me full on the lips, an old habit.

"I gotta roll, Miranda. Date in an hour with Ingrid." She tapped her phone, held it up, and snapped a selfie of us in the bathroom of the Barking Dog. It was my only wedding photo.

"Who's Ingrid?"

"Tall, Swedish, and gorgeous," she said, blowing a lock of red hair from her eyes. And with that mystery solved, she wiped the lipstick smear from my face and hustled out the door, boots clicking on the tile.

I spent the rest of my wedding afternoon listening to Nick and Pete hash out deployment plans for their latest app, something they called BearHug. It was supposed to guarantee double-digit returns in the stock market.

And for a long time, it did.

The wedding evening went better than the wedding afternoon. Once Nick tore himself away from his brother, he drove us into the city and treated me to the biggest steak I'd ever seen.

"Get used to it, babe," he said when my eyes nearly popped out of their sockets. "I said I'd take care of you."

My mouth waters just thinking about that steak, glistening with butter, charred on the outside, pink and perfect in the center. The baked potato on the side needed its own plate. A real meat-and-potatoes kind of person, you used to say when you were talking about someone simple, unpretentious, down-to-earth. The only people who have been eating steak for the past few months are anything but. I wonder if the president gets steak in whatever bunker he's holed up in. Probably he does.

So we stuffed ourselves full of three courses and downed two bottles of Veuve Clicquot. "La Grande Dame," Nick said, "just like my bride." Then we drove home, got to business for the first time as husband and wife, and cozied up on the sofa with popcorn in time to see my mother on the television.

"Turn it off," I said.

"Are you kidding? She's a riot." Nick held the remote out of reach, finally burying it under the cushion he was sitting on. "I mean, like, a certifiable riot."

Mom was all of that.

Tonight she was on some stage in San Francisco — her excuse for not being there for me when I tied the knot — opining about all things Femdom. She didn't seem to get that her group's pet name was in the Urban Dictionary as a category of sadomasochistic female-domination porn.

Or maybe she did. Maybe that was the whole point.

Mom — Win Somers to every other human — had the crowd roaring. She needed to pause after every few words just to let the applause die down. When she spoke, she seemed to be glaring out of the screen, her eyes boring a hole into Nick.

He cuddled closer. "Man, she's on fire tonight."

If she were any more on fire, our house would have burned down.

"Do we have to watch this?" I said, pushing the popcorn away. By twenty-two, I'd had all the indoctrination into modern feminism a girl could take. *Don't get married. Don't get pregnant. Don't let a man anywhere near your money. Blah blah blah.*

Nick ignored me.

"Some women," Mom said, quieting the audience. The cameras cut away from her, showing a full house at whatever arena she'd picked for tonight's show. "Some women still don't get it. So let me say it again: We are living in a patriarchy." Only she didn't say "patriarchy" — she pronounced each syllable with a pregnant pause in between; it came out like *pay-tree-ar-key.* "And you know what, girls? All you have to do is switch that first letter to an H. What do you get then?" She raised her arms, a classic Win Somers gesture to get the crowd going, to stir them up into a froth of excitement. A frenzy. "What do you get then?"

The single word boomed from the set. *Ha-*

triarchy, the audience screamed.

"That's right, girls. That's what we get. And are we sick to death of it?"

YES. WE. ARE.

"How sick are we?"

SICK. TO. DEATH.

Nick laughed. I groaned. Mom was barely getting started.

She went through the usual warm-up, making sure everyone was hot and angry, what Mom called "spitting angry," before trotting out her version of a Mini-Me.

I hated this part.

Jennifer Jones had a walk that was more like a goose step, and a voice as strident as a banshee's. The only part of her that — if you squinted — looked remotely like me was her straight blond hair. With bangs. I always wondered whether my mother picked her for that or whether the haircut was an afterthought, a way to perfect the illusion.

But it was Jen's eyes that got under your skin. They were deep set and large, and they always seemed to be looking directly at you, like one of those trick paintings where the subject holds its stare no matter where you are in the room. Tonight those eyes were looking at me, pulling me in, smiling as if they knew my secrets.

It was all far too creepy. When Nick got

up to grab another beer, I made a lunge for the remote.

"Too slow, Miranda-o," he sang out tauntingly. And off he went, taking the clicker with him, leaving me to watch my fucked-up doppelgänger take center stage.

The lights dimmed, and the scrim behind Jennifer glowed neon yellow on a black background. One word shone behind her, not a real word, but real enough that you could guess its meaning.

Femlandia.

Nick, back from the kitchen with a craft beer he said was a steal at six bucks a bottle, translated it in his own way. "Freaks. Welcome to Camp Dyke-orama!"

"Nick. Really?" I said. But I laughed along with him.

"Think of it like Disneyland for women," Jennifer said from the stage. "A place for us — no more men, no more inequality, no more hatriarchy. Just us girls."

"What do you say, babe? Want to leave me and set up house in Femlandia with the double-X set?"

"I'd rather eat dirt," I said.

Nick smacked his lips. "I can almost taste the kale smoothies now." He took a swig of his beer and winced. "Mm, mm, mm. Tasty."

"Cut it out, Nick," I said when he did it

again. But I didn't mean it. Nick was good to me, better than any other guy I'd dated. To begin with, he wasn't treading water in a credit-card-debt hole. Or, like the last man I'd lived with, not even bothering to tread, just sinking, pulling me down with him. *Can I borrow some money, Miranda? Just for a few days, Miranda. Promise I'll pay you back with interest, Miranda.*

Not that the four-bedroom house with its granite-and-stainless-steel gourmet kitchen or the twin BMWs in the garage or the spur-of-the-moment trips to New Orleans and Paris and Spain and Fiji changed my mother's mind. To Win Somers, every man was a bastard, beginning with her father and ending with mine.

"You can't trust 'em any farther than you can throw 'em," she said. Over and over and over.

And now this. Femlandia. Some crap-ass colony out in the sticks of Virginia, where women and girls could live in bliss without hairy, whore-mongering men. Jennifer's description sounded like hell. The pictures were worse: a dozen log cabins, a cluster of old-fashioned water pumps, a toolshed that looked put together with the leftovers from Home Depot. Women tugging weeds from a patch of brassicas, women pumping water, women repairing generators, women splitting logs and piling up cords of wood for winter fuel.

It all sounded like Disneyland if your idea of Disneyland was running around scrubbing clothes on a wooden board.

"Self-sufficiency," Jennifer said. She laughed a little. "Or I guess we could call it 'self-sufficien*SHE.*' "

The crowd roared. I wondered at the time if it was canned.

It's a thing I don't wonder anymore, not nineteen years later, not when fifteen states in the union have their own Femlandias and another ten are in the pipeline. I've no idea where my mother is, but her legacy lives on.

Three

We had a joke once about the three Safeways in town. In the first one, the Social Safeway, you were guaranteed to bump into someone you knew, usually in the frozen section near the petite peas. Then there was the Unsafe Safeway, the place where most of the ground beef teetered on the brink of being out of date and the cauliflower heads sported an interesting variety of brown. Nick's favorite wordsmithing, though, was the Soviet Safeway — the supermarket that always, always had run out of whatever you needed. Bread crumbs. Worcestershire sauce. Lettuce.

"What's today? Odd or even, Emma?" I've completely lost track. The last time we trekked to Safeway, it was an even day and the place was closed.

"Odd, thank God."

Well, thank someone. "Let's go," I say, locking the front door and starting down the porch steps.

Half of the houses on our street are already shut up tight as a virgin, either foreclosed on or abandoned. The Italians up the street, the ones who'd worked for the World Bank before it ran out of money, left three months ago for Europe. I guess they saw the early signs, but I don't know what they expect to find in Rome. Liz and Mary, the two nurses at 234, moved into a camp for medical staff at Sibley Hospital. Liz said they won't be paid much this year, but at least they've got steady work and a place to stay and jobs to come back to when things settle down. If you believe the papers, there's tons of work, especially in the emergency rooms.

The house I hate looking at is Mr. and Mrs. Sullivan's, the big, boxy Queen Anne two doors down from us. All their roses have a withered, witch-broom look about them now that Margie Sullivan moved out. I couldn't blame her. Who would want to cook in a kitchen after finding her husband's brain splatter on the appliances? Nothing against suicide — I've thought of that escape myself — but you really need to put that shit where it belongs. In a seldom-used office. A guest bedroom. The cellar.

Or in a valley in western North Carolina.

Emma and I walk past it without speaking.

Some of the houses are fine, for now, although the number of fine ones seems to be half of what it was last week. Sweet air blows from the dryer outtake at the Connells' place, a sign they're still above water, afloat enough to keep the appliances going and buy fabric softener sheets. It's also a sign they have a twenty-kilowatt generator and they're still able to feed it natural gas. Nora Connell's curtains shift to the right as we walk by and then fall to the left just as quickly, which is fine with me. A closed window is a hell of a lot better than listening to Nora scream at us about what a mess my husband made, how she hopes he rots in hell, how a good, eternal roasting would be exactly what he deserves.

It's an eye-for-an-eye mentality, I guess. Nick burned the majority of our neighbors and friends, so why wouldn't they wish him the same treatment?

"You think Safeway will be as crowded as last time?" Emma says when we turn the corner onto the main road, leaving Nora and her evil eye behind us.

"Probably," I say. *Probably worse.*

"Think we'll find any vegetables this week? I mean, that don't come in a can?"

"Maybe some potatoes. We can bake them tonight if the gas is still on." I don't hold out a ton of hope for anything else. Two weeks before, just days after the president made his speech announcing the bankruptcy ruling, the shelves looked like they had suffered a mild pre-blizzard run. Milk and bread aisles took the hardest hit, but the produce stayed on the shelves. Last week was a different story: bananas ripened to black, bruised apples and pears, limp lettuce. The cabbages were okay, though. And those indestructible tomatoes bred to withstand lousy transport conditions. I don't know what we might find in week three, but I'm sure the prices will have inched up again.

While we walk Arlington Road, Emma keeps her head down. The locked shop doors with their *Absolutely No Credit* signs are depressing. You can still buy things at a few places, but nothing opens until early afternoon, and then only for a few hours at a time when the police walk their beats. Nothing is open at night anymore, for all kinds of reasons. And now, nothing is open at all.

"I miss the library," Emma says when we pass the building.

"You miss Jason Griffith," I say.

"No. Not that much."

Well. This is new. Jason was all but a permanent fixture in our house for a year and a half. I kept waiting for the shiny diamond ring to show up on Emma's finger, even if they are only sixteen.

"Does he fall into the sonofabitch camp, too?"

"Nah," she says without looking at me. "Just Dad. And those jerks who took our stuff."

Most of them, I think, but I don't bother correcting her. It's difficult liking men when you've been financially ruined by one of them. Two, if I count my former boss, who decided to let the female researchers go first when the funding dried up.

I realize I'm about to become one of those people, the men and women with nowhere to go except a busy street corner, hawking the only wares they have left. The problem is, there are so damned many of us. Tanya Jordan, who owns the used bookstore on Walsh Street, sits on the patch of brown grass outside the shop, a weather-beaten sign clapping its rhythm on the door behind her. It's like a never-ending round of sarcastic applause for the bastards who got us here. Of course, Tanya Jordan threw her money into whichever shitty investments

Nick happened to tout at the time.

Clap. Clap. Clap, the sign says. *Nick Reynolds, take a bow!*

Tanya seems not to see us as we pass. I don't know where her partner is, and I've learned not to ask these questions. The answers are all starting to sound the same anyway. Went back home to her family. Got sick. Threw herself off a bridge.

At the corner where Emma's bus used to stop, there's Dr. Ramirez, the high school principal who sometimes plays the organ at early mass on Sundays. I've heard she's good at it, even got a taste of one of her Bach toccatas when I ran by in the morning on my loop through town. My personal church of preference has always been the Starbucks, the one near the park. Four dollars and eleven cents for a latte. Make it an even five with tip.

Five dollars to waste on coffee three times a week. Pure, unadulterated luxury.

"Hi, Dr. Ramirez!" Emma calls out. "See you on Monday morning." She's learned to humor the principal since the crisis closed the schools. The woman has kept her nonpaying organ gig, but she's shit out of luck as far as a steady salary goes. I think perhaps the church thing keeps her going, but just barely.

"You got a date, young lady!" she calls back. "Doors open at seven sharp. Got a letter right here from the Department of Education." Dr. Ramirez pats her purse before going back to stretching, or practicing tai chi, or whatever she was doing.

I smile back and toss her an encouraging line. Why ruin a gal's Saturday morning if you don't have to?

"Do you think she really has a letter?" Emma asks. There's zero hope in her voice.

"Do you?" I say.

"Nope."

A few of the people we pass still have their houses. Dr. Ramirez is one — for the time being. The old couple next door, the Schafers, also seem fine; they don't have a mortgage, and Mr. Schafer didn't over-invest in failing state pension funds like Nick did. The Schafers haven't come out of their brick box for a few days, at least not that I've seen, but the lights stay on at night in most parts of the house. You can't see the lights from the front because of the plywood, but if you come at the house from an angle, there's the incandescent glow of electric sun through the windows that still have glass panes.

The plywood patches — and the broken shards scattered through Mrs. Schafer's azaleas — are a reminder of why we need to get off the streets after dusk, a Houdini-esque trick when the bank notice that arrived yesterday announced its two-day deadline for us to move out. It's hard to take shelter in a house whose locks are about to be changed.

Mostly, I think the night people are looking for looting opportunities now that the police force is half what it used to be and the better part of the military has been deployed to the capital. But there are always other targets. Not the kind of targets that fill a belly with supper, but the kind that empty a head of its worries, at least temporarily. At seventy-five, Mrs. Schafer is an unlikely distraction. At sixteen, though, Emma is perfect. Food of a different kind for the starving sharks who walk the streets.

The last time we shopped at the Social Safeway, there were plenty of bread crumbs and Worcestershire sauce in the condiments aisle, but not a single head of romaine or Boston or iceberg. Only a hand-printed sign saying *Coming soon. Thanks for your patience!*

I should have planted a vegetable garden, I thought at the time.

There are potatoes in the bin today, bruised and pockmarked with rotting sprouts, and a few bags of onions I don't know what to do with. Emma picks out two russets I'll throw in the oven for dinner. We still have what's left of the olive-oil spread in the fridge, and some salt. Bacon would be fantastic, but the expiration dates on it are borderline.

Anyway, after the movers came, I no longer have a frying pan for the bacon. And the bacon might be rancid.

Said the fox to the grapes.

The truth is, I can't afford the bacon. I checked the last of my money I keep in a sweat-stained canvas belt around my waist, under my jeans. Emma and I discovered early that purses aren't a good bet, not against a hungry man on a motorcycle. There's room again for the money belt now that I've dropped ten pounds, but for a while I was worried whether I'd soon run out of clothing that fit. I thickened quickly around the middle when I was pregnant with Emma, so why should this time be different?

Don't think about that now, Miranda. You've got too much other shit to think about.

Tuna, the light flake kind, is barely still in the budget, so we head to the canned fish and meat aisle, following what must be half of greater Bethesda. Ten cans go into the cart before we move on to the rice and beans. I pick beans, and an hour later it's our turn at the checkout line.

"This is hell, isn't it?" Emma says.

"Yeah. The ninth circle. The one with the embezzlers' wives and the corrupt politicians."

Three checkout guys are working today, another testament to the unspoken men-need-jobs-more-than-women-need-jobs policy. It's like the entire glass ceiling has turned to iron.

"You're that lady who teaches the animals how to talk, right? I saw you on TV last year," the guy in our lane says. He's thirty-something with a gold band on his ring finger.

"Taught," I say. "Really it was sign language. And only one gorilla. It's not like I'm some twenty-first-century Dr. Dolittle." The line behind me doesn't look as if it wants my story.

He scans the tuna and beans and potatoes and loads them into our backpacks. "Yeah. Hard times, ma'am. You could try the Food Lion south of town. Heard they're still open. But we'll pull through."

Some of us more than others, I think. But I keep my mouth shut, pay him with my dwindling supply of twenties, and move out of the way.

"You think he's right, Mom?" Emma says. "That we'll pull through?"

"Sure, hon. One way or another." I help her get the backpack on. "Pack too heavy, hon?"

"Nah. I'm cool."

She doesn't complain much for a girl in the ripest years of the troubling teens, but her eyes are wide, a little hungry. Somewhere inside the tough exterior she fakes, she's a scarecrow of a girl — nervous as a crow and scared shitless. I stop outside the closed doors of the grocery store, take five cans of tuna and a liter-sized bottle of cranberry juice out of her pack, and stuff them into mine before shouldering the beast again. It's what I've been doing every day, lightening Emma's load, adding a little to mine, wondering which can of tuna or beans will be the final straw, the one that breaks me.

Four

We reach the far edge of town and the cluster of three country clubs — the golden triangle of suburban Maryland affluence whose fees were so high, Nick said they could pave the fairways with dollar bills. The fairways aren't green today.

"I wonder what happened to her," Emma says, looking toward the gates. "You think someone helped her out?"

She's talking about the girl we passed last week, a thin and feral-looking child, but it might have been the dirt on her face and the leaves sticking to her hair that made her so. The girl could have been blond for all I knew. She was perhaps ten years old, possibly younger. Emma thought younger.

One thing I know, she was crying when we found her crouched outside the gates to the Burning Tree Club, which isn't very far from the Congressional Country Club and the Bethesda Country Club. You could get between the three with a golf cart in low gear if you wanted, or if you had multiple memberships. So many country clubs, so much wealth.

I'd planned for us to cut through the golf courses instead of taking the long road around to the hardware store that morning. Pounding fifteen miles on tarmac every day had begun to numb the soles of our feet, and the grass was inviting. Also, it's cooler on the fairways, especially once the sun hits noon height. If we tired of walking, there were places to sit. Benches at the fourth tee. Tables and umbrellas at the nineteenth hole.

But we never made it into the sanctuary of the clubs.

Emma saw them first, the lines of men at the Bethesda Club's entrance with their guns slung over a shoulder and their ammo belts worn low around their hips. As we approached, they stood up a little straighter, squared their jaws. Someone must have told them not to talk to the foot traffic, maybe because that someone feared talk might lead to sympathy, an open gate, another mouth to feed and another body to protect. It's easier to be unkind when you don't interact. It's easier to think of the ones on the outside as feral. Like stray dogs. You feel sorry for them, but you know you've got to stand tall and tough.

You know lines have to be drawn.

I tried. That was the best I could do, try to use Emma as my pawn, stir some pity in those cold eyes of the men. I didn't even rate a "Sorry, ma'am." So we moved on to Burning Tree, and we met the same welcome.

The club had been living up to its name. Two dozen trees had been felled from the woods around the main building. Men and women who had once worn Armani suits and Bruno Magli loafers or pumps and drove their Lexus SUVs from one meeting to the next now worked like lumberjacks, sawing and splitting and piling. Once in a while, a former partner at a private DC firm, maybe a lobbyist, would stop to wipe a brow. The men went shirtless, white skin toasting to pink under the punishing July sun. The women grimaced.

It had to be hard to stockpile firewood when fire didn't seem at all necessary. But, of course, it would be. Soon enough.

I cursed the men as I passed. Some of the women, too, but mostly the men. That unhappy marriage of finance and politics is still mostly a big boy's game.

Was.

You don't see this shit coming down, sliding toward you in an ugly, fetid avalanche. No one pays attention to state pension funds, whether they're underfunded or overfunded, or how California is supposed to meet a half trillion dollars of retirement obligations when it's only got three billion in the bank. Nick paid attention, of course, when he wasn't busy lying to me about his trading losses and remortgaging our house, but I didn't. I left it all to him.

You want to know how we got here? Follow the money trail. Always follow the money.

Emma and I walked toward the girl squatting near the gates. I thought maybe we could take her home with us or, if she wouldn't come, we could give her some food. But it would be better to take her back to the house before night came. Night had become too scary a time for girls.

I slipped off my pack, rubbed feeling back into my arms where the straps had cut in and stopped the blood flow. Then Emma and I searched through our supplies. We could spare a bottle of water and some canned fruit, maybe half a bag of banana chips. I kept the peanuts back, though. They've got protein, but the only ones left in the stores were salted. If the girl decided to join us, we could share them later on when we reached the house and had access to water.

The worst part, the part I hate myself for now, is that I really didn't want her to join us. She was so small and weak, and we had barely enough food for two. Especially when one of us was already eating for two.

There. I've said it.

Emma reached out first, approaching the girl with the food and water under the steady gaze of the men behind the gates. She shrunk back the way a stray cat does when you stretch out a hand, refusing our offering, scuttling into the thick brush.

And we trudged on our way.

Last week seems more like last year.

"I don't know what happened to her," I say now, looking back once at the gates. They're still closed, but no longer guarded. A few abandoned tools dot the brown grass, and half-sawn tree limbs lie where they fell. The parking lot, once full of Lexuses and middle-age-crisis Porsche roadsters, is empty today, a sign of exodus. "I don't know what happened to any of them."

Part of me doesn't really care.

The Food Lion's silhouetted logo rises from the pavement at the next corner. It looks more like a ravenous dragon than a lion, and I have my doubts that the long walk over here is going to be worth it when Emma points to street level. A crowd of desperate shoppers snakes from the front door around to the back of the building, where one lonely truck idles as one lonely teamster unloads four crates from it. And then the crowd is on him, pawing and clawing their way over his body, onto the ramp. A fistfight breaks out between two men I recognize from Emma's school, soccer-dad types no longer. At least their wives are cheering them on.

"Let's get the hell out of here," I say, grabbing Emma's hand and spinning us in the direction toward home.

By the time I realize I've made the wrong decision, it's too late. A pair of hands rips the pack from Emma's shoulders with enough force to knock her to the sidewalk. There's a sickening crack, a weak and dry wishbone-after-Thanksgiving kind of a crack, and for a moment I think it's her arm, but then I see the star-shaped shatter on her iPhone's screen.

"Help!" I cry out in the direction of the Food Lion. A few heads turn toward us, almost bored, and then they turn back to the fistfight at the yawning mouth of the delivery truck as the thief who stole half our groceries runs across the street, Emma's pack swinging with each step.

Five

Win was losing her only daughter, and there was nothing to be done about it. It hurt, this rift. It hurt more than the sharp, strangling contractions, more than the incessant pound of her head through thirty-six hours of labor, more than the episiotomy that allowed what she thought must have been a basketball through her as she lay sweating on the bed, cursing Carl for getting her into this shitty situation and cursing her own father even more for insisting on the marriage. But that pain was long forgotten. This new pain was fresh, and it renewed itself each time Miranda rolled her eyes, each time the girl shrunk away from a hug or turned her cheek so that Win's lips met with the space just behind her daughter's right ear.

Miranda winced at kisses, skulked off to an upstairs room when she came home from school in the afternoon and Win had set out a tray of milk and cookies on the cheap gold-flecked Formica of the kitchen counter. So what if they were the slice-and-bake kind? You cut corners where you could, but it was the thought that counted, the effort. And Win, with two jobs, no husband, and a grassroots project that took more hours than remained in the day, put in her share of effort.

She didn't know what Miranda's problem was. The girl was taciturn on her best days, picking at her meals in silence, avoiding Win's questions about classes and friends, reluctantly allowing herself to be led through department stores on back-to-school-clothing missions.

"I don't want *pants,* Mom. I want a dress," Miranda would say, standing with her arms folded in the aisle of Target or Walmart. "Why do I always have to wear what you wear? It's ugly. And it makes you look like a guy." And then Miranda would run off and pick out some fluffy pink thing to try on while Win stuffed the oxford shirts and chinos back into the racks. Other mothers watched them with raised eyebrows before turning to their own daughters and saying — a little too loudly — "You go ahead and find whatever you like, dear."

Miranda loved her dresses, and she loved

the candy-colored lip gloss and the sandals with the daisies on the buckles that her father bought for her, along with the dollies and the houses for the dollies and the god-damned sparkly, girly, stupid outfits for the dollies. When Carl wasn't around anymore to veto her, Win put those fucking dresses and dolls where they belonged.

Jen was different. Jen didn't skulk around and turn her nose up at instant food or unisex clothing. Jen laughed at dolls, preferring erector sets and Legos. Jennifer Jones liked her name short and boyish, like her hair and her nails. Jen hated boys, and didn't hate Win Somers, and that was more like it.

They say you can't pick your children, you get what you get, and you love them anyway. When her daughter was fifteen, Win decided that was bullshit.

SIX

They said the national suicide rate went up in 1929 and 1930, in the year after Black Thursday. They said people stood in line for bread, and teachers hadn't been paid for nearly a year. They said there was only enough money to fund welfare to one in four families.

They said a great depression would never happen again. I don't know what was so fucking great about it, but it happened a second time.

So here we are, with the suicides and the grocery store closings and the school hiatus, all of which they told us were temporary. Here we are, Emma and I, in a lottery that has run dry after two months of waiting to find out how much money we might get and when we would get it. Zero. That was the magic number. And "Never" was the other answer.

I've learned that a lot can happen in six weeks.

The grocery stores can close, having run out of everything.

A high school principal can go mad.

One elderly couple without a mortgage can have a last meal together before self-execution.

The police can give up, or get shot, or both.

And whatever was left of the National Guard can disappear.

Which is why we haven't left the house since the seventeenth of May.

It's hard to remember how many small things went wrong, or when they occurred. My timeline is fuzzy these days, because it all seemed to happen at the same time. I remember economic turmoil in Asia. I remember the European Union fell apart, losing one member at a time as its states slipped into isolationism. I remember the nationalization of tech companies — because, of course, a bunch of idiot politicians in Washington definitely knew better than the CEOs of Microsoft and Google. America was like a windshield with a chink in it that kept expanding, a tiny starburst that got hit repeatedly by other pebbles. Anemic, we still bled out money. To France and to

Greece. To the nongovernmental organizations that took our cash and handed it over to the more needy. To anyone with an open palm and a sad story to tell.

I remember the day when three of the largest states declared Chapter 9 bankruptcy and set the country on a tailspin to fiscal hell. We know the date — Black Wednesday, April 1, in the year of our Lord two thousand and something. If I were in a laughing mood, I'd laugh hard and long at that one. It was a black day, we were fools for not seeing it, and no lord was around to help.

I remember Nick telling me it would all be fine, that the machine was too big to fail, that we'd weather this hiccup.

I remember our president saying he didn't believe in federal intervention, that the spirit of the American people would pull us through.

Most of all, I remember the day Robert let me go, when I signed a goodbye to Bunny for the last time before packing up my books and leaving him in the primate house. Bunny couldn't cry, not like we do, not like I have every day for the past six weeks as another brick slammed against the plywood I nailed up over the living room windows, and the cans of beans and tuna became countable on two hands. Bunny, like the rest of the nonhuman primates, doesn't have tear ducts. So he mimed crying through the glass window as I walked down the hall with my box of no-longer-needed stuff. Gorilla-speak for *I'm sad, Miranda. I'll miss you.*

Yeah, me too, Bunny-boy. I've known him longer than I've known my own daughter. I taught him his first words.

What I can't remember is exactly what date it is today, how many turns the earth has made since I saw the first line snaking around the corner outside our branch of Maryland Bank and Trust. *We treat your money as if it were our money!* the slogan said on their pamphlets. Looking back, they weren't really lying. My money was as good as their money, or at least all our money was in the same place. Going, going, not worth what it used to be worth.

We might have been better off, Emma and I, for the beginning of this temporary hiatus, if Nick hadn't run our bank accounts dry and sold the furniture and car and everything else from under us. We would have been like Mr. and Mrs. Schafer, hiding out indoors, waiting for things to go back to normal, hoarding our cash, waiting for the next brick or rock to sail through a window. Or, maybe, we'd have been like Dr. Ramirez, going about our daily routines, strapping ourselves down until the headlines spun to a happier message in the next morning's papers.

Our delusion would have lasted as long as our cash, which — as the Schafers and our high school principal found out — wasn't long at all, not when ground beef shot up to twenty-five bucks a pound and gas hit an all-time-high of twenty-five dollars a gallon. Nick might have left us a lifeboat, but Emma and I would have ended up in the middle of the ocean eventually, drinking turtle piss and fish blood to get by. He made it possible for us to get there a little sooner than everyone else, but he didn't make this chaos on his own. I tell myself to remember that negligence isn't the same thing as evil. Not at all.

Dr. Ramirez took her own way out, choosing delusion over reality. The Schafers had a better idea — two shots, the second delayed by whatever amount of time it took Mr. Schafer to kiss his dead wife goodbye and turn the gun on himself.

Confession time: when I heard those shots, I went into Nick's office and opened the wall safe. I thought long, hard thoughts about whether, if the time came, I could use what was inside.

I've heard about murder-suicides. They come in two types, the insanity motivated and the thoroughly thought out. Those second are mercy killings, and they require a bravery I don't have. I don't think I could kill anyone, much less my only child. Even with things as bad as they are. Still, I held the heavy piece for a time, considering its heft and its cold, quick power. Then I put it in a high kitchen cabinet, a place where I could retrieve it easily if I needed it.

Now I'm in this same kitchen, face-to-face with Emma, staring at the bare walls.

I suppose my mother would laugh at me for depending on a man who cheated first me, then our neighbors, out of everything we had. I know my old friend Sal Rubio is laughing, not at me, but with me.

Maybe at me, too, I think as I straighten out two scratchy blankets on the living room floor. I kiss Emma goodnight, wash out a few things for the morning, and get ready for another fitful sleep, mentally counting our remaining food and candles and rolls of toilet paper.

People are sheep. Nick predicted the first things to fly off the shelves would be paper products — select-a-size paper towels, Kleenex, toilet paper. "Gotta stock up on the Charmin, baby. It'll be like gold." He was right. Then they all raced for the milk and the ice cream, which require a working refrigerator and freezer; the flour, which requires a functional oven unless you want to mix it with water and eat paste; the pasta, which requires boiling water to make it edible. No one bothers to think of what really matters until it's too late: protein with a long shelf life and a can opener that won't break. When Nick took his literal dive off the cliff a couple of months ago, I loaded the car with tuna, beans, and Charmin. We've still got a full shelf of the squeezably soft stuff, so Nick would have approved.

I rather wish he were here so I could soak it in water and serve it to him in a soup bowl.

SEVEN

Emma wakes on the hardwood floor next to me. I feel the chill, too, as if it were a gray, midwinter morning instead of the beginning of another July scorcher. My throat feels like it's been rubbed with sandpaper, and I automatically go to the kitchen sink to fill a glass.

Nothing comes out of the tap except a trickle.

"We're out," Emma says from behind me. "As of a few hours ago."

So much for working toilets.

"We have to go, honey," I tell her, throwing cans and bottles into my old backpack and the one I stole from the Schafers' garage until they're ready to burst. I climb up on the granite counter in the kitchen — Verde Butterfly, they called it at the interior design office — reach to the top cabinet over the built-in fridge, and take out Nick's gun box. I'll need to remove a day's food supply to make room for the piece and the extra clip, but I tell myself it's worth it. I counted two more bricks last night, and I know the world out there isn't what it used to be.

Emma looks at me with wide, frightened eyes. "Where?"

"I don't know yet. What I do know is that we'll last three days without water. Three." I check the sky outside. Sunny with no chance of rain. I can already feel the mercury climbing to its daily high, and it's only eight o'clock in the morning.

Emma groans. "We could get some bottled water from Safeway, maybe."

All I can do is stare, openmouthed. Even if Safeway still had water, trying to get it would be as successful as the Gallipoli campaign.

"Can't we just stay until tomorrow, then?"

"No. No, we can't just stay until tomorrow, then."

"Why?"

"Because I fucking said so. Now, get dressed, get your shoes on, and get moving." I hate myself for talking to her like this, but someone has to be the bad guy.

She gives me the silent treatment for the half hour it takes us to walk into town. Whatever. I'm in full survival mode now, doing what Nick should have stuck around to do. He had a way of doing the necessary without being overbearing. When Emma bucked, he reined her in, but gently.

"You know," I say, "if your father were here, you wouldn't be pouting."

No response. So we walk on in silence until we reach the Safeway where the checkout guy told me we'll all pull through.

This morning, we won't be adding anything to our packs from Safeway. No one will. Shattered glass that used to be windows sparkles on the pavement like discarded jewels. The shelves, as far as I can see, are bare.

While we've been hiding out in our empty suburban mansion turned fortress, the city has drained itself of most of its life. A few skinny cats, seal-point Persians that must have cost a few thousand as kittens, scrounge among the piles of uncollected garbage. They come upon a carcass of another of their kind and hiss at one another, the larger male laying a proprietary paw on the find. I turn my head, but not before seeing the tom bury his own head into the dead cat's flesh. When I risk a glance back, he's eaten everything. Fur, skin, and the crawling white maggots that had nested there.

Emma sees it, too, and screams. She hides her face in the damp cotton of my shirt, and I think, *Maybe I'm not the bad guy after all.*

"Shh, baby girl. It's okay," I tell her, and we walk on, leaving the cats behind us.

Noise from the other side of the almost-empty parking lot sounds something like an outdoor cocktail party, but when I look, it's only two rope-thin men with beards down to their chests arguing over who owes whom how much for the pack of cigarettes they're splitting up and where the hell did the lighter go. What was that old saying? Smoke 'em if you got 'em. They're the first two humans I've seen today.

I'd like a cigarette now, even with the heat, but I'm glad I quit sixteen years ago. Sixteen. Long years and short at the same time. At sixteen, Emma's old enough to deal with the world falling to pieces around us, young enough that she shouldn't have to. Even when she sleeps, that way she curls one hand under her cheek, she looks more like a newborn than a teenager. An innocent. Some dark place inside me hurts as I watch the rise and fall of her chest while she walks next to me, the trembling of a lock of blond hair as she exhales. It's scary to think that I wasn't much older than her when I found out I was pregnant.

"You'll be fine, babe," Nick said that morning over coffee. "We'll be fine. What do you need another degree for when we're already rolling in dough?"

"It's not what I need, Nick. It's what I wanted."

"The ivory tower is dead. What counts now is the ability to manipulate money," he said, tapping the phone on the kitchen island. It stayed with him, that phone, like it was attached by an umbilical cord made of high-tensile wire. Something was always going on, some new deal always ready to jump on. The next big thing.

According to Nick, people like me — or people like what I'd wanted to be — were obsolete. Dinosaurs. I prepped myself for the usual lecture on machine market analysis and automated commodity trading and all things money management.

Not that I had any reason to complain. Nick took care of me. While my college girlfriends met for a weekly cry-in about law school exams and med school debt and how much they spent on ramen noodles while they were banging out their doctoral theses on Chaucer, like it was some kind of contest to see who had the shittiest life, I did whatever I wanted.

My routine at twenty-three years old:

Manicures on Monday.

Watching Rita and Mary clean the house on Tuesday. ("Never trust a maid," Nick warned.)

Ten loops in-line skating around Hains Point on Wednesday, Friday, and Sunday.

Shopping. Tons of shopping.

I still met them for coffee on Saturday mornings, but except for Sal, not much connective tissue held up in the first couple of years after I became Mrs. Nick Reynolds. Sal said I worried too much; we were all still friends, still looking out for one another like we did in college. "Just us girls," she said. "Sticking together."

One weekend, I showed up late at the Starbucks.

"You think she'll be wearing another thousand-dollar pair of Gucci boots?" That was Mary Jo Farrell's voice.

"Don't even get me started." Sue Sanchez.

"Little Miss Rich Girl. I'm surprised she even bothers to hang out with us anymore." Gret Soderberg.

"Wait until she hits forty and has stretch marks and he leaves her for a younger woman." Pamela Jackson.

I slipped outside without ordering, texted Sal that I couldn't make it, and raced home.

I think I cried for a half hour in the driveway before Nick stuck his head through the kitchen door and found me.

"Bitches," he said, taking me inside and pouring two mugs of coffee. "Forget them. Besides, my coffee's better than that Starbucks crap."

It should be. He spent enough money on it.

"Will you still love me when I'm forty?" I asked.

"Yep."

"Even if I have stretch marks?"

"Yep."

"Promise?"

"Yep." He stopped drinking and set the mug down between us. "Spill it, Mrs. Reynolds."

I knew Nick was smart. I didn't think he could read minds.

There was a script in my head that morning as I drove to the coffee klatch. Sort of rehearsed, sort of not. I'd planned to tell the girls my news and then sneak off to Planned Parenthood with Sal. Easy, simple, one, two, three. What Nick didn't know wouldn't hurt him, I'd go get the doctorate, and we'd move on to family making in a few years. I'd even made sure to hide the pee stick with its damning blue cross in my bag before I left the house.

And then I had to go open my big mouth and mention stretch marks. Not a smart move for a chick who had just been accepted to Georgetown's applied linguistics doctoral program.

"Girl or boy?" Nick took my coffee away and poured it down the drain. Steam clouds came up from the sink. At least the aroma was still there. "Don't worry," he said, seeing the look on my face. "I'll run out and get you some decaf. But first — let's spread a little joy."

"No way."

"Yes way."

Which is how I ended up on the phone with my mother.

Nick left the room, coffee in hand. "To give you girls some privacy," he said. The second his footsteps started one of their usual pace-and-think beats over my head, I poured a cup of high-test.

"What's wrong, Miranda?" Mom said. Airport noise filled in the pause after she spoke. That was my mother, always leaving on a jet plane to the next gig, the next road show.

She would think something was wrong. When you don't speak to your own mother for more than a year and then call out of the blue, it's usually not to chew the fat about the weather. So I blurted it out.

"I'm pregnant."

"Oh, Christ." This was a favorite of Win Somers, an all-purpose blanket response to what she called "unpleasant shit." "Tell me you're getting rid of it. Please tell me that much."

Well, that was the original plan. I let the pause speak for itself.

Mom settled down, and her voice became quiet, conspiratorial, the calm before the storm. I'd heard it before. "Does he know?"

"Yes."

"And?"

"And we're talking about it," I lied.

Then the storm rolled in. "You don't need to talk about it, Miranda. You just need to act. On your own."

"But he —"

"Fuck him," she said. "Goddamned men. Let me guess, he's mansplaining, right?" It was Mom's favorite new term. "Telling you how wonderful it's going to be to have a family while you're young, that you can go back to school later — like that's going to happen — and he'll take care of you and your little bundle of joy always and forever. Does that sound about right?"

By the time she'd finished, my ears hurt. I

poured another cup of coffee and sucked it down. It was hot, and it stung, but it gave me a moment.

"Well, Miranda? I've got a plane to catch."

"Go catch it, then," I said.

Deep breath, long sigh, a few final mother-to-daughter parting words. "You know, if you were more like Jen, we wouldn't need to have this conversation."

I sat in the kitchen after hanging up, wondering how long it would be until I spoke to my mother again.

It turned out to be years. Even then, there was only the one last time, the final knock-down, drag-'em-out scene that seemed a kind of mother-and-daughter anti-reunion. Two weeks later, Jen Jones broke the news that Femlandia's founder was dead.

I didn't cry.

EIGHT

Win was eighteen when she went to college, nineteen when she met Carl Finley of Finley Motors, and three months away from twenty-one when he raped her. He said all the things a man says on the morning after. *Sorry. Thought you wanted to. I didn't know.* And so on. Ya-de-ya-de-ya. It wasn't the kind of rape she could report, because Carl's kind of rape, the kind where Friday night presents itself with a few too many drinks and there just happens to be a sofa nearby and the answer to "Will you still love me tomorrow?" is always an unequivocal "Yes," wasn't really assault. There wasn't any date rape in the seventies because if you didn't have a label for something, the thing in question didn't exist.

"I don't want to marry you, and I don't want to have the baby," she told Carl on her twenty-first birthday. "I'm sorry, but I don't. I have plans. Besides, I think I'd rather be with a woman."

He pouted, he sulked, and then he did the unthinkable. He called Win's father.

Win spent the next month under her mother's nose, stifling the last remnants of morning sickness while being dragged through bridal shops and patisseries, nodding tacit approval at the flowers Mrs. Finley picked out, forcing herself to agree that the lemon cake really was the best choice. Not that her opinion mattered. Win was out of choices. Win was under house arrest.

They had a February wedding, both mother and mother-in-law sacrificing hopes for June nuptials in favor of saving themselves the embarrassment of explaining Win's inflated belly to five hundred guests. Instead, they ended up explaining why the blushing bride cried through the hour-long ceremony.

"She's overjoyed," Mrs. Finley said.

"It's her biggest day," Win's mother explained, pinching the soft flesh on her daughter's arm. "Right, dear?" When Win didn't respond, she pinched harder.

Win didn't like men, not that way — despite Carl reading all the signals wrong and thinking he could convert her, just as her parents thought Win's predilections toward girls had been a phase she would grow out of. But she had never hated men. Men brought home the bacon, took care of their families, doted on their daughters and wives. By twenty-two, Win realized men also wrote the law, enforced it, and had the final word.

She was twenty-two when she started thinking about a way to live without them.

NINE

The blacktop on the road shimmers with heat. We should be tucked inside the Porsche, blasting the AC and the radio, arguing over whether the Beatles or the Stones were the best band, not sweating our way down Arlington Road with a backpack full of canned food and cranberry juice. The juice is the mostly artificial kind, no refrigeration needed, not the organic stuff I used to buy.

"Rest stop?" Emma says, picking out a shaded bench in the park.

"Definitely." For a foolish moment I wonder whether I could track down the maintenance people, trade a few hours of weeding time for some cash. What's the going rate? A penny a dandelion? And I remember there are no maintenance people anymore.

Then Emma asks the question that's been lingering in both of our minds, the one I've been avoiding because the answer is too ugly. "Where are we gonna go, Mom?"

"I don't know."

"We could try the shelter again," she says.

I shake my head. The Unitarians are less than a mile away, back up the hill toward the house that will become a tomb once the food runs out and the little rain that will trickle in for the rest of July dries up completely when August rolls in, turning the entire metro area into a desert. Neither of us wants to walk there for what we expect will be nothing. The last time we tried, we got a handshake, a bottle of water, and a wish for good luck.

It's possible, even with the hatred that divided me from my own mother, that I'm happy Win Somers isn't here to see what's happened. She wouldn't be old now, not so very different as an early sixtysomething, but still. The days are hard enough on a middle-ager. I dream of softer days, or I would dream of them if I could sleep at night.

Emma screws up her forehead, thinking. "A different church?"

I shake my head again. "Look around, sweetie," I say, turning in a full three-sixty. "Everyone's already gone." *Or dead,* I think, but it's the same thing, isn't it?

This is the first time I think of another way out, an escape.

Liar.

"There has to be someplace that will take us in," Emma says.

She doesn't know how many calls I've already made.

My first try was an old college classmate, one of the women I used to meet for coffee when meeting for coffee was a thing. Pamela Jackson hung up on me before I even got started.

There were a few lackluster house calls, lackluster because I didn't think for a minute that any of our neighbors would take us in. Sheila Williams offered to let Emma come with them in their RV, though. "It's not her fault," she said. Emma turned her down. But that was weeks ago. Emma might rethink the idea now that we're at the end of the rope.

Some more dead ends: a second cousin on my father's side out in California (*No problem! As long as you can find a way across the country.*); the Episcopal church on Wisconsin Avenue (*So sorry, ma'am. We can barely house our members. Maybe try the Unitarians?*); a friend of a friend of my erstwhile boss Robert's sister-in-law (*Who are you, exactly?*).

And so on. And so on.

You want to know how people end up homeless, how anyone could turn away or shut a door or hang up a phone? Just start asking for help.

Pamela Jackson, though, that one stung like stepping on a bee, a sharp attack right into soft flesh.

Emma leans her head against my shoulder, points at a fat pigeon scarfing up worms or bread crumbs or whatever pigeons scarf, and I think about the last time I went out for coffee with the girls. It isn't hard to remember. The Starbucks is right behind us, door bolted shut, espresso machines down for the count.

Those machines were running at full speed seventeen years ago. If I listen closely, I can hear them.

"You're really knocked up?" Pamela said, pouring a second packet of Demerara sugar into her small coffee. What do they call that? Tall? Grande? One of those. I never could figure out why "tall" was the name for the smallest size.

"Five months." I tugged up my blouse to show off the maternity jeans.

"What about the doctorate?"

"Oh, you know, I'll get to it later. Or not. Nick takes care of me."

"Must be nice." Pamela's mouth made the word "nice," but the sound that came out was on the other end of the aesthetic spectrum. It hurt.

And what do we do when we hurt? When the cat's claw scratches our skin? We scratch back. Sal almost beat me to it, but she was too slow. My reflexes were finer, more practiced.

"Maybe if you had a husband, Pamela," I said, "you wouldn't be such a fucking bitch."

Sal's jaw dropped. Pamela's didn't; it kept moving.

"I hope he leaves you one day, Miranda. I hope he walks out and leaves you with zero." Pamela stood up and wished the rest of our little group a happy day before walking out herself, leaving her small-tall cup of java on the table. She turned back at the door. "You can have my coffee. Maybe it'll sweeten you up."

Sal came to my rescue, as she always did. She didn't like Nick, but she loved me enough to tolerate him. It must have been hard on her when I was so goddamned intolerable.

"She started it," I said when we were outside, away from the others. Still, my hands were trembling and my heart raced like I'd been in a girl fight.

"No, Randa. You started it. Take a look at yourself." She pushed me sideways until I faced the window. It wasn't a gentle push.

"What?" I said. But I already knew what Sal wanted me to see. I had *Rich Bitch* painted on from my head to my toenails. Beige highlights, Prada bag, Versace sunglasses, gel polish changed once every ten days. This week's color was Orange You Jealous, which about said it all.

"You get it now? I mean, listen, hon. We were all pretty thick in school, right? Just us girls, sticking together."

"So it's a crime to get married? Jesus, Sal. What am I supposed to do, swear off men so I don't upset the single set?"

"That's not what I'm saying, and you know it."

"Then what are you saying?"

Sal ran a hand through her cropped hair, a sort of helicopter-blade cut she said made life easier but I thought looked like she'd stuck her head into a wind tunnel. "They think you abandoned us." She paused. "I think you did, too."

"You're being ridiculous."

"Am I, Randa? You know, you should listen to yourself sometimes. 'Nick did this.' 'Nick says that.' 'Nick thinks the baby's a good idea.' 'Nick tells me I don't need a job.' Nick, Nick, Nick. There's such a thing as balance, girl." And then, the worst of it: "What if he did leave? What if all those eggs you piled into the great big fucking Nick basket tumble out and crack?"

I laughed at her. I actually laughed hard enough to turn a few heads of the people coming out of Starbucks. "Then I'll make an omelet, Sal. That's what you do with broken eggs. Anyway, Nick's not going anywhere."

"Sure hope you're right about that."

I left her outside the Starbucks and walked to the park where I'm sitting now.

Beside me on the bench, Emma peels off a hangnail from her pinky finger. My own nails are clean and pale, uneven. When I tap them, I get a dull thud now, not that pretty clicking sound I love. The thing of it is, I lied about Pamela hanging up without a word. She had words for me when I called and asked for help, words that still sear and sizzle in my ears.

You made your bed, Miranda. Have fun in it.

There were no more calls to old friends, and there's still no answer to Emma's question. I don't even know where we'll sleep tonight. The only person who I know would help is Sal Rubio, and she left for the Virginia Femlandia colony ten years ago.

Ten

There's a gas station I used to go to at the next corner. The nozzles from all six pumps lie like dead snakes on the ground, ugly black hoses cracked from the heat. On the bulletproof-glass window where the cashier used to sit and study molecular biology during her night shift, a note is taped up. *All finished. Like we are.*

As if I needed a reminder. As if the lifeless hoses and broken windows and empty cigarette racks weren't explanation enough. Do we really need a verbal statement detailing the situation for us? I don't think so.

I wonder how it ended for the girl from the gas station, if she sat sweating behind that glass as another angry customer shouted obscenities and demanded the "regular price," three bucks a gallon instead of the market rate. I wonder if she dared to come out and face the mob that was surely waiting for her when the sun went down.

Emma reads my mind. "I just bet she was scared out of her wits while all those assholes beat on the window and screamed at her to unlock the pumps. Assholes."

I brush shards of glass away with a filthy shop towel that was lying near defunct pump number one, and we sit down on the concrete, backs to the door so I can watch the road. Not that I expect to see anyone, but I know cities are the worst places to be when there's a meltdown — too many people in too little space. Open country is better. Emma cracks open a bottle of fake cranberry juice and we pass it back and forth without saying anything. In the tightened lines of her face, I see more hatred than worry. It chills my heart to think that at sixteen she's already learned the hard life lessons that most of us can happily evade until we're of a much older age. It bothers me more that every one of those lessons has, even if coincidentally, been taught by a male.

"Where do you think Jason is?" I ask, peeling the foil seal from the can of peanuts.

"Who cares. I think I'm gonna marry a woman. Less trouble."

"They're not all bad, honey. It's not like evil and assholeness are encoded in the Y chromosome. And I thought Jay was one of the good guys."

She shrugs, and I notice her shoulders have become sharp, forming hard points under her T-shirt.

I broach the one subject that's been on my mind since I woke up this morning. "There's a Femlandia commune near Paris. In Virginia. We can't make it there in a day, but we can get started. Camp out overnight on the way. We'll find a farm once we're past the airport. You up for it?" In my own voice I hear hesitance. The last place I want to be is in my mother's conception of some radical feminist utopia where everyone eats wheatgrass and screams about shitty men and plays angry Janis Joplin tracks on endless repeat. That's just not me.

Emma provides the only answer that makes sense. "Do we have a choice?"

"Probably not."

So we pack up our cranberry juice and our peanuts, refill two empty milk cartons with water from the reservoir at the do-it-yourself car wash station, and start walking again. Emma takes measured, calculated strides, putting each foot flat on the ground, instead of a more natural heel-to-toe step. I know she has blisters. I know they'll be worse after sixty miles. From her stilted walk, I know she understands this, too.

Here is what I know about my mother's intentional-living-community brainchild: Femlandia, whether the Virginia brand or the Nebraska brand or the Vermont brand, is pretty much as advertised. Female-run, and female-populated, self-sufficient existence. Initially, she had wanted to call the communes "Somersville," which I imagined was her way of procreating when what she had actually procreated no longer seemed promising, unable to live up to her standards. Beyond the obvious double-X-chromosome-centric lifestyle, I don't know what to think — aside from the assumed Joplin mania and kumbaya-ish daily rantings about the evils of patriarchy. Who knows? Maybe I'll be surprised.

In any event, Emma is right. We probably don't have a choice.

I take out the folded letter from Sal, the one I stuffed into my pack before we left the house.

The first correspondence I had from Sal Rubio arrived almost nine years ago, a cheery note in her elegant, spidery script telling me she made the right decision, that she and Ingrid (tall, Swedish, and gorgeous) were happy in their new home, even if it was a little less like the promised Disney resort and a lot more like low-budget camping with porta-potties and poison ivy and more rules than a federal prison. Sal didn't say much else, only wished me well with Nick and Emma and told me where to find her if I ever needed anything.

The note I hold now is much more recent and far from cheery. Ingrid wasn't happy, Sal said, and had been making noise about going back into the real world. Sal wanted them both to stay, fearful of what might happen if they left the sanctuary of Femlandia.

My own worst fear is that Jen Jones might be there. And the ghosts of that old tug-of-war will be waiting for me. I don't want that, and I don't want to have to face Jen. Or her self-righteous I-told-you-so shit.

"We'll find a farm," I say to Emma, making the decision for us.

We toe our way down the hill away from the town center, passing the banks with their busted ATM machines and the Re/Max real estate storefront with its advertisements for million-dollar homes (*Ask inside about super-mortgages!*) and the Dog & Cat Veterinary Hospital, its backyard kennels empty. Or I think they're empty. I don't really want to know, in the same way I don't want to think of Bunny the almost-talking gorilla.

The bus depot is empty, save for a few hungry souls in tattered sleeping bags on the floor, tucked up on the side of the building where shade continues to coddle them into a delusion that all will be right when they wake. The sun will hit them soon enough, and they'll roll over, see the day through the shot-out windows with the gray-dog silhouette, and roll back over again once they realize today is no better than yesterday and that the buses are still and silent in their yellow-lined spaces. Emma and I hurry past it, as fast as the building heat and our heavy packs allow. If we keep this up for another few miles, we'll reach the highway. And from there it's straight west through Virginia, far enough away from the capital for a farm.

I'm thinking roast goat. Roast pigeon. Roast fucking squirrel. Anything hot, and I'll take it. Who am I kidding? I'll take it cold.

They say it all tastes like chicken, right?

Eleven

Like most people my age, I grew up with maps, accordioned paper whose creases wore thin with every unfold and refold. And, like most, I kept those maps. Some were souvenirs of trips to Spain and southern France with Nick; some vestiges of our first road trips, where I played navigator in the passenger seat of our old car. No one needs maps anymore — or, I should say, no one needed maps when everything down to the closest dry cleaner's could be summoned in a millisecond by Siri or Alexa. But we kept them. Perhaps to retrace our younger steps along the highlighted squiggles of roads and rivers. Perhaps we thought something so concretely utilitarian was simply too good to throw away. Perhaps, after reading enough novels about modern-day pandemics, some deeply entrenched survival instinct told us to keep them.

So we have a map. Two, actually. One of

the greater Washington area, one of Virginia. Each is filled with lines I imagine speeding along in my Mazda, covering quarter inches of terrain in the blink of eye. I look at those quarter inches now and realize they represent miles.

It's an easy downhill trek to the river, where we'll follow the C&O towpath south into DC, cross Chain Bridge into Virginia, and work our way through the McMansion-lined streets of McLean. Five hours to travel what used to take me twenty minutes.

The things we take for granted.

Emma notes it, too, as we pass clumps of virgin land, still wooded after centuries of occupation. "Imagine the first people here," she says. "And all they saw was this." She points to a patch of trees dripping wisteria.

Briefly, I wonder whether the lavender blossoms are edible.

By high noon, we're at the towpath, strands of loose hair sweat-stuck to our cheeks, T-shirts turned translucent and clinging to our skin. To our right, trampled weeds and running-shoe tread marks signal a route down to the Potomac River.

What goes down must come back up, I think somewhat illogically, measuring the vertical relief. But the water's invitation is unrefusable. A smile paints itself on Emma's face when I mention a swim, and down we go, following the caked-mud tracks of the footpath.

There's a small stone structure at the edge of the river, three walls and a platform. Inside it, I shed my clothes down to bra and panties, and Emma nearly does the same. She pauses, squints up at the bright sun, and decides to keep her T-shirt on.

"Sunburn," she explains.

I find it odd but don't push her. It's a strong sun today, and the sky seems to radiate fire.

Both of us crane our necks out of the structure, peeking right and left like a pair of frightened woodland animals expecting to find predators. There are none to be found. Ninety-five degrees and the region's usual atrocious humidity have kept everyone indoors. Also, the last shops with wares to sell will be opening soon for the daily two-hour rush. I don't imagine much will be left worth rushing for by week's end.

Emma steps gingerly off the concrete platform. Her feet seem to dance over the rocky shore, but mine do the same as soon as I set a bare foot onto the hot, uneven surface. And then the bliss of water on my skin, the cooling evaporative effect, the feeling of being cleansed of the day's dirt. I wish we could stay here forever.

My stomach disagrees.

"I needed that," Emma says while we let the sun dry our bodies. A lone scooter buzzes along the parkway several yards above us, and she scrambles back into her shorts. "How much farther are we going to walk today?"

The mall at Tysons Corner — really two malls, one for the upper-middle-class Nordstrom's shopper, the other for the upper-upper-middle class, who prefer Saks and Neiman's — is eight miles to our west. It's the last place I want to be at night. Last month, it might have provided a marginal amount of safety, possibly a few supplies, bicycles. But I've been through Bethesda today — twice. I know there's nothing left in the cycle shops. And I know the kind of people out after sundown. They aren't the Saks Fifth Avenue types.

"Two hours to Tysons," I say, pulling on my own clothing, ears cocked like a dog's for any more sounds from the parkway. "Then another hour to Wolf Trap. That's if we hoof it, so let's say four hours total." Even after a bath in the Potomac, I have my doubts we can handle a steady clip of four miles an hour. "We can make it to the airport by nightfall."

Just pronouncing the words "Wolf Trap" takes me back to an evening with my mother, before she traded me in for the better model of Jen Jones. Win was opening for a B-list band at their request, and I sat in the wings listening as she threw verbal knives at whichever male targets were the flavor of the day. The president. The chief justice. The secretary of whatever. My father.

And what would have been my younger brother, although I didn't realize it at the time.

"I will not, ever, willingly bring another male into this world," she screamed into a microphone at the end of her rant.

The assistant stage manager, a twenty-something pale man with freckles bridging his nose and quiet gray eyes, flinched on the stool next to me. "Wow. Harsh."

"That's my mom," I said, dangling my feet in the air.

"Hey, kid, your shoe's untied," he said. I thought it was a joke, the kind where someone makes you look down and then flicks at your nose with a *Gotcha!* or *Made you look!* But then he knelt to tie a bow after hanging his headset on his own stool.

Win went ballistic when she left the stage. "You get your filthy hands off my daughter, you pedophile." She spat the words at him. Quite literally, in fact — I watched spittle fly from her lips, glittering in the bright spotlights that had followed her. It looked like snow.

And then I was off the stool, my legs trying to find purchase on the floorboards, as she dragged me out of the wings and into center stage. "Nine years old, and still not safe." Win's eyes cut sharply to her left as I prepared myself for another tirade about a man's world. But Win had something else planned. "He was peeking up your skirt, wasn't he, Miranda?"

"N-n-no," I stuttered. "He was only —" *tying my shoe.*

Those lights blinded me. I still don't know how people can stand on a stage with only the glare of white before them, the audience an amorphous, roaring shadow. Win had my wrist in her hand, and she turned it as she squeezed. "Tell them, Miranda. Now."

In those moments, with the lights and the roar and the smell of summer sweat all around me, with my arm twisted so far I thought it might detach from my shoulder, I told them the lie Win wanted.

I don't know what happened to the pale assistant stage manager who was only trying to tie my shoe — I suppose he lost his job

— but that was the last time Win Somers was invited to speak at Wolf Trap. She moved on to more receptive audiences after that.

"I said, 'I'm ready,' " Emma says, shouldering her pack, bringing me out of the daydream. But she heads up the footpath reluctantly, looking back at the stone structure on the bank of the river at least three times.

In another few hours, I'll wish we'd stayed in that little hut.

TWELVE

Win blinked hard, her sight still filtered through a series of floating spots. Bright whites, coal blacks, primary reds and greens clouded her vision as she walked offstage to the roar of the audience. The Wolf Trap crowd was gearing up for the headlining band, but Win knew most of the applause was hers. Those few men in the orchestra section who had hissed had been quickly drowned out by hundreds of female voices.

Trapping the wolves, Win thought.

"Wow," she said. "That was a trip, Miranda. One day it will be your turn."

She had barely finished her sentence when she saw the young stage manager on his knees. He couldn't have been much more than twenty-one, fresh out of college, but twenty-one was still a dozen years older than Miranda, who was blithely kicking the air with her Mary Janes. Her thin, down-covered legs were spread, giving the young man a private show.

"Get up," Win said as she yanked Miranda to her feet. "Get up get up get up get up!"

"He was only tying my shoe," Miranda said.

Christ, her daughter was a stupid little thing.

Win knew what men were like; Miranda didn't. She knew the department store Santas and the elderly priests and the well-meaning uncles weren't all benevolent, that their hands and eyes roamed over female bodies, and damned if nine years old was too young a target. Nine years old hadn't been too young for Win.

It happened on the morning when Father Black asked her to help him clean the chalkboards after Sunday school.

Win couldn't reach the top of the board, not even halfway up, no matter how long she stretched her arm and how high she stood on tiptoe. She was erasing a verse from Genesis, the part right after God cursed the snake to crawl on its belly and eat dust. Win liked that part, mostly because she didn't like snakes, and after all, the snake had tricked Eve. But the lines that came after about making Eve sorry, about hurting her when she was the one who had been deceived — Win didn't like that part at all. Especially since the snake was a man in the first place.

She was thinking these things when she heard the lock click on the far side of the room.

Father Black came up behind her, lifting her to the high part of the blackboard the way her own daddy used to hoist her up on the kitchen counter when Mother was cooking. But Daddy never went under her skirt. Daddy never lifted up the material of her dress and put his hands around the bare flesh of her waist.

That day, Father Black did so many things that her daddy had never done.

Thirteen

All the parking lots at Tysons Corner are empty. Mostly empty. Those few cars that remain behind sag, with their doors open and their tires stripped. God only knows why their drivers came here — perhaps, like the mall closer to my former home, this one turned into a refuge in those early days. I can hear the Bloomingdale's elevator now: *First floor, Women's Lingerie. Second floor, Children. Third floor, Emergency Medical Services.* The cars tell other stories. A University of Virginia license plate with LAW-23 on it in bold blue lettering. Somehow I don't think Mr. or Ms. UVA Law is going to get any job offers this coming fall. A Toyota hybrid advertises its former owner as a *Believer in Climate Change!* with one bumper sticker; another sticker informs me the clock is ticking and I have only a few years left. If only the Extinction Rebellion people had been monitoring pension funds as closely as carbon dioxide. The worst, the vehicular decoration that forces both Emma and me to an abrupt stop, is the bright new *Baby on Board* warning sign in the rear window of a Volkswagen — the slate of an entire future wiped clean by the stroke of a bureaucrat's or judge's pen.

Shattered glass litters the pavement around the cars, like diamonds on black velvet. I look at the rock on my left hand, another of Nick's follies, worthless as a chunk of coal now. But, of course, back then we never thought we'd come to this.

Then, we were having tea at the Ritz-Carlton, now a twenty-four-story tower overlooking a ghost town. Then, Nick was taking me to Neiman's, whose display windows today are blank, lifeless eyes staring from its brick facade, whose mannequins lie sprawled in a grotesque tableau, each of them assuming its own death pose.

Emma and I walk in the open, avoiding cars and corners, avoiding anything that might provide shelter.

"I don't understand," she says.

"Me neither."

But I do. I get it. I want to tell her civilization is a construct, an abstraction dependent on thousands of trivial variables. It's a triviality to walk out your front door without fear, to jog along a running trail with nothing on your mind but the Stones playing through wireless earbuds and your electronic personal assistant congratulating you on another mile well run (*only two more to go, champ!*), to stuff your wallet with fresh twenties from the ATM knowing they won't be stolen, only accepted in exchange for a Starbucks coffee or a pair of Nikes or the new azalea you'll plant in the front garden. The minutiae of daily life are wrapped in plastic salad bar containers and paper La Brea bread bags. In octagonal signs with the power to halt cars and green lights to make those cars go. In the Mister Landscaper irrigation system that will keep the azalea green during summer's dog days. In free-flowing gasoline paid for with invisible money. In daily mail delivery. In stocked supermarket shelves, clean laundry, and the rule of law.

It's a shitty thing when you end up mourning weekly manicures and the entire judicial system in the same breath.

"Dad said it would never happen," Emma says as we leave the detritus of the twin malls behind us and head north toward the airport toll road.

"Chávez probably said the same thing. It's what we do, honey." Really, it's what we don't do. We don't think anything will ever change.

At the on-ramp to the toll road, we rest again. A lone pickup, its muffler in bad need of repair, rattles by. There's a sign on the rear window. *Sorry. No room. Good luck.*

So we walk on, alone, following the single white line at the edge of the highway, watching our shadows grow longer as the day moves on.

This road used to be so well traveled with cars and taxis. The new Silver Line rail service carried twenty thousand riders a day to and from Dulles Airport. Twenty thousand, nearly the population of the nearby bedroom community of Herndon. With a few hundred thousand cars added to the mix, it's like the entire city of Minneapolis moving back and forth along this road.

Today, there are two of us. Plus the pickup with the shitty muffler that didn't bother to stop.

The anonymous SUVs don't stop, either. They don't even slow as they pass us, only whiz by westward, a long convoy of black steel snaking its way along the highway. The bodies inside them are invisible through heavily tinted windows. It's what remains of Washingtonian power — invisibility behind dark glass and armored metal.

"Where are they going?" Emma asks, stretching. Her shirt is soaked all over again, as is mine. We both look like contestants in a wet T-shirt contest. It isn't a pretty sight.

"Mount Weather, probably. Too bad we can't hitch a ride." The not-very-secret emergency operations center in Bluemont is a stone's throw from Paris, and fifty ugly miles from where we stand. It's where Dick Cheney hunkered down after 9/11, and where Congress will hide out during this new disaster, safe underground dining on meals ready to eat while the rest of us first search for food, then fight for food, then kill for food.

It's nearly beyond my ability to understand how a country can turn from first world to fourth world overnight. Nick always said we were bulletproof. I suppose Venezuela, sitting pretty on all that lovely oil, once thought the same.

Another several dozen black cars motor by, their occupants worrying into walkie-talkies while being blasted by AC vents. I wonder what they say to one another when they see us. I wonder if some of them turn their heads away so they don't have to.

Finally, the snake of cars comes to an end, and the highway is as quiet as a morgue. Time to run my thoughts past Emma.

"Listen, honey," I say. "I think we'll manage if we can get to a farm. We don't have to go to — that other place."

The words are barely out of my mouth when the first thump hits the ground behind me, followed by at least four more. My peripheral vision catches a pair of work boots, their leather scuffed and cracked. Then — a voice.

"Lookee here. Two for the price of one."

Another voice, deeper. "Make it one for the price of one. She's too old."

A chorus of laughter responds.

I register everything at once. The sound barrier wall to my right, separating this stretch of highway from the lonely woodland on the other side. The thumps of five or six men, men who were sitting on that wall watching us, waiting for the parade of government vehicles to end. Emma stretching her limbs, a sixteen-year-old body inside cotton gone transparent.

Oh God.

"Emma! Run!" I scream, but it's a hoarse, dry scream, as cracked as the boots now running past me and toward my daughter.

There are arms, and hair on those arms, and tattoos underneath the hair, all dingy green and grayish black serpentine shapes that come alive with every flex of muscle.

There is Emma, crying out to me, cursing at the men pulling at her clothes and dragging her like a rag doll toward the ditch that drops down from the verge. There are grunts and cackles and fists that find my own body, forcing me backward onto coarse gravel. There is blood in my mouth and on my lips, hot and ferrous.

And then they are on her, their laughter the sound of wild birds. One, a broad, bearded man in a plaid shirt, says, "We'll take their food. After."

A wetness seeps into me, soaking my clothes as I turn to one side, cheek pressing into the loose stones on the side of the highway. I can feel each one of them, each irregular shape as it pushes into my skin.

Get up, goddammit.

The beaten, bleeding woman I've become says to stay down. Rest. The mother inside me hears Emma scream, and I wrestle my arms from the straps of my pack, sliding open one zippered pocket after another, reaching with road rashed hands for Nick's gun, finding the safety and thumbing it off. Emma's screams have turned to sobs, throaty, mournful heaves as the men egg each other on. They aren't laughing anymore, and they aren't speaking. They've become something unhuman, primal.

I'm on my feet now, skidding along the stones, sucking on my bruised lip to stop the blood. It's useless, so I let myself bleed. And when I raise the gun toward the first of my daughter's attackers, I let him bleed. Without a warning.

He doesn't deserve one.

Fourteen

Four pairs of eyes watch me from the ditch. There are five pairs, but the ones belonging to the bearded man currently lying motionless where he dropped don't seem to be registering much of the world around him. Perhaps, I think morosely, those eyes are staring into the shitty eternity that's waiting for him.

Good.

I haven't yet lowered Nick's pistol. It's heavy in my grip, the metal of the barrel hot and the grip slightly tacky from my own sweat and blood. I must look like a one-woman murder scene.

"Beat it," I say, surprised at the steadiness in my voice.

I honestly expect them to laugh. I expect another chorus of cackles and a few dismissive waves in my direction as they get back into the game they've started. I expect the gun to jam, or the clip to be empty, or the bearded man in the plaid shirt to suddenly come to life and dodge any remaining bullets before he takes me down with an easy, one-handed swipe.

But they do the unexpected. They run. And they don't stop running until their hulking forms are distant, wavy lines in the rising heat of the highway. When they're far west of us, barely visible, one stops and shouts something about bikes. Another shouts back. There's a pause in the action, like the still time just after high tide when the water is slack, when you're not quite sure which way it's moving. Then they become nearly invisible.

"Mom?" Emma's voice is weak.

I don't think I can look toward the scene. Sometimes, expectations play out. I step forward, eyes half-closed and half-open, trying to veil them with my own lashes so the next several images might remain fuzzy, impressionistic pictures that I'll always be able to reprocess into less traumatic ones.

"Mom!"

Now I'm running, tripping over a surfaced root, in the direction of her voice. Another part of me wants to run down the highway, heatstroke be damned, and unload everything else I have into four faces, enough to turn them into bloody Rorschach blots.

"Mom."

And again, my expectations defy me. Emma is on her back, hair wild and strewn with clumps of mud and weeds, her shirt stretched thin around her even thinner body. But there's no blood, no limbs bent into impossible angles, no clothes torn off and discarded into a puddle of material. My baby is all right.

Of course, they would have played with her first, like cats toy with mice before the kill. It's no fun, I suppose, if the game ends too quickly.

I've never feared men. I've never had cause to. Nick, who could play rough in our bed only because we both saw sex as a no-holds-barred, anything-goes-as-long-as-it-feels-good kind of experience, never laid a hand on me, never raised his voice, never treated me as the weaker one or the dumb blonde or the wife to be seen and not heard at company parties. The few boyfriends and lovers I had before marriage were the same. They wore *This Is What a Feminist Looks Like* T-shirts and ate kale. It's hard to fear a man who eats kale.

But I can imagine being afraid. Every time I ran a 10K and watched legs with muscles I would never have stride on by, every gym visit where a man twice my size dipped his entire weight and raised it back up with only his arms, every wild, breathless hike up foreign mountains when Nick would reach back and take my hand, pulling me along with what seemed to be an endless supply of strength, I sometimes imagined less benevolent legs and arms and hands, and what they could do to me if the will to harm were in them.

Or even if it weren't.

Bunny, my great ape who I'd come to think of as a second child, who I hope went peacefully after the prick of a syringe and is not starving and thirsty in what used to be the National Zoo, was a peaceful type. But I never forgot he outweighed me by 250 pounds. An overenthusiastic hug could have cracked a few ribs. An accidental stumble over one of his toys, and he would have crushed me. The intent meant nothing, only the mass and muscle. And, I learned, animals are capable of intent.

I had just begun working with Bunny when the attack happened, all ninety seconds of it. Only the video, afterward, gave me a hint of the actual time. During, while I watched, the attack spanned both an endless ocean of time and no time at all.

A chimpanzee, one of the younger males, had been swinging with his mates from branch to branch. There was only a sharp crack, then a thud, then what sounded like screaming.

A child, about ten, cried and turned her head into the folds of her mother's dress. A group of teenagers, mouths gaping as their phones recorded, stood in a sort of wondrous silence. Two zoo staff in khakis tried to herd the crowd away from the nine-foot fence with its barbed-wire coils running along the top. They failed.

I was as rapt as anyone else in the great ape enclosure. After the thud, five full-grown chimpanzees scurried across the ground toward their fallen mate. Later, when I listened to the confused audio, I would hear things like *They're helping him! They're cooperating! They're saving the chimp!*

But no.

What the mob (for it had fast become a mob) was doing was biting. And stomping. And tearing.

Underneath the hoots of the attackers were cries of pain, almost human, as the five descended on the fallen chimp and ripped into him. Blood-matted fur flew from the cluster in a gruesome trajectory; the water in the shallow moat turned turbid with pink, then red. There was the hiss of fire hoses and the pop-pop-pop of Robert's tranquilizer gun being fired as more chimpanzees stormed out of the inner enclave first to inspect, later to join in.

Then came the stones, showers of them arching up and over the barbed coil at the top of the fence, raining down on the spectators. I stood with my back pressed against the gibbons' enclosure, across the pedestrian path that separated the monkeys from the chimps, my eyes wanting to close but staying wide. Two children and their parents huddled to one side of me, the confused parents frozen with fear.

"The males are barbaric," someone said softly.

They were all of that. But I saw more than barbarism. I saw intelligence and strategy and planning.

The rocks being flung over the fence by the band of chimps numbered in the hundreds, scattering the onlookers in every direction, funneling the crowd to narrow passageways now blocked by other curious zoo-goers trying to push their way inside the great ape house. A Japanese tourist with a Nikon strapped around his neck fell, and both man and camera disappeared under the crush of moving feet.

I pulled the two children near me forward,

away from the gibbons and closer to the chain link that separated the chimps from the humans. Their father pulled back, but the mother saw my logic — a vacant bench was there in the open space. She and I pushed the others down and under the wood seat planks. Whatever the father might have been saying was lost in the noise.

The pure horror sickened me, but I held my phone steady, zooming in and panning from the far right of the enclosure to the far left.

Much later, after it was all over, I would watch the security footage from earlier in the day, watch the chimps working together, building ten neat pyramids of stockpiled stones.

They had planned the attack.

Fifteen

Win understood from an early age that men were animals. She would have called them pigs but found no reason to insult a perfectly good pig with the comparison. Hyenas, maybe. Jackals. Anything wild that ran in a pack and looked out for itself first. But not anything that could be considered cute, edible, or useful.

There were man-babies, like Carl, who couldn't pick up his dirty underwear without being reminded — Win did everything but staple a note to his nose once they moved into the house their parents had bought for them after the wedding. And there were man-wolves, like her father and Carl's father. They were the ones to be frightened of. Because they were the ones Carl and the rest of the man-babies turned to for help.

During her pre-wedding sequestration — and afterward, until she was far enough along with the baby that the Finleys and the Somerses no longer feared an abortion — Win sat for hours in her mother's sitting room waiting for Carl to arrive from work. He had been able to finish his degree, he had been able to score a job at his father's company, and he had the freedom to leave the house unattended. No one treated Carl like a disobedient pet, tethering him to the confines of the Somerses' suburban fortress. No one balked when he kept his shoes on and tracked grass cuttings over the parquet floor or sawed through his meat at the dining room table like a barbarian wielding a primitive tool. It was during these hours, these long, boredom-filled stretches only occasionally interrupted by Mrs. Finley's daily phone call to check on her, that Win thought.

She thought of her father, the way he would walk in the front door and kick off his boots, leaving them for Win's mother to pick up. She thought of the stack of plates he would ignore in the kitchen, passing them by as if they were invisible to his man's eyes. She thought of the mornings her mother would tiptoe around the house, squaring up papers and books and mail into neat little piles.

Mostly she thought of the grunts that

seeped under her parents' bedroom door at night, creeping along the carpets, finding their way into her room and into her ears. On the mornings after such nights, her mother was always quiet, subdued. "Tamed" was the word that came to Win's mind.

When she was young, she understood that men and women got married and had children, and that everyone was supposed to be happy about it. All the animated movies said so. Princesses were the thing to be, and the thing for a princess to do was catch a prince.

What Win couldn't understand was why anyone would ever want to catch a wild animal and have to live with it afterward.

SIXTEEN

I have one eye on the lonely stretch of the highway and one on Emma as I help her to her feet and check for damage.

"I'm fine, Mom." She says this casually, as if she were refusing dessert or telling me she's all hooked up for a ride to school. But her voice is more than casual. There's a vacancy in it, a deadness. It's a doll's voice after a string is pulled, like Chatty Cathy saying *I love you, I'm sleepy,* and *Ow, that hurts* all in the same unemotional tone.

I recognize the other signs of shock, Emma's wide eyes that seem to see me and not see me at the same time, the tilt of her head to one side as she regards the gun I set down on the gravelly verge, the curiously inquisitive half smile when her gaze falls on the man in the plaid shirt. Only a small disruption in the black-and-red pattern on the breast pocket gives any clue to where I hit my target.

Emma lets me pat her down, staying still and wooden while my hands roam over her body searching for tender spots. When I reach the small bump on the back of her skull, she doesn't wince.

But she says, "Ow, that hurts."

And she sounds like Chatty Cathy, mechanical.

What isn't still or wooden is Emma's left foot swinging back and then forward, landing hard on the perfect bull's-eye of the dead man's temple.

"Emma!"

Her foot swings back once more in a graceful arc, a ballerina's malicious arabesque, and comes through again, harder. And again. And again. The toe of her left sneaker takes on a bright cherry tinge, and when she sees it, she smiles a wolfish smile.

And she continues kicking.

I think, *I should stop her.* I think, *The sonofabitch is already dead.* I think, *Why the hell not?*

I join her.

There are no clocks in this world of frenzied violence, no bells to signal the end of the round or referees with their color-coded cards to halt us. Here, on an empty stretch of a highway that once carried bumper-to-bumper traffic in and out of the capital, we are on our own to do what we will. And our will in this moment, in these long, unmeasured moments, is the will of savages.

Below me, in the chaos of kicked-up dust and unearthed weeds and blood — so much blood — the thing that used to be a man's head lolls and rolls with each kick. A single fly settles on one eyelid and buzzes off at the next contact of my shoe. A crack, small, like the snapping of dry kindling, almost vanishes among the other sounds. Squishing sounds. Liquid sounds. The sounds of soft tissue losing cohesion. Nearby, Emma grunts.

Inside me, different things are happening. Each breath of hot, stale summer air is a cocktail of dirt and sweat. My vision blurs and refocuses, then blurs again until colorful starbursts appear, like fireworks. I can feel my heart in my chest, really feel it, not just its rapid, aperiodic rhythm, but my actual heart, the muscle contracting and expanding. With every new swing of an arm or a leg, with every grunt — I can't tell whether these grunts are mine or Emma's or whether we've somehow merged into one larger organism, the child reabsorbed into the mother — there is a kind of ecstasy. An orgasmic pleasure.

And still it builds.

The face in the ditch is now pulp, and we continue our kicking, mixing blood and earth, feeding off each other, and feeding off the violence. It's so pure, this violence, so raw and primeval and instinctual.

I feel somehow like a god, only destruction, not creation, is my game. But there are gods who destroy, aren't there?

Seventeen

I do not feel like a god anymore.

Emma is up first, and this time she pulls me to my feet before running along the sound barrier wall, dragging me behind her.

"Don't look back there," she says. "It's — never mind. Just don't."

"I need your dad's gun."

"I've got it." She jerks a thumb over her shoulder, indicating the backpack, then cocks her head, listening. "Oh shit. I think they're coming back. Come on."

"Give me the gun, honey."

Emma doesn't answer, not right away. She pulls me closer to the wall, crab-crawling on the ground, getting as low as she can and as far away as possible from the body. "No. Not them. The other ones. The ones in a Hummer. An olive drab Hummer. Like maybe they could have been on patrol thirty minutes ago? Fuckers."

We crouch here, at the foot of the wall,

and wait. The low rumble of a motor turns higher-pitched as the army vehicle approaches, slowing. In the still of mid-afternoon, its sound is all but deafening. One uniformed soldier stands in the ring mount, half-exposed, head covered with a combat helmet. A weapon rests over one of his arms. I don't know what it is, only that it's heavy and long and ominously pointed in our direction. The image is apocalyptic. All we need is Mad Max and a motorcycle gang to complete the picture. In my mind, I hear the word "bikes" again, the shouting of the man who wanted to turn back toward us. Maybe the Mad Max image isn't so far off.

They were everywhere at first, these trucks, prowling the suburban streets and avenues, the men and women in them alerting us to sundown-to-sunup curfews through bullhorns. *Temporary measures,* they said. *No cause for alarm,* they promised. I felt safe with the trucks and bullhorns and the uniforms, all symbols of an accustomed order. It never crossed my mind that such measures are only deployed during wartime, and war is, I think, the absence of order.

Finally, the truck passes by. There's the whir of the engine accelerating and the telltale diminished pitch as the airport access road takes it away, west. Everyone, even the army, is escaping.

My watch tells me it's nearly five in the afternoon. Three and a half more hours of daylight. More than enough time to reach the airport and set up camp for the night. We've barely put a chink in the fifty-plus miles I want to cover, and all of a sudden I'm realizing it will take days.

"We have to go back," I say. "We have to search him for a car key."

Emma goes pale, and for the first time since our rampage, I'm really seeing her. The spatters and streaks of blood on her face and clothes give her a horror-queen look. I'm thinking Carrie after the prom. When she returns my stare with a grimace of her own, I know I look just as bad. Maybe worse. I've half a mind to retrace our steps and go back to the river to rinse off, but I wonder, after what I've done, if all the water in the mighty Potomac would be enough.

We work with our eyes closed, breathing through our mouths as we pat down the body, swatting away the flies that have come to feast on the remains. Together, we roll him over, and it's only then I see the real effects of my handiwork, a horrid mess of cloth and tissue and blood, as big around as a grown man's fist. Emma screams.

I find two keys — a silver-toned Schlage, probably for his house, and a smaller one that looks like a mailbox key. There's also a wallet in the left hip pocket. I slide the wallet out and scoot backward in the ditch, putting as much distance as I can between the man and myself. The flies are wicked, and what was a lone hawk circling over our heads has now been joined by two more. The flies and the hawks have enough to eat, I think absently. More than enough.

The man's driver's license introduces him as Howard Joseph Tebbetts of Vienna, Virginia. Inside the billfold are three crumpled fives, a twenty, and a few quarters. I take it all, even the license. The credit and debit cards I leave behind. They're useless. But the keys — the Schlage means a roof over our heads for the night. All we need to do is cover the three miles back to Vienna, adding another hour to the trip's total.

Emma comes over, inspecting my stash, careful to avert her eyes from the dead and mangled Mr. Tebbetts. "That's a bike-lock key," she says.

"How do you know?"

"It says Kryptonite on it. Kryptonite makes bike locks."

I wonder, briefly, which Madison Avenue genius came up with that. On second thought, I don't care. I'm all about playing my own brand of Superwoman and figuring out how to scale the sound barrier wall separating us from the bike path I know is on the other side.

It takes us thirty minutes of our remaining daylight to find a break in the wall, and another half hour to double back eastward along the former railroad that was converted to a recreational trail some years back. When I see the shiny steel of the five mountain bikes, glorious primary colors spattered with mud, I want to find the ancient Greek or Sumerian who invented the wheel and give him a prize.

"Which way?" Emma says.

"The house in Vienna is closest, but it means backtracking," I say. *And the unpleasant possibility of running into his pals,* which I don't say. Emma doesn't need a reminder, and I really don't want to shoot anyone else before the sun goes down. "We'll go to the airport and camp out. Plenty of open space there."

"And tomorrow?"

I'm not sure when I made the decision, or if I made one at all. I think maybe the choice was made for me, by Emma's attackers, by fear and by fury, by a small voice inside me that thanked Win Somers for teaching me how to protect myself. The .45 I took from the house might have belonged to Nick, but it wasn't Nick who taught me how to shoot. That was all Win's doing.

"Tomorrow we go to Femlandia."

"I'm cool with that," Emma says.

So am I.

We ride west along the converted railbed, stopping only once at another defunct gas station, where we hose ourselves off from head to toe, scrubbing madly until our skin is rid of the red and begins to turn a bright pink from the friction.

It's like washing off war paint, and I wonder if I will ever be able to rid myself of it all.

Most of it, I think, is on the inside.

Eighteen

Win couldn't remember when she started to hate the thing growing inside her, but today she hated it more. She wanted it out, partly because it was another link in the chain that kept her tied to Carl, partly because she saw no good reason to bring another male into the world. There were enough of the bastards already.

She didn't think she would be able to love a son, not the way she loved Miranda. And an unloved baby was a recipe for disaster. He'd grow up to be some unsocialized monster, take the inevitable spin into crazy land, and probably shoot his family one night after dinner while they were snugged up watching television and scarfing down rocky road ice cream. Also, Win had plans. And her plans didn't leave room for months of sleepless nights breastfeeding a colicky baby. An eight-year-old daughter was enough.

The appointment was scheduled for this morning, the soonest Win could get in. She kissed Carl on the cheek and told him she had to run a few errands and would lunch downtown with a friend.

"Celebrating?" Carl said. He sat reading through paperwork at the dining room table, shoes off, one foot propped up on the tablecloth Win had laundered and pressed only yesterday. Win noticed an ugly coffee ring staining the linen near his elbow and thought of the last conversation with her mother. "Boys will be boys" was the answer to any complaint. It always had been.

"No. Just lunch," she said.

"That's funny." Carl looked up from his work, beaming at her. Win hated this look of his, as if he were gazing at a well-deserved trophy. "It sounds to me like you've got something to celebrate." Now he got up and drew her close, circling his arms around her back. "Six more months. I can't wait."

Win winced over his shoulder. Carl took it as an invitation to further intimacy.

"What shall we name my boy?" he said, releasing her and firing up his laptop.

His boy.

"Look, Carl," Win said. "I don't know how you found out —"

"I called your doctor."

"I see."

"How about our fathers' names? David Jonathan Finley. Like it? Or Jonathan David. Yeah, I like that one better."

She should have walked out the door then, picked up Miranda from school, and driven as far as the car would take them. She should have done all those things. What she shouldn't have done was tell Carl she didn't want the baby. But she did, and he pouted.

And this time, having learned a thing or two from the big boys in the Finley-Somers dynasty, he threatened.

He did this with a smile, as if they were consulting on where to go for a holiday or which restaurant she might like for dinner. "Win," he said. "You're tired and you're not thinking right." Carl steered her to the living room, sat her down on one of his mother's antique Chesterfield sofas, and knelt before her. He took each of her wrists in his hands. To Win, the pressure around her wrists felt like handcuffs.

"Now, what kind of husband would I be if I let you go off and do something that can't be undone?" he said.

"It's not up to you to let me." She felt herself sinking lower into the sofa cushion, growing smaller. If it continued, Win might float upward, light as one of the dust motes dancing in the morning sun through the front window.

His grip on her wrists only tightened. "I'm the man, Win. It is up to me."

"It isn't." Even her voice had turned weak, kitten-like.

"I'll call the office and put in for some time off." His eyes brightened, and a childish grin spread across his face. He snapped two fingers together. "That's it. Time off. We'll go somewhere. We'll go sailing, Win. Leave Miranda with your folks, just you and me on a bareboat. By the time we're back, you'll feel better about this." He released her other wrist and cupped two hands over her stomach, claiming it as his own.

NINETEEN

Washington Dulles International Airport once handled sixty thousand passengers every day. We leave it as we found it, an empty and motionless structure, its control tower standing sentinel over absolutely nothing. The last time I was here, Nick was with me, having conspired with a still-friendly neighbor to take Emma for a week while my husband whisked me off on a surprise trip to Paris. I remember the activity, the travelers rolling their wheelie-bags along miles of busy corridors, the moving walkways transporting us from one end of the terminal to the other, the weird buses with their hydraulic raising and lowering mechanisms that made *whoosh-whoosh* sounds as they prepared for loading and unloading of another hundred travel-weary passengers.

I remember we flew first class. I remember I had the filet mignon on the flight over.

"It's only money, honey," Nick said when I saw the ticket receipts on his phone. He said it as if money were worthless.

Nick was more right about that than he could have known.

While we ride west on a deserted Route 50, town house communities giving way to a different, thickly forested landscape, I think about money. I think about the abstraction of a ten-dollar bill, that green mix of cloth and paper that I used to slide into a hairdresser's apron pocket, or hand over in exchange for two cups of coffee. I think about the quarters, some shiny, some with their heads and tails rubbed dull, that I fed into parking meters thinking *Who cares if I put a few extra in? They're only quarters.* I think about the pennies I left in the little trays next to cash registers. *Take a penny, leave a penny.* I must have left hundreds of those thin pieces of copper.

I don't know how to think about money when it's not in use, when there's nowhere to spend it and nothing to spend it on.

So I stop thinking about it.

Emma cycles on ahead of me at a lazy pace, lost in her own thoughts. She hasn't spoken more than a few words since yesterday afternoon after we found the bikes, and in the early hours of the morning she slept fitfully, turning sharply to each side as if trying to shake off something, swatting my arm away whenever I reached out to soothe her. But this isn't the worst of it. At six o'clock, just as the sun began peeking over the wing-shaped roof of Dulles' main terminal, Emma woke up paler than usual, refusing to eat even the dry melba toast I found at the bottom of my pack. The crackers were crushed, an apt metaphor for how I'm feeling. When I offered her the few bits that were still intact, insisting she eat something, Emma shook her head.

"You need to have some breakfast. We've got a long trip ahead, even with the bikes."

"I don't want to. And I don't want to go anywhere right now. I'm tired."

I looked around at the emptiness of the airport lot. What bothered me was that the place wasn't empty enough. There were cars and vans, a rank of taxis that should have been idling but weren't. All around us stood concrete Jersey barriers, perfect for hiding. Perfect for hunkering down behind until something or someone worth waiting for appeared. Like us.

And I wasn't the only person walking around with a handgun. A panic washed over me, cold and prickly, as I stared out at the parking lot, at all those obstacles that could be concealing anything at all, a thought that hadn't worked its way into my addled brain when we arrived here yesterday. "We're going, Emma. Now."

She stared at me as if I were a stranger.

"I said, 'Now,' Emma." It was the first I'd ever raised my voice to her. When I reached out to grab her by one arm and yanked her to her feet, it was another first. I'd never manhandled my daughter before.

Emma jerked away, landing with a hard thump on the pavement, her eyes widening with fear. Then she held one hand out, index and middle fingers up, thumb down, and clamped them together.

The baby sign for *No.*

"You don't want to go?" I asked, allowing her regression without making a big thing of it, even though the sense of needing to get out of here, get going, get anywhere, was starting to suffocate me.

Again, the fingers shut, quicker this time, with finality.

"Why not?"

Emma continued mutely and held both hands in front of her chest, elbows out, then let the elbows fall to her sides. *Tired.*

"I know. Me too. But we have to. It's not a choice, Emma, tired or not tired."

Her next sign I knew well from the time

Bunny had scarfed down five bananas at once, taking advantage of a moment when I was distracted with paperwork. Emma pointed one hand to her head, the other to her stomach. *Sick.*

"Oh, come on," I said.

She made one final gesture before swinging a leg over her bike and leaving the corner of the short-term parking lot where we spent the night wedged between two cars that won't be driving anywhere soon. Fingers pointing toward her chin, flicking fiercely outward. *Hate.* And then the rooster crest that stopped first at her forehead, paused, and moved down between her breasts.

Man.

Apparently, I had taught her well. I wonder if Win would be proud of me.

"I get it, honey," I said. "But we're going. Both of us."

She repeated the same sign — in a way. But instead of moving the rooster crest of her hand down, she only tapped her thumb against her chin. That insignificant change might have been a mistake, Emma misremembering her signs. Because the new sequence didn't mean she hated men.

It meant she hated Mommy.

An hour after leaving the airport behind

us, we approach Middleburg. This is horse country, or it was. The paddocks on either side of the rural roads are overgrown now with tall grass, all gone to seed. Water troughs provide the only relief on the flat land, and they look like child-sized coffins. To my right, a roan mare and her foal lie still, the foal's spine pressed up against the swell of her dam's belly like spoons in a drawer. In my mind hangs a question that will never be answered. *Which one went first?*

If I had any doubts about the decision to try the Femlandia commune, they mostly evaporate as I watch Emma's long, coltish legs pedal steadily on. When she finally settled down last night, we slept together like those horses, the curve of my daughter's body fitting in the concavity of my own. There's another body, of course, the one inside me, and when he or she kicks for the first time, all my other doubts turn into nothing, replaced with a new energy and a fierce will to pedal onward for the two remaining hours.

I keep my head down, following the double yellow line on the empty road, and I don't look for any more horses on the way.

TWENTY

My legs are jelly, but I will them to keep spinning as we climb the not-so-gentle slope up into hill country.

I think I can. I think I can.

You could call what I've been repeating to myself over this twenty-four-hour journey a mantra, but that would defeat the point. That first syllable, in all its forms, left my vocabulary this morning when I watched Emma regress back into childhood. The attack could have been worse — much worse — but an assault remains an assault, a threat of bodily harm. They say the best way to put an end to tyranny is by not using the name of the tyrant, right?

So I'm not saying any goddamned mantra.

I'm saying a repetition. A series of sounds with meaning. A *femtra,* maybe.

We follow the fence with its *No Trespassing* and *Danger — High Voltage* signs for about a mile, maybe more than that, cycling slowly, trying to peer inside the compound. The other side of the fence is thick with tall evergreens too dense to allow for spying. I suppose it's intentional. But it doesn't look any more like Disneyland than it did the first time I saw it, a quarter of a century ago. Back then, there were no electric fences and no warning signs aside from a few boards with *Keep Out — Private Property* hand painted on them. The modern additions aren't much more than lipstick on a pig.

Oh, Mother, I say to Win's ghost. *Is this really your idea of paradise? A barricaded thicket in the middle of nowhere?*

Emma slows, then stops, balancing the bike between her legs. She points to her left without looking back, and when I ride up to her stopping place, I see it.

After a day of travel, we're done. We're home. Even if it isn't really home.

I shouldn't call what we left "home," either. This is our new home, this place, this community. They say home is where they have to take you in, no matter what. So I guess the gates Emma found lead to somewhere like home, if I think of home as a refuge, a door that will open when all other doors have closed, friendly arms waiting with welcomes. Home or not, the village behind the gates — whatever it might be — is the only place left to go.

They also say X marks the spot, and the metal gates separating us from our new home bear two Xs, solid steel letters, unembellished with flourishes or serifs, one on each side. An apt logo for an all-female enclave. Behind them is another double gate with close-fitting panels. The whole setup reminds me of those airport security passages, the ones that can trap you in a no-man's-land between each set of doors.

Think of it as a ranch, Miranda. One of those dude ranches where city slickers pay their money to try something different.

And this will be different, only no one will be asking me for my money. A damned good thing, since I'm down to the last worthless pair of Hamiltons, a Jackson, and a few Lincolns in my money belt. A shame those bad boys aren't reproducing. Maybe I should have pocketed a few Susan B. Anthony dollars and let them go at it.

That's okay, guys, I tell the bills tucked into my cargo pants. *You're not needed where we're going. Take a rest.*

Fine advice, rest. I should try it sometime.

Soon, Miranda. Breakfast, bath, bed, in that order.

I need all three, and I know Emma does,

too. The hunger cramp in my side, the blood-matted hair in my eyes, and the rough salt on my skin all tell me I've needed this holy trinity for a good long while.

To my right is a bell, a heavy chain to pull hanging from it, perfectly plumb. If I draw an imaginary line and continue the chain, where will it emerge? China? Thailand? The eastern border of Russia? I reach out to the chain and pull my hand away. Ten in the morning and the metal is already hot, as if it's recently been drawn out of the forge that made it.

Emma takes a spare T-shirt from her pack, wraps it around one hand, and yanks down on the chain.

There's no sound.

She yanks again, harder this time, putting all of her muscle into it. When she pulls once more, her eyes are wild, unseeing, glazed over like they were yesterday when she kicked her first kick into the head of Howard Joseph Tebbetts of Vienna, Virginia.

From nowhere, I have an image of the Shakers. Devout, separationist, and celibate, they didn't last forever. It's hard to last forever when you don't fuck. And even if you do, there's bound to be an equipment deficit in the Femlandia communities. Lots of Slot As, no Tab Bs to insert into them.

Adoption is one way of getting around that biological inconvenience. Artificial insemination is also a possibility. For all I know, there's a refrigerated truck making the rounds from one Femlandia to another, a kind of sperm dispenser on wheels, although this wouldn't work, either. They'd have to dispense embryos already in development unless the women wanted a surprise Y chromosome thrown into the mix. It's the first I've thought about the logistics of it all, and it's too much goddamned work for a day when I have more work ahead of me.

Of course, if Win didn't think about it, then there's a good reason no one is answering the bell.

"Emma," I say. "Enough. There's nobody here."

You know where to find me if you need anything, Sal wrote in her letter.

Well, I'm in need, and I can't find Sal.

I don't get back on my bicycle. I don't want to. These wheels have brought us here, to nothing. We can't continue the climb west, not with the Blue Ridge rising like a forested wall; and back east there are only dead horses and dead men and permanently grounded airplanes that might as well be dead. To our north is Mount Weather, and I figure on a snowball's chance in hell of getting inside that compound without a plastic government ID card. South means more heat, and as it is, Emma's face has taken on a clammy cast, as if her skin has a thin film of paste on it.

That face now looks at me, forehead creased quizzically. She drags one finger through the air, tracing an invisible map. *Where?*

I've no answer to her question.

The thing of it is, I'm supposed to have an answer. I'm the mother. We're the ones who have all the answers, who fix the scrapes and cuts from sudden falls, who know what's for dinner tonight, who tidy up life's messes, the large and the small. We're the last words on the parched lips of men in foxholes, the final resource when resources have run dry. We're gods to our children, and I wonder what we become when there's no more power to heal or cook or clean, if when stripped of our powers, we become nothing.

A frenzy takes over, raw and primitive. It starts deep inside me, in my cells, bubbling like the innards of a volcano waking from a long dormancy. I kick the bike over with one swift swing of my foot, tripping as I do so, scarring myself with grease from its chain. I kick it again, as if this useless piece-of-shit transport held all the fault. And then I'm on the ground, crying into the dirt, wishing the earth would open up and swallow me whole.

I think I say the word "Mommy."

Twenty-One

"That's no way to treat a perfectly good bicycle."

At first, I think Emma has come out of her selective mutism, grown suddenly older, and developed a husky, Lauren Bacall–type voice, but when I raise my head and see the woman behind the outer set of iron gates, I rethink this.

"What do you want here?" the woman says, standing in the no-man's-land as the second gate swings closed behind her. She's more or less my age, a redhead with wisps of gray at her temples and twin tattoo sleeves covering each bare arm from shoulder to wrist. Colorful and complicated, they remind me of the tropical gardens I encountered in Hawaii on a trip with Nick. There's no anger in her words, only a matter-of-fact bluntness matching her stance — hands on hips, akimbo. Those arms, I think, look like they could bend the iron bars between us without so much as flexing. Emma stares at her, as awestruck as I am. From my vantage point on the ground, this woman is huge.

Amazonian, I say to myself. And they said it was an extinct race.

"You see that?" She points to the left side of the gates, to the *No Trespassing* sign that's more rust and gray than its original red and white.

"Yes," I say, picking myself up and dusting the road grit from my bare skin. Some of the dirt and remaining blood seems to have embedded itself and taken up a permanent, subcutaneous home.

"Well, then."

Any relief I felt at seeing another human being where I thought there were none melts away. "Is this Femlandia?" I say.

No response. The hound dog, who has been panting at the woman's side, growls softly.

"Look, I have a friend here. Sal Rubio. And her partner, Ingrid." I leave out the part about not having heard from Sal in almost ten years.

She doesn't nod, but the corners of her mouth twitch in a half smile.

"Do they still live here?"

"I can't give out any information about our residents."

I hear the subtext. *You're not coming inside.*

"Look," she says, speaking to both me and Emma. "I'm sorry. We have some women here who don't want to be found. I don't know who you are and — more importantly — I don't know who you know."

"You mean whether I've been sent by an angry husband," I say.

"Or father. Or brother. Sometimes it's their own son."

"Jesus."

"He doesn't always come when he's called, does he?"

She's wearing a shawl, gauzy white cotton slung over her shoulders and hanging down over ample breasts that might be lactating. Around her waist is a sarong that looks like homemade batik. The white shawl shifts a little, revealing naked flesh, free of tan lines, underneath.

She sees me notice and smiles. "We're free here. From many things. If you wait, I'll get you some water." Her eyes move over Emma's and my bodies. "And a bite to eat. Then you need to be on your way."

"On my way to what?" I spit the words at her. "There's nothing out here. Nothing." I'd pulled Emma close, but now I release her, shoving her forward, startling the dog. "My daughter was attacked on the road. In broad fucking daylight. We've been showering in gas station car washes, filling water bottles from rivers — when we can find one without too many floating animal carcasses. I have enough food to last for two more days. And that's if we don't run into another asshole who tries to take it from us."

"I'm very sorry." The woman regards Emma with something approaching pity. "Really. I'm sorry. We don't take visitors, and we don't take new members without referrals. Ever."

"You're *sorry*? That's terrific. Just rich. Isn't your whole goddamned project supposed to be about women supporting women and girl power and all that shit? Escaping from the hatriarchy? Being sick to death? Well, one of us is sick and both of us will be dead within a week because we don't have — what? — *references*? How sorry are you going to be about that, you and your closed community?" *This is it,* I think. This is the moment when I realize it won't take a week. I already feel like I've started the death process. When I look into the woman's face through the thick bars separating us, I find no hope. No hope at all.

Unless.

Unless I play the one card still lurking up my sleeve.

Nick knew about my mother, as did Sal. I've never told another soul, not even my daughter. I didn't want her growing up knowing she had an angry, misandrist crackpot for a grandmother. And I didn't want our friends and neighbors to know because, well, people have a way of talking, a way of associating the innocent with the guilty. All it takes is a direct bloodline, as if the propensity for violence is nothing more than another inheritable trait. *You have your mother's eyes* or *I see you've got your mother's green thumb* might as well be *You have your mother's insanity.* There's no room for nurture in this way of thinking. Nature trumps all.

I took every step possible to shield Emma from playground taunts and the jeers of high school classmates. In the process, I suppose I protected myself as well.

And Win Somers did a few things worth talking about, ending with killing her own husband.

Twenty-Two

Win hadn't wanted to kill him. She only wanted a bit of freedom, a taste of the autonomy her mother hadn't known. But Carl was Carl, and the bareboat charter was booked, and their plane to Nassau left tomorrow morning, so something had to be done. Three and a half months at sea was three and a half months too many by a matter of days. When they returned, the only doctors who would touch her would be the unlicensed kind — Win would simply be too far along.

During the week leading up to their departure, Carl worked from home, setting up shop on the dining room table, from which he managed whatever automotive industry magic there was to manage, but always with a careful and protective eye on his wife.

Win spent her days gardening. If rain was in the forecast, she ironed.

She was a fair sailor, having grown up on her father's boats. She was also physically strong and capable of mimicking her husband's handwriting, which, when the time came, would prove more useful than being able to drive the boat back to a marina singlehandedly. While she deadheaded roses and pressed Carl's work shirts, while she cooked their meals and straightened the papers he left scattered around the house, Win mentally prepared herself.

On their second night at sea, she dosed Carl's wine with powdered over-the-counter sleep aids, sprawled on the deck lounger, and feigned interest while he had his way with her under a canopy of stars. It was the same as it had been on that first night, missionary, mechanical, and meaningless — except on that first night there hadn't been any stars. Carl busied himself with his usual thrusting and shuddering, and she thought he looked like a pig with his face gone all pink and his nostrils flaring so wide, she imagined she could see all the way to his brain while he hovered over her body.

He fell asleep mumbling something about baby names, and Win went to work.

The diver's weights were easy enough to cinch around his wrists and ankles, and she forced herself to murmur wifely "I love yous" and enough sweet nothings to lull him back to a complacent sleep. Hoisting Carl's deadweight onto the gunwale as the forty-foot boat rocked in Caribbean waves wasn't as easy. Plus, Carl woke up.

"Win? What the heck?" It came out slurred and slow. *Wha za heh?*

She smiled into his eyes one last time, surprising herself at the tenderness she felt, then braced her foot against the side of the lounger where he had fucked her, and pushed. In the middle of the night, eight miles from Nassau, the splash was deafening. His gurgled calls for help, not so much.

Win went below, shutting the companionway hatch to the night, opened a bottle of the champagne Carl had brought with them (*Only a drop for you, my dear*), and began to write his suicide note. It took her seven tries to get the script just right, like Carl's but with a hint of uneasy panic in the hand. One by one, she ripped off unsatisfactory attempts from the thick block of his monogrammed stationery. Win didn't use monogrammed stationery, only crappy mass-printed cards from the Dollar Store, preferring them to Carl's gift of expensive paper from Pineider with — of all things — a monogram of his own last initial. No S as in Somers, only an ornate, calligraphic F that made it seem as if even her own handwritten notes were coming from him and not her. She struggled with his fat-as-a-cigar Montblanc pen. Sleek as it was, she had never gotten the hang of writing with such an awkward implement. Once, she ripped a ragged slash in the paper from pressing a little too hard. It took an hour before she satisfied herself that the short but poignant note (he had, of course, expressed his unending love to Miranda and to his parents, mentioning Win last) looked enough like his handwriting. She laid this sheet aside and made one more attempt, changing the order of the sentences, adding in a few poignant details, trying it on for size. No, the other note was better. More spontaneous, less purple. She then took the half dozen practice copies, including this last try, where she had allowed her creativity to get away from her, into the head and burned them to ashes, waiting a full minute between flushings until all traces were gone.

She thought of leaving the stationery and pen on top of the small fold-down desk in their cabin, where Carl would have penned his final missive. But that was so un-Carl. Leaving things strewn about didn't match up with a man who crossed off the days on a calendar each night at eleven PM, or who demanded his daughter put away her toys in neat rows on their shelves. In the end, she placed the pad back in its leather case, sliding the pen into the inside loop, and laid it among the rest of Carl's neatly packed work materials he had brought along. The final copy she folded neatly and placed on the built-in wooden table next to her side of the bed, where she would find it in the morning.

Twenty-Three

"And if I were Win Somers' daughter?" I say, thinking the consequences of Emma knowing her own heritage might be a fair price to pay in exchange for getting off the streets and avoiding starvation. Still, I whisper the question. "Would that be enough of a reference for you?"

The woman blinks. "It would. If I hadn't heard the same story before." Now a smile spreads over her face — the lower part. Her eyes don't quite reflect it as she explains. "We had a woman here some years back. She made the same claim, telling us her mother was a close friend of Sister Win."

Sister Win? What a benevolent way to think of my mother.

"Another of us was on gate duty then," she continues, and I see no need to ask why that other woman was replaced. Her tone tells me everything about the incompetence of her predecessor. "This woman came messed up. I'm talking shiner on one eye, fresh burns on her forearms — think cigarettes, honey, purple bruises in full bloom on the wrists and biceps. If it were me, I would have been suspicious, but we had a new girl watching the gate."

I don't ask why bruises and burns raised her suspicions. It's not as if I've been living under a rock for forty-plus years.

Suddenly chatty, she leans in and gives me the rest of the story. "Eva let her through as soon as the woman mentioned Sister Win. Funny thing was, her strip search didn't show marks in any other places. Not one. You ask a woman who's been living her life as a human punching bag, and she'll tell you the sonofabitches always try to hide their marks. Always. I mean, they still want their wives to be able to get out to Safeway without raising eyebrows, right?"

"Strip search?"

My question is ignored, although from Emma's wide-eyed expression, I can tell she's as nervously curious as I am. Maybe more.

"And if you get a guy stupid enough to leave bruises right out where God and everyone can see, you can bet he'll leave a shit ton of them where they can't be seen. Ass. Thighs. Stomach. But there was nothing. You work in a shelter as long as I did, you get to know the patterns.

"Sure enough, next morning I catch the newbie asking around. 'When did Sister Linda arrive?' 'What's Sister Linda's last name?' Oh, Sister Linda's from Gaithersburg? Me too!' Shit like that. She was collecting, see? Except she didn't make it *look* like she was collecting; she made it all seem like she was just another battered-up fugitive from a crappy home, doling out sympathy to anyone who would take it. So I follow her for the rest of the day, right? By the afternoon, she was at this gate, lurking around. Waiting. By nighttime, they were here. Complete fucking shitstorm." She accompanies this last bit with a full-body shake, as if trying to rid herself of the memory. The shawl slips again. "Anyway, that's why name-dropping doesn't work here. You got ID?"

"They who?" I say.

"Who do you think?"

"Husband?"

She nods. "And two of his brothers." My gaze follows the line of electric fencing, easily ten feet high and topped with coiled razor wire. When she notices me looking, she answers the unspoken question. "Yeah, we had one of these installed back then. The newbie sabotaged it — at least that's what I think. This one is, let's say, an improvement."

Now that I'm looking more closely, I can see why. Two parallel fences, not one, extend from either side of the gate. Between them is a bed of gray river rock, a few yards in width, and beyond the inner fence another swath of rock, then a dense hedge of Leyland cypress trees.

"It works for keeping people out," the woman says.

Or for keeping them in, I think.

"Wait here, and I'll get you that water and a few sandwiches. Do you both eat meat? Because I think you need some." She looks over Emma, who has been standing silent, listening, then sweeps her eyes over my own body, pausing at the thickening around my waist. The rest of me has been thinning as this other part swells, feeding off my stores of fat and muscle, which were never in abundant supply — even before the crash reduced them to rare commodities.

It strikes me I haven't really looked at myself, or at Emma, recently. Our mirrors drove away in a truck, along with everything else, leaving only the ones in the bathrooms. I never could stand my reflection under that harsh light, where every blotch and pore would stare back at me, a quiet reminder I wasn't twenty anymore and never would be again. And our expeditions to Safeway before it shut down didn't exactly necessitate a full-blown makeup job. My cosmetic endeavors limited themselves to soaping up and rinsing off. The moment I caught my chipped nails and hanging cuticles in the mirror, I thought anything beyond a quick wash was tantamount to putting lipstick on a pig.

But I'm looking now. Emma is a different kind of reflection, part me and part not me, as if a pair of skilled hands had deconstructed each of her parents and reassembled the elements. The word I think of when I study her face, formerly somewhere between childishly cute and pre-adult beautiful, is "gaunt." I don't like this word, but it's the right one. It looks like how it sounds.

The woman behind the gate tilts her head, and I can't tell if it's patience or exasperation in her voice. "I said, 'Do you eat meat?' There might be some bacon left from breakfast if you don't mind it cold."

Cold? I'll take it raw.

"That would be fine," I say. Then, in a final act of desperation: "I really am Win Somers' daughter."

"I'm afraid I need more than your word, honey."

Emma speaks up in her newly reacquired baby sign language, thumb to chin, forefinger swiping down. *Who?* Then, with more deliberate movements, as if italicizing and bolding and underlining the question all at once, she asks again. The look on the woman's face before she turns toward the inner gates tells me we might not even get food and drink now.

"My daughter never knew her grandmother," I explain. "Long story, and it's not one I'm ready to explain to her on a dirt road in the middle of nowheresville when all we've had to eat is a tin of congealed pinto beans and some melba toast crumbs. Look, can you call someone? Can you call Jen Jones? She'll know me."

The woman, whose hand has been resting on the brass lever of the inner door, turns slowly back to me. "We don't have a way to make calls here. We aren't like the outside."

I'm reminded of another trip with Nick, the first afternoon of which I spent asking random Madrid residents where I could find an open shop that might repair a broken shoe strap. Each question was answered in patient, overarticulated English that nothing would reopen until five, the subtext a loud reminder that I was clearly not from these parts.

"But," she continues, "I'll tell her you're here."

The inner gate swings open barely wide enough to allow her through, and a bolt slides into place behind it. Once again, we are alone, strangers in a strange land, only the metronome-like click of the bicycle wheel Emma spins absentmindedly to keep us company. So Jen Jones lives here, in Paris, Virginia, not more than an hour's drive from my former home.

That's super. I'm dying to meet the daughter my mother wished she'd had instead of the one she was stuck with.

Like hell I am.

Twenty-Four

The entirety of me feels filthy. The soles of my feet sweat inside running shoes that were once white with aquamarine stripes and are now caked with red Virginia clay. My hair, which hangs in tangled strings down to my shoulders, has become something I want to pull out or shave off completely, if only it would stop my scalp from itching. My fingernails are a horror show, ragged and of impossibly different lengths. You'd think at least two of them would be even, but no. They're ten varying shapes of ugly. I wipe dried skin from my nose — maybe it's skin, I can't tell — and at the moment I think I can't possibly feel any more vile an excuse of a woman, the gate opens. Jen Jones casts me in a whole new brand of pathetic.

Strange that I used to think we looked alike.

To begin with, the woman is clean. More than clean, almost glowing, as if she'd emerged from a bleach bath only moments ago. Her hair is so blond, it's hard to tell where it ends and where the white embroidered kaftan begins. Her sandaled feet show no sign of having trod on anything but sparkling floors — ever. And her nails, clear of color, are buffed to a high shine, almost reflective.

I loathe her.

Need, however, displaces loathing in my current universe.

"Miranda?" Jen says, stepping forward — no, *gliding* forward — across the vestibule between the inner and outer gates. "How lovely to see you." She takes some time assessing the state I'm in, and then adds, "I wish it were under better circumstances."

I wish it were under no circumstances at all, but I force a smile, cursing myself for not cleaning my teeth this morning as she slides the heavy bolt on the first set of gates and holds her arms out in a ridiculously overdone welcome, her smile showing perfect pearly whites. My tongue slides around my mouth, tasting pinto beans and sensing something akin to wool.

"And this must be your daughter," Jen says. Emma has reached her first, and Jen wastes no time. Her eyes draw Emma forward, and pale white arms wrap themselves around my daughter in what seems like a maternal hug, but to me it looks more like a constrictor's embrace, suffocating its small prey before the kill. "Oh, you're so thin, child. We'll have to see about fixing that, won't we?" Jen looks over Emma's shoulder at me. "You too, Miranda. What on earth have you been living on these days?"

"Whatever we can get," I tell her, and pull Emma back toward me. There's some resistance, like wresting a small hunk of metal from a weak magnet. Not impossible, but evident. I can't say I like it. Emma is my daughter. Mine.

But Jen is accustomed to trespassing these little biological boundaries, of denying the laws of filial relations. Of course she is; she learned the trick from my own mother.

I was younger than Emma when it happened, when Win Somers first allowed another daughter into her life. At first, I welcomed it, this idea of a sister, a girl to giggle and gossip with. Until a few years later, when I came home to find them discussing me in the kitchen.

"Miranda hasn't woken up yet, not like you have," Win said.

Jen and I were both sixteen then, well on our way to womanhood after the awkward years of adolescence. At least they had been awkward for me, a late bloomer who had no use for tampons until I was halfway through high school. Jen, on the other hand, seemed to have already navigated the waters of sexual maturity by eleven. But in my sophomore year, I'd changed. I had crushes. Plenty of them.

My mother must have been washing up or working on dinner preparations, because the sink faucet was running as she talked. "Every day, it's 'Phil's so cute' or 'Do you think this dress makes me look pretty?' Or 'If Kevin doesn't ask me to the homecoming dance, maybe I'll just ask him myself.' Sometimes I think Miranda studies boys more than she studies anything else."

"She'll figure it out one of these days," Jen said. "Right now, her hormones are doing the thinking for her. I might have gone through it, too, if I didn't have a cocksucker for a father. He should have a custom T-shirt with 'Old enough to pee is old enough for me' printed on it. Asshole."

Win laughed, but it wasn't a cheerful laugh. "I know, honey."

There were some other sounds then, a shuffling of feet and a scrape of kitchen chair legs on tile, then sobbing.

"I promise you won't ever have to go

through that again," Win said. "And I hope you're right about Miranda. I mean, that she figures it out soon."

"Give her a year or so," Jen said.

"A year? Ten seconds is long enough. Plenty long enough when we're talking about these young guys who shoot their wads before their trousers are even down." The water stopped running and plates clattered as she cleared the dish rack. "Then you end up like me. Young, dumb, and full of some jerk's cum." More clanking of plates; then the refrigerator door opened. "And Miranda isn't clever enough to do what I did. She'll stick around, even if the guy's a complete douchebag." A pause, then: "I don't know. Maybe it doesn't have anything to do with being clever. Maybe, when it comes down to basics, it's more about survival instinct. You know what I'm saying?"

"You gotta do what you gotta do," Jen said. "Even if the rest of the world doesn't understand it. Even if it seems wrong."

"Yeah. That's it, girl. They say freedom isn't free. I say, it ain't only not free, it's goddamned expensive. People wouldn't understand that I had no choice. I had to get rid of him."

There was some silence, broken by a

heavy sob. I couldn't tell which one of them the noise came from. Then Jen's voice whispered, "I understand. And I love you for what you did, Win."

It was all too much, more than I wanted to hear. I stood at the front door, keys in hand and violin case tucked under one arm, listening to my mother and my best friend take turns psychoanalyzing me. And then it became more than too much.

"I wish you were my daughter," Win said. The words came out like a sigh.

That was the day I started referring to my mother as Win. If she wanted to be called Mom, if she wanted filial affection beyond a perfunctory peck on the cheek on Christmas Day, she could go right ahead and start the adoption process. I'd even print out the forms for her.

Which is what Win Somers eventually did.

"I see Mom in your eyes," Jen said, holding out both arms and waiting for me to fall into them. "I miss her so much, I can't even think how you must feel."

Time to play the loyal daughter. "It still hurts," I lie. I'm about to savor a small victory, though. Some of the day's filth that has accumulated on me is about to rub off on Jen.

She pulls back when I get close, a kind of

cobra move, retracting from my less-than-pristine body as if I might be infectious. "Let's get you cleaned up and fed, darlings. Sister Kate can take care of the formalities and I'll see you later this afternoon in my quarters. We have so much to catch up on." There's a flurry of white linen as she sails back through the inner door, only pausing long enough to throw a coquettish smile at Emma. And to lock eyes with her.

Emma, to my horror, smiles back, entranced.

Kate steps out to the road, picks up the bikes, and wheels them both from the road before locking the main gate. And then we follow her through the inner door, into our new sanctuary. Into Femlandia.

Twenty-Five

When the heavy door swings shut behind us and Kate taps a code into the security panel, I know we're not in Kansas anymore. I'm not even sure we're still in Virginia.

Emma stands beside me, openmouthed, her left hand slowly curling closed in front of her face. What she's saying is more "wowsa-wowsa" than the literal "beautiful."

I expected a shantytown, not a paradise.

"This is the visitors' area," Kate says. "Inside is much nicer." She looks us over from top to bottom, slowly. "If everything checks out, you'll see."

"What needs to check out?" I say.

Kate points one of her tattooed arms toward a row of wooden cabanas. "You can use those if you like. Or you can just take everything off here and hang it on those." She indicates a cluster of low benches, also wood, with high, latticed backs. "Whichever you prefer."

Emma looks me a question.

"Take what off?" I say.

By now, Kate has shed the gauzy shawl completely, wrapping it into a loose turban around her mane of auburn hair. Not a single tan line marks her upper body, not even the thin white thread of a bra strap or a bikini tie. She has a lean, feral aspect, and if she weren't speaking to us with the slight traces of a northeastern urban dialect, I'd think she was a wild woman, born and raised in these wooded parts of the country.

"We have rules," she says. "No mobile phones, no cameras, no devices of any kind. Not that they work anymore, but still."

Emma digs into her backpack and brings out her phone.

"And yours?" Kate asks me.

My iPhone turned into a brick weeks ago. I wiped it before I sold it for a tenth of its original cost, a final goodbye to my former life. The pictures on it, all those selfies of Nick and me on deserted Caribbean beaches, in the bars of the Paris Ritz and the palm-shaded lanais of unaffordable Maui resorts. There, in the storage depths of my phone, were portraits of Nick, dashing and devil-may-care in a Brioni dinner jacket, of me, newly coiffed and highlighted after a day at a Fifth Avenue salon, a collar of diamonds and sapphires circling my neck. I kept them all, all the shots of Emma as a baby, tucked into her bassinet in the room we spent thousands renovating — who cared about the cost of the custom paint or the trompe l'oeil windows looking onto scenes from the Moscow Art Circus and the earthy expanses of the Maasai Mara, elephants lumbering in the distance, zebra galloping, as if with a long enough arm, our baby could reach through the artistic trickery and touch them.

These things were all gone now. Keeping them seemed psychologically risky. So I deleted them all, removed the SIM card, and got rid of the damned thing. I suppose keeping our history might tempt me into hoping I could return to it. But these are the hopes of children — the hope that Santa will always bring the gift at the top of the list (because he did it once before); the surety that all summer holidays will end in a Lancaster-Kerr beach scene worthy of immortality in the annals of cinema; the knowing that if anything good has already happened, it will, without fail, occur again.

We who have lived a little longer know the realistic — and thoroughly depressing — truth: we talk of history's propensity for repetition, but there are no guarantees. Or maybe there are. Maybe the guarantees only apply to the shitty parts. Anything even marginally pleasant is doomed to be a one-hit wonder.

Emma, given time, will learn this, too.

"I haven't had a phone for weeks," I tell Kate. "Search if you like."

What happens is a kind of airport customs search, bags opened, unzipped pockets proffered to the eager nose of a hound, whose name, interestingly enough, is Buffy. Not exactly what I'd expected as a first choice for a radical feminist commune — or a police dog. Buffy sniffs, taking her time, exploring each crevice and cavity. She finds the last few melba crumbs, laps them up from the bottom of my backpack along with some crumpled fast-food napkins, and then, her day's work done, the dog plops down at Emma's feet, licking salt and blood off a bare ankle. She's made a clean spot, which serves only to highlight the rest of Emma's road-weary patina.

Meanwhile, Kate has been turning Nick's gun over in her hands. "We can't let this in either," she says, turning toward the cabanas. She unlocks the first in the row, searches for an empty pigeonhole, and comes back minus one phone and one .45, and plus one plastic numbered ticket, after locking up the storage case again. "Keep this. In case you want your things back when you leave." Her eyes move from us to the locked inner gate. "Not that there's anywhere to go these days. Thank God Win had such a vision."

"Yes. Thank God for Win," I say, still wondering exactly what my mother's vision was, and why it requires a full-body strip search.

And I think of the road just beyond the solid gates. Really, I think of what might be on that road, or who. Another gang of bicycle-thief road bandits? But there's no one here except the three of us, the solidly built cabanas, and a copse of cypress that have grown into one another. No one to see me in the buff.

I'm the first to take off my clothes, peeling them off and heaping them in a pile beside the wooden bench. Ugly white bikini-top patches where no sun has ever penetrated make my breasts stand out like bright high beams, and the skin on my ass is pale enough to be called blue. It's the curse of the fair blonde; no matter what, we always end up looking like skim milk.

Kate catches me comparing our bodies and spends a tick longer than necessary studying my waistline, as if she's trying to decide whether I've put on some middle-aged pudge around the middle or whether something else might be going on. "You stay here long enough, you'll get darker. But for now, I'd recommend SPF 90. And a hat. One of the others can fix you up with some supplies once we're inside."

Terrific. I'm about to trade indoctrination into a semi-nudist colony for room and board. My mind doesn't like it, but my stomach is dancing a happy little jig. "Can I put my clothes back on now?"

"In a sec. I need to pat you down, okay?"

She doesn't wait for an answer before snapping on a pair of latex gloves and giving me a thorough, clinical grope starting with the soles of my feet. I protest, or my muscles protest, as she moves up.

"Relax. I'm not going any farther than necessary," Kate says, moving her hands up my thighs and gently forcing my legs apart. "Think of it as a quick gyno exam."

"What do you think I'm hiding up there, heroin? Little sachets of plutonium?"

She slides one finger inside me, and then she's out. I feel guilty, although I'm not sure of what.

"No one's going to blink if you smoke a little Mary Jane now and then, but Sister Jen draws a bright line on the hard stuff.

No opioids, no coke, no Ecstasy or other meths. And she doesn't give warnings, so if you're traveling with that shit, you need to give it up now."

"I'm not."

Kate studies my belly again, then nods toward Emma, who is shaking her head so vigorously, I'm worried her neck might snap.

"Emma's clean as a whistle." I lean in close and whisper, "In every way, if you know what I mean. Do we look the type of women who shoot up?"

Kate gives me another one of her smiles. "No. But drugs aren't the only problem."

"What is?" I say, putting some of my clothes back on. The shorts and tee are even more foul than I thought, so I bundle them up using only my thumbs and forefingers and hold them as far away as possible.

"Let's put it this way," Kate says, pulling the gloves off and disposing of them in a small canister next to the locked cabana. "Sister Jen has a strong preference against anything with a dick."

I look at Buffy the hound, presently curled in on itself licking at a pair of intact testicles.

"Oh. Dogs are fine. And useful," Kate says. "We need to maintain the population, don't we?"

I'm flummoxed. "You need a half-assed

gynecological exam to satisfy yourself I'm a woman? Really?"

Kate frowns at me, creating lines in a forehead that was, until a moment ago, smooth as a newborn's. "I need to satisfy myself that you were always a woman."

"Let me guess. Another one of my mother's stipulations?"

"No. This is Sister Jen's rule. She likes things to be black-and-white. Gray, not so much."

"Sounds pretty exclusionary to me," I say.

Kate shrugs. "Let me ask you something. You see how we are here, right?" She waves one hand over her bare breasts. "How free do you think we would be if we started letting in male residents?"

"If they identify as women, though —"

I'm cut off before I can finish. "They can identify as a fucking hedgehog for all I care. I'm talking about what they are. Not what they think they are or what they want to be. It's a slippery slope. You let in one, you have to let in all. There's a reason your mother called this place Femlandia. Get used to it." She's obviously finished explaining the facts of life to me and faces Emma. "Your turn, honey."

Emma has never been a shy girl, never the type to hide herself from me or demand separate dressing rooms when we made our annual back-to-school pilgrimages to the department stores in Chevy Chase. Around her father, she kept up a healthy habit of modesty, but when it was just us girls, our bodies weren't dirty things to be kept from view. She'd even confessed to going topless once on a beach trip with a few school friends, shocking the hell out of them, and finally asking what the hell the fuss was all about since they all had the same equipment.

But today, she's different. She repeats her baby sign for "no" in exaggerated movements, two fingers and thumb clamping shut, opening, clamping shut. Again and again and again.

"She's had a shock," I explain to Kate. "Those men yesterday. I thought she was fine, but there was a delayed reaction. Do you really need to put her through this?"

"Okay," Kate says with a certain finality. "Let me put this all out front so you understand. We're a womyn's commune. That's 'woman' with a Y, not an A. We have rules, the same rules your own mother laid down a quarter of a century ago. We don't ask for any money, only in-kind contributions. You live here, you eat, you rest. You have rotations of chores, same as everyone else. What you don't get to do is rewrite the fucking rules. And the rules say everyone gets checked out." She stops. "There are two doors here. One leads inside; the other takes you back to where you came from. There's no third option."

"Give me a minute." I take Emma by the hand, leading her toward one of the benches.

"Why so shy, hon?" I say. "It's just like going to the doctor."

For the last time, Emma signs *No.*

Shit.

"All right. We can go. If you really want to, we can go back out there. We'll find something." Although I'm wondering how warm a welcome we'll get when we walk up to a farmhouse in our road-weary, blood-stained clothing, looking like a pair of murderous hellcats. I think back to the girl squatting outside the country club gates, her hair greasy and matted. I think about the relief I felt when she shirked away from my outstretched hand. The fact is, she frightened me, and I was glad to turn my back.

What I want to say to Emma is this: the worse things become, the more backs we'll see turning from us. It's a curiosity of human nature, and not one I'm proud of.

I think, as I stroke my daughter's hair and will myself not to beg her to turn her body over to Kate's roaming hands, that if we leave here the same way we came in, we'll both be dead within a week.

This all-too-realistic realization propels me over the line from protective and understanding mother to the kind of mother I need to be today. Protective, yes. To hell with the understanding business. My hands stop their calm stroking and lock onto her upper arms.

"Emma, do what she says. Now."

Emma wrenches herself from my grip with a force I didn't think she had in her, pulling away and taking us both down to the grassy space between the bench and the cabanas as Kate looks on, nonplussed. It's a meltdown, in the literal sense. Emma goes lax for a moment, then balls up into a fetal position with her thin arms wrapped around her knees. Her eyes continue to watch me, so wide I see more white than brown. If I didn't know myself, I'd say she was preparing for a hard kick to the ribs.

"What's all this?" Jen's syrupy voice cuts through the air in the enclave, severing the tension. Her kaftan floats toward Emma, and when my daughter holds out her arms to this stranger, when my view of my own girl is blocked, it seems the white cotton material of Jennifer Jones' dress severs something else.

Twenty-Six

Nick used to take me places, and he had his own way of showing me the world's wonders, ancient, modern, and natural. When we visited Agra, he insisted I follow him with my eyes closed until we stood at the far end of the long and narrow pool. Then he made me wait.

He took his usual half-smug, half-childish eternity before saying, "Open 'em up, hon." And when I did, when I saw nothing but the ivory white of that marble mausoleum, I went into a new space, only seeing the double images of the Taj Mahal, one real, one reflected. It was the same story with other places and other exoticisms. Chichén Itzá's towering temple of Kukulcán. The miraculously intact frescoes of Pompeii and Herculaneum. And, closer to home, the stark nothingness of Death Valley, the endless depths of the Grand Canyon, the violent white water of Niagara Falls.

Each time, I thought myself a child again, looking through a lens at impossible freaks of nature and engineering, not really believing my own eyes. It delighted Nick, this showing off, even if it ended up crumbling our lives to the level of some of the ruins he took me to see.

I'm in that same place right now, allowing myself to be led through the wide door from the visitors' enclave into the inner refuge of Femlandia. I never considered the tiny towns tucked into Virginia's green mountains and thick forests exotic — they're towns surrounded by hills and trees, for chrissake — but here I am, staring with wide eyes and a gaping mouth at another of the world's wonders. That my own mother created it is in itself a wonder. I didn't think Win's anger left much room for beauty.

Or magic, which is the first word that comes to mind.

"It's only confusing at first," Jen says, taking note of my roaming eyes. "Think of it like a partial clock face, only compressed on the lower half. We entered at six o'clock, walked north from the main gate, and now we're coming into the center of our little village."

"I get everything except the little part," I say. We're standing in what looks to be at least an acre of open land. The makeshift huts and sloppily slapped-together kit homes I imagined are absent. Instead, a variety of buildings, all of which a skilled hand might have finished repainting this morning, dots the deforested area like jewels on a bed of green velvet.

Jen points them out one at a time.

"That's our meeting place on the right, kind of a town hall, I guess. We can seat two hundred comfortably, and the stage is multipurpose. Last year, some of the girls put on *Steel Magnolias.* I think they're doing *The Children's Hour* this fall. And we have a chorus," she says, "for those of us who can sing but can't act our way out of a paper bag. Like me, I guess. Do you still play violin?"

"Not much."

"Well, if you want to get back into it, Marcia can set you up with an instrument. I can't promise anything like an Amati or a Guarneri, but she's a decent luthier." Jen turns to Kate. "Can you take Miranda to the shop once she's settled in?"

Kate has been hanging back as we walk, keeping quiet, but now eyes Emma with a mix of suspicion and exasperation. There was, in the end, no strip search, not after Jen Jones intruded and acted the savior.

"Sure, Jen," she says. "I'll go on ahead and see about a bungalow. I was thinking Sarah's place."

"Put them with Nell. There's more space, and Nell could use a little socializing these days," Jen says, and Kate walks off with her hands raised, palms to the sky, evidently accustomed to taking orders and not arguing.

I feel like I've landed on another planet. Only an hour ago, I pegged Emma and myself for dead, either from quick, get-it-the-hell-over-with violence or a slow, depressing starvation — a Hobson's choice I still don't want to think about for very long. Now I'm standing in something rather like a luxury resort while a woman who might as well be my sister discusses commissioning me a handmade violin and seeing about bungalows with people who need company. I half expect her to invite me to high tea this afternoon. At this point, I don't think my eyebrows could creep any farther up.

Again, Jen reads my mind, and laughs lightly. "What did you think your mother set up, a few shitty shacks around a swimming hole?" She turns toward me and takes both of my hands in her own. "Let me tell you something, Miranda. Win planned for everything." Her eyes glint with something between mischief and wonder.

"Everything? Like the rest of the country turning into post-Chávez Venezuela?" I say. "Because even though the juice is still on out there, it won't be for long." I cock my head toward the gates behind us. "How many more weeks — days, maybe — do you think people can survive in a vacuum?"

What I'm really thinking is that my crackpot excuse for a mother might have thought brightly painted buildings and a private orchestra were enough. But Win wouldn't have foreseen the total infrastructure collapse. She wouldn't have gotten that far. She wouldn't have had the foresight to make a project built to last.

A little of the light leaves Jen's eyes. "You're underestimating Win. And you're underestimating me. Don't do that." The light comes back. "As for juice, we have solar-powered generators. Enough for normal activities and then some. We have an intranet for local communication — messages, phone calls, announcements. Stuff like that. All the tech is in sector one, over there." She points to our right, and I follow the length of Jen's arm toward yet another gate, this one of solid steel with a keypad lock below its handle. "It's limited access unless you're certified. How are your computer skills?"

"Shitty," I say. "Think early Iron Age."

Emma tugs on one of Jen's sleeves, points to herself, and bumps one fist on the other twice. *I work.* She does it again with even more emphasis at the first sign of a placating smile from the woman.

That's my girl, I think. *Now if you'll only start talking to me.*

But Emma isn't even looking at me. She's staring up at Jen Jones like a pagan would stare at an icon on a pedestal. Rapt.

"She hasn't been talking," I explain. "Not since yesterday."

"What happened yesterday?" Jen says. She stoops down to below Emma's eye level and asks again. "You can tell me anything."

Emma's hands make two more signs, the descending rooster crest meaning *man,* and the dual index fingers pointing at each other. *Hurt.* When Jen looks the question at me, I explain.

Man hurt. Hurt man. It's ambiguous, but true in either interpretation. A man hurt us, and we hurt him right the hell back. At once, I'm back on the side of the highway, listening to the men as they shove Emma into the ditch, listening to their cackles and boasts. The memories of twenty-four hours ago are all sounds: the rip of fabric, the deafening crack of Nick's gun, the thump of our shoes against flesh and bone, the squish of a man's head as we kick it over and over.

What frightens me most isn't what we did, but the realization that, in some sick and twisted way, I enjoyed doing it. Worse, I think I could do the same thing all over again. I think I might enjoy it even more.

I shake off these unpleasant audio memories and find Emma folded in Jen's arms. And now there are different sounds. My daughter, who hasn't spoken a word to me since we found the bikes yesterday, who has insisted on communicating only in the baby sign language I taught her more than fifteen years ago, has decided to be vocal again. It seems a switch has been turned on.

"Not yet," Emma says to Jen.

"Not what?" I say, putting a hand on Emma's shoulder. Like this, we make a strange little tableau here in the wide-open space of the commons, a familial still life: mother, daughter, and this non-sister of mine. I catch our reflection in the spotless glass of the meeting hall and think of another trio on another day, decades ago, when Win would take Jen and me out for ice cream, my mother in the middle with one of our small hands in each of hers. The proverbial monkey in the middle, the object of an undeclared tug-of-war. In the long run, Jen came out ahead and I got stuck with the bitter end of the rope.

A chime sounds from one of the larger buildings across the green, opposite what Jen called the town hall, and several dozen women pour out the door, some arm in arm, all chatting and laughing. They pause to check us out, but Jen dismisses the crowd with a wave of her hand and a slight shake of her head. The women disperse, falling out into smaller groups. About half wear sarongs around their waists like Kate does, letting it all hang out. It's stupid, really, but I feel my face go red, as I did when I was a child and one of my father's *National Geographic* magazines arrived in the mail, chock-full of the kind of exotic photojournalism that would have been pornographic in any other medium. Being *National Geographic,* I suppose, made the exposed tits and asses okay.

They're of all ages, from babes swaddled in tie-dyed slings and snugged up against their mothers, to teenagers like Emma — narrow-hipped and long-legged — to middle-agers like me, to those who have given up worrying about stretch marks and crow's-feet. It isn't only the loose kaftans and colorful fabrics that mark them as different from the women I'm accustomed to; it isn't anything they have or wear at all, but rather what they don't have. An absence. I don't think I ever realized until now how uptight we city women are — or were — how we constantly, incessantly protect ourselves by keeping our heads bent down at our phones or by examining an imagined hangnail, our subconsciouses expecting danger lurking around every corner. We make ourselves look older and uglier than we are, as if youth and beauty were attributes to be hidden away from the world. These women don't have any of these tics, because what these women don't have is fear. And being fearless, they must possess a sense of freedom most of us have never known.

Score one for Mom, I think, even if thinking it disturbs me.

Kate walks toward us from a sector opposite the way we came into the colony, still bare-breasted, sarong hitched up above her knees now that the midday heat has become too much for even that extra length of material. It's the first time I've noticed her sandals, sturdy flats with ribbons crisscrossed all the way up the calves. The rest of the women seem to be sporting the same medieval-bondage look.

She calls to a few of the women. "I'll see you at the pool, Maria. And this time I'm going to kick your ass in the butterfly." With those arms and legs, I have no doubt there's going to be some serious ass kicking.

All at once, the shame melts from me, and something else replaces it. Envy. Standing here in my stained clothes, reeking of whatever filth I've managed to soak myself in since our swim in the Potomac, I want to be Kate. I want to be all of these women. I'll even try out the funky gladiator shoes.

"Do you swim?" Kate asks, approaching us.

"A little. I don't think I'll be challenging you in the butterfly anytime soon. Maybe the dog paddle."

She laughs, and this time it's genuine. "You'll get strong here. You'll see." Turning to Jen: "I told Nell she'll be having some company. Bungalow's all ready for them."

Jen releases Emma, but it seems there's an invisible tether between the two of them, in the same way there was always some magnetic force between my mother and Jen, a feeling that I was being squeezed out. "Why don't you take Emma home? I want to have a word alone with Miranda."

The tether doesn't break; it simply stretches as Emma walks away from us, hand in hand with Kate, at the same time Jen takes my arm and leads me toward a bricked patio and a cluster of umbrellaed tables.

My daughter looks back once, but not at me.

Twenty-Seven

Win cried at the funeral.

It was the right thing to do, and damn if it didn't pull at a few familial heartstrings to see the young widow in her simple black dress and lace veil as she stood quietly by the empty coffin. She rested one hand on the mahogany, keeping the other pressed to her lips, a tiny silk handkerchief hiding the smile that might break out again at any moment as Reverend Forsythe talked about Carl and the better place he was in, and the open arms of Jesus, and all that other good shit people made up to deal with the horror of death.

Win knew where Carl was. He was in the open arms of the Caribbean Sea, about eight miles north of Nassau, sleeping with the fishies. She stifled a giggle at the image of those Jesus-fish bumper stickers, one of which she had seen today when one of Carl's aunts pulled into the church lot. It was like fate.

The funeral had gone well, as did the requisite show of grief afterward, during which Win and Miranda gratefully accepted casserole dish upon casserole dish, lining them up in the refrigerator until no room was left. It was silly to bombard her with premade dinners, as if Carl, not Win, had been the one doing the cooking for these past eight years and now all of a sudden she would need an institutional quantity of tuna tetrazzini and not-really-from-scratch lasagna to get her through the days. When the mourners left, Win scraped the contents of one Pyrex after another into the garbage bin, tied up the bag, and took it out to the garage.

It wasn't so hard being on her own. She could take out garbage as well as the rest of them.

Miranda was the problem.

"But everyone needs a daddy, right?" Miranda said, tucked into her bed with Carl's dollies next to her. She had been crying all day, and Miranda's tears were real.

"I don't see why. Plenty of children grow up with one parent, and usually that's the mommy." Win pulled up the covers, set the music box on the night table to play "Beautiful Dreamer," and kissed her daughter goodnight. "See you in the morning."

She spent the rest of the night awake, packing up Carl's clothes and books. She wrapped up his watches, several pairs of gold cuff links, all the Victoria's Secret shit he had brought home over the years believing her oohs and aahs over each bra and panty set, and stuffed her husband's earthly left-behinds into boxes destined for the attic. Then she sat in the living room with a bottle of wine, and thought.

The house was paid off, as were her car and Carl's car, which Win intended to sell next week. She would have to live without the insurance money for a while — the company was balking at the suicide payout — but the Finleys had enough money to keep their daughter-in-law and grandchild going in the meantime. Naturally, Carl's parents had broached the subject of Win and Miranda moving in with them, and Win said she would think about it. For now, she needed to be in the place she had shared with her beloved husband.

She wouldn't, and she didn't.

Everything else happened by accident.

A week after the funeral, Win terminated her pregnancy. A day after that, she held her first coffee hour with two women from the clinic. The two became four, and the four became eight, and by the first anniversary of Carl's untimely death, Win was forced to move the meetings to a rental space downtown. It was a shabby excuse for a women's club, but the rent was cheap. And no one cared whether the paint was peeling or the boiler made annoying thumping noises or the chairs were hard enough to give you cramps after sitting in them for too long. The talk was what they came for, the camaraderie. Win's spiked punch didn't hurt, either.

The talk, like all real talk, like unfiltered truths spoken somberly, had an effect on Win she didn't see coming.

"He made me end the pregnancy," Amy said from her chair in the circle, drawing nods of sympathy from three other women.

"He told me I'd get the promotion," Dee confessed. "Yeah, I know. But I went ahead and slept with him anyway. And you know what? He promoted a guy who didn't even have a master's degree. What was I supposed to do? Quit with two kids to feed and a mortgage to pay?"

"He always said he was sorry the next day," Alfie told the group, keeping her head down, hiding the yellow-and-purple bruise blooming on her left cheek. "I still believed him a hundred times later."

He was my uncle.
He was my boss.
He was my doctor.
He was my brother.

Win would go home after these meetings, worn and defeated, the weight of all these women and all their problems on her shoulders.

And she would cry real tears.

Twenty-Eight

"So," Jen says, sinking into one of the garden chairs before offering one to me. She stretches out, her legs forward and her arms arching back, taking up more space in a classic alpha move.

I feel myself shrinking, hunching down, and will my back to straighten. It doesn't help. "So," I say.

"What a clusterfuck. Out there, I mean." She calls over her shoulder to a young girl, a few years younger than Emma, who has been standing inside the archway, half in shadow and half in light. "Two lemonades, Leila. Light sugar." Then, turning to me: "Oh, do you want extra sugar in yours?"

I do. I want mountains of it. But I measure the difference in our skin and our flesh, and I feel suddenly lumpy. "No. What you're having is fine."

The girl nods and turns inside, but not before giving me a curious once-over, another silent reminder that I desperately need a shower and a change of clothes, both luxuries Jen has either forgotten about or purposefully delayed. Leila comes back out with a tray and two tall glasses garnished with lemon slices and mint sprigs, sets it down, and disappears back under the arch.

"What? No cocktail umbrella?" I say to Jen.

"We have what we can make and what we can grow here, Miranda. And all that crappy kitsch is made in China anyway. Even if we wanted it, we're so far off the international trade grid, we might as well be on the moon."

"They don't have lemonade and mint on the moon," I say, taking a gulp of my drink.

Jen sips hers, but the volume doesn't seem to decrease even a millimeter. "We're a working community, honey. Your mother was a genius. She had it all planned out back when you and I were still worrying about acne and SAT scores. God, I miss her."

"Me too." I'm not sure how many more times I can tell this lie with the appropriate sorrowful timbre in my voice and bittersweet shine in my eyes, but everything about Jen makes me think it might be worth the trouble to keep up the act.

Or not. Jen beats me to the punch.

"You two didn't really get along, did you?"

"Not since I found out what she did to my father." *And not since you came into the picture.*

She leans forward, bright eyes boring into mine. "Carl was a bastard."

"So Win said."

"So Win knew. The problem, Miranda, was that you didn't want to believe her." Jen takes another microsip of lemonade, notices my glass is empty, and calls for Leila to refill it. When the girl has done the job and ducked back inside, she continues. "You still don't want to believe, do you? Like you didn't want to believe that husband of yours was taking you for a ride. What was his name? Nick? Dick?"

"Nick," I say.

"Right." There's zero agreement in her voice. "You were always so forgiving of the other side."

"Nick was good to me."

"No. Nick was good to Nick. You were an excuse for him to self-indulge." She waves a hand, dismissing the topic. "Anyway, it doesn't matter now. The country would have gone to shit with or without him."

I think of the house and the two men with their furniture-crammed truck, and my car that was towed off like a piece of scrap metal. All Nick did was pull the rug out from under us a little bit sooner and tell us the lies that made us think there might still be some hope. Nick didn't single-handedly throw the entire island of Manhattan into starvation when the food ran out. No one person could do that, bastard or not. Sooner or later, Emma and I would have ended up like everyone else. Desperate. Hungry. An endangered species.

Or like Mr. and Mrs. Schafer, who I assume are still lying where they fell.

I nearly arrived in that dark place myself, and here I am sipping lemonade in a courtyard that belongs more in a resort than in a feminist intentional community. Maybe it's time to start being nicer to Jen, taking this gift horse as a gift and not looking for hidden Trojans. "You're right," I tell her. "Nick was a dick." But the words taste sour in my mouth. Nick wasn't all bad. No one is all bad.

"Glad you finally saw the light, sister," Jen says. "As for Carl, well, I don't think you could have known what was going on between your parents. You were eight when it happened, right?"

"About. I knew enough, though."

"The same way you know about what's

going on with your daughter?"

"She regressed," I say. "After the shock of yesterday." I don't really want to talk about yesterday, not ever again, so I stand up, smoothing out the clothes that have stuck to me under my arms and breasts, a sign to Jen that I need more hospitality than lemonade.

She gets the point, checks a small book she's taken from one of the sleeves of her kaftan, and says, "Let's meet at my place this afternoon." One unpolished finger scans the lines on the page. "Will four o'clock give you enough time to change and rest? We can go over the rules then. Just you and I, if that's okay. Nell can take Emma to the pool."

Jen may keep an appointment book, but four in the afternoon is the same to me as any other hour of the day. "Sure. Four it is. And really, Emma's fine. Or she'll be fine soon." I'm about to ask if Sal is here when Jen cuts me off.

"Oh, Miranda, you really don't know, do you? Are you and Emma close?"

"I'm her mother. I know everything," I say.

"Then you know she's pregnant." The sentence falls flat, but in Jen's raised eyebrows there's a question.

I force myself not to blink, not to let my voice waver. "Of course."

"Yes," Jen says, summoning Leila back to the table and asking her to show me the way to the bungalow. "Yes. Of course you do."

TWENTY-NINE

I shoulder my own backpack as well as the one Emma left behind and follow Leila along a brick-in-sand pathway lined on both sides with heat-tolerant portulaca. A few women come into view out of a sector to my right, the same direction Maria of soon-to-be-ass-kicked fame walked earlier. From behind the copse of trees comes the pleasant din of splashing and laughter. Summer sounds. The notes of a song that sings of no school, beach bonfires, the barbecues and beer and fiery sparklers of Independence Day. I remember today is the Fourth of July.

"Is it a party?" I ask Leila, nodding over toward the noise.

She shrugs. "No. I don't think anyone has a birthday until next week. Why?"

"Don't you celebrate the Fourth?"

"The fourth of what?" She asks with such complete innocence, I know she isn't pulling my leg.

"July."

Another shrug. "Why would we celebrate the fourth of July?"

I stop in my tracks and look at her. "Um . . . history, maybe?"

"You mean 'herstory.' That's the only story we've got." Again, Leila's eyes tell me she's dead serious.

I'd first heard the term from Win, not very long after Congress declared March Women's History Month. Win hated the term, calling it a stupid contradiction.

"And besides," she had said, taping the posters at my school with overlays that asked *And what? After March we go back to Men's History Year?* I remember the principal made her take them down and pay for a new printing. Win didn't give a shit. She'd gotten her message across.

From then on, it was "Herstory this" and "Herstory that." By the time I got to college and started Morphology 101, I came back at her with the utter ridiculousness of the campaign. "It's not parseable, Mother. It's one goddamned word." I left out the part about the original Greek meaning "wise man," but she persisted, getting pissed off if I referred to a mailman or a fireman, turning as much as she could of the English language's lexicon into a forced gender-neutral soup. Manhunter became personhunter; human became huperson. She made up bizarre-sounding pronouns instead of using "he" and "she," causing most people of the late 1980s to stare in confusion and respond with something like *Ich spreche kein Deutsch.* Naturally, Win's preferred spelling of "woman" was the variety with the Y in it.

"You're like a one-woman linguistic police force," I told her during one of her rants.

Win mumbled something about changing the thinking by changing the words. I insisted it didn't work that way, she insisted it did, and that was the last conversation we had on the subject. It was one of the last conversations we had at all.

"We're in the United States," I say to Leila now, "and whether you like it or not, we've got a common story. His, hers, or whoever's. We can call it anything, but that doesn't really change its nature, does it? Like Shakespeare's rose."

"Shake what?"

"Speare," I say. "As in that little play called *Romeo and Juliet.* Don't tell me you haven't heard of it."

Leila looks at me with the kind of weary patience a person might have when talking to a foreigner with only elementary English skills. She speaks slowly, deliberately, overarticulating each consonant and vowel sound. "We are not part of the United States. Not since I've been here. We don't conform to their laws, we don't pay taxes, and we don't get anything from them. This isn't some random fly-by-night intentional community with a bunch of hippies running around playing at veganism until they get tired of it. We're the real thing, ma'am." She's earnest, but something in her tone smacks of rote recitation.

"I see. So, no Fourth of July fireworks."

We continue walking along the path until it forks into three branches. Leila steers me toward the left. "You're in sector B. Sector C's the other residential area." She points toward our right.

"What about the middle one?"

"That's Sister Jen's private compound. Totally off-limits. Unless you're invited."

The path straight ahead ends at a gate not unlike the others I've walked through, although this one is partially obscured by a tangle of red climbing roses, maybe to soften the industrial look. As we approach, I see the thick, thorny limbs of the plants. Only the flowers are soft, and even they are the color of old blood.

Sector B's sole barrier is an arbor of

morning glories, their blossoms closed now in the heat of midday. We pass through it, and Leila continues her strange tutelage.

"Sister Jen doesn't want anything to do with men, though you've probably figured that out already. So we don't study them in school here. And we definitely don't celebrate them. Basically, it's women's herstory month the whole year round."

"There's a school?"

"Yep. A good one. You can work there if you have a master's. Or you can do something else. Everyone here has a job. I do part-time at the café since it's open in the afternoons. On weekends I might do a dinner shift at the restaurant. They let me start when I turned thirteen. Before that, I helped out in the piggery and chicken coops, or I swept up the common areas. What do you do?"

"I teach animals how to communicate. Correction: I did. But not pigs. Apes."

Leila shoots me a sideways glance. "We don't have any of those here. I suppose if we had men, you could teach them. Sister Jen says they're all animals. I believe her."

"There are some good ones," I say, even if I can't think of a specific example from my recent experience. My thoughts move to Nick again. If he'd been with us on the side of the highway when those men took Emma, I know he would have defended us with his life.

"Maybe." She shrugs again. "I wouldn't know. Never saw one."

"You've never seen a man? Ever?"

"Why would I want to?"

We walk along in silence for a few minutes, passing neatly hoed vegetable gardens and a grid of laundry lines where linens and towels are hanging out to dry. "You got kids?"

I've had enough of the anti-male dogma for one morning, so I'm relieved she's changed the subject, even if the subject is about to get an earful from me. "Yeah. A daughter. Emma's sixteen."

"I'm fourteen. We might be in the same classes. School here is kind of accelerated. The sixteen-year-olds are basically doing university math and science."

I suspect there's probably a shitload of extra time for advanced calculus and astrophysics once you knock out most of the past few hundred years of history and literature. Absently, I wonder how they manage to work around Pythagoras and Euclid. But I only smile at the girl. "How long have you been here?"

She straightens, making herself taller than

she already is, then arches her back with her arms raised, stretching like a cat in the sun. Under each arm is a tuft of pale blond hair, and I think of how cranky Emma gets if she emerges from a shower and finds that she missed a spot while shaving. "All my happy life. I was born in Femlandia."

"So you've never been — outside?"

"Nope."

"Do you know a woman named Sal Rubio? She came here with a woman named Ingrid. I forget Ingrid's last name."

Leila's face goes blank. "I'm not supposed to talk to you about the other women. Not until Sister Jen goes over the rules with you. Anyway, we don't have last names here."

A trio of women in their early twenties runs out of a house carrying towels and sun hats, probably on their way to the pool. They wave a hello to Leila and throw me a set of pleasant, if cautious, smiles.

"I guess some of the women come here already pregnant," I say. Not that I notice any; kaftans are perfect for hiding baby bumps.

Leila points toward a low house with a wide porch. "That's your place. And yeah, some do. Some don't. My mom lived here for a few years before she had me." She turns back toward the morning glory–covered arbor before I have the chance to ask my next question, the obvious one. "Gotta head back to work now. Nice talking to you." With a wave of her hand, she's gone, and with her the answers to all my other questions. For now.

THIRTY

There are four steps leading up to my new home's porch, and every one of them feels like an endless climb, a perpetual-motion Stair-Master designed to torture my thighs and calves, to make me feel weaker than I am. How completely absurd that I used to spend two hundred dollars a month for the dubious benefit of saying I belonged to Bethesda's luxury gym, and that didn't include the twice-weekly sessions with my private personal trainer. If my forty-something self could reach back in time to her younger version, she'd tell her to save the C-notes, throw a bag full of bricks over her back, and start hiking.

According to the note stuffed into the handle of the screen door, my new house-mate has already taken Emma out to the pool, so I can put off the mental exercise of a difficult conversation with my daughter for the time being. A good thing, really, because I don't have much left in the way of stamina — either physical or mental. The second I'm in the door, I let the packs slip off my shoulders and breathe in the smells of cedar and wildflowers.

They're the last things I remember. Then I'm out cold.

While I'm asleep, I dream.

Emma and I are on the gravelly verge at the side of the interstate. She's just laid down a picnic blanket, the old red-and-white-checked kind like the tablecloths you find in Italian restaurants. It matches her pinafore. I've roasted a chicken and cut it up for salad, and we've got a spread fit for a king to go along with it: lemonade, apple pie, a cheese board that smells faintly of sweat socks, so I know it must be the fancy French sort. Emma's contribution is a basket of buttermilk biscuits, although I can't remember ever seeing her with flour on her hands or near a rolling pin.

"Even better than last week," she says. "And the week before. Do you think they'll come?"

I nod. "They always do." The conversation is so automatic, it seems we've had it multiple times.

As if on cue, the men arrive on their bicycles, plaid shirts rolled up to the elbow revealing sinewy forearms. Their muscles look like snakes have been trapped beneath their skin. They slither and twitch as the men pull on the handlebars, climbing their way up the hill to where we sit. Emma smiles at me, and my hand reaches for Nick's gun. It's been sitting quietly between the chicken salad and the stinky Morbier while we've waited. I don't even need to look to see where it is.

The leader of the pack — there's always one — is a mountain of a man. As he nears, I can smell him, and he's worse than the Morbier. Ripe. He swings a leg as thick as a tree trunk off the bike and lets it fall, all the while keeping his eyes trained on the cleft between Emma's breasts. She's left her pinafore unbuttoned at the top, the better for him to see.

"Hello, ladies," he growls. Wolflike. Feral. But the sounds aren't really human sounds; they're what a wild dog might sound like if it tried to articulate our language.

What we do next varies. Some days, I let them get close, let them catch our scent and drink us in. I watch their trousers bulge as they come closer, as they get a good long whiff of woman, and I know what they're thinking. They're thinking sex. They're thinking rough, dirty, animalistic fucking with your face so far down in the dirt, you're breathing it. They're thinking that having us in whatever way they want is their right as men.

Now, this is the fun part of my dream.

I stand up, arching my back like Leila did earlier today, throwing my breasts out toward the men, letting them see the stretch in the sheer fabric and that gap between the top two buttons. Emma also stands, raises the skirt of her pinafore, and peels down her underpants, stepping out of them lightly before dangling the white cotton in front of the men. They've changed, though, these men. They're no longer on two legs, but down on all fours, howling and barking. Drool melts in a long, syrupy icicle from the leader's lips. They want us. Everything about them tells me so.

You can play this game too close to the edge, though. It's happened before, when Emma and I are high on teasing and let the space between us and the man-dogs narrow. Like that sorry end the Crocodile Hunter came to when he let go of his fear. We keep ours. We keep it within spitting distance.

I never know which comes first, the shot or the fall. They seem simultaneous in this dream, and in my dream's memories.

There's a crack and a thump, or a thump and a crack. And then there are more of each, four, five, six. As many as it takes until they're all down.

And how they howl. Emma and I dance to it, as if their pain were music.

"Mom?" Emma says.

This time, I've made a mistake. I haven't taken them down hard enough, haven't spent enough bullets in the right places to keep them from their steady advance. A strong hand grasps my arm, shaking me, and I see Emma's face, wide-eyed and worried.

"Miranda? Wake up." Another voice.

The men, or the wolves, or whatever my subconscious conjured, are gone, as is Emma. Only a small, birdlike woman is here. Her head, hair tied up in a bright bandana, interrupts the clockwise whir of a ceiling fan as it spins above me. Two hands pull me up to a sitting position.

"You must sleep hard," the woman says. "I'm Nell. And this" — she sweeps an arm around the room — "is home, sweet home. Complete with bedrooms."

I rub my eyes, blinking the sleep away. "How long have I been out?"

"I don't know. When did you fall asleep?"

"No idea. Where's my daughter?"

Nell walks the short distance from the place where I've been lying to an open kitchen. I hear water running, and then she reappears with a glass, offering it to me. "She's fine. I walked her over to the farm area and then she went off with Sister Jen to the café." There's a pause. "Nice to have a daughter." She says this as if daughters were a rarity.

"Sometimes," I say. I'm not sure how nice it's going to be after Emma and I have a talk, assuming Emma will talk to me.

"They're a gift, babies. Maybe you should be grateful instead of complaining about her."

I remember Jen saying something about Nell needing more socializing. So. There's one thing Jen and I agree on. "I just meant it's hard sometimes. It isn't all a rose garden."

"Would you give her up?" Nell says.

"No way."

"Then, there you are." Nell takes off her gardening gloves. Her voice doesn't match the rest of her. She's tiny everywhere, with wrists that look as if they might snap while she's weeding a flower bed. I expected more of a chirp than a flat monotone.

"There I am," I say, picking myself up off the floor. "Sorry, but I had a hell of a nightmare. Emma's great." *Great with child,* I think, but don't say.

Something about Nell — it might be the dark circles under her eyes or it might be the way the corners of her mouth pull down when she smiles — tells me not to continue the baby conversation, so I drink my water, pick up the two packs I dropped at the front door, and survey my new digs.

"Where do you get the water?" I ask. I refill my glass from the kitchen sink, and what comes out is cold, clear, and the kind of tasteless I used to pay for when I bought cases of Evian.

"We have wells. Only problem is the plumbing sucks, so you can't put anything down the sink or the toilet. Pee and poo make it, but the last time someone tried to flush a wad of Charmin through the pipes, we had a major problem. Sister Jen had a fit, Sister Rosalyn got a tongue-lashing, and we all had to use the old porta-potties after Jen ordered the water shut down for a month." Nell shivers. "You from around these parts?"

"Bethesda, Maryland," I say. "Home of Saks Fifth Avenue and the McMansion."

"Yeah, well then, you know what January is like in Virginia."

"Hold the fuck on. She made you use

outhouses in January? All of you?" I'm trying to imagine my bare ass on a frozen toilet seat in winter. My own McMansion had heated seats. Six of them.

"Sister Jen likes her rules," Nell says. "You must be hungry. Want some chicken? Cheese? A salad? You name it, we got it. That is, if we can grow it, milk it, or butcher it."

I opt for the chicken, and Nell takes a plate from the small Euro-style fridge, setting it on the woodblock counter between us. "Yeah. She could have just punished Rosalyn, but she didn't. We're all for one and one for all in this place, kinda like the hundred and fifty Musketeers. By February, I think most of us were too frightened to even shit once Jen turned the water back on. And no one spoke to Rosalyn until late that summer." She takes a thigh from the plate and gnaws on it. "By the way, make sure you use the 'Sister' thing before names here. It's not completely laid down in law, but you never know. Best to stay on Jen's good side, if you get my drift."

The chicken is the best I've had, golden skin and ivory meat, the kind that comes from corn feeding, I guess. I finish off the breast and go for a wing, savoring the crisp saltiness. "You sound like you're not happy here," I say.

Nell smiles another one of her upside-down smiles. "I am. The past month's been hard." She finishes the chicken, chases it with a tumbler of water, and washes her hands in the sink. I note the pains she takes to wipe off on a thin, irregularly shaped towel hanging near the faucet. "Besides, it isn't like I have any other choices now, is it?"

Nothing down the drain, I remind myself. After a lifetime with a built-in garbage disposal and the Roto-Rooter man on permanent retainer, I'm not looking forward to the transition. Then again, what good is a goddamned garbage disposal if there's no food to wash off your hands? I'll get used to it.

"We might as well get everything out in the open," Nell says. "Seeing that we're sharing this place." She puts a kettle on one of the two electric burners and takes two mugs from hooks over the stove. "First of all, there isn't really any coffee or tea here. Not officially. So brush your teeth before you go see Big Sister this afternoon. And don't ever let anyone catch you calling her that until you know who's who. Especially the younger ones. They can be a little, well, radical."

"But you've got teabags," I say, thinking of Leila and her lifelong indoctrination. "Tea doesn't grow in this climate."

She dangles two Twinings bags in front of me and lets them fall into the mugs. "Nope. But we had other ways to stock up on creature comforts before the shit hit the fan in May. Femlandia isn't the fortress Jen thinks it is." For the first time, she really does smile, and I see that she's beautiful. Also, Nell seems normal, thoroughly un-Jen- and un-Kate- and un-Leila-like. "Of course, now it is. Now you could take the fucking electric fences down and everyone would still stay put."

"I thought the fences were to keep the big bad wolves out."

"Yeah. That, too," she says absently. "Second thing. I lost my baby in June. Stillbirth. Or sort of stillbirth. The little bugger was breathing when I delivered her. And then she wasn't." The smile fades, and her voice returns to a dirgelike monotone as she pours out boiling water.

"Oh, jeez. I'm sorry."

"I'm sorrier for you. You're the one who has to live with me."

I could think of worse housemates. My mother, for instance. "You probably don't want to hear this, but I'll say it anyway.

You're young. What are you, twenty-five tops?"

"Twenty-six. And that's what the midwife told me, so if what you're about to say is that I can still have plenty of children, then you'll need to get in line. I've heard it all. Come on, let's sit on the porch where it's cooler. We might have lights and fans and refrigeration, but what this dump really needs is coolant. Five million cubic feet of good old Freon." She looks me over. "Actually, you should rinse off. I'll hold off on the tea for now." She looks closer. "And change. What the hell did you fall into on your way here?"

"Ran into a stray dog," I call over my shoulder on the way back to the sole bathroom in the house. "But I don't want to talk about it right now."

Thirty-One

The shower is one of those half-inside, half-outside setups, rustic, the kind they put in ultraluxury island resorts so the guests can feel like they've gone back to nature and forget that they've paid a grand a night for a shack on a beach. For a minute, I wonder how Jen Jones managed to rig functional plumbing, and then I remember even the Romans had pipes. I'm counting on the ones feeding water to me right now to be made out of something other than lead. I've heard it's incompatible with long-term survival.

I towel off with a rough cloth that seems to be handwoven and laugh out loud at the thought of being put on loom duty. The unpleasant realization is that I don't have any skills aside from teaching animals basic sign language, and I doubt there's much of a market for that here. I can't butcher a hog, my carpentry experience is limited to putting together a do-it-yourself picture-frame kit, and I'd be the person most likely to electrocute herself if you put me anywhere near wiring.

Maybe I'll end up waiting tables with Leila. We could talk about Shelley and Austen and the Brontës. Probably not about Shakespeare.

Nell has left a kaftan for me on my bed, and I pull it on. It's softer than the towel, maybe made by the advanced weavers. What the hell do I know? It could have come here from Bloomingdale's with one of the women. I can see Win now, stockpiling kaftans and sarongs. I check my watch and it says three. An hour before the meeting with Jen.

I can't freaking wait.

Still, I can't deny the wave of gratitude that runs through me as I check myself in the mirror and look around at my new bedroom. It's rustic, but comfortably so, kind of like glamping. Rattan blinds cascade from the tops of the two windows; a few dozen well-read books lean on one another on a shelf; twin peace lilies soften the hard lines of what looks like handmade furniture in mission or Shaker style, simple but elegant. There might not be a Starbucks within walking distance, but there's a café with more character. And the gardens I have to meander through to reach it aren't exactly unpleasant.

A word comes to my mind: *utopia.* Not that almost anything wouldn't be perfect after the wrecks Emma and I passed on our way here, but my mother's world is miles better than I expected. Who knows? Maybe I'll even enjoy getting my hands dirty in the garden. It beats getting them dirty in other ways.

"Come on out here," Nell calls from the porch. "Let's see what you look like when you're not playing an extra in a horror movie."

I do feel a lot less like Carrie after the prom and a little more like my old self when I collapse into one of the matching Adirondack chairs on the porch. The wood is cool and smooth and blond, sanded to the texture of baby skin.

Nell notices me noticing. "I made these. Adirondacks are easy."

"Uh-huh," I say, thinking of the picture frame that ended up more trapezoidal than square.

"Really. I'll teach you. We're gonna have a lot of time on our hands." She sighs and leans back, sipping her tea. "No more midnight excursions to the great outside world. Even if we could get over the electric fence, I don't think the stores will be stocked with Earl Grey anymore. Is it as bad as we've heard?"

"Worse."

"Ah, well. Here's to Femlandia." She raises her mug and clinks it against mine. "Don't worry. I got something stronger for later on."

"Like what?" I say, thinking that a double shot of anything would be welcome.

"Gin. Wine. Beer, if that's your thing."

"Where do you get all of it?"

"Juniper berries, grapes, hops, and barley. The rest is just chemistry and time."

I may like it here even more than I thought. "You're kidding, right?"

"Nope." Nell points to a roof in the distance. "You see that building? Well, behind it is about two hundred acres of sweet Virginia farmland. I don't know what they do in the Alaska Femlandia, but we can grow pretty much anything here." Now she points at me. "Just don't get drunk. You get drunk, Sister Jen gets pissed off. And a pissed-off Sister Jen isn't a pretty sight."

"I know." She looks puzzled, so I explain. "Jen and I go back awhile. We were in high school together." Now she thinks I'm the one who is kidding. "Really. We were. We were best friends until my mother decided she wanted to trade me in for a shinier model, someone who would buy into this whole w-o-m-y-n fantasy of hers." I shrug. "So now it's out there. My big, ugly secret."

"I don't get it." She pauses. "Oh, you can't be serious."

"As a heart attack." I smile, turn my palms up in a show-and-tell gesture, and dump the rest on her. "Miranda Reynolds, née Somers. Pleased to meet you."

"Holy shit." Nell clamps a hand over her mouth. "Look, I'm sorry if I said anything —"

"Say all you want. I haven't seen my mother in fifteen years. We were — let's say we were never close. In any aspect."

"But here you are."

"Yeah, well, like you said, the great outside world has come a-crumblin' down. Did you ever meet her? Win, I mean."

Nell answers with a shake of her head. "Sometimes Jen talks about her at our meetings. But always in the past, you know? Win was this; Win did that; Win used to say such and such. I asked once if she was really dead or maybe hanging out in the New Mexico Femlandia. Jen only gave me one of her beatific smiles, like I'd just asked where the Virgin Mary was hanging out."

In all these years, I never thought Win might still be alive, that Jen's announcement could have been a fabrication to protect my mother. And now that I'm thinking of it in real terms, I realize I feel absolutely nothing.

A screen door slaps shut in the bungalow across the way, and two women come out. They wave a cheery hello before gathering up towels and a picnic basket and heading back toward the entrance to our sector. It's hard to tell exactly how old they are from a distance, but they have a schoolgirl lightness about them, even though their school years must be decades in the past. The taller of the two reaches up to loosen a clip in her hair, and a waterfall of caramel curls falls down her back, uncombed and wild. I think of all the money and hours I spent in salons perusing magazines, looking for the perfect suburban housewife cut, the exactly right shade of honey-beige highlights.

What a waste of time.

"There's something utopian about it," I say, following the women with my eyes as they amble down the path and lose themselves among the gardens.

Nell smiles over her mug of tea and sighs. "I read somewhere that everyone's utopia is someone else's dystopia."

"Who said that?"
"Fuck if I know. Does it matter?"
"How long have you been in this place?"
Nell stares up at the ceiling fan set against a typical Southern porch blue ceiling, counting silently. "Four years this November."
"Are you happy?" I say.
"For the most part. There's a thing my ex-husband used to say — 'Ain't no rose without thorns.' I guess it's like that. No matter what, you always trade something." She looks up again and bobs her head from right to left, left to right, as if she's weighing two invisible, but nearly equal, masses.
"Did you trade something?" I ask.
She leans in conspiratorially. "I had to go somewhere. One of those flyers made it into the mail slot about a year before I left home. I thought it was a joke, honestly. But I kept it, buried it in the closet with all the cleaning stuff. Like Ronnie would ever look there. Things hadn't been running very smoothly up in Brooklyn."
"I thought I heard a few absent Rs," I say. "Not much, though."
"I lost most of it since I've been down south. You should have heard me before. I sounded like one of the Sopranos." Nell laughs into her mug, then starts to cry.

I've never been good at this woman-to-woman stuff. The truth is, I don't know that I like women. Those old roundtables at Starbucks went in one of two directions, toward complaining or toward competition. Usually a medley of both. But I reach a hand out toward Nell all the same, and she takes it gratefully.

"I married one of those hot-blooded types," she says. "All red roses and charming talk — until he gets a ring on your finger and you get knocked up. Then he's off with his *putana* of the week. The last one was named Lola." She makes a gagging face. "Lola. I mean, you can't make this shit up, right? So he comes home one night, late, and the dinner I'd made was cold, and he says to me, 'Yo, Nellie, you little Irish twit, where's my dinner? I'm starvin' over here.' Seriously. That's how he talked. Like Joey Fuckin' Buttafuoco. Not a very nice guy, in the end."

"They aren't all like that."

"How many times you been married?"

"Once."

"Where is he now?" Nell asks, looking at me as if she already knows the answer.

"Dead. He drove his car off a cliff when he heard the first announcements about the crisis."

"Pussy."

"Yeah."

She's over the crying now. "Maybe he wasn't like Ronnie, but there are a hundred flavors of jerk. You got the pussycat kind. I got me a fucking tomcat. Had the scratches to prove it. More than scratches, actually." Nell moves one hand protectively over her stomach, and her eyes glaze a little in the remembering. "That was the first time I lost a baby," she says. "After Ronnie punched me."

There are supposed to be words for this situation, a soothing and comforting response, but I can't find them. I should say *I'm so sorry for your loss* or *It's okay to grieve* or any one of those old chestnuts you find in Emily Post's lists of things to say and do when confronted with the uncomfortable. I am sorry, and I should tell Nell it is okay to grieve, to let the sadness out, but I stop myself. The words, hanging there in my mind, seem trite and meaningless. I doubt Post or Baldrige would approve of what I actually say.

"Fucking sonofabitch."

"It was worse than that. I hit him back, and you know what Ronnie did? He called the cops. Said I went crazy on him, started a fight, and ended up falling. His family backed it all up. I wanted to get a divorce, but you know how it is."

"Bye-bye, financial security, right?"

Nell narrows her eyes at me. "No. I'm an engineer. I could have gotten any job I wanted and left that asshole broke. The problem was his family had one of their closed-door powwows. Ronnie came out of it smiling, turned on the charm, and told me if I even set one foot wrong, he would kill me. Family honor and all that shit." Nell gets up, stretches, and looks around the gardens. "And here I am, four years later. I hope the bastard starved to death."

I find myself hoping the same thing, and then I stop in my tracks, thinking of what Leila said about her mother being here for a few years before Leila was born. "Wait," I say. "The stillbirth — you weren't pregnant when you arrived."

"No. I conceived here. Not that I wanted to have the baby here. We've only got one midwife, and sometimes there are — well, I guess you could call them complications. There isn't much medical infrastructure beyond the basics."

I think of indoor plumbing and solar-powered generators and gin stills, all primitive in comparison to things like magnetic resonance imaging equipment and a fully stocked pharmacy. "How did you get pregnant?"

"The usual way. Sperm," Nell says.

"Yeah. I know about that. But where does the sperm come from?"

She shrugs and looks away from me. "They had it delivered. From the outside, I guess. Sister Sal's in charge of all that."

"But Leila told me you're completely self-sufficient, that you don't give or get anything from outside."

Nell raises her mug. "We managed to get a few cases of Twinings. I guess Sal managed to get a few cryotanks of frozen sperm. Like I said, she takes care of all things midwifery. And Sal runs the lottery." I must look confused, because she goes on. "Obviously, we don't have any men here. Which means the sperm supply is finite. Which means we have to apply. And there's a waiting period before I can reapply, so I'll be thirty by the time I can put my name in again."

"Huh." It's all I can think of to say.

And then it hits me.

Sal.

"What's her last name? Sal's?"

"No idea." Nell checks her own watch. "When do you meet with Big Sister?"

"In about ten minutes."

"Then you don't have long to wait. She'll fill you in on the last-name deal. We don't use them here."

I get up, too, follow Nell into the kitchen, and rinse out my mug, wondering if Sister Sal is Sal Rubio. It would be nice to have an old friend in my corner.

THIRTY-TWO

Building the place wasn't easy, but Win knew it was worth every dollar she'd managed to beg or borrow, every week she had to wait, and every mishap and misadventure along the way. She knew this the instant she stepped over the threshold, right now nothing more than an imaginary line dividing inside from outside. She knew because she felt the relief wash over her in waves, lapping at invisible wounds like a loyal dog. She knew because she saw the other women's faces, formerly lined with worry and care, now somehow more youthful, almost virginal.

She didn't need to hear the words of gratitude or to taste their tears as they came forward, one by one, and kissed her. The place hummed with a vibe that was the truest peace Win Somers had ever known.

He'll never hit me again.

That's the last time he'll run my bank ac-

count dry.

I can have my baby. I can be a mother.

Seven years after Win held her first coffee meeting, Femlandia, initially built on a hundred-some acres of tangled scrub and brush in the back of nowhere, was open for business.

Win had spent those years in hunter-gatherer mode, hunting for information and gathering funds. The research proved easier than she thought — Femlandia would be just one more intentional community, one more purpose-built haven for like-minded people. There were precedents: Shakers, Amish, Christians, yoga freaks, gun freaks, sex freaks. She had little in common with the inhabitants of the places she visited and toured, but commonality wasn't the point. Win needed exemplars, prototypes of off-the-grid collectives that had succeeded in skirting the tax laws and that had succeeded at the longevity game.

On opening day, the Femlandia compound near Paris, Virginia, had a population of thirty, not counting Win. Some of the women (Sister Betty was one of them) had big dreams and little skill. But the majority were picked carefully. It wouldn't do to feather the nest with lawyers who knew nothing of medicine, or with doctors who couldn't understand business. Win started with a well-rounded team, plus a few Sister Bettys because, well, the Sister Bettys of the world needed help, too. They needed a safe place, and they would learn. Already Betty had volunteered for one of the cookery jobs.

If there was a cloud obscuring this bright new day, it wasn't Jen, who stood at Win's side to welcome the women, shaking their hands and passing out information booklets with a smile. No, the cloud was the other fifteen-year-old, the one lazily shaking dirt off one pink sandal at a time, studying the ground and the women with alternating stares.

Miranda was bored out of her mind and not trying to hide the fact that she would rather be anywhere else.

"I don't get it," Miranda said. "Who would want to live here? It's like a crappy camping trip, except instead of coming home after the weekend is over, it goes on. And on. And on." She picked a burr from her sweater and flicked it to the ground. "Plus, there aren't any boys."

"That's the point, honey," Win said. She took the girl aside, out of earshot. "Some of these women have had a rough time. I'm giving them a chance to be happy."

"I bet Jim Jones said the same thing."

Win slapped her then, a hard crack of a slap that sent Miranda's head spinning to one side and left a bright red print of Win's hand on her left cheek. "Don't you say that."

Miranda stood quiet for a moment. "Whatever." Then, turning to the crowd of women who were busily shaking hands and swapping sob stories, she said, "You won't last. Any of you. You'll live your make-believe lives and then you'll die out and I'll laugh like hell. See you in the car, *Mom.*"

Thirty-Three

Nell takes me back along the path from our bungalow and through the morning glory–choked arch. We turn right, and once again I'm facing the heavy door surrounded by red climbing roses.

"The bell's here," Nell says, pointing toward a small panel that has been cleared of thorny limbs. "Ring, wait, and someone will come out to get you. See you at home." She walks away, and before she disappears through the tightly closed flowers, she calls over her shoulder. "Good luck, Sister Miranda."

I feel as if I've been dumped inside a bizarre kind of convent, a nunnery shut off from the rest of the world. My finger finds the bell and pushes it. Whatever sound it makes must come from deep inside Jen's compound.

The roses are thick and dense, their thorns making an intricate keyhole through to the space on the other side. A forbidden, locked space, and although I get Jen's need for a private retreat, I don't get the Fort Knox thing. It seems like overkill. While I'm waiting, I think of the Bluebeard story, of the new wife entrusted with the keys to every room in the house, even the forbidden cellar. It was a test of loyalty, the mad and violent man's way of assessing his bride's trustworthiness. Her curiosity, of course, won out in the end, and when Bluebeard left her with his ominous warning, Little Miss Nosey Parker just had to check out the basement. It was like an itch that needed to be scratched, even if under the surface lurked blood, terror, and the corpses of her husband's former wives.

The door I'm standing at is not a test of loyalty or trust. It's locked tight, and as I wait for it to open, I wonder which stirs up more curiosity, a threshold I can walk through for the asking, or one that bars entry, keeping its secrets safe behind it.

While I'm wondering, the mechanical click of the bolt makes me jump. And here is Jen Jones, radiant and lovely, beckoning me forward.

"Right on time," she says. "I hope you don't mind my stealing Emma for a while."

"No, of course not." What I mean to say

is *You bet I do.* "Where is she?"

"At the café. I asked Leila to walk her home." The door opens wider, and Jen sweeps out a hand to invite me in.

"It would have been nice to have some time with her," I say. "She's my daughter, after all."

Jen's eyes narrow to slits, crinkling at the edges, showing her true age. "We're all family here, Sister Miranda. We share."

What do you share? Children? Bathwater? Secrets? But I keep my mouth shut as I follow her inside the compound. I hear a bolt slide back in place behind me, and Jen takes my elbow, turning me toward the widest of three narrow paths. One of the other two is also traveled, but the third isn't, not well enough to keep the weeds down to ground level. They sprout up, lonely green sentinels that seem to say *Don't tread on me. I dislike it.*

She notices my gaze and hears the unspoken question. "Oh, that. It's an eyesore, I know, but we're working on it. There's so much land here, so much to maintain. I've had this area at the bottom of my priority list for too long."

"What area?"

"Just storage. Detritus from our earlier times that we don't need on a regular basis.

Tents, tarpaulins, fire pits. Things like that. We tend to forget about it. Out of sight, out of mind, as they say."

Still holding my elbow, she leads me along the first path. Bordered with high hedges, twisting like the insides of a serpent, the walk seems to go on forever, and finally we reach a rambling bungalow three times the size of the one I'm sharing with Emma and Nell. There are obvious perks to being what Nell calls Big Sister.

"We'll have a drink out on the porch," Jen says.

"Porch" is a strange word. It conjures images of young lovers sipping iced tea on a swing, of old couples in twin rocking chairs, of the family dog curled up on slow mornings and sun-drenched evenings. This porch looks like it could accommodate a small airplane. And that's only the part on the front of the bungalow.

Jen offers me a seat at one of the wicker seating clusters on the right-hand side, rings a bell, and sits down herself. After a minute, a woman comes out of the front door with a tray of glasses, a pitcher, and several small bowls of snacks.

"Thank you, Sister Barbara," Jen says, waving the woman away. Then, turning to me: "It's not the Ritz, but we do what we can." There are two slim folders on the table between us. She pushes one toward me and opens the other. "Let's go over some ground rules, and then if you have any questions, we can cover those. Lemonade?"

"Sure."

She pours out two glasses and opens her binder. "Right. First, we're self-sufficient here. I think you've already figured that out. That means we get no help from the outside. Not that I expect there's any to give anymore, if the starving stragglers who've been pounding our gates for the last month are telling the truth. But we haven't taken a cent from the government for fifteen years, not since we filed for the new 501 status with the Internal Revenue Service. And you know how that works."

I have absolutely no idea how that works. "I'm not really a financial expert," I say.

Jen explains. "It's not so different from the former 501d rules we started with. Pooled income, asset allocation on a per capita basis, every member files her own tax return, and since the individual assets were shared, each one of us technically stayed under the poverty line. So no taxes owed and no taxes paid. When the government initiated the new tax status, we were able to secede. Think of it like the monasteries that went completely autonomous. We don't interfere with Uncle Sam, and Uncle Sam leaves us alone."

"And that's gotten you all this?" I say, sweeping one hand over the gardens and the porch and the overhead fans.

"Like I said, we didn't start out as autonomous, but that was Win's plan all along. Your mother was a smart woman, Sister Miranda. Very forward thinking." She turns a page. "So. A few housekeeping things. We've modeled ourselves on established intentional communities that we know have survived well over the past fifty years. I don't like the word 'commune,' but that sums up what we are better than any other term I can think of. We all work, and all our work is valued on an equal basis. If you have medical skills, you earn the same number of credits as Leila does in the café. And we're extremely flexible when it comes to jobs. Say you teach in the school. Terrific. But you don't only have to teach. If you want, you can take a shift in the piggery, or milk cows, or work on the maintenance team for a few hours. Our midwife, for example —"

Bingo. She's touched the subject I'm most interested in. "I was meaning to ask you about that. About children."

Jen straightens in her chair and gives me a

look that says she's running this show. "We'll get to that. There aren't enough births to keep Sister Sal busy for forty hours a week, so she does other things."

"Like?"

"Like taking care of the animals." Jen seems eager to rush over this part. She flips to another page and picks up a pen. "What skills do you have? I think we've already ruled out infotech." Her eyes show a hint of disdain, as if I'm useless. Her next question confirms it. "Did you work outside the home?"

I nod. "I was part of a research team at the National Zoo. We studied animal communication."

"Interesting," Jen says, not sounding at all interested. "And what did that entail?"

"Mostly training a 375-pound gorilla to use sign language."

"We don't have any primates here."

I can't help but bark out a laugh. "Of course you do. You told me you could seat two hundred comfortably in the town hall meeting room. So that's at least two hundred primates."

Jen winces, obviously uncomfortable being compared to an ape. "I see."

"So I could teach the babies sign language," I say, turning the subject back to children. "I did it with Emma, and she started communicating at four months. It's a fantastic tool to get kids socializing early in life."

She makes a few notes. "Good. We can find something for you in the care center. Do you have any other experience with animals?"

"Not really. Nell said she'd teach me basic carpentry."

More notes. "Right. Let's put you down for ten hours in the care center, ten in the woodshop, and twenty on agricultural detail. You can shadow the women with more experience, and we'll take it from there."

She turns another page, and my new life as teacher, carpenter, gardener, and apprentice cow milker seems to be all planned out. I can't wait.

"Next thing," Jen says. "We have a policy of nonviolence. It doesn't mean there aren't squabbles among us, but it does mean we don't act out. If you have a problem with one of the sisters, or if you witness a problem between two or more other sisters, I expect you to come to either me or one of the planners. There's a list of them on page five of your binder. You've already met Kate."

I think Kate could settle all arguments without breaking a sweat. "What happens if there's a problem?"

"We mediate it. If that doesn't work, we have a few isolation rooms for extreme situations. They don't crop up often." Jen taps her pen to her lips. "Let's see. Plumbing. It's delicate, this system. Doesn't like the paper we make, so absolutely nothing goes in the toilets except the necessary. The restaurant is open for lunch and dinner, the café from eight in the morning until ten at night. Everyone has access to everything with the exception of the bungalows they aren't assigned to. We tried it the other way but found it helps to keep some spaces private."

Like your little sanctuary, I think, and once again I'm imagining Bluebeard's secret room in the cellar, wondering what could possibly be so sacrosanct as to necessitate the kind of security Jen has installed. Looking around, I don't see anything here worth stealing. Even if I wanted to pinch the wicker furniture or the handmade candlesticks perched in the bungalow's windowsills, there's no place to take them. Theft without the prospect of profit is pointless.

"I asked if you had any questions," Jen says.

I do. But I can't ask all of them. "Nell mentioned Sister Sal. Is that Sal Rubio?"

Jen shakes her head. "We don't use last names here. I think you might already have been told that."

"Fine. Sal, then. Can I meet her? I'm only asking because I had a good friend —"

"Sister Sal is very busy."

"But you said there weren't enough births to keep her occupied." *Gotcha.*

"She does other things," Jen says. She's gone a bit stiff, as if she isn't used to being contradicted. "I'm sure you'll meet sooner or later. Given your daughter's situation."

And mine. But I keep my own situation to myself for the moment. I don't know why; I only have an odd feeling, an idea that less information might be better. I swallow the last of the lemonade in my glass and change the subject. Sort of. "How many children are there?"

"Oh, about a dozen high schoolers. A few more in the lower grades. And ten or so in the care center. No newborns, though. Did Sister Nell tell you what happened?"

"She said the baby died."

Jen's lips press together in a thin line. "We try. We don't always succeed. The important thing to remember is that there's always another chance. Did she tell you anything else?"

I shake my head. "Not much. Only that there's a lottery."

"I know it sounds clinical, Sister Miranda, but we have to work with what we've got. I can't have half of the women here pregnant at the same time. For obvious reasons. And we won't be receiving any additional sperm from outside because there isn't any more outside." She pauses, takes a long sip from her glass, and looks straight at me as if she's about to share a state secret. "On top of that, we can't use fifty percent of the sperm." She smiles. "Let's say they have incompatible chromosomes."

"You mean not enough Xs," I say.

"Exactly. So we mete out what we have in a way that I hope is fair to everyone. Your mother intended for Femlandia to be a long-term proposition, not some flash-in-the-pan dot on the face of history."

I think about the Shakers again, how they hoist themselves with their own moral petards in the form of strict moratoriums on procreation. Simple living and celibacy only get you so far — about one generation. Without a replenishable sperm supply, every last one of the Femlandia colonies will go the same way, a handful of gray and bent old women watching themselves die out, one by one. Jen's fooling herself if she thinks her control extends far enough to stop it.

The mention of history takes me back to my conversation with Leila. "I've also heard you don't teach certain subjects," I say. "Was that Win's idea or yours?" I'm trying my damnedest to sound vaguely curious without coming across as confrontational. It isn't easy.

"That's right. We're womyn oriented here. And that's 'womyn' with a Y. It isn't going to be a problem, is it?"

"Of course not."

"Good." Jen closes her binder and stands, looking down at me. "Win would be happy to know you came to us."

"Me too," I say, thinking the mother-and-child reunion would be about as warm as Greenland in winter. I stand up as well, meeting Jen's stare at an even level, wondering what the hell I'm doing in this place.

Not starving, Miranda. That's what you're doing. Not starving.

THIRTY-FOUR

A bell rings, two short and sharp trills that rattle my bones, at the exact moment I'm ready to step through the gate and leave Jen's enclave. I look around for the source, but, like all loud and unexpected noises, the sound seems to come from everywhere. Underground. Over my head. Directly in front of me and behind me at the same time. It rings again, and now I feel it in my ears, reverberating like an unwanted, unpleasant song.

The third time, Jen calls out to me from the path. "It's fine. Only the front gate. Come along with me. We can walk and talk. Sister Kate normally has gate duty, but she's helping out with another job this afternoon."

We retrace my earlier steps through the heart of the compound, passing the party noises from the pool and the café, where a few women have now gathered, all of them lounging in the shade, sipping from tall glasses. I recognize some of them from this morning and give them a friendly wave. It isn't returned.

"Everyone is suspicious of newcomers at first," Jen explains. "They'll love you once they get to know you. By the way, I thought I'd call a meeting tomorrow to introduce you and Emma. Get the ball rolling. Okay by you?"

"What a super idea" is what I say.

Jen unlocks the inner door, the one with the keypad, and holds it open for me. When I reach the vestibule where I first met Kate, my blood turns cold.

The two boys are lean and filthy from head to toe, so dirty I can't tell the color of their skin or hair. Only the whites of their eyes, wide and scared, give any hint of humanity. The left arm of the smaller one, whom I'd put at seven or eight, hangs like a dead branch from his shoulder, the elbow jutting at an impossible angle inside his shirtsleeve.

"Help us," the younger boy says. "Please help us."

The older one puts an arm around him, looks at me with a wild and hungry expression. "Please, ma'am." His voice is deep, almost husky, and tells me he must be at least fourteen, maybe older, but his body is thin with hunger, making him look more like a young girl than a boy on the cusp of manhood. A stripe of dried, caked blood runs from the hip of his jeans all the way down to his ankle, and his T-shirt, bright red, is torn so that it bares his left shoulder. "My brother's hurt bad. Real bad." At this, the younger one begins to cry, tears carving silvery rivers on his dirt-smeared cheeks.

I want to cry with him.

Nick used to mock me, calling me overly sympathetic to any kind of human distress. "You're such a softie, Miranda," he would say when I went pale at the sight of a homeless panhandler on the streets of Washington. We might be coming out of a museum or walking up the stairs to our favorite restaurant or picking up Emma from her private school, and there he would be, destitute, hungry, malodorous as forgotten fish on a warm day.

What struck me then, and what strikes me now, was the thought of that man — sometimes that woman, but usually that man — once being someone's baby. And just that word, "baby," would make me want to cry. I would imagine a woman in a clean hospital bed, pushing until she couldn't push any longer, sweating and swearing as her child came out into the world, and I would try to trace all the miserable steps that might take that tiny, helpless thing toward the vagabond holding out his hand and asking for a dime, a coffee, a cigarette, anything to get him through the next hour of his miserable life. I'd name those steps: neglect, abuse, ignorance, hunger, each one closing the gap between the baby and the man it would become.

At my side, Jen's body stiffens, and I can feel her answer before she says a word. There's no apology, no emotion in her voice, no explanation, only a flat and final "No" as the two boys stare up at us through the bars of the gate. If either of their faces held a glimmer of hope, Jen's one syllable is enough to dissolve it.

"Jen," I say, putting a hand on her arm. "Come on. They're only children." No one, not even a women-only commune, could fail to sympathize with a couple of boys who look as if they've emerged from a war zone. The younger one, especially. He's so small, the kind of boy who only a few years ago would be taken into the ladies' room at a department store by his mother, not yet world-wise enough to venture into the grown-up land of the men's toilet.

Jen pulls her arm close to her, away from my hand. There are goose bumps on her skin. "They may be. But they aren't welcome here."

I can handle rules. I can handle milking cows and scrubbing moss from the garden paths. I think I can even handle Emma snuggling up to Jen Jones — at least she's talking to someone. I don't know how I'll handle this, how I'll be able to sleep a wink tonight wondering where these boys are and what will become of them, which monster will claim their lives. Gangrene, dehydration, violence, and starvation are all in the running. It's only a question of which one will reach the finish line first.

All at once I'm at the gate, fingers fumbling for the bolt. A nail on my right hand rips off down to the quick, and, absurdly, I try to remember when my last tetanus shot was as my hand slides over a rough, rusty part of the weathered iron. Somewhere, off in the distance behind me, Jen cries out, and in front of me the faces of the boys regain some of the hope I saw in them before.

"It's okay," I say. "It's okay."

But it isn't okay. Nothing is okay. I lose my grip on the iron bar and fall to one side, the metal slicing a long and ugly gash through Nell's kaftan, down the length of my left thigh. I'm down in the dirt, in the leaves, and the warm, ferrous taste of blood fills my mouth at the moment my teeth gnash together. When I raise my head, there seem to be four boys instead of two, double twins, and the younger of them screams.

Jen's voice is controlled and calm as she speaks, but I don't understand a word, not with the steady pounding in my head beating into my brain like a wrecking ball. It's minutes later — impossible to tell how long — before I realize she isn't speaking to me. There are others here now, three pairs of sandaled feet on the dirt near me. And there are whispers, some of them from me.

"Those boys will starve. Or worse. Jen, do something. Jen —"

I let my left arm be lifted and stretched out, feel the icy cold of alcohol in the crook of my elbow, and then the prick comes, short, perfunctory, expert in its quickness. I barely feel it when the same arm falls to the ground. A warmth comes over me now, radiating underneath layers of skin, and the throb in my head begins to drift off, leaving me. I've fallen, I've bumped my skull, I've bitten into my own lip enough to draw a gush of blood, and yet — I feel good. As good as new, as right as rain.

The women around me are talking in low tones.

"Thank you, Sister Sal. Perfect timing."

"She'll be fine by tonight."

"Sister Kate, I'll leave you to deal with those other things."

And then the warmth inside me seeps into my bones, melting them to jelly, and silence falls over me like a blanket.

Thirty-Five

When I wake, it could be any time of night. No sun filters through the rattan blinds in my room, and the air around me is quiet as a grave. I reach one hand over to the left side of the bed, where Nick always slept, and find only the cool cotton of a pillowcase, soft and lifeless under my fingers. Nick wasn't soft, and he wasn't lifeless, and I long for him in a way I don't understand. I should hate the sonofabitch, but all my hate has already been doled out today. Every last shred of it, I've spent on my mother and Jen Jones.

In the dark, I check myself over, running a hand over my body, feeling the lump at the back of my skull and the bandage covering what has to be the mother of all flesh wounds along my leg. My lower lip has ballooned and no longer seems a part of me. When I reach up touch it, my other hand meets resistance and a twinge of pain forces me fully awake. I'm on a tether, a line leading from under the skin of my left hand, along the edge of the bed, and over to a metal stand that glints like a shiny coatrack next to me. An IV drip.

The afternoon comes back in a rush of sights and sounds and smells. The clean, linen white of Jen's dress, the emphatic "No" in her voice, the odor of dirt and rubbing alcohol. Then a sting on my arm and the glint of a steel needle in strong hands before everything went dark and silent.

I came, I saw, and I was oh-so-easily conquered.

They come back to me also, those boys, ragged and bleeding in their torn clothes, closer in time to having been some mother's baby than the adult vagrants who once walked the urban streets of the capital. I remember thinking I wanted to help them, not because they were mine, only because they were. They *were.* They existed, and it didn't — or it shouldn't — matter whether you called them boys or males or blokes or lads. It didn't matter what their chromosomes looked like or whether they had waists or breasts, whether they would one day menstruate or bear children. They were two hurt beings. Only that. Beings. And so that made them no different than me.

I thought the same about Bunny, and took a few hits for that from the other researchers on the team, all of whom had more letters following their names than I ever would. I was the one who would share my lunch with a gorilla, split a banana, let him have half of the yogurt I'd brought along, feed him popcorn and the odd cookie. So what if the team laughed. The idea of munching away on my own while we worked out sign combinations and new vocabulary seemed somehow wrong.

So there I would sit, cross-legged on the floor of Bunny's playroom, my cashmere sweaters getting snagged whenever my giant-sized pupil got it in him to reach out and give me a pat on the shoulder, the researchers with their doctorates rolling their eyes as they passed through the windowed corridor. I knew what they were saying. And I didn't give a shit. I was doing something, and it felt good.

There's not much I feel good about now, not after I sat by and allowed three women to let two boys die.

I roll to one side and stare out at the darkness beyond my window. There's a cocktail party noise, a chattering from a place that feels both close and distant. It reminds me of the nights I spent at the zoo after closing hours, the time when visitors had packed up their cars and driven home, leaving the animals in peace. Or so the humans thought. Most of the wild things lived a nocturnal existence, sleeping their way through the days and coming out to play when dark settled. The sounds seeping through my window remind me of listening to the big cats and the coyotes, the hyenas and the dingoes. I could almost forget they weren't like us. If I concentrated, my mind could invent words to go with the nonverbal sounds.

The sounds cease abruptly, as if Mother Nature pressed pause, and then they recommence. I cock my ear toward the cracked window and listen. Hard.

There were coyote sightings in the Tidewater area a few years back. Coyotes swimming in rivers, coyotes making dens under tool benches in suburban garages, coyotes loitering behind Burger Kings and Taco Bells. They bred like wildfire, those coyotes, and when they sensed their population was in danger, they bred even more. I imagine hordes of them migrating up from the southern parts of the state, owning the land again, crying during the night like lost children.

I imagine there's no one to stop them

other than two young boys.

Now I'm wondering where those boys might be, asking whatever god might be in charge if they've found safety for the night, if the little one's arm causes him pain. I suspect it does. And I suspect whatever god there is couldn't care less. He or she or it didn't exactly rise to the occasion when Emma was attacked, or when the Safeway ran out of food, or when the lawyers turned sentinels at the country clubs stood by with their rifles slung over their shoulders and their heads shaking a silent "no." There was no divine intervention when the pensions went bust. No invisible hand kept the water running or the telephone networks alive. Why should I think anyone is protecting those boys?

Thirty-Six

"I told you I don't want to talk about it," Emma says, pulling away. She's perched on the edge of my bed, arms tightly crossed over her breasts, her blond hair braided into twin ropes that fishtail down her back. Emma has never worn braids. Not that I can remember.

There are other things off about her. Instead of denim shorts and a faded T-shirt, she's wearing a kaftan. I take a second look through eyes that need several more hours of sleep. Yes, my daughter is draped in a fucking kaftan. It gives her an aloof, regal look, the kind that says *Don't touch me,* and *I'll speak to you when I goddamned feel like it.* Worse, the garment is about a foot too long for her, so it isn't Nell's. And the embroidery on the sleeves looks suspiciously similar to the handiwork I saw on Jen yesterday.

"Where'd you get that?" I say, fingering

one of the intricate floral designs on her left arm.

Emma retracts her hand. "Mother Jen let me borrow it. She said I could keep it if I want to."

I've only just realized my daughter is speaking again.

"Mother Jen? I thought she was Sister Jen," I say. "And welcome back to the world of spoken English, by the way."

"Oh, that. Mother Jen says I have to communicate if I'm going to fit in here. And all the girls call her Mother Jen."

"Leila didn't."

"Leila's not me." She does a lazy, one-shoulder shrug, which I ignore.

"What else does Jen say?" The false smile on my face is so frozen, it may crack at any moment, falling off me in shards, revealing the grimace underneath.

"*Mother* Jen says it's important to talk about my feelings."

"That's terrific, sweetie," I say, the smile almost hurting now. "Why don't we start with how it feels to be pregnant? Then we can talk about how it feels to lie to your mother — your real mother. And if all that goes well, we can talk about how you feel you might have gotten pregnant and what you feel you're going to do about being sixteen years old and expecting a baby."

"I don't have to talk to you if I don't want to."

Suddenly, I'm speaking to a stranger. This woman-child sitting next to me isn't my daughter. My daughter has been abducted by aliens. Or infested by parasitic body snatchers. Or kidnapped by a secret federal agency for experimentation. Or brainwashed by the ghost of Charles Manson. What the actual shit?

I sit up now, wincing as the wound on my leg rubs the wrong way on the bedclothes, then fall back and wince all over again when my head makes contact with the wood behind me. I feel a scream work its way up inside me, and I stifle it. Screaming would only show how weak I am.

"Okay. Let's start over again," I say. This time, I'm more careful about sitting up. "I get that you didn't want to tell me. And I guess I even get that it's easier to talk to a stranger. But, honey, this is me here. Mom. You know you can tell me anything."

Emma rises from the bed, making a show of walking extra slowly around the room, pausing every now and again to smooth out the material of her kaftan or pat one of the braids in her hair. She stands at the mirror in the corner next to the window and talks to me through it.

"I didn't tell Mother Jen. She just — I don't know — figured it out. Like she's wise or something."

"That seems to imply I'm not wise," I say.

"No. You're smart. But Mother Jen does therapy work, so she's got a kind of intuition. She's an . . . what's the word? Empath?" Emma is still talking to my reflection.

"There aren't any empaths, honey. I think you mean she's empathetic." I see the boys at the gate again, their haggard faces and bloodied, broken limbs, and I want to tell Emma about the real Jen Jones, the one I saw yesterday afternoon.

"Whatever. She says I can start sessions with her in the mornings," Emma says.

"Which mornings?"

"All of them. If I want to."

Super.

I'm seeing them now, Jen and my daughter, having a little fireside chat, all cozy and snuggled up to each other like a brooding hen with a stray chick. They'll talk about me, of course, in the same way Jen and my own mother talked about me. This time, I'm still the bad guy, the one who doesn't understand, the evil autocrat who forced Emma to hole up in the furnace that was our house once the air-conditioning ceased working, who could have come to Femlandia two months ago but delayed the decision until the last minute. I'm the mother, which inevitably means all fingers point to me when things turn to shit.

"You can talk to me, Emma. Anytime. Was it Jason?"

She shivers in front of the mirror, almost imperceptibly, at the mention of his name. "Can we not go there?"

"Sure. We could not go there. Or we could discuss it. Last I heard, Jay was ringing all your bells."

Emma spins around now, looking at me squarely. She throws her head back and laughs, the fishtail braid jerking with the rhythm of her body. "Oh, he rang my bell all right. And when I didn't answer, he let himself in."

"What? Are you telling me he —"

"Raped me? Yes. And no. We were fooling around at his place one night after studying. I mean, we'd already done it a few times, so it wasn't a big deal." The way she says this makes me shudder more than the throb in my leg does, but I let her go on. "And Jay said we should try it bareback — you know, without a condom —"

"I'm familiar with the term," I say drily.

She goes on. "And if I'd just had my period, there wouldn't be any problem and so we got to it. How was I supposed to remember when my fucking period was? Like, to the exact day?"

I can't believe what I'm hearing. "Um, because it's your body? So there's a sort of shared responsibility there."

"*He's* the one who lied to me. He's the one who said it would be fine. No problemo. Asshole."

Now I do sit up, pain be damned. Off goes the coverlet on my bed, and I sit straight, giving myself some extra height, some extra authority. "Emma, he's not an asshole because you didn't take any precautions."

"Mother Jen says he is."

"Oh, terrific. A complete stranger tells you white is black or two plus two equals five, and you're cool with that?"

Her bottom lip plumps out in a babyish pout. "I knew you wouldn't get it."

I once heard the same words from Win in a bizarre role reversal of the present situation with my daughter. I'd come home from school, high on double As in a couple of pop quizzes, higher on the invitation from Rafael Marino to his senior prom. Rafael, or Raffie as everyone called him, was the tall, dark, and lightning-fast star of my high school's track team. I didn't think he had even known my name. And now I, a lowly junior, would be on his arm at the dance of the year.

Win stood in the dining room turned workshop, her back to me as she collated print material for her next rally. "He says he wants to take you to the prom. What he really wants is to take you. Typical."

"It is, actually," I said, setting my bag of books down. The thud on the wood floor might have served as punctuation enough, but I had more to say. "It's a dance, Mom. Boys ask girls to it. You can't get more freaking typical than that. Not in high school. Why do you always have to turn everything ugly?"

She did turn then, toward me. "Because I have experience. You don't. Anyway, we're driving down to the beach that weekend. Jen's coming along."

"I don't want to go to the beach. I want to go to the prom. It isn't as black-and-white as you think it is. Not all guys are jerks and not all girls are saints."

"Oh, honey. You just don't get it, do you?"

The conversation ended there, with Win going back to her anger-rousing paperwork and me stomping up to my room. I spent prom night in a shitty beach cabin on the

Outer Banks of North Carolina, and Rafael took my friend Ginger to prom. By the time I got back, Rafael and Ginger were the hottest talk on the high school dating scene.

Win told me to get over it.

I'm sick and tired of being told to get it and get over it and get with the program. Especially by my daughter, who used to pass for sane.

I turn on Emma now, ignoring the stab of pain in my leg as I stand up. "Get it? What am I supposed to get here? Five minutes ago I asked you if Jason raped you. You said yes. Sorry, honey, but the facts don't seem to support the claim. And it's a serious claim."

She does the worst thing in the world. She laughs.

"What's funny?" I say. I'm holding one of the bedposts for support and feel my nails digging into its soft wood. "What's so goddamned funny, Emma?"

"Mother Jen said Jason acted coercively. And that's a form of abuse."

Christ. A thousand hideous scenarios flash through my mind. Emma at college, putting the wrong kind of slant on a professor's comment, finding coercion and abuse in his innocent offer to walk her through a calculus problem. Emma at her first job, spinning an argument with a co-worker into a harassment allegation. Emma, married, deciding that killing her husband is the best way to guarantee her having the final word. "What else did Jen say?"

She corrects me once more on the honorific, and I want to slap her. "That you would get all worked up about it. Like you're doing now."

My nails dig deeper, and Emma studies the skin of my hand, the white mountains of my knuckles. "I'm not worked up." But I am. You don't try to engrave a piece of oak with your fingernails and talk through gritted teeth when you're calm.

"You seem pretty violent to me, Mom. Maybe you should lie back down and rest." She pulls back the sheet and fluffs a pillow for me before standing back, creating a safety zone between us. "I'll get you some dinner."

I sit on the bed but don't bother lying down. After I woke in the middle of the night, I must have drifted off again and slept through the day. In those twenty-four hours, Jen Jones has worked on my daughter, turning her into a person I no longer recognize. "I've been here since yesterday afternoon, Emma. I need to get up and move around."

"What?"

"I said I need to move around."

"No. Before that. You said you've been here since yesterday afternoon." Emma screws up her face. "I'm starting to worry about you, Mom. Maybe I should get Mother Jen."

"What are you talking about?"

She's already headed for the door, kaftan swaying around her legs as she moves. "We got here on the fourth, Mom. This is the seventh. Lie down and I'll get someone."

I've been in this room for three days.

Thirty-Seven

While Emma is out rounding up what I expect might be a former accountant with a degree in witch doctoring, I gather up fistfuls of bed linen, squeezing them until the cotton goes damp and the muscles in my fingers start to pulse with an arthritic ache. It's a poor substitute for one of those stress-reducing balls Nick used to keep on his desk while he crunched numbers, but it will have to do. If I don't squeeze the life out of something, anything, I might have to scream. I might have to get all worked up about things.

Who am I kidding? I already am all worked up about things.

I knew Emma and I would be close from the moment I first held her tiny, squirming little body against my own and looked into those blue eyes, so clear it seemed I could see all the way into her, know all of her secrets. We would spend minutes like that, seeing each other, both of us full of questions and searching for answers in the depths of each other's eyes.

"You're kinda scaring me, Randa," Nick would say, but he didn't mean it. He was as mesmerized as I was, although I never sensed the same connection when he and Emma played the staring game. They looked. Emma and I fixed on each other like pagans worshipping an icon, like an addict considering the first hit of crack that would soon course through his veins, like Sunday churchgoers raising their eyes to the mystery of the consecrated host. I needed a word with more heft, more magic.

Emma and I didn't look. We gazed.

In her eyes, I saw perfection, and I think sometimes I saw the future, as impossible as that sounds. I saw Emma's first toddling steps, pudgy starfish hands grasping at invisible support in the air, but always aimed toward me. I saw her first haircut and her new pair of one-inch heels, white with small blue bows on the straps. I saw her dancing at her wedding, pushing out a baby of her own, crimping a piecrust while we chatted away at her kitchen counter, me bouncing my grandchild in my lap. Mostly, I saw us together doing all the crazy, girly, bonding things mothers and daughters do. Antiques shops on rainy afternoons. Walks along the beaches of Chincoteague, laughing at the wild ponies. Selfies in the Smithsonian museums with dour portraits photobombing us in the background.

In my strange, time-reversed memories, I saw us close, stuck together with Krazy Glue, no solvent available.

Now I wonder if Win once thought the same thing about me.

While I'm working over how quickly the rift between Emma and me has occurred, there's a knock on my door. The air stirs when it opens, creating a cross breeze in the room, and a familiar face walks in.

Sal's taller than I remember, although it might be the low ceiling creating this illusion. It might be the fact that I'm lying down.

"How's my favorite patient today?" she says, striding over in a few quick steps and holding her arms out toward me, careful she doesn't dislodge the IV line. "Man, you gave us a scare, honey." Sal takes me into an embrace, a Sal-like bear hug, but it's light, as if I'm made of glass.

"I'm okay. Really. You can hug harder if you want."

She does, and for a while we're both young again, sharing stolen cigarettes and trading lipstick. For a while, I forget I've been knocked out for seventy-two hours.

She finally releases me and sits on the bed, fiddling with the IV tube in my left hand, not looking directly at me as she dislodges it and sticks a bandage over the tender spot. "I'm sorry. But your leg was in bad shape and you were thrashing in your sleep. I had to give you something to keep you still while it healed. And a saline drip to keep you hydrated." She slides the sheet aside. "Can I have a look?"

"I thought you were the resident midwife," I say.

"Midwife, triage nurse, camp surgeon. Although my surgery is mostly limited to removing splinters. Any shit heavier than that and Dr. Miriam gets called in." She palpates the wound on my leg, running a finger down its length. "Looks better. I was worried for a while. Do you remember when your last tetanus shot was?"

I nod. "I got a bad scratch at the zoo a few years back. They gave me a shot then."

"Tell me you didn't stick your hand into the hyena enclosure."

"No. One of the chimp babies in the language lab decided to try grooming me. She got a little overzealous about it."

Sal stares at me as if I'm making it up.

"I started out as an assistant on a research group."

"So you got the big doctorate after all?"

"Not even the small, lowly master's," I say. "School and baby weren't exactly compatible activities then. I'm mostly self-taught, but they handed me a gorilla to work with and I ended up on the team," I explain to a confused Sal about my Pygmalionesque work.

"Can't see much of a need for that here."

It's strange. People keep telling me there's no need for an animal communication specialist in Femlandia. As if I thought there would be.

She wrestles one hand into a latex glove, unscrews the cap off a plastic tube, and applies a thin layer of some substance to my leg. Even the light touch makes me wince.

"Hurt?"

"Only when I think about it."

"Good. Pain is a sign you're not dead," she says, laughing. "Seriously, this is ugly, but you'll be fine in another few days." She recaps the tube, drops it into her bag, and pulls the sheet up over me. "I came to talk to you about another matter."

I let out a long and overdue sigh. "Emma."

"No, actually. You. I'm guessing nineteen weeks. How far off am I?"

"How do you know this shit?"

"Night school. Ingrid and I went together." She pauses, then adds wistfully, "Back when Ingrid and I were together."

"So she ended up leaving after all?"

Sal nods her head. "Yep. Cited irreconcilable differences. So here I am, single again." Now it's Sal's turn to sigh. "I'm okay. I keep busy. And speaking of busy, I've spoken to Sister Jen. You'll be doing half days at the care center until I'm satisfied there's no risk of infection. Think you can start tomorrow?"

"Sure." I'm thinking anything that will get me out of this room is appealing right now.

"Terrific," Sal says. "Be there at nine. And I want to schedule you for an ultrasound this week." She takes a tiny notebook from her bag. There's a larger one inside the leather case, but she buries it out of sight.

"What about Emma? Sal, she's so young. And she doesn't tell me everything like she used to. Has she talked to you?"

Sal shakes her head. "She's sixteen, Randa. Did you tell your mother everything?"

"My mother was a crackpot."

"Most teens think their parents are crackpots." Sal turns back to her notebook without giving me the answer I want. "I can do tomorrow afternoon when you get off work. Don't imagine you've had many checkups in the past few months."

"Not since the end of March. Should I be worried?" It isn't the first time I've thought about giving birth without the benefits of modern medicine, without epidurals and shiny stainless steel instruments, without an army of white-coated doctors monitoring every one of my bodily functions. But it's the first time the reality of having a child off the institutional healthcare grid has hit home. I'm seeing myself in this room, a wad of bedding clamped between my teeth, a pot of hot water at the ready while Sal sterilizes Nell's kitchen shears with a Bic lighter. Someone yells *We're losing her!* but I don't know whether she's yelling about the baby or about me. Then I think of the episiotomy, how it will hurt and hurt and hurt, how there might be more blood coming out of me than my body could possibly hold, how I sneak one quick glimpse of my newborn before a hand touches my wrist, feels for the weakening pulse, and the voice that belongs to those hands speaks the last words I will ever hear.

I can overimagine things sometimes. But still. Right now I don't care that my own immigrant great-grandmother went out to dig potatoes, paused to squat, popped out a nine-pound living thing, and returned to hoeing through rocky soil with a newborn strapped to her back. If there's a god, he or she or it stopped forcing that natural crap on us girls after the beginning of the last century. And I'm okay with that.

"I see you've managed to work yourself up, Randa," Sal says. She laughs and takes my hand. "You'll be fine. The baby will be fine. And so will Emma's. Leave it all to me, honey." She plants a kiss full on my lips, like old times.

The paranoia I felt eases. And the ridiculous scheme I concocted when I thought Sal had kept me doped up to give Jen time to move in on my daughter seems all the more laughable in light of our easy conversation. Being with Sal is like old times, and it's all good.

Everything will be fine, I remind myself as I roll over on my nonhurting side and drift off to sleep.

I'm curious if Sal once said the same words to Nell.

Thirty-Eight

Nearly fifteen years had passed since Win rolled her husband over the side of a chartered sailboat. They were good years, all of them. She fielded Miranda's questions with sadness in her voice and in her eyes, with a quiet shake of her head whenever she said the words *Daddy left* or *I don't know why, honey* or *Of course it isn't your fault.* This last was not a lie.

She had thought that, without a male figure in the house, Miranda would come around to see Win's side of things. The dolls would be put away, the sticks of candy-colored lip gloss forgotten along with frilly dresses and twirly skirts. They would go on in the world, making their way as independent beings. Not humans, not women, but beings without ties to the male population, not even linguistically.

The dresses and the lipstick and the dolls never disappeared while Miranda was a child. Now they had been replaced with more expensive dresses, more expensive lipstick, and a life-sized doll named Nick Reynolds.

It was a rift, a breaking, but the real cataclysm happened much later.

Win was away at a rally when her daughter texted.

Coming over this afternoon to go through old boxes. Want the crocheted baby blanket.

Sure. I'll be home at 6. We can have dinner!

OK.

There were no exclamation points in Miranda's messages. No emojis. No love hearts. Win wasn't surprised; there hadn't been much love between them since the argument over her daughter's sudden pregnancy. But the baby would change all that. Babies could work magic.

And, after all, Miranda's baby was a girl.

Win walked in her front door that evening in a wired and tired state, two hours after she was due. Her flight was delayed, but the gig at Berkeley had gone well. Better than well, really — she and Jen had stirred up the crowd, a stirred-up crowd meant donations, and donations translated into two more Femlandia locations, one in New Mexico and one in north Florida. Upstate New York had proved a failure — even tough women had a limit as to how much snow they could wade through for six months of the year — so Win settled on sites in more temperate zones. They would follow the model of the first colony near Paris, Virginia, and if luck stayed on their side, Jen could begin scouting for more land in the mid- and southwest before the end of this year.

"Got some good freaking news, Miranda," she said as she let her bags fall to the floor and sank into one of the living room chairs. "Get that bottle of bubbly out of the fridge and pour us a round." She tapped her phone, bringing up the number of one of two dozen takeout restaurants. "Thai okay? Or do you want Mexican?"

Miranda didn't answer.

"Miranda? Oh, honey, I'll get it." She went to the kitchen, found the bottle on the top shelf of the wine fridge, and took down two flutes from the glassware cabinet. She poured the first glass without any problems. The second bubbled over, foam rising in the confines of the crystal, hovering for a microsecond before the tension broke and the kitchen island became a sea of Möet. Win didn't notice. She focused on the shadow of her daughter. Miranda was sitting in the small task chair at the workstation in the kitchen corner.

The bottle fell from Win's hand. She didn't notice that, either.

What she noticed was the phone in Miranda's left hand, the block of stationery with Carl's monogram in her right, and the look of absolute hatred on her face.

"Miranda?"

"Dad used to write me notes on this paper. He tucked them into my lunch box," she said absently, her fingers working over the edges, caressing them lightly. "I always wondered where his stationery ended up." She had a faint, almost wistful, smile on her lips, as if the paper itself had transported Miranda back to an age of innocence.

Win could see Carl pushing his young daughter on the backyard swing set, her shoes scarring the dirt with each backward and forward pass. She saw him blending ice cream and milk for thick vanilla shakes on warm Sunday mornings, saw Miranda smiling through a frothy white mustache as he spoiled her rotten. It was easy to fool a child, Win thought. So easy to hide what you were from her. But Win knew the monster behind the mask.

Miranda's voice brought her back to the kitchen. "You know how my father wrote. Hard and fast, like he was attacking the paper with his pen. Sometimes you could see the writing on the next two sheets." Her fingers still worked the edges and surface of the notepad. "I told Jen about it when we were in high school, and it gave her an idea about how to get around cranky Mr. Frey. Remember him? The history teacher who ran his class like he was Pol Pot?" She laughed then, but the laugh was hollow and wooden. "Jen's idea was to write invisible notes. You bore down hard with your pen, but you didn't pass the real note, you passed the blank sheet underneath. The one that didn't have any writing on it. Not any obvious writing, at least." She tapped the paper. "Until you shade over it. Remember that?"

"Vaguely." Win swung away, toward the sink, one hand outstretched for the dish towel she knew would be hanging from a cabinet. "Let me clean up this little spill," she said. But as she spoke the last word, she knocked the bottle of Möet sideways and the little spill became a much larger one.

Miranda did not move from the chair.

The champagne began to spread out like a sea at Win's feet, seeking its own level, and she thought of another sea and another bottle of bubbly. She felt the gentle rocking-swaying motion of a boat as she pressed down hard with Carl's awkward pen onto

Carl's pretty stationery. But there was no boat. The rocking and swaying was inside her now. She steadied herself with a hand on the counter's edge to stop this motion. Yet it didn't stop. It became more violent. A squall was rolling in. Now she was in this same kitchen again talking to a different girl, a sweet sixteen-year-old who would become her second daughter. They were talking about men as they waited for Miranda to come home from her violin lesson. No, that wasn't exactly right. They were talking about Carl.

Miranda isn't clever enough to do what I did.

Had she said anything else to Jen that day? And, more important, had Miranda come home while they talked? The unhappy answer to both questions was in her daughter's eyes.

"You're the devil. You're the fucking devil incarnate," Miranda said. There was no emotion in her voice, none of the girlish lilt Win remembered, only a steady stream of monotone, robotic and inhuman.

More cold champagne dripped from the counter onto Win's shoes. She ignored it. "Randa?"

The monotone continued, now detached and far away, as if Miranda were speaking through a child's string-and-Dixie-cup telephone set. "You killed him. All those years ago when you dropped me off at Nana's and said you and Dad were going sailing. You fucking murdered him."

"Miranda. It was a suicide. I told the police, I told Carl's parents, and when you were old enough, I told you." She spoke quickly now, repeating the story. "He wasn't a happy man. His note said as much. You know that because you've seen it."

"Which note are we talking about?" the voice said. In the dark corner of the kitchen, Miranda's hand opened, and the stationery pad thumped to the floor. One edge landed in the champagne puddle, and the expensive cream paper began to swell as Win stooped to retrieve it. Something was wrong with the top sheet. It wasn't the vanilla she remembered, but a flat, dull gray.

Mold, she thought. *Only mold from the attic. Or dust, maybe.*

Win went white as she picked up the block of paper. Even her hands had taken on the color of old chalk. Those hands dropped the stationery immediately, as if the touch might burn. She had no words, no response, nothing to say at all, as she read the faint letters standing out like ghosts against the background of pencil shading. They were her words. Well, they were supposed to be

Carl's words, the ones she had decided were too forced to pass for authentic. Now they were here again, staring at her.

Miranda tore off the top sheet before Win could reach down and retrieve it. "It's a different letter," she said. Her voice was cool and remote. "Who writes two versions of suicide notes, Mother?"

"I don't know what you're talking about."

Miranda laughed. "Maybe someone who needed to practice? To get it just right? Not only the handwriting, but the tone." She waved the sheet casually in the air. "This one's not right. Too flowery. Too — I don't know — forced. Dad wouldn't have gone on about the doll he brought home for me at Christmas or how much he'd miss seeing me grow into a woman. That wasn't like him."

"People say strange things under stress, darling," Win said.

"Uh-huh. And some people try too hard. What happened? Did you spend a few hours practicing? When you got the penmanship to look like Dad's, then you started on the stylistics?"

Win said nothing.

"I think it was the right move, Mother. Going with a shorter version. More Carl, less Win. Also makes the handwriting analysis trickier. Smaller sample. But you should have destroyed the sheet with the indented writing instead of putting it in a box up in the attic." Miranda winked and picked up her phone. "I'm calling the police now," she said, and the clockwork tones of her telephone counted off the seconds.

They would arrive soon, Win thought. Men would come for her in their white cars with the flashing blue lights. They would cuff her in front of her daughter and they would manhandle her out the door. She would feel the firm hand of one of them as it pushed down on her head, and she would hear the words of a different Miranda. *You have the right to remain silent.*

Not now, she thought. *Not when I'm about to take off. Not when everything I've worked for is about to fly.*

What would they do to her? Lock her up? Of course. That's what happened to women who killed their husbands. Other things happened, too. Win had heard the stories in the group sessions she led. Prison was no joyride for a moderately attractive female, not while the prisons employed male guards. The thought of a man's groping hands, of a prick in a uniform having his way with her body, of God knows what being done to her — all of it unseen and unheard and unheeded by those in charge — made her feel violently ill.

"You can't do that to me, Miranda. Please. You don't know what it's like for women in this world," she said. Her voice was small, no longer Confident Win, only Mouse-Sized Win.

"I don't give a shit, Mother."

"I'll die before I go to prison."

Miranda shrugged and lifted the phone to her ear. "Don't be so melodramatic." She spoke again, but this time not to Win.

There wasn't much point in trying to make Miranda see her side of things. Oh, she could tell her about the shotgun marriage — it might have been a mass at the Washington Cathedral with a reception for five hundred in the Willard's largest ballroom, but it was still a shotgun wedding, and the barrel had been aimed at Win. She could tell Miranda about Carl's cute trick engineered to keep Win pregnant with a child she didn't want until there was no more time for choices. She could talk until she was blue in the face about the women who needed a sanctuary. Win could say all this and more, but what was the goddamned point?

And so she flew. Away from the kitchen counter, away from the spilled Möet, away to the foyer where she had dropped her bags. With one hand, she rummaged through the little table's drawer until she found what she wanted. Both the .38 and a box of cartridges went into the laptop case, the cartridges clanging a metallic tune as they spilled out. Win hefted the two bags and ran out the door, stabbing Jen's number into her phone, leaving the house open behind her.

If Jen didn't come, if Jen was late, Win would do the necessary.

As she ran, she was screaming on the inside.

THIRTY-NINE

I've woken up with hunger and thirst battling inside me in a death match, but that isn't the main concern on my mind right now.

I heard them again tonight, the animals. They seemed close enough that I could detect their scent, a heady mix of blood and excrement and musk. A zoo smell. Nell said we were sitting on two hundred acres of farmland, but the acreage reaches out from the far end of our sector, past the house across the way where I saw the women walking with their picnic basket. My window is at the back of our bungalow, facing in the other direction, perhaps closer to the perimeter, closer to the wild things.

One thing I'm sure of, I won't be hopping any fences to go on midnight runs in search of Earl Grey tea. Not with coyotes nesting nearby.

Or whatever they are.

Nell is bustling around the kitchen when I come out of my room, toweling off my hair with one hand, sliding on a pair of flat sandals with the other. The clock on the wall tells me it's already eight thirty in the morning, and I have no idea where the care center is, or what I'll be doing.

"Sal told me you would sleep hard," she says. "So I let you. But you're not walking out of this house without something in your stomach besides a bag full of saline." Nell slides two fried eggs and a miniature mountain of bacon onto a plate, tops it off with slices of wheat toast, and sets it on the kitchen counter. "Feeling better?"

"Yeah."

I don't remember the last time I had bacon. Or eggs. Or butter and jam. The absurdity of my own body rebelling against anything other than canned food crosses my mind. Still, I eat like a wolf. And this reminds me of last night. "Have you heard the coyotes?"

Nell makes up a plate for herself and sits next to me on one of the stools, picking at her food. No wonder she stays so thin. One egg, one strip of bacon, a half slice of toast. I feel like a glutton watching her. "All the time," she says. "It's been going on since I've been here. Gets so bad sometimes I can't sleep." She takes a bite of unbuttered toast, chews it about fifty times, and continues. "Like being in the middle of a daycare center where all the kids are jumped-up on coke."

Nell has no idea how close her comparison is. "They're exactly like that," I say. "Everyone thinks they howl, but coyotes aren't wolves. They sing. They're lyrical."

"Too lyrical, if you ask me. How do you know all this?"

"You learn all kinds of shit working in a zoo."

I finish my breakfast and steal another piece of bacon from the stove. A third plate is in the sink, Emma's probably, and I start washing it, my hands operating on autopilot, moving in slow circles around the rim as I stare out the open window. I've always liked having a window over the kitchen sink, but when a breeze blows through and I catch a fetid smell, I shut it. "What's out in that direction?"

Nell shrugs. "Depends. If you go right, you hit the wall to Jen's inner sanctum. Go straight ahead and you hit the same wall, only a different part of it. Left takes you to the perimeter fence. It's the one we used to scale when there was still a world worth scaling a wall for. Not that there was much right over the fence, but one of the girls had a car stashed outside and it's only forty-five minutes to town. Why?"

"Shh. Hang on a sec." I open the window again and listen. "Where's the care center?"

"Opposite direction. Back through the arch and to the right. You're gonna need a map for the first few days here. I know I did."

"Nell?"

"Yeah?"

"You said you've been here four years, right?"

Four long years.

"Four years, one month, fifteen days."

I nod absently and strain my ears. "And you've been hearing coyotes since you arrived?"

"Every night. Sometimes during the day. Mostly at night."

"Strange."

"Jen says we don't have anything to worry about. They can't get over the fences."

No. But they can burrow under them.

One thing grates at me as I walk along the path in our sector, pass through the arch of morning glories still glowing their eponymous electric blue, and turn right toward the care center.

Coyotes don't stay in the same location for four years.

FORTY

If I didn't know the coyote pack was far behind me, back past the arch and the cluster of bungalows, past what Jen calls an unclimbable fence, I'd think I was about to walk into it.

The stumbling toddlers yelp and squeal as they mill around a sea of plastic toys so dated, I remember them from my own childhood. Some manage to stand up and navigate the playroom; some cry with minor pain or surprise as they sit down hard on their little bums. Babies can sound so much like animal young.

When I walk in, a woman greets me. Her eyes are wild, as if ten short people have taxed every shred of patience she brought with her this morning. She introduces herself as Sister Luca.

"Like in that old song," she says. "But with a C, not a K."

I remember the song, the boppy, upbeat

tune of the 10,000 Maniacs genre of social commentary masquerading as danceable pop music. We nodded our heads whenever it played on the dining hall jukebox until finally someone figured out Suzanne Vega was singing about an abused kid. I didn't listen to the Luka song much after that. It put me off.

"Okay," Luca says, wiping a film of sweat from her brow. "I'll make a deal with you. I'll take the whiny ones if you can figure out some way to keep me awake until the afternoon shift gets here." Underneath the haze of what looks like sleep deprivation, she's beautiful. Young, fit, happy. And the children seem to adore her.

Three run up, clutching at Luca's skirts, regarding me, the intruder, with wide eyes and fascination. *Gazing,* I think, remembering Emma as a toddler. Two skitter away, as best as their spastic little legs can carry them. One stays behind and tries to crawl underneath the material around Luca's legs.

Luca bends down toward the girl. "This is Maya," she says, and pats the dark-haired child on the head. She mouths a few words to me. "Maya's a bit clingy." Then she kneels down, putting herself at Maya's height, fixing a loose pigtail and retying the bow. "There you go, Maya. Good girl. Now, go play with Sister Jasmine."

"Sisters," Maya says. It doesn't come out quite right; the Ss are heavily lisped and the final R vanishes among the other sounds. But there's no mistaking how many Ss there are. Three. Not sister. Sisters. I try to remember the exact age when Emma began adding the sound to plurals, maybe around two and a half. Maya looks younger.

It takes another dozen gentle pushes to get Maya out from under Luca's skirts and settled into the group. She toddles off, swaying left and right, checking at least five times over her shoulder. "Si-tuhs," she says again.

I look a question at Luca.

"Oh, she's fine. Developmentally, at least." Luca looks as if she's about to cry. "She was a twin. Maya came out first. Her sister —" She stops now and turns away from me, unable to choke out the words. One hand goes to her mouth, as if it might prevent the rest from being spoken aloud, as if words unspoken might undo the truth. She takes one deep breath and goes on. "Her sister died shortly afterward."

I start to ramble, citing some story I read in one of those pregnancy self-help books that I think do more harm than help, the kind that induce Technicolor nightmares of last-minute complications and unexplained heart failures and everything else designed to blow a future mother's blood pressure right through the roof. "They say twins sense a loss, that the surviving sibling knows there's an absence. I guess after nine months living in close quarters, anything's possible." I look over to the spot Maya has chosen, and when I look back, Luca has turned away from the children, her shoulders shaking with the jagged rhythm of uncontrollable sobs.

I am such a fucking idiot.

"Oh, honey," I say, and rest an arm over those shoulders, absorbing some of the movement into my own body. "I'm sorry."

"The thing is," Luca says, hiccuping out the words one at a time, "I think she does know. I think that's why she's always trying to crawl back inside, like she's lost her favorite toy."

We stand together, strangers turned into sudden friends, if only because we're the only adults in the room. I watch Maya in her corner, playing pat-a-cake with an invisible partner, thankful I'm wearing Nell's shapeless spare kaftan to hide my swelling waist, partly because it's more comfortable than the pinching elasto-bands of maternity wear, partly because I don't want to be the one to catapult Luca into another crying fit.

In a corner of the room there are two high shelves with an electric burner and a kettle that looks as if it was foraged from a 1950s garage sale. I spy instant coffee in a jar next to it and go to make Luca her promised caffeine fix.

When I move, the baby inside me moves with me.

It's a feeling I haven't experienced in more than sixteen years, but I know it. I remember the first time it happened.

Nick and I were on the sofa, a bowl of popcorn between us, two glasses sweating on the coffee table, beer for him, lemonade for me. I reached over and I let out a small, surprised sound.

"Oh my God, Nick. Oh my God."

He must have thought I was crying, but I wasn't. I was laughing loud and long, almost howling as I pressed both hands against the fabric of my sweater, willing it to happen again.

I'd heard the term for this, read about it in baby books and Supreme Court opinions. *Quickening.* It had a magical cast to it, a witchy sound, but I didn't believe in the magic until that moment on the sofa while I was executing the supremely mundane task of reaching for a glass of lemonade, while a crazy kind of miracle was happening inside me.

It's happening again. But this time I'm not laughing.

Maya runs up to us once again, making Luca smile with love and frustration, a *What am I going to do with you, sweetie?* kind of smile. This time, the child says a new word:

"Bruvvuh."

Looking around at the ten children in the playroom, all girls, I'm suddenly scared to death.

Forty-One

"Well, that's fine," Sal says, stripping the ultrasound wand of its condom and then sliding off surgical gloves from her own hands. "I think you'll have a healthy little girl in a few more months." She glances down at a clipboard, and her mouth moves as she reads off numbers to herself. "I'd say we're looking at early November based on the measurements." Her eyes roam over my stomach, mostly flat below the sheet. "The baby's. Not yours. You're too thin."

I'm not listening to her. I'm staring at the frozen ultrasound image on the small screen to one side of me that looks like it was harvested from a hospital graveyard, the same as most of the equipment in this one-windowed room. There's a steel instrument tray in the corner, clean, but it has the patina of having been scrubbed a million and one times. Bottles of bleach and antiseptic stand on an upper shelf, their pink and blue contents down past the halfway point. The box of condoms for the ultrasound probe is almost full. The expiration date stamped on one side in numbers large enough to read says December of last year.

Sal flicks off the monitor, and the grainy image fades to a dull black. "I don't know what I'm going to do when this piece of shit bites the dust. We've got two backups, but this is my favorite. Better detail."

My mother couldn't have planned for everything. She couldn't have planned for an economic fallout that makes Chernobyl look like a minor gas leak. Sooner or later, everything here will run out, break, or deteriorate. Sooner or later, we'll be back in a place as dark as the monitor of the ultrasound machine.

But.

How much of this shit do we need? I'm remembering the timeline murals at the zoo, the unfathomable temporal distance between the *Then us* and the *Now us.* We survived a few hundred thousand years without cars and synthetic chemicals and air-conditioning. We bore children without test tubes and ultrasounds and progesterone creams. We endured, maybe not in luxury, but we went forward all the same.

As long as there are males and females, as

long as there are just a few of them, it seems like we'll go on.

Sal brings me out of these ponderings. "Anyway, we need to fatten you up. I pegged you at five months, but you're a few weeks ahead of me." She stares at me hard. "Because you haven't been eating. You need to do that, girl. You eat, baby eats. It's not some fucking mystery. I said the same thing to Emma a few hours ago. Meat is about to become your best friend, so get used to it."

"How far along is she?"

"Sorry," Sal says, shaking her head. "Doctor-patient privilege. Not that I'm a doctor, but the rules still apply. Let's have a look at that leg of yours."

"She's my kid," I say.

"And she's my patient." Sal presses lightly against the bandage on my thigh. "Also, she's sixteen, which means even if we were on the outside, I'd only be able to involve you if there were a serious threat to her health. Or if she consented."

"What do you mean, 'even if we were on the outside'?"

Sal sighs. "Look, Randa. I don't make the rules here."

No. Of course you don't.

"Ah. I think you can take this off in a few days. Let the skin breathe. I'll give you some antibacterial cream to take home. Thank the gods we still have a mountain of it." She smooths the sheet back down over my legs and crosses her arms. "That's it. Eat, sleep, take care of baby, and I'll see you next month. I mean, I'll see you before that. I meant for an appointment. How about we go get some lunch tomorrow after work? Leila makes a killer BLT at the café."

"Sounds great." I'm thinking I could tolerate a bacon-heavy diet, maybe even an all-bacon diet. As long as I don't have to be on pig-slaughtering detail. Ketosis I could take; entrails not so much.

"Any questions?" she asks while I get dressed.

Oodles. But I start with one. "Sal? What if it isn't a girl?"

"She's a girl, all right. Two eyes, one nose, ten fingers, zero penises."

"Yeah, I know." *I don't. You turned off the machine.* "But what if it weren't?"

"Well, that's a new one." Sal helps me to my feet and encloses me in a bear hug. "You never worried about contingencies before. Remember what you said when I asked what would happen if all the eggs in the Nick Reynolds basket ended up being broken? You told me you'd make an omelet. Then you told me they wouldn't break. So here's me telling you that you're having a bouncing baby girl in a few months, and here you are asking questions that don't matter." She stands in front of me, one hand on each of my shoulders. "Read my lips, old friend: *You're having a girl.* Trust me. You can start knitting tiny pink booties."

"Can we do another scan?" I say. "I didn't get a good look. Guess I was dozing off."

"Next time, hon. I've got a patient due in a few minutes." She pats the ultrasound monitor as if it were a sick child. "Plus, this little baby needs to nap between playtimes."

"But we're not a hundred percent sure, right?"

"First rule: medicine is an art, not a science. Second rule: trust your doctor. Or, in this case, certified midwife."

I don't know what I expected, but the full gamut of scenarios crosses my mind, from the scientific to the statistically implausible to the Swiftian grotesque.

We screen proactively for chromosomes.

We're just lucky, I guess.

Male babies? Oh, yeah, we eat them. You like pork, right? Well, wait until you try baby!

I laugh in spite of myself. "It's a hypothetical question, Sal. I was only wondering if there's some policy in place. Scenario: I have a baby boy, Jen isn't exactly hot on the whole XY thing, so I get shown the door. Or the gate." I pause by the entrance to Sal's makeshift clinic and come back into the room. "You know I'm going to keep asking you, right?"

She gives me a friendly poke in the ribs. "And I'm going to keep telling you to eat. Now, shoo on out of here and I'll see you tomorrow."

"It's a date. And I'm buying."

"You can't."

"Why the hell not? I might as well spend my last few bucks on someone I actually like."

"Didn't Jen go over this with you? There isn't any money here. You work, you earn credits. I don't think three hours in the care center today is going to cover lunch for two. You can treat me next time." She must see the perplexed look on my face. "It's in your paperwork. Honestly, girl. Do you not read shit?"

"I have a hard time concentrating when I'm unconscious," I say, making a mental bookmark to read through the paperwork back in my room. Again, I pause at the door. There are other things I want to ask. While Sal scrubs off and preps the exam room for her next patient, I take a seat on the rolling stool.

"Sal? Can I ask you something else?"

"Fire away." Her voice tells me to go ahead, but the constant scrubbing and wiping down, and the clang of the biohazard container as it slams its metal jaws shut, tell a different tale.

"What do you think will happen to those boys? The ones at the gate."

There's a moment now, long and quiet, while I wait for her answer. It seems to hang in the air between us, floating, being weighed.

"I honestly don't know," she says. "We can't help everyone. If a few dozen women showed up at the gate tomorrow, Jen would have to turn some of them away. Maybe all of them."

But we're talking about kids. Two kids.

I change the subject. "Okay. One last question, and you have to promise not to laugh."

She crosses her heart. "Promise."

"Do you ever hear — um — coyotes?"

"I don't think so. Do they sound like wolves? Because there aren't any wolves in Virginia. Not anymore."

"No. Coyotes are different. Higher-pitched, more singsong. Wolves howl like someone's doing a bad Halloween ghost impression, but coyotes — I don't know how to explain it — they're more talkative."

"Huh." Sal says this without much interest. I could be reciting instructions on how to fix a leaky water tap for all she cares.

"It's weird, Sal. I heard them again last night and I thought —"

"Aw, hell," Sal says, shutting off the water and slapping a sterilized, but still wet, hand to her forehead. "I completely forgot." She takes a spiral notebook from the pocket of her white lab coat and flips through it. "I have something tomorrow. Can we grab lunch another time?"

"Sure," I say, thinking my social schedule isn't what it used to be. "Want to do Thursday instead?"

There's a long pause before she answers. "Sorry. Thursday sucks, too. I'll call you, though." She laughs. "I mean I'll come find you. Hard to put a lifetime of phone culture behind us, isn't it? Christ, I miss my iPhone."

Walking out of the clinic into the warm July air, I don't miss my phone. Not one bit. Instead, I miss other things.

Like straight answers.

Forty-Two

According to the paper schedule Nell tacked up on the fridge door, tonight is my turn to cook. I got a reprieve in the form of strict orders to go to my room and rest while Nell and Emma sliced up vegetables from the garden behind our bungalow. Carrots, new potatoes, the glossiest zucchini I've ever seen, their golden trumpet blossoms still attached, although Nell said she'll be cooking them separately, stuffed with sausage and fried in fat. I think I might have drooled.

It all looked and smelled like summer, so much like life, I'm almost afraid to eat it. The hunk of marbled cow on the counter, on the other hand, was appropriately dead, so I could always stick to the paleo diet. I've got what amounts to doctor's orders on that front.

As I lie in bed, the distant song of the coyotes, less active in the late afternoon, soothes me like a lullaby. It shouldn't, but

I'm accustomed to animals. I find them better company than some humans. Animals — with the exception of a few devious chimpanzees who like to stockpile ammunition — don't lie. They don't show one face when it suits them and another when they want to hide secrets. Animals are transparent.

Unlike Emma, who is sitting at the edge of my bed, shaking my shoulder to waken me.

I've counted seven words from her since she arrived home: uh-huh, okay, uh-huh, fine, some, yeah, and uh-huh. Our conversation before I retreated to my room seemed lacking.

Our conversation now is anything but.

"I told you, it's too soon to tell," Emma says for the second time. "Sister Sal wants me back in a few weeks to check. Then we'll discuss my options."

I'm up now, de-crumpling the bed after a power nap. "You know I've always said it's your decision. Whatever you decide, I'll support it." What I want to say is *You're too young. This is a no-turning-back kind of decision. You can have another child later.* But I keep my mouth shut. I've always been in favor of choice, and the choice is Emma's, not mine.

"You mean that?"

"Of course."

This prompts a hug. Not only a hug, but a full-out I-love-you-Mom-you're-the-best-ever embrace. I turn my head away from Emma's cheek and wipe a stray tear with my sleeve before she can see. We're back to normal, we two.

"I'm so glad," she says. "I didn't think you'd be on my side."

"You know me better than that, honey. I'll never push you into anything." Coax, maybe. Push, definitely not. I've seen where that gets me. "Ever. So, what does your gut tell you?"

"Mother Jen says I can still go to school. You know, after. She'll even set up private daycare at her house if I want. And she says I'll probably have a blonde. Like you and me. Won't that be cool?"

My daughter must have missed the class on Mendelian genetics. Nick was half-Greek. Jason is black Irish, more Mediterranean than Celtic. I have a feeling nature is going to favor the jet hair and eyes of the men in the family.

"Mother Jen says —"

Behind my smile, I can feel my teeth grinding together, all thirty-two of them. "That's great. But what does Emma say?

That's what I want to hear."

She sits in the rocker near my room's window, slowly moving back and forth. "If it's a girl, I'll keep her. If it's a boy, I won't."

It takes me a full five seconds to digest this because Emma's tone makes her sound as if she's picking ice cream flavors from the frozen-food section of Safeway. Or deciding between the vinaigrette and the ranch dressing on her salad. Or weighing the merits of printed sheets instead of plain white when what she's really talking about is a choice worthy of Styron's doomed Sophie.

Emma flashes me a grin. "So. Should we eat? Whatever Nell made looks mega-yummy."

"I'm still trying to process what you just said."

She stands now, whirling around to face the window, staring through it at the gardens outside. I imagine her trampling over the green growth, stamping out whatever doesn't appeal to her tastes, killing the living things she doesn't care for. The metaphor makes me want to be sick.

"I knew you'd say that," Emma says.

"I haven't said a goddamned thing." *Yet.*

"Mother Jen knew it, too." Now she spins toward me, her eyes narrowed into slits. "It's called *Fem*landia, Mom. Fem. Not Manlandia. Not Malelandia. Not Boylandia. Fucking FEMlandia. If you didn't like the idea of it, why did we come here?"

"Watch your language, Emma."

"I'll watch my language when you start making sense. You said it was my choice, didn't you?"

I don't answer this.

"Didn't you?"

Sitting on the bed, facing her, I force my hands to relax their hold on the coverlet. I put them in my lap, one on top of the other, my right hand keeping my left from mischief. It's hard to do, hard to maintain enough pressure so that my striking hand doesn't fly off with a will of its own and find the target of Emma's right cheek.

"Let me ask you a hypothetical question," I say, keeping my voice steady. "You want a blond girl. Suppose someone told you there was zero chance that your kid's gonna come out looking more like Zorba the Greek than you or me. What do you do then? Abort her because she doesn't look enough like a Barbie doll?"

Emma rolls her eyes at me. "That's not the same thing. Besides, they do it in other countries. All the fucking time. You think Chinese families with that one-kid rule don't kill the baby girls so the dads can strut around talking about how great it is to have a son? You think poor people in India who can't scrape up the money for dowries just take whatever comes along? No way, Mom. People have been getting rid of girls, like, forever. I don't understand what the big deal is."

"If you can't see how selective breeding teeters on the knife-edge of supremely — and I mean supremely with a capital S — fucked-up, I'm not sure I can talk to you."

"And if you can't see it our way, then maybe you should pack a bag and leave."

Our way.

The words sting. They burn into me, crawling under my skin, numbing and innervating me at the same time. I don't know when it happens, if I make the decision or if my left hand finds a will of its own. Out it flies, swift and sharp, and a clear crack fills the room as my palm makes contact with Emma's face. The smile falls from her like a mask, melting off, becoming a grimace.

"You shouldn't have done that. You really shouldn't have done that," she says.

I call out to her as she darts out of the room, slamming the door behind her hard enough to rattle the walls around me. "You deserve more than a slap."

It's all I can think of to say.

Forty-Three

Win was childless now, and that was the best way to sum things up. No sugarcoating, no spoonful of excuses to help the medicine go down, none of that shit. As she hid in the shadows of parked cars five streets over from the house she would never return to, she swallowed the truth, took it inside her, buried it.

I don't have a daughter. I've never had a daughter.

Jen arrived twenty minutes later. She rolled her secondhand Honda to a near stop, opened the passenger door, and flung it out, pausing long enough for Win to creep from between the executive sedans standing sentry in front of houses where other families — intact families, for whatever that was worth — settled down to their weeknight suppers. She flung her bags into the Honda and then folded herself inside, staying low as Jen slid the car into gear and powered away.

That was what Miranda had to look forward to, she thought as they drove through the suburban neighborhood. Mr. Right, or Mr. *God I hope he's right,* pulling up to the curb, locking the car behind him as he walked along the path toward his castle, leaving the public world he ruled behind him and entering the private world, which he also ruled. There would be kisses and greetings, maybe a few children running up to dear old daddy and giving Mrs. Right, or Mrs. *What the fuck did I do in a past life to deserve this?,* a ten-second reprieve from a day filled with children and laundry and *Don't forget the Smiths are coming for dinner on Friday night.* Mrs. Smith would be a smiling milquetoast of a woman, starting to spread out through the hips, oblivious to her husband's affair with his twenty-year-old secretary. Or worse, thoroughly aware of it and willing to overlook this slight transgression in exchange for title, home, family. On Friday night, Mr. Smith would dominate the dinner conversation, and Mr. Right would let him. Mr. Smith would, of course, be Mr. Right's superior in the public world.

Well, they can have it, Win thought. *They*

can have it all.

"Okay, Win," Jen said. "Spill it."

So she spilled it, beginning with Miranda finding the forged suicide note and ending with her threat to call the police. "I gotta get out, Jen. I need to bury myself so far under the radar, she won't find me."

Jen had already turned the car west onto the interstate, darting through traffic, then meandering over secondary roads once they were out of the metro area. Win watched, her head pressed hard against the cold of the window, as the Honda pushed farther from the city and farther from the grown woman Win would never understand. The only warmth in the car came from the heating vents on the dash, and from Jen's hand clasped over her own.

She should have been crying. That's what you did when you lost someone close. You grieved. But not if you convinced yourself the person had never really existed. Then it was okay. You could go on, create a new life, choose a fresh path.

Win didn't have a daughter — perhaps she'd never had one — but she found some small comfort in knowing a granddaughter was on the way.

One day, she thought, *I'll meet her.*

Forty-Four

Nell and I eat in silence with only the occasional interjections of "mm" and "delicious" to break up the awkwardness. The third plate on the table stays untouched because Emma left the bungalow more than an hour ago with a change of clothes and a canvas bag of schoolbooks over her shoulder. She had a sullen goodbye for Nell, nothing for me.

I can practically smell Nell's disapproval. It makes what otherwise would be a fine meal taste bitter. She doesn't have to say anything, but if she did, I know what it would sound like.

It would ring with the same self-righteous tone of a woman in a grocery store chiding an exasperated mother for telling her wailing child to *Just stop wriggling, would you?* It would be the dual-income-no-kids couple at the movie theater rolling their eyes when the parents in front of them say *That's enough popcorn, Billy,* and take the tub away before the kid overloads on chem butter and pukes it up all over row five. It would be the whispers trailing around the neighborhood like kudzu when a woman has to yell *I said NOW* because saying it five times in a normal voice didn't work so well at getting the kid inside for supper. It would be the sound of every non-parent's scolding of every parent because the non-parents just don't fucking get it.

You don't know how it is until you have one of your own. Until you hear the words *You're a bitch* and *I wish you were dead* and *Leave me alone* just because you're trying your damnedest to keep your baby safe, to protect her, to lead her into this crazy world step by step instead of letting her plunge into the waves face-first.

So I don't have much to say to Nell this evening, and I suppose that's fine, because as soon as I get up to clear the table, there's a knock at the door.

It's Sal.

She doesn't look happy to see me.

"Miranda."

Kate stands behind her, arms folded under her breasts, her squarish jaw set. Somehow I doubt these two have come to reassure me about the coyotes.

"Miranda," Sal says again. "I need you to come with me."

"We're still finishing up the dinner dishes," I say. A glance over my shoulder shows Nell shaking her head slowly. So much for us girls sticking together.

Sal holds out one hand. "I told Sister Jen to let me come. To — well, to keep things on a friendly basis."

So we're back to 'Sister Jen' now. What a difference a few hours make. Of course, there were other differences. My big mouth. The argument with Emma. A slap.

"Am I coming back here tonight?" I ask, already knowing the answer.

Neither Sal nor Kate responds.

"I see. Can I pack a few things for overnight, then?" Jen's warning has come back to me.

What happens if there's a problem?

We mediate it.

This time it's Kate who speaks. "We'll send someone later. You can make a list if there are any particulars you need."

"What the hell would I need?"

She shrugs. "Vitamins. Medication. Books."

"You want me to bring books to a mediation session?"

The women outside my door exchange a

look, and I remember the rest of what Jen said.

If that doesn't work, we have a few isolation rooms for extreme situations.

It's a stupid move, but I do it anyway. I turn from the door, bolting back into the bungalow toward my room. When I find no lock on the door, I'm not sure whether to be surprised or not. I think not. For a full minute I stand here, sweating and panting, my back pressed hard against the wood, as if this would be enough to bar the two women from entering. Kate would be enough on her own. More than enough.

And so she is.

"Sister Miranda, you need to come with us."

I search Sal's face for some sign of sympathy, some shred of absolution or understanding, but I come up with a handful of nothing, only the faintest replay of her words from earlier this afternoon.

I don't make the rules here.

No, Sal, you don't make the rules. But you carry them out. These are the words I want to say. Some part of me, some survival-bent reptilian remnant in the base of my brain, tells me to shut the hell up and do as I'm told.

Forty-Five

For the second time in the five days I've been here, I walk through the rose-covered gate into Jen Jones' private domain. There isn't any lemonade on this occasion, not even water. Her porch has been turned into a makeshift tribunal, one long table set up with four chairs, and one single chair facing it. Genius-level processing isn't required to know the lone chair is meant for me.

"Have a seat, Sister Miranda," Jen says as she takes one of the center chairs at the longer table.

I'm struggling to think of the right word to describe her expression. "Pinched" might work. But something else colors her face, aging Jen beyond her forty-one years. When Emma walks out the front door and brushes past me, I don't have to try very hard to find an appropriate descriptor. It's smug. Totally freaking smug. She sits next to Jen, who takes one of her hands and squeezes it.

Then Kate and Sal join them. Their faces are masks.

"Violence," Jen says, "isn't part of our life here."

I start to speak, but she holds a hand up. "You'll get your turn. We'll hear from Sister Emma first. Go ahead, dear."

"All I was trying to do was talk to her. And she slapped me." Emma talks as if I'm not on the porch with them, putting on her best little-girl voice, a voice that couldn't be more different from the one she used with me only a few hours ago. She even throws in a few hesitant stutters to ramp up the self-victimization. "Hard."

Sal makes a tutting noise and shakes her head. Kate stares directly at me and remains expressionless. Both of her fists clench, turning the muscles in her forearms from slack to ropy.

So much for nonviolence, I think. Everything about Kate says she'd love to get those hands on me.

"Do you deny this?" Jen asks.

"I don't see how it's your business. Emma's my daughter, we had an argument, and things got out of hand. It happens." I'm trying desperately to stay calm. It's not working.

Jen folds her hands together and leans

forward on the table. She speaks the next words slowly, hyperarticulating them as a kindergarten teacher might do with an unruly child who has focus problems. Or speaks another language. "I asked you if you deny it. Yes or no?"

"If you'll give me a chance to explain —"

"I don't want an explanation, Sister Miranda. I want an answer. One clear answer. Yes or no. So let's try this again. Did you slap Sister Emma?"

"This is ridiculous," I say. "It was a slap. A tiny little slap. You're treating me like I pulled some *Mommie Dearest* shit and throttled her. And she's not my sister. She's not my *peer.* She's my teenage daughter."

She ignores me, turning first to Kate, then to Sal. "Sisters, I'll take recommendations now."

Sal doesn't hesitate. "Isolation. Two weeks."

"Four," says Kate.

My mouth drops. There's a hint of a smile on Emma's face that only I can see as Jen nods agreement. I could slap her all over again.

It's a shitty way to think about my daughter, but something's not right. Emma and I have had our share of arguments, usually over some crap like a T-shirt that dips an inch too low, or a Saturday night curfew of ten PM when the party at so-and-so's house "won't even get rolling before midnight." The teenager facing me now seems like she's been body snatched by an alien.

And she seems to be enjoying it.

Jen pats Emma on the shoulder. "You did fine. Now, go inside and ask Maria to fix you some supper. I think there's mushroom soup tonight."

The worst part of this charade isn't Emma smiling at me as she stands. It isn't the wink she throws my way, or the posture that's a little too upright, a little too nose-in-the-air. The worst part is that she bends down and gives Jen a kiss before she walks into the darkness of the house.

Jen also stands, looking taller than she has before. "You'll be in isolation for one month. If there's something you need from your bungalow, I can have it brought to you. Leila will bring your meals from the café."

And that's it. My trial is over. One witness, three judges, no counsel for the defendant. I think fleetingly about running. Down the porch steps, across the gardens, through the gate. I think again about this when I realize the gate is locked, I'm surrounded by electric fences, and Kate's legs look like she might have been a contender for an Olympic medal in track. Of course, even if I outran Kate, defeated the locks and electric fence, tasted the freedom of outside, I'd be worse off than I am now. The devil you know is better than the devil you don't know.

Shit.

"One more thing," Jen says as Kate and Sal lead me away. "I know about the discussion you and Emma had. What you need to know is this. It's her choice. Not yours."

I get the choice thing. I really do. But the kind of choice Emma is set on makes me ill. "It isn't right," I say. "It's no better than what people have been doing to female babies."

Jen has only a few more words for me when Kate takes me by the arm and turns me toward my temporary — and secluded — home. "It isn't your decision."

So this is how things operate in Femlandia.

What frightens me most is that I have a feeling this is far from the worst of it.

Forty-Six

I can deal with quiet. I can handle a room not much bigger than a jail cell and only the barest of amenities. I can survive without so much as a word from Leila when she brings a tray to my window at breakfast, lunch, and dinner.

The food is surprisingly good, if a little strange to my palate. There's nothing on my plates that hasn't been recently pulled from soil or plucked from a plant — no bananas from Mexico, no kiwis from south of the equator. The eggs in my omelets are richly golden, not the pale yellow I'm accustomed to from the Whole Foods in town, and the greens carry a mineral undertaste that makes me think everything I've eaten in the past forty years has had the life processed out of it. Meats come in small portions (I think: *No wonder the women here are so fit — we're back to three-ounce servings*), but when every morsel is an explosion of flavor, perfectly cooked, when every sauce is so simple I can count the ingredients, the portions no longer matter. I'm set.

And I have my books, three small mountains of them rising from the floor of my tiny home. Jane Austen. Octavia Butler. The Bröntes. Angela Carter. Women I've read a hundred times over and women I've never heard of. I'm not sure I ever realized how many female authors inhabited the literary world — how much I could enjoy a life without Shakespeare or Bradbury or King. These ladies keep me company, and I think I might love them for it. Currently, I'm speeding through *Jane Eyre.* It's better than the movie.

So I can deal with captivity. But there are other things I'm not prepared to deal with.

Like losing my only daughter.

I expected we would have moments, the two of us. Any mother with even the weakest grasp on the reality of having a teenager expects at least one relationship trauma. When Emma started high school, I had paranoid fantasies of a million possibilities. Hooked on Oxycontin. Anorexia. Long and black episodes of depression. Unwanted pregnancy. Okay, so I wasn't far off the mark on this last nightmare. But I thought of other tragedies. I thought of Emma getting her hands on a gun — maybe even Nick's — and going postal on her classmates one afternoon, like that Kevin kid from the book. I imagined horrible, disfiguring accidents in other people's cars, my little girl left paralyzed or brain damaged. Or both. I worried over every routine blood test, thinking her white cell count would skyrocket or her marrow would suddenly stop churning out the other kind of blood cells. In my crazy mother's eye, I saw her abducted a block from the house, shuttled into a windowless panel van, and driven toward a life of forced sex.

I did not expect her to be stolen from me, brainwashed by a woman who used to call herself my friend. Who expects that shit?

Silently, I wish for Nick. But I've lost him, too.

Today may be the first time I've had a chance to absorb that he's gone, that he isn't coming back.

Go on, Miranda. Say it out loud. He. Isn't. Coming. Back.

Here in this room, I mouth the words, first to myself, then out loud. I say them over and over. Ten times. Twenty times. Fifty times. I say them until they aren't words anymore, until they become a string of meaningless sounds, stripped of their significance, the way an ordinary English word or phrase can sound like babbling if you overthink it. What does *he* mean? What is the sense of *not*? What if I added another short string at the end of this sentence? *He's not coming back today. He's not coming back yet. He's not coming back soon.*

Or I could just leave that part off, replace it with something else.

He's not coming back, stupid.

As the last lights in Jen's house on the other side of the compound blink off to darkness, I lie back, listen to the coyotes, and think about something new. It's as unpleasant as my thoughts of Nick.

Emma is seeing Sal again in three weeks. I get out of here in four.

Choice is such a tricky concept, maybe a little like freedom. Freedom is fine, until you add another word at the end of it all. *You're free to do what you want . . . but. Sure, go ahead . . . unless.* Some inner philosopher of mine asks what happens to choice if we qualify it.

I suppose it becomes something other than a choice.

Still, it irks me, this inevitable slippery slope. I'm supposed to be fine with choices, fine with women deciding what to do with their bodies. But I remember a conversation with the girls over coffee, one that left me without answers.

"So," Sal said, one arm loosely draped over Ingrid's shoulder, the other hand pointing a finger at the rest of us in turn. Gret, Pamela, Mary Jo, and I were the four subjects closest at hand for Sal's latest ethics poll. "So here's a question, and I want straight answers from y'all. Suppose you're pregnant. You go for a checkup, and the good doctor tells you with one hundred ten percent certainty that your kid is going to be fuck ugly. Like elephant-man ugly. Or walrus ugly. What do you do?"

Mary Jo spoke first. "Well, you can't know for sure. There's that saying 'ugly at the cradle, beautiful at the table,' right?"

Sal shook her head. "Appreciate the insight, honey, but it's my hypothetical. I'm stipulating total certainty. From birth to death. Next answer." She looked hard at Gret Soderberg.

"Well," Gret started. "Well, I don't know. That seems kinda harsh, Sal."

We went around the table, ending up undecided and uncomfortable. Sal gave us another scenario.

"I'll make it easier this time. What if the doc tells you the kid's going to be a mass murderer? Or Hitler. Or that fat guy who runs North Korea. What do you do then?"

This time there were nods of agreement, a few "Yeah, I don't think I could go through with it" answers.

"All right," Sal said. "Now let's flip it around. What if you're the doctor and you know for absolute sure the kid's going to turn out all fucked-up." Sal stabbed a finger in the air to emphasize the absolutely sure thing. "But the mother doesn't. Should you get to decide for her?"

"No fucking way," Pamela said. "My kid, my choice."

"And if we're not talking about squeezing out a baby Hitler," Sal said, "but — I don't know — maybe you're having a girl and you want a boy. Maybe the opposite. What about then?"

Pamela waffled for a moment. The rest of us were silent, and I remember wondering whether Sal was trying to trick us into the answer she was looking for.

Sal unwound herself from Ingrid and made a sort of balancing gesture with both hands. "That's the point, ladies. Choice is either absolute or it isn't choice. Because the minute — no, the *second* — we start putting a qualifier on reproductive rights, we're headed into some murky-ass, subjective waters. And that's how the anti-choice people trap you."

It wasn't the most relaxing coffee hour we'd spent together. But memorable, yeah.

I asked Sal later on if she really believed what she had said.

"Theoretically, yeah. But if you're asking if I could actually do it" — Sal shook her head — "probably not. I'm not that fucked-up."

I fall asleep asking myself if I had any right to say what I did to Emma.

I don't expect I'll ever really know.

Forty-Seven

Four weeks and forty books later, I walk back to my bungalow with all the shame of a college coed trudging home from a one-night stand knowing the asshole she just slept with has zero intention of calling. It's a humiliating walk, and the women who watch and whisper *That's her — She's the one — Sister Jen told us to steer clear* are not my allies. A few of them show sympathy. Most flinch and turn back to their chores.

So I walk on, away from the rose-choked arch, now growing brown with fungus in the humid days of early August. The roses aren't flowers anymore, but dried and powdery whorls that crumble to the ground when I brush past them, a reminder that we're in the dog days, the time when everything seems to be dying. From somewhere to my left come the sounds of splashes and late-summer fun. It's the swimming pool I still haven't seen.

My first month in Femlandia hasn't exactly been a holiday. Even if I did make it through a record-setting forty novels.

The empty bungalow seems like a small palace after my single room in a far corner of Jen's compound. Nell must be out building chairs or running wood through a lathe or whatever it is she does during the day. I never had the chance to ask her. It's also possible she's avoiding me. When I wipe my forehead of a thin layer of sweat, I almost expect to feel the mark of Cain. Maybe a scarlet letter. Some stigma that warns people off.

My room looks the same as it was when I left it one month ago, but after a quick unpacking of the clothes that Sal and Kate threw into a suitcase for my solitary stay, I leave it and go to Emma's at the front of the bungalow. It's barren. No kaftans, no schoolbooks, only a stripped bed and an empty chest of drawers, as if my daughter had never been here.

I return to my own room, stretching out on the bed, not bothering to turn the covers down. Back here, without the ambient sounds of the busier parts of the colony, I can hear nature at work. Orchestras of cicadas humming with their gossamer wings. The racing of a squirrel through branches as it collect acorns, promising a harder-than-usual winter — if you believe the old *Farmers' Almanac* myths. The muted, distant voices of the coyotes that seem to have set up a permanent camp on the outside.

I was told not to talk about the coyotes. More than that, I was told to act as if they don't exist.

It was Jen herself who came to see me halfway through the long and lonely month of my confinement. I remember looking at her eyes on the morning she entered my room. They were cold, icy, without a glimmer of friendship. She didn't mention Emma at all, only told me that if she caught me spreading any more fear to the women of Femlandia, she would be forced to start thinking about my exile.

"But there's nothing out there," I said.

"All the more reason for you to work harder at fitting in here."

Jen left, and that was the end of it.

Forty-Eight

It was nearly midnight when they reached the back gate of Femlandia, where Jen parked the car in a cleared lot next to three Jeeps, a herd of pickups, and one flatbed truck meant for hauling loads the pickups couldn't handle. There was no greeting party for the founder, no champagne bottles popping their corks, only full dark and silence.

"Everyone's asleep," Jen said. "We've had long days and short nights. Oh, and don't get your hopes up. We're not finished yet."

Win didn't need the warning. The porta-potties reeked of old urine and shit, the newest kit home had been slapped together with nothing more than wishful thinking to keep it from collapsing, and the vegetable patch Jen shone her flashlight on as they picked their way through the brush was more mud than vegetation.

We'll get there, Win thought. The thought

fluttered in the back of her mind, weak, a once lively bird grounded by a broken wing. They had to get there. Win had nowhere else to go.

She was quite sure Miranda had made good on the threat to call the police. Miranda hated her, hated everything Win had stood for and everything Win had built. Silly, stupid Miranda, who had spent her youth playing dress-up and now spent her adulthood in the same way. The girl — Win supposed she would have to get used to calling her own daughter a woman now — didn't know about hard knocks. She didn't know shit about what the world was like, how the men and women in it really behaved, how a natural pecking order emerged.

This, Win thought, wasn't the worst of it. The worst was that Miranda did know and didn't care. If a thing wasn't happening to her, the thing wasn't happening at all.

"Penny for them," Jen said, opening an inner gate and waiting for Win to pass through it before reattaching the chain and locking the entrance to the central compound.

"You're going to need more than a penny."

Jen led her to the bungalow, brought out blankets and bourbon, and they settled into chairs on the porch. The two of them sat in silence, watching the stars, tracking the moon as it found its hiding places behind trees that had begun to lose their leaves. Win thought about death as she stared up at those trees.

When Jen's hand found hers in the dark, when, moments later, their lips pressed together in a warm kiss, Win started thinking about life.

Forty-Nine

I'm not sure when I made the decision to break into Jen's enclosure, or even if it was a decision. What I know is this: after an uncomfortable dinner with Nell, after I helped her clean up and watched her leave the bungalow, I'm here at the extreme edge of our sector facing an electric fence that could shock me to kingdom come if I so much as brushed against it.

I waited until full dark. Then I packed a bottle of water, pocketed a box of matches I found next to the propane heater in one corner of my room, and let the chatter and whining of the coyotes draw me.

They're like nothing I ever heard in my years at the zoo. The higher-pitched ones, the cubs, bleat weakly, their vocalizations like the sounds in a crowded and colicky nursery. The older animals emit ear-piercing screams from time to time, as if wounded or caught with their paws in a trap, unsure of how to escape, only knowing an indescribable pain.

It hurts me to hear them, but I've kept going. Closer, all the way to the section of the fence where the crying is loudest.

I don't know much about physics, or how many volts a human body can take before the heart stops, or where to find the control panel that powers the compound.

But I know a few things about electric fences.

I know monkeys can defeat them.

It was the talk of the week at the zoo when Katrina, one of our Sulawesi macaques, managed to short out the wiring in her enclosure. Some said she was lovesick after her mate had been moved to another area. Some said she was bored. Some said it was a complete accident, a freak occurrence that had nothing to do with emotions or smarts. "Don't anthropomorphize the animals," one of the biologists said. She was the one with the doctorate, so we listened. "You can only socialize a beast so much. Especially once it's reached maturity."

I don't have a doctorate. I don't even have a master's degree. All I know is Katrina screwed up the circuits with a wet blade of grass, crawled out, and brought five more monkeys with her. They spent the hours before we found them having a hen party at the other side of the zoo.

When I brought Robert over to see them, he laughed. When we herded them back through the zoo, passing Katrina's mate's new enclosure, we both did. Katrina stopped, checked over her main man, Kimbo, and mimed what she had done with the electric fence and a single wet blade of grass.

So I figure, if a monkey can do it, I shouldn't have a problem. I've got grass; I've got a water bottle. I might not be lovesick, but curiosity is as good a motivator as any.

The first long, thin blade of grass slips through my fingers on the other side of the wires, disappearing in the dark. The second, now that I'm trembling, joins it. When I try for a third time, letting the limp piece of green fall over first one wire, then the next, it trembles for a moment. I hold my breath, listen to it sputter as electricity tries to find its natural course, and place another next to it.

All the while, the coyotes howl in the black of night.

On the fifth try, there's more sputtering. And then there isn't. A light on one of the fence posts goes dark, its connection severed, leaving me night-blind. As I wait for my vision to adjust, I rehearse my next steps. These are coyotes, after all, no matter how human they sound. My scent will hit them even before their sharp eyes find me in the dark, and when they sense their territory has been invaded — and it is their territory, that place on the other side that they've claimed — all hell will break loose. I might as well set off a few fireworks and announce myself with a bullhorn.

I reach out with one hand, tentatively touching the wire, ready to pull back the instant I feel the buzz of electricity course through me. There's nothing, not even the prickly jolt I got as a kid when on a stupid dare I let my tongue rest on a nine-volt battery. The system is as dead as Elvis.

Easy peasy.

Except for the barbs on the wire. One catches first on my shirtsleeve, then bites into the skin underneath, tiny teeth razoring the tender flesh on the inside of my right arm. I've been bitten before — twice, actually. The first was a baby spider monkey who was teething. Not bad. Really nothing more than the nip you might get from a suckling newborn. The second was Bunny, who, despite all his years of sign language tuition, never did get a thorough grasp on his own size or strength. That bite was bad.

This is worse.

I nearly let the pain get to me, nearly cry out in a howl that would do the coyotes proud, then push my face down into the wet grass to stifle the scream welling up inside me. I lie still, as still as I can, for what seems like an hour but must only be minutes. My left hand finds the barb, feels the sticky slickness of blood. There's an ocean of it, coating my arm and drenching the cotton of my clothing.

Do not pass out, Miranda. That's an order.

But, oh, the smell of my own blood. I never could stand it.

Lying here, semi-nauseous and sweating, makes me think of Emma, of the time I had while waiting for her to make her debut appearance in the labor ward at Sibley Hospital. I cursed every person in the room, from Nick to the obstetric nurse to my doctor. I may even have cursed Emma, poor thing, for putting me through the pain and suffering. Absently, I wonder if mothers are entitled to damages, if any woman has ever put in a claim for restitution.

Right now, the way I see it, my daughter owes me.

The coyotes continue to sing and chatter to my left, beyond the fence at the northern end of Jen's enclosure, the part that divides her slice of Femlandia from the outside world. Once I've squeezed through the fence, I turn right, away from them. I need to think. I need to get my bearings.

I need to stop the bleeding before it sends the coyotes into a frenzy.

There's a small hut, hard angles outlined against the night sky. My feet pick their way over twigs that snap and crackle under my weight. Walking slowly, using the fence as a marker, it takes me fifteen minutes to reach the outbuilding, fourteen more minutes than it should because I feel a fresh wave of nausea coming on with each step forward. When I find myself at the door, I realize the structure is much larger than it seemed. The building stands low and long, stretching out far enough that its roofline vanishes in the dark. I follow it, my right hand guiding me along its length, feeling for the recess of a door or a window. I follow it until my right arm protests and demands I switch to my left.

As I turn, ready to start a slow, backward walk, I realize I'm at a door.

And I think, crazily, of Bluebeard. Of his horrible secrets.

In every adventure — and this, whether I like it or not, is an adventure — a choice presents itself. Like in those old first-generation computer games, everything is binary. *Open the door? Y/N? Go inside? Y/N? Turn back? Y/N? Door locked. Use tool? Y/N?*

Do you really want to see what might be beyond this door, you stupid cow?

Remember what happened to Bluebeard's wife?

Remember the dried blood and the frozen screams on his wives' severed heads?

Remember what he did to Little Miss Nosey Parker when he caught her snooping?

Y/N?

Yes.

I feel like Eve with her apple, or Pandora with her box of horrors, or Lot's wife with that last look she had to take.

Eat it?

Open it?

Look at it?

Y/N?

They all answered "yes," those silly women, bringing sin into the world, loosing evil on humankind, turning themselves into a pillar of salt (what the actual fuck?). They just had to know, had to find some truth.

Women are shamed for this kind of curiosity, cursed for its devastating, world-ruining effects. Much more than men, I think, as I feel the cool metal of the doorknob in my fist. Where are the Bible stories and myths about men screwing everything up? Why are women always compared to cats, curious and relentless, happily wreaking havoc because they just. Want. To. Know the goddamned answer? Why all this, and never a thought to the fact that more men have torn up the world than women?

Look at the world outside these fences, for chrissake. Look at the peaceful bliss inside them. Look at the fact that men are the reason I'm here, bleeding, and on the brink of losing my daughter. Maybe a world without men isn't all bad.

Turn back?

Y/N?

But now I think of Maya, the girl in the care center who lost her twin sister. I think of Nell and her dead baby. And I think of Emma, of the isolation room and the long days I spent inside those walls, knowing my daughter was being turned against me, one degree at a time, until she would stand at a hundred eighty degrees from where the two of us started, a face-off. An adieu. The exact opposite of a meeting of minds.

If there's a remedy, if there's a way to repair this break, it has to be with the truth. And the truth is eating an apple, opening a box (a door), turning my head in a direction I'm not supposed to look. So screw the evils of curiosity. Curiosity is what we need if we want to know what's real, terrifying or not.

Behind me, the coyotes sing out their agreement.

Turn back?

No fucking way.

The door to the outbuilding doesn't turn in my hand and I've no key from a sadistic, test-happy husband. What I have is a pane of glass to my left, and a rock at my feet.

That will do.

I take off my shirt, wincing as the fabric tears away from the open wound on my arm. Who knew blood could set so quickly, sealing fibers to my flesh, making my clothing a part of myself? With the rock wrapped inside it, there isn't much in the way of protection, only thin strands of cotton between my knuckles and the glass pane of the door. I use my right hand in case it all goes badly. At least then I'll still have one fully functioning arm instead of two battered ones.

My first try with the rock fails. Instead of crashing through, it bounces off the glass like a tennis ball. I arch my arm back farther on the second attempt, ignoring the pain as the tender skin above my elbow, already desperate to knit itself back together, stretches and unravels the pathetic work of cells and tissue fighting to mend. The rock bounces again, falls away from my hand, and lands with a dull thump on my foot. It's a refreshing change from the white-hot burning on my arm.

Turn back?

No.

Remember Bluebeard's wife?

Go screw yourself.

This time, I swing back like a pitcher warming up for the bottom of the ninth with three men on base and needing, oh man, *needing* that comeback triple. I open my mouth in a silent scream as the skin stretches again, widening, protesting, yelling at me to stop, to give it a rest, to let that pitching arm fall to my side and sleep it off.

This time, the rock goes through.

And I'm in.

I'm not sure I want to be.

Turn back?

Y/N?

FIFTY

Inside the building, I forget what creatures of habit we all are. My right hand still clutching the shirt-wrapped rock, my left hand moves automatically to my hip, to my back pocket, expecting to find the phone I gave up months ago, fingers ready to touch and swipe and tap for instant light. Finding nothing but a few damp leaves stuck to my trousers, the same hand glides over the wall, first on the right side of the doorway, then on the left.

Bingo. A light switch I don't dare turn on.

I unwrap the rock and put my shirt back on before dropping to my knees. The floor is clean and dust free — not what I expected for an outbuilding with who knows what purpose — and I crawl forward. One of my palms is slick with sweat; the other isn't. It takes a while for me to process this situation, these effects of a simple cause: rock meets windowpane, forgetting all about the human hand in its way. Blood is such a stealthy little bugger, invisible in the dark, even when what seems like buckets of it are flowing from the slice between my right thumb and forefinger. I'll be a hot mess in the morning.

If I don't pass out right here, right now.

Use tool?

What tool?

Light fire?

Do I look like Prometheus?

Turn back?

I can't. Not yet.

Matches. I do have matches. I can make fire along with the best of them.

Sitting back on my heels, I search my trouser pockets for the box I took earlier from my room. God knows how old they are, and as soon as I register the moisture that seeped into my clothing — from damp ground or from warm blood — my heart sinks. It sinks all over again when I can't find the goddamned matches.

They were there when I went through the fence.

They aren't there now.

Turn back?

Oh, shut up.

Working back along the fence line, retracing my steps, I keep my eyes on the ground.

It's like searching for a blue tile at the bottom of a swimming pool, and I switch senses, crawling now, sweeping my sore right hand in wide arcs in front of me, supporting my weight with my left arm. It's working well, until the edge of my hand finds the matchbox and sends it flying off into the leaves.

"Dammit," I say, a little too loudly.

A voice, thin as the air, answers. "Help us. Please help us."

It sounds childlike, almost a falsetto. I think back to the boys at the gate, to the young one with the broken arm and the sticklike jagged bone protruding from his skin who said the same words. With a sudden swiftness, all my own pain melts away. What are a few cuts and bruises compared to wandering around the outside chaos with a broken bone and no one to give a shit?

Nothing. That's what. Nothing at all.

"Help us?"

Another howl — a long, wailing cry — cuts into the night. The coyotes. I shut my eyes to visions of small limbs, yet to grow into a man's legs and arms, clenched between teeth, being pulled in a tug-of-war between an alpha and the lesser coyotes. Closing my eyes only makes the image all the more vivid, so I open them.

And a light goes on as if I've commanded it. Squinting into the black, which isn't so black anymore thanks to a risen moon casting its wan light through the canopy of leaves above me, I think I make out a figure.

"Go see what the problem is, Kate. I can't think straight with that shit." Jen's voice, normally composed, cracks on the last words.

My eyes squeeze shut again at the sound, an instantaneous reflex I'm barely aware of. That old child's lie comes to mind, the one we use for monsters in the closet and boogeymen lurking outside bedroom windows: *If I can't see you, you can't see me.*

There are more lights now, a bright and blinding swath of incandescence that makes the bungalow in the distance come alive. A screech of door hinges introduces another voice. Kate, this time. She's talking to herself. And she's angrier than Jen.

"Damn it all. Every single goddamned night. Every single morning, for that matter. Knock it off, or I'm hitting you fuckers with the hose again, and I don't care what she has to say about it. And who the hell turned the lights off? Jesus."

As if the coyotes can process this.

I flatten my body on the ground, now dewy from the change in temperature, as fast as sore limbs will allow. My breathing quickens, and it's a trial to control it, to get everything back into a steady rhythm that won't give me away. Kate's feet, in sturdy wellies instead of sandals, plod across the ground to my right, approaching. I'm cursing the moon that decided to rise, as if its sole purpose were to betray me.

"Goddamned animals," Kate says, passing within a few feet, swinging a flashlight right and left. "Can't live with 'em, can't live without 'em." The beam from the light comes close, so close, and I shrink away from it as if the contact might burn. Then it sweeps back in an arc, away from me and away from the long outbuilding. Away from the broken pane of glass.

My body is completely still. The only sign I'm breathing is the warmth of each exhalation on my shoulder. I count each breath silently and let Kate travel on, crunching the leaves under her boots, marking the beat of my heart, until her outline begins to fade in the shadows and she becomes one with the trees.

Another crunch sounds to my right, but Kate can't have turned around already. I make out the small, oil-spot eyes of an animal, a raccoon, maybe. Or an opossum. I'm hoping for the latter. Opossums are crazily resistant to rabies. Raccoons, though, not so much. Hell, what's a little rabies virus on top of all the other flavors of bacterial infection I've allowed into my bloodstream? I think back to Sal's examining room, to the dwindling supplies of antiseptic and the long-expired condoms, to one of the colony's doctors shaking her head and telling me how sorry she is there isn't any medicine left.

Femlandia has a magical feel about it, but magic isn't real. All magic is artifice. A veneer of illusion over a simple reality.

The air in front of me is noiseless, and then the screams come. Bloodcurdling, pain-wracked yelps and screeches. Kate is doing something to the animals to quiet them.

Something unspeakable and cruel.

It takes three rolls of my body before I feel the matchbox at my hip. I slide it into my pocket and reverse the crawl back toward the door of the outbuilding.

As I reenter the darkness and shake off clinging leaves, there are two more howls.

The first tricks my ears and sounds like "Please." The second is an unmistakable "No."

Fifty-One

Before the collapse, before the water shut off and the brownouts gave way to prolonged blackouts and the blackouts became a permanent thing, I never thought much about light. Light was there, whenever I wanted it. I flicked a switch in the hall, or gave Siri a nudge from my car, or — in most cases — did absolutely nothing. Timed streetlamps flickered on at dusk, airplane cabins glowed bright during descent, the solar-powered landscape disks along our garden path led the way from the roses to the azaleas and back. It was as if every day — every hour of every day — some god, somewhere, commanded *Let there be light.* And all of us, the little people, saw the light, and saw that the light was good, and took it for fucking granted.

Which is why I'm now squatting in the dark, which is not good, hoping like hell the matches still work.

Kate has passed by again, on her way back toward Jen's bungalow. She called out once, and the sound was loud enough to make me jump. But she moved on, and once more the creak of a distant door served as a punctuation to the end of her night wanderings. There were other voices coming from the house, too. Jen's and Emma's I recognized. Another woman, not Sal, not anyone I've met here, spoke a few words, and then all was silent.

Time to get to business.

The matches do work, well enough to singe my fingertips if I hold them for too long. In the dark, I can't count, but the box feels half empty, and it's one of those I've seen in kitchen junk drawers, the large, industrial size of strike-anywhere instant light. Maybe there are a hundred matches inside, maybe more. One hundred more chances to burn my fingers.

Nell told me when I first arrived that all the bungalows had at least three flashlights and a store of batteries to feed them.

"You never know," she said, "when the juice might run out. Could be a generator fail, could be a wiring fault. But it happens." She took me around the place and made me memorize the locations. "We can usually get it back up in an hour or so, but that doesn't help when you gotta go pee at three in the morning. Or if there's a fire and you need to leave. If you forget, or if one doesn't work, check next to another door. They're always by the doors, Miranda." Then, in a whisper: "And if Sister Jen should come in and find one somewhere else, well, let me put it this way: just keep the buggers by the doors and keep the batteries fresh, all right?"

We never needed them, not that I've been around the bungalow much since I arrived, but the rule comes back to me, and instead of striking another match on the cold tile floor, I turn, feeling with my hands around the frame until I find the casing with its built-in handle.

Click.

I'm nearly blinded by the whiteness and click it off again.

My shirt has turned into an all-purpose tool, a kind of Swiss Army Knife made from cotton.

Use tool?

Hell yeah.

Tripled, the shirt damps the light, and a gobo effect of stripes falls on the walls and floor of the outbuilding. When my eyes adjust, I see I'm in an office so neatly arranged, it doesn't seem to have a specific purpose. It could be the workplace of an accountant, a lawyer, anyone. I won't know until I start digging. Until I start acting less like myself and more like Bluebeard's wife.

So I dig. First in the desk drawers, which contain neat piles of Post-it notes that long ago lost their magic stickiness. The twin file drawers on either side of the desk's kneehole yield more interesting fruit.

Within fifteen minutes, I have ten thick folders stacked before me on the desk. What I don't have is enough light to read them by. Another quarter hour goes by while I tape up the door's window panes with a patchwork of pastel-colored sticky notes and cover the broken glass with a manila envelope. My ears strain for foreign sounds, but there's nothing, only the muted whimpering of the coyotes.

I wonder what she did to them. Kate mentioned a hose, but I heard no water, no jets or rain-like patter, nothing. The boys would have run off, as best as their legs could carry them, at the sight of her. The coyotes, though, they would come back. They would keep coming back, searching for food, a way in, a coyote sanctuary.

Unless she did something else.

Each of the files has a woman's name on it. *Nell. Luca.* Others I don't recognize. The last two, and the first I pulled from the drawer, are labeled *Emma* and *Miranda.*

With a shaking hand, I open the folder with my name. It's slim, like Emma's, perhaps because we're newcomers. Inside is a medical chart with a few numbers — height, weight, date of last menstrual period, age. Nothing I don't already know, even though I am a little iffy on the whole LMP issue. On the next page are Sal's handwritten notes from my appointment. I don't read them, not quite yet, because my eye is drawn instead to the large red X on the bottom of the page. It's the kind of X a child might make, two deliberate strokes, angry in their boldness. Underneath the X are words in Sal's script.

July 8
Ultrasound, vaginal
Heartbeat: 140 bpm
Nuchal fold: 4.5mm (within normal
range) Gender: XY (male)

I read them several times, in the way you read the same paragraph of a book, eyes glossing over each word, measuring the shape of it, mouth silently sounding out consonants and vowels, without actually absorbing the content. You start over, from the top, read through again, thinking *This time I'll pay attention, this time the black serif letters will all fit together and make sense.* But they don't. The more you read, the more the marks on the page take on a foreign look, nothing more than lines and curves, until you question the language and whether it's your own.

I try again. And again. Try to clear my mind and focus. I'm having a baby, and that baby is strong and perfect. I'm having a son, and in this place, son spells imperfect, something to be crossed out.

Something to be deleted.

Sal lied to me.

I think of Nell, of Luca, of Maya.

She was breathing when I delivered her. And then she wasn't . . .

She was a twin. Maya came out first. Her sister died shortly afterward . . .

Si-tuhs.

Bruvvuh.

And then of Emma miming what could only have come from my mother, passed down through Jen Jones:

People have been getting rid of girls, like, forever. I don't understand what the big deal is.

Sal, my oldest friend, lied to me.

Emma's folder is nearly a duplicate of my own with slight variations in dates and measurements. In the space after *Gender,* Sal has written *Undetermined.* There is no X obscuring the writing, but the paper is stained with a red ribbon of blood.

Nell and Luca are next, although I'm not at all sure I want to open their files. I take a minute, more than a minute, to steady myself, gripping my knees with both hands and letting my head hang. The cut sings with a bright, clear pain, and when I hold my right hand up to the flashlight, I see why. One ugly shard of broken glass is still lodged in the pad of my palm. It comes free easily, and my hand feels suddenly warm from the new blood.

Time to put the shirt to use again.

I douse the light, unwrap it, and tear one sleeve of my shirt off, tourniqueting it around my wrist, folding the last section over the wound and tucking it in. Already, the cotton has turned dark and wet, forcing me to fall into the desk chair and sit with my head between my legs until the worst of the nausea passes.

I should go. I should turn back and scramble through the fence while the current is still down. I should retreat to my room and think.

As if thinking would do any good.

One by one, the scenarios run through my

mind, color pictures of choices and their outcomes. I see myself confronting Jen, Sal, Kate. Trying to convince Nell of what I've seen. Breaking Luca's heart all over again. Every way I look at it ends with me back in isolation — or worse. Jen could kick me out, send me into the wide and barren world on the other side of the gates. Would I last long enough to see my boy? Maybe. I'd end up squatting in some field west of Middleburg, the carcasses of dead horses in sight, pushing a child out, mind reeling with the struggle and the euphoria and then, finally, the absolute desperation when reality presents itself.

We'll be like that mare and her foal, spooned together, without food or water.

We'll be waiting to die.

There's no amount of thinking, no process, no pro-con list, no flow-chart, that ends any other way.

Unless.

Unless I follow Jen's advice and work harder at fitting in here. If I play my cards right, there might be a promotion in my future.

Hi, I'm Sister Miranda. Welcome to Femlandia, where every day is a blue-ribbon day! It's like Disneyland for women, a lifelong picnic. Over here we have the community center, and beyond that hedge is a beaut of a swimming pool. Oh, look! Here's Sister Sal. She'll tell you all about that bouncing baby girl you're going to have. Chances are one in two the kid won't survive. But come now, don't look at it as a glass half-empty, look at it as a glass half-full!

I can almost feel the false smile plastered on my face as I drone the welcome spiel, doing my best to fit in, watching my soul turn black as I become party to infanticide.

I think I might be out of options.

Turn back?

Not yet.

Fifty-Two

As I leaf through Nell's and Luca's files, reading the notes Sal made and tracing the lines of the red Xs with a fingertip, I have a gruesome thought.

At the zoo, I learned how to make supplies last. "Grant money doesn't grow on trees," Robert used to say. "If you think you need something, order it before the fiscal year ends. Hell, order it even if you don't think you need it. And for God's sake, don't ever throw anything away." They were lessons in planning, those supply orders and warnings to hoard the junk. Bunny had five brand-new sets of flash cards, three yet-to-be-used touch screens with stored vocabulary, everything he and I needed. But if a few dollars remained as the end of September approached, I put in my orders, squirreling away equipment in case next year's financial forecast turned out to be dry with no chance of rain. And I never threw anything out, not if it had life left in it.

What if . . .

I push the thought away, burying it, and turn to the next page in Luca's folder.

Multiple. Dizygotic. XX and XY.
Mother: Luca Schwartz. Father: unknown.
XY neonate Generation-ID B-4 transferred to Building 3, Sector A.

I'm in Sector A. Jen's closed-off part of Femlandia. But there's no number on the door, no maps, no building identification. The shirt I've tied around the flashlight isn't tight enough, and I crouch down in the dark kneehole of the desk to redo my work, unfolding and refolding. I think of the flashlights in our bungalow, the ones Nell told me to keep by the door, to check the batteries once a week. I imagine Nell has that job now — I haven't been home much.

This light also has a label. Not *Sector B, Bungalow 14,* but *Sector A, Building 3.*

Building 3 is a long, large space.

I realize I'm inside an old tobacco barn and the office, at one end, is only one part of it. With my back to the desk, I sweep the flashlight low, and the outline of a closed door comes into focus. *Another of Bluebeard's secrets,* I think, except I don't expect to find dead wives.

I expect to find worse.

The door isn't locked, which surprises me and doesn't surprise me. The women here are a tight group, a group within a group, and I remind myself I've already defeated two levels of security. Once I'm through, I'm in a narrow corridor with tall, boarded-up venting windows to my left. A shiver runs through me, and I unwrap my shirt from the flashlight, easing myself back into it, already regretting tearing off one sleeve. The ceilings are high here, probably to let warm summer air rise.

With the light free of its filter, I can make out a series of doors to my right, each one old and scarred, each one a forest of invisible splinters. The knob on the first door turns easily, and inside the smaller room are shelves, some wood, some metal. It looks like the cleaning section of a shitty supermarket. Bottles of Lysol and Windex stand like bright green and blue soldiers on the racks, dust marks indicating the places where more bottles once stood. In the toilet paper section there are a few dozen mega-roll packs.

There used to be more.

Dwindling supplies, I think, and the idea of stocking up on necessities again comes into my mind. What will they do — what will *we* do — when the inventory runs low?

Make soap from animal fat, I guess. Let the grapes sour into vinegar and wash windows the old-fashioned way. Lysol and Windex aren't strictly necessary. They aren't basic elements, not like air and wind and fire and rain, all of which carried us through millennia before the chemical companies convinced us we needed pine-scented and streak-free cleaning solvents. In another generation, the children here won't miss them. The concept of wiping your ass with squeezably soft embossed paper will have gone the way of the buggy whip, Kodachrome, the crystal ashtray.

They'll make do. We'll make do.

Of course, there needs to be someone still around to make do.

I move on to the next door in the line. Like the first, it has no label, nothing to indicate what might be behind it. The beam of my flashlight finds a different section of the supermarket — #10 cans holding ketchup and pickles, sacks of flour and sugar wrapped tight in clear plastic bags to keep the vermin out, tins of active dry yeast.

Again, I think of the next round of children, the ones who won't know processed foods, only fresh tomatoes and crisp cucumbers from a garden, put up in glass jars for winter. We'll get by without ketchup. Easily. We'll go gluten and sugar free, make our bread from the natural yeast in fermented grape skins. We'll bring the arts of ancient Rome into the twenty-first century.

But we'll need to be here to do all of this.

Door three holds bolts of material and skeins of yarn. In a cupboard to the side are boxes brimming over with sewing thread and dress patterns from *Vogue* and *Simplicity.* I recognize another pile of tools as latch hooks, tatting shuttles, double-pointed knitting needles. Two small, portable looms lean against one corner of the room. Emma's daughter — if she has a daughter — will wear simple clothing, fasten it with buttons or hooks and eyes, wrap material around her like a sari or a sarong. She won't miss ready-to-wear or back-to-school specials at Nordstrom's. She won't know such things ever existed.

But.

But, but, but.

The answer is in my mind already. It slows me down, makes me want to take my time and open each of these doors, to waste minutes and hours inside this old barn turned warehouse. I pass four more closed doors without turning the knobs and shine my light down the corridor toward the far end of the building, where four panes of glass mark another door leading outside.

Easy access, I suppose. To the more necessary supplies.

I'm still fifty feet away from the last door when I hear the sound.

Fifty-Three

Win worried.

She worried about the crops and she worried about the livestock, both of which had suffered badly from blight and disease in the three years she had been living in Femlandia. She worried about electricity and outages and stopped-up plumbing. She worried about education and medical supplies, about the occasional squabbles that broke out among the women. She worried about growing older.

Already the change had started, her periods becoming increasingly irregular and her waist thickening. She didn't want another child, didn't want to start all over again at forty-seven, but wanting or not wanting to conceive wasn't the point. No, the point was that nature had made this choice, altering Win's chemistry for the second time in her life, unceremoniously dumping her into the category of dried-up and finished.

Win wasn't the only one affected.

She rarely ventured far from the central compound, and when she did, she was never Win Somers. Jen had spread the story of the middle-aged woman with the delicate constitution through Femlandia, and Sister Rose, as Win was known to the community, played the part well. She attended few community meetings and limited her work to light maintenance in Jen's bungalow. No one questioned this because no one questioned Jen's word. Ever.

But she had to get out once in a while, if only for a change of scenery. A year was a long time to be confined, and although Jen was a good partner — the best of partners — Win missed the camaraderie of other women.

There was no question. The population was aging. Sister Betty, not a spring chicken when she arrived twelve years ago, had streaks of gray in her dark hair. Sister Jeannine, Femlandia's first doctor, was down to one day of work per week. Two of the residents who had come to the colony in their seventies died last year, one following the other.

When the Paris, Virginia, Femlandia opened, there were thirty residents. That number grew to one hundred over the years but was slipping ever downward. Only one baby had been born — a girl, thankfully — and the two tweens who had come with their mothers were now in their mid-twenties, nearly Miranda's age, and eager for children of their own.

"I hated telling them 'no,' " Jen said one night at supper.

Sal agreed. "Same here. Especially since I promised there wouldn't be a problem when the time came. That was two years ago. And it's not just the younger girls." She pushed her plate away as if the food disgusted her. "Sister Rachael's talking about moving back with her ex."

Win paled. To the extent she had favorites, Rachael had always been that woman. It wasn't that Rachael went back all the way to the first coffee group, or that she had always been the one to bring something to the meetings, even if that something was a half-eaten bag of stale Oreos. Rachael epitomized change. She had come here thin and tired, a wisp of a girl, afraid of her own shadow. A single raised hand, meant only as a gesture, and Rachael would shrink back into her chair, often leaving the group in tears. Raised hands were her husband's hands, and raised voices were her husband's warnings. The bruises on her body disappeared within a few short weeks, but Win knew there were other kinds of bruises, the kind you can't see and the kind you can't reach.

Rachael, only twenty-five when she packed a bag and executed a midnight run from her house to Jen's waiting car, was a bruised woman, too damaged — by her own assessment — to even think about motherhood.

And then, something changed. The twenty-five-year-old became a thirty-five-year-old, and middle-aged Rachael showed no fear of raised hands or raised voices, no fear of conflict. At Win's urging, Jen had put the woman in charge of new intakes, and now she was strong. Strong and ready to have the child she had been wanting before nature's clock struck its final warning chimes.

Jen had to say no.

"I thought we'd have more supplies by now," Jen said.

Win looked hard at both of the women. "And why don't we?"

"Regulations," Sal and Jen said at the same time.

"It's sperm, for chrissake. Not plutonium." Win stood and circled the dining table. "What regulations?"

"We got the news last December," Jen

said. "We didn't want to tell you until we were sure."

"Tell me what?"

"The cryobanks are refusing to screen sperm for sex chromosomes, Win."

"What?"

"I mean, they can't do PGD anymore."

Win sank down into her chair between Jen and Sal, wishing it would swallow her. "They can't do PGD anymore," she repeated. "Oh, fuck."

Jen took her hand. "We knew preimplantation genetic diagnostics was spinning out of control, honey. That's why we stocked up when there was still time, before they limited PGD to medically necessary cases." She turned to Sal and mouthed, "Help me out here."

"It's no one's fault," Sal said. "But the last batch that came in was recalled. Chromosomal abnormalities. The bank said they would ship a replacement batch and . . . boom. The legislation against designer babies passed. Their hands are tied, Win."

"But I don't want designer babies. I want girls. Black girls, white girls, brown girls. I don't give a shit what color their eyes are. How goddamned difficult is that?" Win stood again and paced the room. "How many samples do we have?"

Jen hesitated. "I'd have to check."

"Ballpark figure. A few dozen? Tell me we have a few dozen." Win didn't need to hear Jen's reply. She only needed to see the woman bite her lip and lower her eyes. "Okay. Fine. Make me a list of the fertile women here. Then contact the bank and see if they'll send us enough samples to go around. If they can cover the demand, terrific. If not, set up a lottery and put Rachael's name at the top of the list."

"But, Win," Sal started, "they won't send us sorted samples. I just told you —"

"I know what you told me. And this is me telling you to get the stuff."

Later that night, Win lay awake next to Jen. She listened to the woman's steady breathing, felt the sheets move with each rise and fall of Jen's chest. It was not a perfect solution, not even close to an optimal solution. Without advance gender selection, half of the new babies would be males, and males in Femlandia defeated the purpose.

It was, one way or another, a fix to their problem. She couldn't let someone like Rachael leave, not knowing what waited for her on the outside. Win would rather die than send one of her girls back to a monster.

There were other things Sal didn't understand. Win didn't really understand them, either. Her grasp on global economics was tenuous at best. But Jen's wasn't. Jen knew things.

A low moan of desperation escaped her throat, and she thought about supplies again, not only the supplies on the inside, but those on the outside.

"You need to sleep, honey," Jen said as she turned under the covers.

"I can't. Do you think the next one will be as bad as 2008?"

Jen sat up and switched on the bedside lamp. A soft glow warmed the room. Still, Win shivered.

It was a good room, a cozy room, and lying here next to Jen, Win could almost lull herself into a kind of easy complacence. They had built a home from nothing, but it was more than that. They had built a community, a family, happily separate from the world.

"I don't know," Jen said. "The predictions aren't exactly rosy." She skipped all the details of mortgage debt and student debt, of automobile debt and global debt, skipped the part about monetization and the flooding of economies with dirt-cheap money. She didn't mention a word about funding gaps in pension plans or manipulated employment statistics. Jen only sighed, and in that sigh, Win understood.

"What are we going to do, then?" she asked.

Jen leaned over, kissed Win lightly on the forehead, and turned out the light. "We're going to stock up. On everything."

FIFTY-FOUR

There's that sound again.

My response is instant and involuntary, a fight-or-flight reaction that keeps me grounded to the floor, unsure of whether to burst ahead through the last doorway of the barn or to turn tail and run like hell. Even Bunny felt this on days when we opened up the research lab to visitors. A woman entered with a toddler at her side and an infant swaddled in one of those contraptions that might as well be a second womb. The baby stirred, yawned, and let out a wail I was sure could be heard on the far side of the earth. Everyone — young, old, humans, primates, men, and women — went rigid and became alert. It didn't matter whether we had children or not.

The thing about babies, sometimes cute, sometimes annoying, is that you can't turn them off. You can't not pay attention. The screeching newborn in the bulkhead of an airplane isn't really a nuisance. The nuisance is our response, the triggering of primitive brain activity in our emotional centers. We can't tune them out and we can't not listen. We're wired that way.

I'd like to pretend I haven't heard. I'd like to run back along the hall, past the boarded-up venting windows and the closed doors hiding their dwindling supplies, and I'd like to crawl through the fence and keep running until all I have around me is middle-of-the-night silence. But I can't do that. I've already listened, and my brain is issuing orders to obey.

Open door?

Do I have a choice?

The knob turns without resistance, and I swing the door open, keeping the yellow beam of my light low. Part of me says this is a kindness, a way to let young eyes adjust to the difference. Another part of me suspects I'm doing it to keep myself in the dark as long as possible.

This room, unlike the storage spaces, is warm and humid, the kind of comfortable temperature that matches that of a human body, a womb of sorts. No dust motes swarm in the beam of my light, and the tile floor gleams as if it had been polished only moments ago. At foot level are two rows of wheels below shiny stainless supports, one row to either side with a narrow walkway in between.

The flashlight floats up, inch by inch, revealing more steel and, finally, the clear plastic of a hospital bassinet. There are twelve of them in all, six on my right and six on my left.

I stop dead when I catch the familiar shape of a baby monitor on each side of the rear wall, my face stupidly held up to one lens like a stunned cat burglar.

The power's out, you idiot.

All but the first bassinets in each row are empty, sterile little receptacles. Nestled inside the two closest to me are babies.

Automatically, I reach out, only to remember my free hand is mess of blood. I set the flashlight into one of the empty cradles and let the yellow beam bounce off the wall, diffusing its light, creating a warm glow in the room. One of the infants stirs in its swaddling, yawns, and pushes a tiny fist into the air. The baby to my left is the one who has been crying, a hearty and colicky howl I remember from Emma's early days when I counted myself lucky if I slept uninterrupted for more than two hours at a time.

I pick the crying infant up and cradle him in the crook of my left arm.

Babies, like most animals, cry for a reason, and hunger is usually the culprit. Either that or a dozen others: wet, cold, hot, sick, tired, not tired, attention starved, overstimulated, or no reason at all. In the corner of the small room is supply cabinet, but when I pry the doors open, I find only neat stacks of diapers, some disposable, some cloth.

The baby lets out another monstrous wail and then settles his head close to my breast, already swollen, preparing itself for my own child.

It won't work, Miranda, I think.

But it might.

It does.

As soon as I wrestle myself free of shirt and bra, the tiny mouth finds its target, sucking greedily with closed eyes. I start humming the old mockingbird song, the one my mother used to sing to me, and the hums morph into sobs before I can stop them. With my back to the wall, I slide down, propping myself up, cradling the unwanted child, and before I know it, I'm crying full out as I trace his round cheeks with a fingertip.

He, on the other hand, seems content. What a trade.

I don't know how long we've been sitting here, joined together in that most basic way.

When I move to switch sides, he's fast asleep. After a quick diaper check, I place him back into the bassinet. It's unexpectedly hard to let go.

The second infant is still sleeping, his barrel chest rising and falling with each breath. I'm tempted to wake him, to preempt his hunger pangs, but I don't. There's that old saying about letting sleeping dogs lie.

This one has a birthmark, an irregular port-wine stain on his throat. Nothing like Gorbachev's forehead, but noticeable all the same, the kind of harmless blemish he'll be teased about in school when he's older. The kind of blemish that, one day, the right girl might only smile at and kiss.

Then I remember where I am.

Above his head, an identification card is fitted into the built-in slot of the plastic. There's no name, only a number, *B-7.* In the space below it, written in block letters, are the words *Nell / Sperm: A-1.* The first bassinet has a similar card with different details: *B-8* and *Helen / Sperm: A-3.*

I check the others for identification. Nine are blank. The last one on the right side has a card with *A-7,* my name, and *Sperm: External.* The bassinet is an empty shell, waiting for me to fill it with necessary — no, vital — supplies. My contribution to the procreative well-being of Femlandia.

Before I leave the nursery, I perform one last task. Just to be sure.

As if I don't already know.

The babies here, of course, are both male.

I hope my mother really is dead. If she isn't, I think I might have to track down Win Somers and put a bullet in her brain.

Fifty-Five

At the zoo, I had one job. I was also the lowest-ranking, least-educated member of our research team, which meant that I had many jobs. I mopped floors, I hauled buckets of shit out from the primate enclosures, I gave baths to baby chimps, and I fetched whatever they wanted me to fetch. Bunny needed break time from our work, and break time for Bunny turned into work time for me.

One of the errands I ran — more often than I cared to — was the most menial of labors. I shuttled between the primate house and the frozen zoo, the place where we stored vials of cryogenically preserved skin samples, eggs, sperm, and fertilized embryos. We kept tens of thousands of future animals in the smallest of enclosures, a bank of freezers in an off-site location outside of the city.

So when I open the door next to the

nursery, I know what I'm looking at.

There aren't tens of thousands of vials behind the glass door of the freezer, only a few dozen, all labeled with an alphanumeric sequence beginning with A. My light finds one of the A-2s and I stare at the sample of cloudy, congealed liquid. I stare for a long time.

The numbers are too simple, too low, and too uncomplicated to be from a sperm bank.

If I'm right, the babies next door are second-generation Femlandians, those born from residents using sperm from internal sources. That's why the card identifies my baby as A-7 — Nick, thank God, was most definitely external, not a denizen of Jen Jones' twisted wonderland. The vial marked A-1 contains the sperm that fathered Nell's child, a B generation. A-1 is not a man, not a human being, only a glass tube resting in its holder, a tiny frozen soldier standing ready to do his work.

I pretend I'm in a different place. A movie, a novel. My character runs through streets, dodging traffic, ignoring the cramp in her gut, carrying evidence to police, reporters, magazine editors. Within days, maybe only hours, the scandal will spread like wildfire across the country. Hashtag FEMLANDIA will trend everywhere. Emma will see her mentor for what she really is. I'll celebrate with a mani-pedi and all the caffè latte I can drink.

None of this is going to happen. If there's still a police force, it's gone deep underground. Emma hates me. Lattes and other niceties don't exist anymore.

I run, though, out of the cryo-storage room and all the way back down the length of the building, out the office door, and along the fence line. As I run, the sounds I've heard before become louder, almost deafening. I think of my conversation with Sal about the coyotes, about how they sing rather than howl. About how they seem almost talkative.

Fifty-Six

A haze of sudden cloud cover has swallowed up the moon, and I trip twice on my way. I should have unwrapped the flashlight, but I wasn't thinking straight. I'm not sure I'll ever think straight again. From ahead of me, a voice calls out, thin as the night air.

"Help us. Please."

I run faster, wanting to know and not wanting to know.

Sometimes, when I would wander around the primate house watching another set of two-legged idiots thump on the glass of the chimpanzee enclosure, hearing hordes of unruly schoolchildren heckle the baboons, I wished for superpowers. I wished for the kind of magic that could swap human for ape, if only for a little while. A few hours. Overnight. Just so the kids could have a taste. Maybe they would come away from it transformed; maybe they would learn some respect.

It wasn't anything more than a fantasy to work out my frustrations. I hated seeing the animals caged up, hated the constant questions that would nag at me. Were they conscious of their situation? Did they hate it? Did they want to cry out, *Help us. Please*?

When I hit the chain-link fence at full speed, I realize I've been paying more attention to my feet than to the space ahead of me. There's no more space now, only the metal pressing its diamond shapes into the flesh of my face.

I hear everything now, and I keep my eyes squeezed shut, as if by not seeing I can somehow deafen the sounds and block the distinctive smell coming from beyond the fence, but the temporary blindness only heightens all my other senses. My right hand burns with new pain, and I realize I've got the metal chain link in a death grip, trying to bend it to my will. Instead, the fence seems to be bending me.

And then there's a softness as something warm and dry wraps itself over my fingers from the other side. My eyes fly open at the sound of a voice.

"Help us. Please."

The boy I first saw outside the gates, the older boy, is eye to eye with me, his mouth only inches from my own. When he speaks, his breath is a mix of peppermint and salt, the most basic form of toothpaste in a world where Crest and Colgate aren't readily available from drugstore shelves. I raise the flashlight, keeping the beam out of his eyes, and study him.

A month ago, when he and his brother first begged for help at the main gate, this boy was in trouble. He was intact, no broken bones, no visible wounds, but he wouldn't stay intact for long. Not outside. Not with muggers and animals all looking for prey that would hold them over for another few days, another precious week. At first, a sense of relief washes over me. Jen let them in, she caved, she's not inhuman after all.

I could believe this, if I didn't see the fright in his eyes. And the banks of low, whitewashed structures behind him, each one emitting grunts and the occasional moan.

They're like doghouses. Except taller.

"Please, ma'am," he says. "You have to get us out. We'll leave. We'll go back out" — he knocks his head weakly to one side — "there. We probably won't last very long, but I'd rather be anywhere than in here. They make us — they make us —" His voice trails off, and tears brighten his eyes before running down his cheeks, cutting shiny rivers in the skin. My light catches faint whiskers that, together with the tears, remind me this boy is in that no-man's-land between youth and adulthood. He sniffs a few times, rubs at his nose with one sleeve, and stands a little taller, as if he's realized he shouldn't be crying, that crying is for babies.

"It's okay," I say. "Everyone cries."

The waterworks start up again, but the boy turns them off. "I'd rather me and Walter die than stay here."

I want to tell him he doesn't mean that, doesn't really want to face starvation and thirst. A look in his eyes, a look much older than this teenage boy, keeps me from arguing.

At the sound of his name, the younger boy approaches. His left arm ends at the elbow, and I sag against the fence. When he's closer, it's clear the arm is still there, only bent and supported by a sling. Someone mended him. I think of Sal telling me she's nothing more than a midwife and I wonder who set Walter's broken bones.

Walter looks up at me. "I can't do it anymore," he says. "I tried, but I can't. Nothing happens. And they say if I don't make it come out, they'll hurt Oliver. It hurts real bad, miss. Like burning."

"He's only ten," Oliver says. "Nothin's gonna happen for at least a couple of years. And he's small for his age, so maybe longer." He scuffs one foot lazily back and forth, studying it, not meeting my eyes as he talks.

Oh, I wish I didn't know what these boys were talking about. I wish, I wish, I wish.

But I do.

The vials labeled A-1 and A-3, the necessary supplies that impregnated Nell and Helen, had to come from somewhere. I let my weight carry me down, grabbing the fence with my injured hand for support, and kneel there, silent. The boys follow me.

"Why are they doing this?" Oliver asks.

I could tell him it's self-preservation, all part of a plan to keep Femlandia going, to populate the colony. The problem is, I don't know how to explain this to two young boys. There aren't enough words and rules in my language to spell it out. There shouldn't be, at least. There shouldn't be any way to tell two children they're being kept prisoners and forced to produce the only thing Jen Jones considers them good for.

"How many others are there?"

Oliver doesn't respond, only turns his back to me and flips the latches on the miniature houses. A few heads appear, timidly poking out of the open doors, then more come, drawn by my light. In minutes, the enclosure is filled with children, some Oliver's or Walter's age, most younger.

The small ones act more like pets than children, chirping playfully, running half-naked around the perimeter of the enclosure. They pull one another's hair and squeak protests when another child pulls theirs. A toddler wobbles on unsteady legs and pushes dark locks of hair from his face. He seems familiar, and I think back to Maya in the care center.

Maya, who lost her twin and wanted her — or him — back.

The older boys, only two of them, squat down before me, regarding my flashlight with unease.

"I'm not going to hurt you," I say.

Walter responds. "They don't understand. We're the only ones who talk here. The rest are like, I don't know, like aliens. Or gorks."

"Don't say "gorks," Wally. Mom wouldn't like it."

"Sorry, Ollie."

" 'S'okay." Oliver hangs an arm over his brother's shoulder. "I know you didn't mean anything bad." Then, to me: "He doesn't, you know. It's just that there are ten kids here and none of 'em talks. They just stare at us and sometimes let out a howl or a weird kinda cat sound. It's like they're trying to say something, but no one's ever taught 'em about sounds."

"They're feral," I whisper, more to myself than to Oliver and Walter.

"And if they make too much noise, that big woman comes out and yells at them. Then they stare and howl some more. I tried to get 'em to be quiet, but they don't know what I'm talking about. They only know the big woman carries a zapper thing, the kind that gives you shocks. They're like that dog the Russian dude had. Pav-something."

"Pavlov," I say. As if anyone gives a shit. I turn my head toward the fence. The lights are still off, but who knows how much longer I've got. Kate noticed the power was out, and already I've spent more time here than I planned. "Listen, Oliver. This is important. I have to go back to the other side."

Walter yelps. "No!"

"I have to," I say. "Just for tonight. Tomorrow I'll talk to some people —" I'm making it all up as I go along, saying anything to reassure these two kids. The fact is I have no idea who to talk to or if anyone will listen.

If anyone will care.

A chill runs through me when I think of another possibility.

Everyone here may already know. Including Emma.

Oliver and Walter plead with me to get them out now, tonight. "We can take our chances on the outside," Oliver says. "Maybe it's better."

"Maybe it is," I say. A voice inside me disagrees.

"Anyway, it's gotta be better than in here."

No one has come to the gate since the day the boys arrived. No bell has rung, no pleas for sanctuary have been cried out. I'm sure there are still people, maybe in the larger cities, maybe on farms, but they aren't here. Femlandia is an island in the middle of Virginia, and like the saying goes, there ain't no one here but us chickens.

I guess a few roosters, too.

A promise I can't be sure I'll keep comes out all on its own, unfiltered. "I'll be back tomorrow. At night. Do whatever they tell you until then, okay?"

Oliver gives me the kind of look I deserve, a lopsided half-smile that says, *Like I have a choice.* He points up to the roof of the enclosure. "There's no way out of here."

Reluctantly, slowly, I move away from the

chain link and watch the boys watch me.

When I turn my back to them, the lights on the fence posts are on again.

FIFTY-SEVEN

I didn't give up last spring when my world crumbled into a pile of debt and worthless dollars. I didn't give up when Nick killed himself, or when Emma and I were too tired to walk another step, or when the gang of men caught us on the highway. But a woman can only keep going so hard and so long.

Time to rest.

Behind me, I hear Oliver hushing the boys and herding them back into their little houses. *Kennels,* I think. What a word. One by one, the clicks of wooden latches sound. Then Oliver speaks to Walter, and all goes quiet.

I try three times to short the fence before I give up and I lie down, holding my throbbing hand close. The ground is hard and damp with nighttime dew, but it's any-port-in-a-storm time, a time when a body doesn't care about discomfort, a time when all a body wants to do is collapse into a pile of bones and wait for sleep to come.

It doesn't take long.

This sleep is dreamless. Almost.

I see women with their legs in stirrups, sweaty and trembling, waiting for the moment when the life inside them is ready to emerge. I hear pants and grunts; cries of *I can't!;* the soft, urgent instructions of midwives and nurses. I smell blood and salt and clean, fresh cotton. I taste their anxiety and feel their pain. When the work is done, I sense everything else.

A first cry.

A smile.

The weight of a warm body.

This is the way it's supposed to go, this process. Pain followed by joy, fear followed by calm, a tangible result of months of wait and worry. Whispers of *Hello, beautiful* and *Your name is Leila. Alice. William.* A collective sigh of celebration, hands holding hands, all the rituals of welcoming. Once upon a time, the passing around and firing up of cigars when a nervous father ended his wait, slaps on backs, baby's first home movie in stuttering and grainy eight-millimeter.

I let these sights and sounds wash over me, try to keep them close, try to hold on, but when I grasp at them, it's like grasping at fog, like trying to embrace a thing that I know is physical but isn't. The pictures bleed, oil colors left out on a hot summer day, and go to gray tones. When I reach out to them a final time, only wisps are left.

Something else replaces them. A whisper behind a cupped hand. A shake of a head. A decision.

I'm sorry, but . . .

Is she okay?

Sleep now.

And I sleep.

FIFTY-EIGHT

I never could stand the sight of my own blood. And it seems to be everywhere. The cloth of my camp pants is stiff and dingy brown. My mock-bandaged right hand is a bloody club. Even my hair hangs in dry, crinkled ropes over my eyes when I manage to sit up. Everything in front of me is filtered through a curtain of rust-tinged crimson. I don't know whether to scream or be sick.

My mouth opens, ready to let something out, and a hand clamps over me as two more hands, stronger, lock onto each of my arms. I'm pulled up quickly, so suddenly that my head swims and bright flecks invade the field of my vision. This is no rescue. Good Samaritans usually don't succor the wounded with violence.

"Take her inside." This is Jen's voice, colder than usual.

The hands gripping me (Kate's?) obey, pushing and pulling me away from the fence line and over uneven terrain, toward the bungalow where, only last month, I faced the false testimony of my own daughter.

You slapped her, Miranda.

So I did.

No one speaks as we walk. In front of me, through the uncombed strands of my own hair, I mark Jen's sandaled feet. On her right is Sal, and on her left a much older woman. They're close enough that I can hear the sibilants of their whispers, and far enough ahead to be sure this is all I hear. Only Kate is with me, her strong hands squeezing the soft flesh of my arms as she marches me along. When I stumble, Kate catches me, but again, it's a violence, not a kindness.

Finally, Kate speaks. "You're in deep shit, girl. You're in a fucking abyss of shit. Hope you can swim." The hand on my right arm slides down, reaches my own hand, and squeezes until I beg her to stop. Femlandia's version of forcing me to cry "uncle." Or "aunt."

"Yell all you want. No one cares," Kate says, and pushes me forward again.

We stop when we reach the steps to Jen's porch.

This is the part where I find new, untapped energy, where I break away from Kate, my limbs flying. Where my fist makes contact with her jaw, and my voice, no longer hoarse, screams a Whitmanesque yawp. Where I stand tall, feeling no pain, and release the boys from their prison. This should be the part where I do all these things.

Except I'm weak. I'm tired. I can't find my voice, let alone make a fist. And I'm outnumbered.

Sal takes the older woman inside without looking back at me.

"I should send you outside," Jen says, turning around. "Before you poison everything we've built. How long would you last, Miranda?"

It's Kate who answers. She picks up my left hand, examining it, running her fingers over the chipped polish of my nails, only one of which isn't broken down to the quick. Then she turns my ring, the rock Nick put on my finger on that day he promised he would take care of me forever, that it was his job, that he would make sure I never had to worry.

"I'll give her a day. Maybe a day and a night," Kate says. "She hasn't seen much of the world other than the inside of nail salons. Have you, honey?"

I get it now. It's the same old crap I took from Pamela Jackson and Mary Jo Farrell and Gret Soderberg at the coffee shop. I have female disdain following me around like a plague, all because I went traditional. But there are things I didn't do. I didn't steal babies and lock them up. I didn't force them to choke up sperm and threaten them with beatings. I didn't turn hoses and Tasers on children who weren't old enough to have done anything wrong aside from pulling pigtails in first grade and stealing cookies from a kitchen jar.

"I've seen plenty here," I say, meeting Jen's stare. "You're not feminists. You're misandrists. Man-haters. You don't want equality, only power."

"And you don't know what the women here have been through," Jen says. "You weren't around when the first ones came, the bruised women, the anxious women, the women who had been robbed of everything by their asshole husbands. You didn't listen to them cry until their voices went hoarse, and you didn't hold them until they stopped shivering. I did that. Your mother did that. So don't stand there and tell me my business."

"I think your business sucks," I tell her.

Jen smiles. She approaches me, and Kate's grip becomes tighter, nearly cutting off the circulation in my arms when I try to break free. With one hand, Jen pushes my hair to the side and runs a finger over my face, tracing my cheekbone. It's a motherly touch, but there's no maternal kindness in the gesture.

"I don't really care what you think, Miranda," she says, returning to the porch and sitting on the highest step. Then, to Kate: "Put her back in isolation."

I'm stunned. I figured they would slap me with a one-way ticket out of here. In fact, I'd almost prefer it to another month in a small room. And maybe Oliver, young as he is, spoke some truth. Maybe things are better on the outside; perhaps a stability has emerged. Even if it hasn't, the walk to Bluemont, to the Mount Weather Emergency Operations Center, can't be more than ten miles. They'll let me in when I tell them about the babies. About the boys. They'll have to.

All at once I see it happening; see the Jeeps riding south toward Femlandia; hear the khaki-clad soldiers issuing their orders to open up, watch the fortress my mother built crumble, one electric-fence segment at a time. I feel Oliver and Walter's embrace, look into Emma's eyes when the boys are taken out of their enclosure. There's still safety in this world, and its name is Bluemont.

I can do ten miles.

I think.

"I'll leave," I volunteer. "Give me Nick's handgun and a pair of shoes."

Jen's face is a mixture of frustration and doubt and hatred. Mostly hatred. Close to my ear, Kate speaks.

"Let her go, Jen. She won't last."

They continue their conversation as if I weren't here.

"We have two now," Jen says. "This one will make three. Sal's done the numbers and she knows our minimum threshold. I can't risk consanguinity."

Kate: "You're forgetting about the two older ones that came in last month. The eldest is already producing. The younger brother won't be long. Maybe a year, maybe less. That's a bonus, Jen. And you need to think about the risk of letting her stay. If word gets out —"

"Word won't get out."

"But if it did —"

Jen slaps her palm against the stair. "I said it won't."

This changes things, ups the stakes, means there are more to be rescued than the boys. For a while, as I dozed and dreamt last night, I started to believe the women here did know, that they were in on the game, that Nell and Luca had put on a show of ignorance solely for my benefit.

"So they don't know, do they?" I say. "They really think their babies died."

Jen stands now, towering above me on the top step of the porch. "Get her out of my sight. No shoes, no gun. Just put her out like a dog."

"You got it," Kate says, and turns my body with her own. Out of the corner of my eye, her smile broadens.

But so does mine. If the women here aren't in on the game, maybe Emma doesn't know, either. And Bluemont is only a few hours away. If I need to, I can crawl.

"Hold on a minute," a voice behind me says. The timbre isn't unlike Emma's, a bit lower, a touch gravelly, as if my daughter has suddenly aged. Or taken up chain-smoking.

Kate, probably sensing my surrender, loosens her grip just long enough for me to wrench free and turn myself around. Another woman has joined Jen at the top of the stairs. She's dressed in cargo pants and a gray camisole so small it should fit, but it hangs on her instead. It's hard to tell where her iron-colored hair ends and where the gray material begins. At her side is Emma.

When I saw her last, I was twenty-four, and this woman was middle-aged. She always looked slightly older than her age, as is the way with some makeup-free hippies and outdoorsy types. Now her skin is leathered from age, from sun, from being at least fifteen pounds underweight.

I still recognize her, even after sixteen years.

Jen and Kate stand stock-still and open-mouthed, looking from me to the woman, and to Emma, who is holding the woman's hand and smiling up at her like they're soul sisters.

Jen speaks first. "What is it, honey?"

Honey?

"Let's give her a couple of days to mull things over and then I'll talk to her." She doesn't wait for a response from Jen before looking squarely at me with something that might be pity or might be indifference. "Miranda," Win says. "Right now, I think it's time you go to your room."

Before Kate leads me away again, I see Emma smiling.

FIFTY-NINE

The way Win viewed things, adult life was all about choices. Constant choices. Every day, every hour of every day, sometimes every minute of those hours, presented a dilemma. Weed the garden or feed the chickens? Eat an extra helping of pie, knowing it would appear on your hips by tomorrow, probably doubled in size, or not? Finish the book that's been boring you to tears or move on to another? Most of these were trivialities, choices that had no real repercussions.

There were other choices, though. Run away or marry a man you don't love? Have the baby or kill your husband? Stick around, waiting for your granddaughter to be born, waiting to see yourself in her eyes, or go into hiding? Win had faced all of these forks in the road and chosen the best path available. At nearly fifty years old, she thought all the tough ones had already been thrown her way.

Except.

Except now, Win was staring the mother of all choices in the face.

"What do you wanna do?" Sal said, arranging her notes and stuffing them back into a folder. "Rachael's two days overdue, and I don't think we can wait any longer. The baby's not getting smaller, Win. If she doesn't go into labor tonight, I'll have to induce."

And there she was, Win staring at the choice, and the three other women in the meeting staring at her, waiting.

She knew what Kate would say, what Kate had already said a million and one times, starting with the day Sal performed the first ultrasound on the now beach ball–sized Rachael. Kate seemed tough on the outside, but that toughness was a carapace, a shield the woman had built one plate at a time over the years.

Kate had come to Femlandia with the first wave, an empty shell of a human being. What held her together was nothing more than megadoses of antidepressants, daily therapy sessions with Jen and one of the psych pros Win had brought in, and a round-the-clock team of suicide-watch volunteers. It was touch-and-go for a while.

Very touch-and-go.

Win supposed that was what happened when you discovered your husband had been diddling his own daughter, and when you discover that daughter the way Kate had discovered hers, bled out and bleached pale in the guest-room bath. Cold as ice by the time Kate returned home from work.

She got Kate's perspective. Kate was voting "yes."

Sal and Jen, on the other hand, were a toss-up. As was Win herself.

The idea was sinister on its surface, barely justifiable only if one looked at it with the most clinical of eyes. Even then, it was a thing they would have to hold back from the other women — for a thousand different reasons. If word got out, if one of the residents should discover the practice and decide to do a little whistle-blowing on the outside, well, Win would be facing a deeper pile of shit than the murder of one man.

Slowly, Jen raised her hand. "I have misgivings, I have to say." Kate started to speak up, and Jen silenced her. "If we can agree to do no harm, either physical or psychological, then I'll vote in favor." She looked sharply at Kate. "We don't have to love them, but we have to treat them fairly. Like pets. They provide a service; we provide them food and shelter and care."

"Minimal care," Kate interjected.

"I don't like it," Sal said. "I mean, I'm not a doctor, I never took the oath, but I practice yoga. And this seems like a harm, any way you look at it."

"What good are your spinning chakras going to do when we have to fold up our tents in another generation, Sal?" Kate said.

Win hushed her, but she knew Kate's point was solid; she had made sure of it. Femlandia was never meant to be a temporary concern, a safe space that would evict its inhabitants once the goodies ran out. She imagined the four of them, bent with age, surrounded by the remaining few who had held on through the years. She imagined no future generations, no daughters or granddaughters to take up the work when the work became impossible for old women. They would all end up right back in the same shit they had started in.

She looked over at Sal with a question in her eyes. Sal shook her head.

Now, with two yes votes and one no, Win had to decide.

She rose from her place at the table, went over to the front window of the bungalow, and looked out at the day. Three women were walking down the path with Sister Rachael between them, all three laughing and trading turns at putting a hand to the expectant mother's belly. At the pool, two other women and their daughters tossed a ball back and forth above shimmering blue water, occasionally splashing their opponents, sometimes dipping their heads backward to smooth their hair. The gardens were busy with Sister Anna's bee project and harvesting of summer's fruits. Everywhere, there was happiness. Everywhere, there was safety.

Win closed her eyes and allowed herself to see other pictures. Rachael was pregnant in these as well, but the hand on her belly was her own worried hand, as if apologizing to the baby for what would surely be a shitty childhood followed by a shittier adult life. There were women cooking food for men who stayed late at work, women answering telephones where the calling party — always a female — would suddenly hang up, women hanging their heads over bank statements and wondering where all the money had gone. There were bruised women and crying women. There were women trapped in marriages and women pushed down on mattresses, told to shut up. Ordered to do their duty.

What Win had decided was, in many ways,

a crime. The alternative, she thought, was much worse.

It would take at least a dozen years, maybe more, if they started now with Rachael's baby. Win came back to the table, nodded to the other three women, and stipulated once more that care should be taken, that no harm be done beyond that which was necessary.

"By the way," Win said before they adjourned, "what will you tell the mother?"

"I'll think of something," Sal said. "And I'll get her back on the list as soon as she's ready."

Win nodded and showed them out. Once more, she looked from the window across the grounds. They would be needing another set of fencing and some additional equipment.

Soon.

Sixty

The walls seem to be closing in on me, inching in toward the center, making this room smaller each minute. I should have been on the road three days ago, heading north across open country, ranting wildly to any gate guard who might listen at the emergency ops center. I should have been leading a raiding party back here to storm the gates, set things right, give babies back to their mothers, and return my daughter to me. I should not be locked in a room.

Call it what it is, Miranda. A cell.

Leila has been bringing me food again — decent food designed to keep me physically strong. Yesterday was pork barbecue and slaw. This morning, three hen's eggs baked in a small casserole with spinach from the garden, their sunny golden yolks the only bit of brightness in an otherwise grim day. I ate every last bite. Leila saw to it.

The first day, I left the plates as they were

delivered, forcing myself to ignore the aromas of meat and herbs and spices. The second day, Kate came along with Leila. She didn't have to speak, only had to tap the butt of the Taser in the holster on her waist. They stood there, backs to the closed door, watching me deliver forkfuls from plate to mouth. I don't believe they care whether I eat or starve, but I'm carrying precious cargo, and they care very much about that.

They'll keep me here for three months, more or less. And then I don't know what they'll do with me.

An hour or so after Leila takes away my breakfast plate, the click of a key sounds in the lock and the door swings open. Win sets one foot inside, then the other, and sits down on the corner of my single bed.

"It's time we had a talk, dear," she says.

I slouch in the chair where I've been spending my hours. "I don't really want to."

"I can leave, then. Maybe return with Kate?"

"Fine. What do you want to talk about? My father? Jen? Emma? Maybe a couple of boys named Oliver and Walter? Go ahead, Mother. I'm all ears."

"Don't be like that," she says. It's unbelievable, but there's hurt in her voice. "I only want to clear the air."

I think I snort.

Win's eyes wander around the room, taking in the bare walls, the single table with its single chair, the lonely wooden knob on the back of the door where a change of clothes hangs. This time, they didn't bring me books.

"I imagine this is about the hardest you've ever had things, Miranda."

This gets a shrug. The threat of bringing Kate back here might force me to listen, but it isn't enough of a threat to make me an eager conversational partner.

Win doesn't seem to mind. Instead of arguing, she talks on in a one-woman-show monologue. "Yes, I guess this is the toughest you've ever had it." She leans forward, checks me over, and continues. "See, you're the kind of woman I don't like very much." Maybe she sees me flinch. "Sorry, honey, but I got to lay this out straight. I didn't say I don't love you; I suppose I do in some ways. But I can't lie about liking you. And I didn't come here to apologize or to sell you some story about why I did what I did. I came here to tell you all the shit you don't want to hear, because it's true shit. And it's about goddamned time someone tells you, so I guess it might as well be me." She smiles. “I am, after all, your mother.

“I’ve known women like you. Some people call you deniers; some people call you other names. No reason to get into a name-calling match, though, so let’s just say it like it is. You’re the kind of woman who thinks that because a pile of shit didn’t fall on you, there was no pile of shit. It didn’t exist, right? It didn’t come crashing down out of the sky like a dump-truck load of manure and fall on anyone else. You didn’t get groped by an uncle or a priest or your own goddamned father, so no one else got groped. You didn’t wake up one morning and discover dried jism on your panties, so no one else woke up that way. You weren’t beaten because supper was late or cold or not what your wonderful Mr. Right had a craving for that evening, so no other woman took a beating.”

She stops, maybe to let this sink in, and folds her hands on her lap. “I’m not gonna call you names, Miranda. All I’m here to say is that you. Don’t. Get. It.”

Time stands still. Maybe for a minute, maybe longer, while we let the silence stretch out between us until it’s so taut, the slightest movement or the shallowest of breaths might crack it, like a thin ribbon of candy that's been pulled too hard and too long.

Finally, it breaks.

"You're right," I say. "I don't get it. But not the way you think. I don't get how you can justify *that.*" I gesture with one finger pointed north, as if the walls of my room have suddenly gone transparent, toward the repurposed barn at the edge of Jen's compound. "Because there is no way to justify it. No way. Not unless you're completely fucking insane."

"I'm not insane, Miranda. Insanity, if you know anything about it — and I doubt you do — is the inability to distinguish right from wrong. Simple, really. What we're doing here, what we've been doing here, is complicated, but it isn't wrong. Only necessary. You think I would send these women back out into a world that hurts them? And I don't mean a little bit of hurt. I'm not talking about a bad breakup or a marital spat. I'm talking about women who have been crushed so badly, I didn't think some of them would ever put themselves back together."

She tells me everything now.

I used to wonder where all the rage came from, how any one person could maintain such anger for so long. As my mother speaks, first about a locked classroom and a priest, later about the night my father forced himself on her, and still later about the weeks and months she spent as a prisoner in her own home, waiting to have a child she didn't ask for, the wonder slips away from me.

When she's finished, she stands, smooths out her trousers, and for the first time, I see how old my mother has become. Her hands are as rough as the cloth underneath them, chapped from work. Once, I saw much more life in her eyes. Now, only weariness and worry. It's impossible to hate her in this moment.

"Mom," I say, and reach a hand out toward one of hers. For an instant, there's contact, skin against skin. Then she retracts with all the quickness of a startled snake. "Mom, you should have told me. Maybe I could have helped."

"Jen helped," she says abruptly. "You were too busy."

The words sting like a slap. "Those boys. It isn't right." What I heard and saw a few days ago is so far from right, it makes my head spin, but I can't think of another word.

"It is what it is, Miranda. And right or wrong, it's too late to do anything. What do you think, that I can give them back to their mothers with an apology and a kiss for good luck?" She shakes her head. "We did what we had to."

"And if you had to do it all over again?"

Another shake of the head. "I need to go."

She opens the door, letting in a flood of late-summer sounds and smells. I could easily push her out of the way and make a break for it. If there were anywhere to go. And if Kate weren't standing within spitting distance, waiting like a guard dog. My mother breathes in the air and puts a finger to her lips. "Listen to that. Listen."

It all drifts toward me. Splashing water, giggles, the lazy chant of a jump-rope game. Somewhere in the distance beyond fences two girls are clapping out Miss Mary Mack. A part of me wants to run from here and join in.

"They're happy here. *We're* happy here. And the other ones are taken care of. If they get hurt, we fix them. If they're hungry, we feed them. We're not barbarians, you know."

I can't help but snort again. "Two of the boys told me Kate threatened to hurt them. And that she carries something like a Taser."

"Boys lie. Oh, don't you get it, Miranda? Won't you ever get it? They all lie."

I stare at her. "What are you, twelve? Girls lie, too."

"Kate went too far. Once. It won't happen again." A kindness brightens her eyes, a look I haven't seen since before my father died. Win takes my hand in both of hers and lingers for a moment at the door, letting me listen again to the world outside these four walls. "You could be out there, too, honey. Think about it. You and Emma, in your own house. You'll have a granddaughter soon, you know."

"I'll have a son sooner," I say. "Three months. What happens then? What happens to Emma and me?"

Seconds before she closes me in, shutting out the sun: "Emma stays with us. What happens to you depends on you."

Sixty-One

A part of me thinks Jen has upped the ante on activity this past week for the sole purpose of driving me batshit. And there's no mistake — I'm nearly there. Without books or work, without anything to keep my mind occupied, there's nothing to do but think.

So I think about Nick, about the broken promises and the disappearing money, the magician's tricks he played with our security, only to take the easy way out. Nick lied.

I think about the pension fund managers and the lawmakers and the judges, the soldiers who drove past us without offering a soldier's protection. All of them, in their own ways, lied.

Boys lie.

Girls lie, too.

Maybe. But I'm not here because of a woman's lie.

The first time I saw Femlandia, I was

fifteen years old. I almost can't process the passing of a quarter century, so I rely on cold, emotionless math. Back then, I would have put bets on my mother's plan folding within a few months, as long as it took for the desperate women who came here first to get a taste of mosquitoes and ticks and August without air-conditioning. Femlandia was nothing like Disneyland, could never be, not in my overly critical — and under-experienced — teenage eyes.

It sucks to be so wrong.

While the women go about their daily routines, while they garden and farm, and build and babysit, I've been listening. But not to the women's sounds. I've been listening to the absence of other sounds.

A conversation where no deep voice interrupts or overtalks. A dinner where no man asks for seconds without bothering to rise from his chair. A construction project without a *Let me do that, honey. It's complicated.*

If I could expand my reach, there are other things I wouldn't hear. I wouldn't hear *I thought you wanted it.* I wouldn't hear cars with only men behind the wheel or the screams of young girls as their clitorises are being amputated. I wouldn't hear that a woman's testimony is worth half of a man's or the forced vows of a young girl compelled to marry her rapist.

I would hear silence. And in that silence, I would hear peace.

They're happy here.

Maybe they are. Maybe I could be, too. The boys did look well taken care of, well fed and clean. So what if they have to jack off in a cup once in a while? We girls have had to put up with more than that. Much more than that.

The baby kicks once, a feeble little nudge of complaint.

Sixty-Two

I've always been drawn to helpless things. The stray cat trembling under a porch on a rainy night. A dozy bird who saw only trees, not the glass of my living room window. Bunny, when he was young, fumbling with his first banana in the primate house, wondering what to make of it until I showed him the trick of ignoring the stem and breaking the bottom off. Nick always said I had a soft side, a runaway mothering instinct. I guess I do.

It's hard to believe only six weeks ago I killed a man, that I spent a frenzied twenty minutes with Emma beating his body to a pulp. I think I could have killed more men on that day. The soldiers, the other bikers, anyone who got in our way. It's contrary to having a soft side, but I remind myself those men weren't helpless, not like Oliver and Walter are.

Not like the tiny life inside me is.

As I pace the length of my room, I think of Emma. For all her tough misandrist talk, I know she's helpless, too. It's the curious thing about living through hell — everything else looks and tastes like salvation. I know this is how cults are born, how people are broken down and built back up by modern, misguided Frankensteins with different names. Manson. Jones. Moon. Emma didn't even need breaking; she was that way when we arrived. An empty and thirsty vessel, ready to be filled by the closest poison at hand.

Which is why I can't talk to Emma. Not yet. Maybe I'll never be able to talk to her again.

When I started working with Bunny, I thought a lot about words, how they were all absolutely meaningless, nothing more than concatenations of random sounds. It's the same with babies. There's no dog in "dog," no flower in "flower," only movements of your lips and tongue, expelled air performing its linguistic tricks as it flows through the varying shapes and contours of a vocal tract. Babies are like apes. You can talk at them all day long; you can describe the color and fur of a collie until you're blue in the face. It's much easier to go out and find yourself a goddamned Lassie.

You have to show them. You have to give them pictures. Even better, you have to show them the real thing. Everyone knows it worked for Annie Sullivan when she finally broke through to Helen Keller at the water pump.

Hell of a job, Annie, I think. *Good for you.*

So I need to get to someone who will understand the words and who can turn them into pictures. Someone who already has a picture in her mind. A birthmark, for instance. Or a family resemblance.

That means Nell and Luca.

There's another thing I learned in my years with Bunny. Before you ask for something, you have to earn trust.

Leila comes right on time, at noon. She's never a minute early or a minute late with my meals. Today someone has made me crepes with chicken and goat cheese, tomato soup with garden basil, and a salad of field greens. I pick at it while Leila stands by the door, watching.

"Do you think you'll have children?" I ask.

The girl shrugs. "Someday. Sister Jen says we should all have at least one baby. And I guess I'd like to have a daughter."

"What if you didn't have a daughter?"

She's been twirling a lock of hair between her fingers, an idle movement to pass the time. At my question, she stops, leans her head a little to one side, and regards me as if I've forgotten we're in the dog days of summer and asked whether we might get snow tonight.

"Well?" I say, eating the food on my plate slowly, chewing each bite until my jaw hurts.

"That's impossible," she says. "Everyone here has girls. That's why it's called Femlandia." Leila starts twirling her hair again, pauses, and leans close to me, whispering. "Sister Sal came to school for health class once. She told us she has a method to make sure."

"I'll bet she does," I say, forcing a reverent smile. "But let's pretend something went wrong."

"Like what?"

Like the natural outcome of a fifty-fifty proposition. "Oh, I don't know. Say you thought you were going to have a girl, but a —"

Lelia titters. "But a boy came out? Hypothetically, right?"

"Absolutely. Completely hypothetical."

"Well, I guess I'd have to take care of him. But I think Sister Jen would make me leave."

I take another microbite of chicken crepe. "Even with — you know — the way things are out there now?"

The hair twirling starts again. In any other

situation, I'd think Leila was stupid, that she'd been late to the party on the day they were passing out brains. But "stupid" isn't the right word. She's simply not thinking because she's never had to.

"I don't know," she says. "I guess she couldn't do that."

"So there would be boys in Femlandia. Sooner or later."

"I guess there would be. Huh." Twirl. Twirl. Twirl. It's as if she's working the gears in her head. "But if we knew beforehand, we could — well — take care of it."

"Would you — take care of it?"

"Hell no," she says. "I mean, I get that some women would, but I don't think I could. It seems kinda wrong. Just because it's a boy, you know what I'm talking about?"

Yeah. I know what you're talking about.

Suddenly Leila doesn't need any prompting. "My mom would never — I mean, never — have another abortion. That's why she left my dad. She got pregnant when she was real young, and he made her get rid of the baby. God, men are dicks." She puts a hand up to her mouth and giggles. "Sorry. Didn't mean to say that out loud. Anyway, this is all hypothetical, right? Just a what-if kinda scenario?"

"Yep," I say, and finish my plate. I don't need to delay the girl any longer.

She picks up the tray and starts to leave. "I'm not supposed to talk to you, Sister Miranda. But I won't tell if you won't."

"Mum's the word." I slide my hand across my lips and give it a little twist, turning the invisible key.

Leila does the same.

"I have one favor to ask, Leila," I say when she's in the doorway. "There's some medication in my bungalow. Do you think you could ask Nell to bring it to me? I'd ask you, but it looks like you're working overtime these days."

"I could ask Sister Jen."

"Oh, I'd hate to bother her. They're just vitamins. Nothing important. Forget I said anything."

"You need your vitamins. This food is good," she says, nodding at the empty plate, "but in health class Sister Sal told us you can't go wrong with a little extra."

"Really, it's okay."

With the tray in her hands, Leila can't twirl anymore, but she pauses, thinking. "Tell you what. I'll ask Nell. She's been kinda down lately what with your daughter not there and now, well, you in here." There's another pause as she processes something else. "She won't be able to get in, though. Not without a key."

"Oh, right. I forgot about that." *Fuck.*

"I could give mine to her after dinner. But you can't tell anyone, all right?"

"Not a soul," I say.

The lock clicks, and I'm alone again. Hopefully not for long.

Sixty-Three

There's a woodpecker banging its beak against a tree somewhere outside. I use him like a lovestruck girl with a daisy, counting off each succession of rapid-fire beats. *She'll come. She won't come. She'll come. She won't come.*

When Leila arrives in the early evening with my supper, I lose hope. She's in a hurry, something about a study group for a summer reading project that she's already running late for.

"Promise you'll eat it?" she asks. "I don't want to get in trouble for skipping out early."

"Cross my heart."

She's out the door before I have the chance to ask her about Nell, and now it's just me and Mr. Woodpecker. Absently, I wonder if I could bribe him to come drill an exit for me.

The rest of the compound is still, the

women having hung up their spades and hoes and gone to dinner. Only a few whispered voices break the silence when a group passes by, not far from my little building.

"That's the one who keeps getting into trouble."

"What did she do?"

"I don't know."

What will they say when they do know?

I stretch out on the single bed, asking myself this question over and over, asking whether there's a woman alive who would give up a baby because it was the wrong sex. It seems impossible to believe, but men have done it. Men still do it. Maybe women, too. After all, it isn't the menfolk who are circumcising little girls in Uganda. That's women's work. The prep, the holding down, the cutting and the sewing back up.

My mother would say women are no different than men; anything a guy can do, a woman can do equally well. But Win says other things, too: Men lie; women tell true tales. Men fuck things up; women mend the broken bits. Men fight; women keep peace. There can't be no difference and a difference at the same time, can there? And if there's no difference, then maybe I shouldn't find it so unfathomable that a woman would abandon her child.

After all, anything a man can do, a woman can do equally well. It must be so; it's written in the gospel according to Win Somers. Jen and Kate and Sal follow that gospel to the letter, but I can't bring myself to believe the other women know.

When Nell comes and hears what I have to say, I'll have my answer.

I fall asleep to the woodpecker's rhythm. *She'll come. She won't come. She'll come. She won't . . .*

At the knock on the door, my eyes spring open. It has to be Nell; no one else bothers to knock.

"Miranda?"

A key scrapes its metallic click in the lock, and the door swings open. With Nell silhouetted in the doorway, it's impossible to see the expression on her face.

"Well," she says, handing me the bottle of multivitamins, "what did you do this time?"

"Guess I went roaming around where I shouldn't have been roaming," I say.

"Oh boy."

"Exactly."

She steps toward me now, leaning her head to one side, looking at me with a quizzical, almost bemused expression. "What do you mean?"

I reach forward with both hands and take

a light hold of her wrists before blurting everything out. "Your baby, Nell. A few nights ago, I saw your baby."

Nell pulls back. "My baby is dead, Miranda."

"No. He's not." I speak quickly now, all the words pouring out in a frenzy. "There was a birthmark. A port-wine stain on his throat." Her eyes widen at this, and I keep going. "And a name tag. But it wasn't really a name tag. It had your name, and where there should have been another name — a name for the father — there was only a number. And the baby has a number, too. I think it's a code, maybe to identify generations so they can keep track. So they don't breed too closely in the future." I pause to catch my breath before going on. "There was another baby there, Helen's baby. Do you know her? Did she have a girl who died?"

Nell nods. "Yes. I know her. I don't understand what you're saying."

"There are boys, older boys, in the back of Jen's compound. They live in small huts, like kennels. Like doghouses, Nell. Some of them are so young, but not all. A few are older. Old enough to produce what Jen needs. They force them to. Oh God, Nell. They force them to masturbate — or maybe they do it for them. And they take the sperm. I saw it. Vials of it. All frozen in the old converted barn."

Nell's mouth drops. "You saw all of this?"

"I swear I did. I got through the fence. And I saw them. Nell, they're feral. Like — I don't know — like pets. Like zoo animals." The panic rises in me like a tidal wave. My throat closes involuntarily, as if hands were locked around my neck, squeezing, but I choke the rest out. "That isn't all. Luca's boy is there. It had to be her boy. He looks just like his sister, Maya, same age, same coloring. And they all know, Nell. Sal and Jen and Kate and my mother. They all know. That's what I asked you to come here for. We have to tell the others. We have to tell the women what happened to their babies."

"Right," Nell says, and finally I feel hope.

"I don't think Emma knows." My head is shaking back and forth as I speak, so fast I must seem like I'm having a fit. "Like you. She doesn't know. Because — because no one would do this, right? I mean, it's insanity."

"Insanity." Nell's skin is bleached pale in the overhead light. She seems to be in shock. "Right."

"We have to get the word out," I say. "We have to tell all of them and we have to rescue the boys and we have to turn this place around before it's too late. We have to stop this before my baby ends up in the same place. I think it might already be too late for the older ones, but the young ones, they'll be all right. I can work with them. I can get them talking." I collapse onto the bed, hard, barely feeling the mattress underneath me, barely feeling anything at all.

"You believe me, right?"

Nell doesn't answer immediately. When she does, it's with a sad smile. "I guess I do." She puts a hand on my shoulder. "Don't worry, Miranda. I'll get the word out."

I sniffle. "Promise?"

"Promise."

Sixty-Four

At first, Win had liked the silence. She liked the way the boy who came from Sister Rachael, the same boy who would one day father a new generation of girls, stared at her with big blue eyes and said absolutely nothing. She had thought he might be deaf, maybe brain damaged, but the rest of him looked okay. He had been able to scoop food from a plate with his hands and shovel it into his mouth; he was able to walk — or at least toddle — around his little house. He had a disconcerting habit of ripping off his clothes and rolling around in the dirt outside until he was covered with leaves and mud, but it could have been worse. The boy they called A-1 could have resisted potty training, and wouldn't that have been a hot old mess. As it was, he managed to take care of things in a more or less sanitary way. There had been accidents (even to this day there were accidents), but they were occasional, no more inconvenient than a cat who thought its litter box was larger than it actually was.

As he grew, they sometimes had to tie him down, if only because Win feared he might harm the smaller ones. They often played rough, and there was no amount of talking or scolding on Win's part that could break up a fight. Once, A-1 had flung himself on one of the toddlers, biting the flesh under the younger boy's neck, pulling fistfuls of hair from his scalp. Win and Kate had been feeding the others, and a moment after they had turned their backs, all hell broke loose.

"No!" Win snapped. "No. No. No."

It was the easiest word, a tiny little syllable, the word most babies learned first. But A-1 didn't seem to register the sound. He kept on going, straddling the smaller one, biting skin and pulling hair until the boy underneath him stopped howling and began a pathetic, defeated whimper. Finally, Kate had to wrestle the larger boy off and shut him inside, away from the others.

That was almost five years ago, and today, when Win unlocked the steel gate and entered the compound, when she peered into the window of A-1's little house, two eyes, dull and doll-like, stared back at her. He let out a sound, not quite a howl and not quite a chirp, but something between the two. An alien sound, Win thought.

He wasn't like the other boys, the new ones whom Jen had found at the gate last month. They talked to each other. They didn't squabble or pull hair or bite. They acted like human beings. She had heard enough to know that the teenager's name was Oliver and the younger boy's was Walter, although she also knew Jen's files referred to them as C-1 and C-2. These two didn't need special handling for the purpose of extracting the necessaries. All Kate had to do was tell them to get to it and get it over with. Then she would leave them, wait fifteen or so minutes, and come back to collect the containers. They were easy, even if the younger boy seemed to be having a little trouble.

She didn't know why it couldn't be easy with the others.

Watching through the window, she repeated the same words she had said to Miranda only a few days ago. "We're not barbarians."

Those dull, lifeless eyes only stared.

The boy they called A-1, who had already sired another boy, Nell's boy, was now fourteen years old. Getting what they needed from him required at least two women, but it was always easier with three. Two could hold him down, and the third would cajole him into taking care of business, sometimes with a carrot, sometimes with a stick. At A-1's age, the business was over within a few minutes.

Sixty-Five

As soon as Nell leaves, locking me back in, I seem to float.

You won't be a number, little guy, I think, running a hand over my belly. *None of you will be numbers anymore.*

In the dark, I invent names for them. Maybe Nell will give hers one of those Gaelic names, lovely in its pronunciation, impossible to spell without a detailed guide-book. Cillian. Padraig. Diarmaid. Luca might go avant-garde, christening her boy with something mysterious and mythical. Moonbeam. Prometheus. Merlin. Emma will go literary, choosing a name from the denizens of Austenland to match her own. As for me, I've already chosen.

I'll call him Nicholas. And I'll tell him why.

Nick had his faults, more than I can count. He lied about things, but I think he lied because he was too proud to tell it like it was. He had a vision of himself, of all men, I think, and that vision didn't allow for setbacks or weakness. It was one thing for women to get knocked down, but men were expected to stand tall no matter what. He saw us as fundamentally different, not stitched from the same cloth. Nick was the protector; I was the one to be protected. He made promises to me, and even in his stupidly misguided way, I suppose he kept them for as long as he was able. When he stopped being the kind of man he wanted to be, he had to leave.

I had my faults, too. Like Nick, I thought we had opposing roles. I kept myself fit and pretty; he kept us solvent. I had a vision of what boys and girls should be, not my mother's or Jen's vision of complete equality, but my own idea. Different, but the same on the most fundamental spectrum. Which I suppose, when you get right down to it, means the same. Nothing more than human beings with all the crap being human entails.

In any case, my boy will be Nicholas.

One by one, pictures run through my mind, future home movies. Nick and Cillian and Darcy at play in the care center, all of us looking on as they roll balls back and forth, stifling behind-the-mouth giggles at their tongue-tied attempts to talk. I see Oliver and Leila together at Femlandia's first mixed social, a kind of cross between a small-town festival and a high school prom. The younger boys will catch up, slowly at first, then like runaway trains, until one day, they're as eloquent as the rest. I'll work with the older ones myself, like I did with Bunny. I'll get them talking.

Maybe we'll change the name of our place here to something more inclusive. "Landia" has a fine ring to it.

Maybe more people will come, men and women, girls and boys. We'll muddle on, we'll have more children, and we'll be all right.

Maybe my mother, when she hears all those voices asking her *Why?* and *How could you?,* maybe even she'll understand how crazy-wrong she's been.

When sleep comes, it comes quick and heavy, a blanket of solace laying itself on top of my body. In the last few seconds before I succumb to dreams, I hear what I once thought were coyotes chatter and sing in the distance.

By tomorrow, everything will be different.

Sixty-Six

At dawn, they come for me. All of them.

There's no knock at the door and there's no breakfast on a tray, only the click of the key in its lock and ten pairs of eyes staring at me through the door. I blink a few times at the bright morning sun, sure that I'm seeing things.

My mother is here, with Jen at one side and Emma at the other, their mouths set in straight lines. Sal, on the left, looks away as soon as I come to the doorway. Kate scowls. Behind them are Nell and Luca. Maya is curled in her mother's arms, fussing only slightly. Leila stands toward the back and shakes her head in a sad, slow rhythm. Next to her is a woman I don't know, but process of elimination makes me think her name might be Helen, the mother of the second baby I found.

As my eyes adjust, I see the others, dozens and dozens of women. I recognize the couple who were headed out on their picnic on the day I arrived, and I think I can pick out Maria, the woman whose ass Kate promised to kick in the butterfly on that same morning. There are so many more I don't know.

A whisper rustles through the crowd like dry, wind-tossed leaves on a fall day. The sounds are indistinct, as if the entire congregation of women were whispering the same words. Win steps forward, away from Jen and Emma, and turns toward the group with one hand raised.

All fall silent, an orchestra waiting for their conductor to lower the baton. Their upward gazes are almost reverent.

"Sisters," Win says. "I think Sister Miranda has something she wants to tell you." She pulls me out the door, into the day. "Go on, then."

I blink again. A few women in the back of the crowd cough. Three others, closer to me, discuss plans for the morning. Emma yawns sleepily and rubs her eyes. They're all staring at me, but not with the reverence they showed my mother.

"Well? Go on," Win says.

My voice cracks as soon as I start. "Good morning," I croak out. An unenthusiastic hum ripples through the group. "I do have something I want to say."

"Then say it so we can all go back to what we were doing," one woman in the rear calls out. "I've got bread in the oven, and it ain't gonna wait forever."

Another, next to her, yells, "Janice has a bun in the oven! Hear that, ladies?" The ensuing laughter fades out slowly, only after Win raises her hand a second time.

I start again. "There's a lot of good here. I can see it. When I was fifteen, I didn't think I'd ever say that. I didn't think Femlandia could work." I look over at Win, who raises her head a notch. "It does, but there's —"

"You bet your skinny ass it does!" another woman cries, cutting me off. More laughter.

"There are boys here," I scream above the noise. "From baby to teenager."

"Oh no! Boys!" Janice says, throwing her voice into a high-pitched vibrato. "Not boys!" The crowd roars.

I look over at my mother. She presses her lips together so tightly, I can see the deep, feathery creases around her mouth. It's as if she's trying to stifle her own laugh.

I've never been a good speaker. I don't know how long to lead in, how much to build up toward a punch line. So everything comes out too quickly, too bluntly. "These women," I say, pointing to Win and Jen and Kate and Sal, "have taken your babies." I look at Luca. "Your baby boy, Luca."

Luca bounces Maya in her arms but says nothing.

"And yours, Nell." My eyes find Nell's in the sea of women. "They lied to you. Your baby didn't die."

Nell raises a mug of what might be tea to her lips and doesn't seem to hear me.

"And Helen's. And maybe more." Before I can finish, the wind goes out of me, and all I manage is a low, voiceless moan.

The women only stare.

My mother, who had been at my side all this time, moves in front of me. "Okay, Sisters. Your turn. Does anyone have anything to say to Sister Miranda?"

They don't believe me. None of them believes me. I force myself to think this because the alternative is unthinkable.

I fly at my mother, my hands becoming claws. "Tell them! You have to tell them!"

At once, Kate and Jen are behind me, cinching my arms, pulling me back into the dark room. I heard somewhere that the thing to do in this situation is to go limp, to not resist, but that only makes it easier for them.

"You have to tell them the truth, Mother!"

Kate wrestles me onto the bed and pins me down. It takes a full minute, maybe longer, before I can regulate my breath. When I'm as calm as I think I can be, I say it one final time, the words coming out one by one with heavy pauses in between. "You . . . have . . . to . . . tell . . . them."

Win sits on the edge of the bed and folds her hands in her lap. She doesn't touch me, doesn't smooth my hair or rub my back; she only sits there looking down at me. I see her shape through teary eyes.

There's no need for her to say anything, but she says it all the same.

"Miranda, you silly girl. Don't you understand they already know?"

SIXTY-SEVEN

I suppose there was some discussion, maybe even a vote. What they discussed doesn't matter.

Sal saw to my injuries the other morning, and except for a few bruises and a long series of stitches along my arm that itch persistently, I'm good to go. That's as it should be, since I'm going.

I don't protest, not with my voice and not with my body, as Kate leads me through the gardens of Femlandia, past the pool that I've heard but never even seen, past the café and the community center, where a few women mill around tending to whatever the business of the day is. They don't raise their heads as we walk by, and there's no need to guess what the topic of the day is.

The topic is me, the first official exile case in Femlandia's history. Or so my mother has told me.

Jen opens the first set of gates, and we're

back in the vestibule, that no-man's-land between Femlandia and the outside world. In the weeks I've been here, nature has been steadily at her work, and wild tangles of weeds now choke the side road that brought Emma and me to these gates in high summer. The native plants seem to have crawled in from the edges and pushed through any weak spots, as if they were reclaiming land once stolen from them.

I had hoped the outside might have healed itself, but the weeds dash every last shred of those hopes. No one has been down this road. No traveler, no car, no bicycle. No dead poet waxing philosophic on the merits of roads less traveled or snow-frosted woods. A lone hawk circles high in the sky, making lazy loops, crossing its own path once, twice, three times.

Suddenly I'm terrified.

Sal presses a pack into my arms. "There's some food for you, and a change of clothes. I don't know where you're going, but I hope you get there." She still avoids looking directly into my eyes, but she whispers in my ear. "You have to come back, Miranda. Just because they know doesn't mean they agree. Come at midnight, and I'll make sure Jen opens the gate."

"I don't care where she's going," Kate says

under her breath, clearly not hearing Sal's message.

I shrug on the pack, careful with my bandaged right hand. It weighs heavy on my shoulders, but not as heavy as the prospect of walking through these gates, of finding myself on a road alone.

Jen unlocks the main entrance, swings the gate wide, and stands back to give me room.

"I'd hoped you would see it our way, Miranda," Win says. "The women here are damaged women. Or they were damaged women. We're only trying to help them find peace. Right, Sal?"

Sal digs into the earth with one sandaled foot.

"Right, Sal?" Jen says.

"Of course, Jen." She throws a sympathetic glance at me. "At least give her one of the bicycles. We can do that much."

Jen seems to consider this, then nods to Kate, who disappears for a few minutes and returns with the bike I rode here in early July.

They turn their backs on me as I walk out the gate, the same gate that looked like salvation only six weeks ago. I start pedaling west, already feeling the sweat on my skin, worrying I'll lose my grip on the handlebars. I pause and look back once, feet flat on the ground, and the double Xs on the iron gate leer at me with their horrible, uncompromising message.

"Don't forget to eat something," Sal calls over her shoulder. "Soon."

I don't respond. Tears begin to cloud my eyes, and a heaviness pulls my shoulders down. If I say even one word, they'll know I'm crying.

Sixty-Eight

Emma didn't come to see me off. She fell away with the rest of the group after Win forced me to confront them, walking back to the bungalow on her own. I didn't see her again. I didn't know if I ever would.

When I'm far enough away from Femlandia, I turn onto a driveway leading toward what used to be a farm. The drive is weed choked and pitted, like the road itself — like everything — but it feels safe in its abandonment. Weary of the cruel jostling of my body, I get off the bike and lean it against the trunk of an oak. I walk along, feet scuffing in the clay dirt, pack sticking to my back like it's been glued to me. I pass chicken coops that hold no chickens, a paddock for horses that aren't here. Something isn't right.

There should be carcasses, I think. There should at least be the evidence, the unsightly debris of death.

Slowly, I shuffle forward until I reach the steps of the farmhouse porch. I nearly sit down here, but the midday sun is high and strong. Inside would be cooler. The front door hangs ajar, telling me there's no reason to ring the bell.

I push the door open and set one foot in, then the other, calling out softly, knowing there won't be a response.

In the front room, in what used to be a parlor, I find the chickens. Or what's left of the chickens. Small, brittle bones litter the carpet, meat stripped clean. I might be tempted to write the damage off to rats, except I've never known a rat to use plates and silverware. Someone dined here not long ago.

Instead of entering the room, I walk forward down a dark hall with café doors at the end.

"Hello?" I whisper, then force myself to raise my voice. "Anyone home?"

It's the smell that hits me first, and I instinctively turn back toward the front door. My pack bumps a frame on the wall, and it falls with a sharp crash to the hardwood at my feet. It's a child's picture of a farmhouse, drawn in crayon. I pick it up, brushing the broken glass aside, and study it.

Two horses stand in the paddock at the right-hand side. On the left, a dozen chickens mill about, a single rooster with its bright red cock's comb at their center. On the porch steps is a yellow-haired woman, young and plump and smiling.

At the bottom of the picture are the sharp, irregular strokes of young handwriting.

Walter Morris. It has to be a coincidence.

The picture hanging opposite the fallen drawing is of the same house, much more expertly detailed. The steady hand that drew it belongs to Oliver Morris. So. Not a coincidence.

I want to leave this house, run from the café doors at the end of the hall, run anywhere my tired feet will take me.

The café doors creak and squeal when I push them, and now I'm in the kitchen, amid the stench of decay and the ugly aftermath of violence.

On the floor is a cast-iron frying pan, an ordinary, homey object. That it's lying next to the body of a woman — no longer plump and smiling — makes me stop short. The pan isn't ordinary and homey anymore. Not in this context. In this context, it's a merciless weapon.

When I see the three sets of boot marks on the linoleum near the back door, when I see the torn ragged strip of bright red cotton lying near the marks, my mind writes a story to go with the scene.

The farmer woman was barely holding on, but she managed. She milked cows in the morning and scattered cracked corn for her chickens before the sun went down. Her boys helped, as much as they were able. The three of them would weather the storm.

Until the men came.

They were hungry, those men, desperados in an already desperate world. One young woman and two boys were easy pickings. They came, they killed, and they ate. Then they moved on, maybe west, maybe south, looking for what they needed, not so different from a band of coyotes.

I stoop to pick up the torn rag of red cotton. I see Walter's arm hanging limply at his side as he stands outside a set of iron gates. I hear Oliver pleading for help. *My brother's hurt real bad.*

And I know I have to go back to Femlandia.

A patchwork apron, frayed at the ends of its strings, is still tied loosely around her waist. I hold my breath and pull it up, covering what's left of the woman's face.

Sixty-Nine

In the hallway, I collect Oliver's and Walter's drawings, the last conscious action I make before running out the front door and collapsing on the porch steps, head between my knees. I let the spasms have their way with me and dry heave until my stomach protests. Then I sit, waiting for the cramps to subside, and unfold myself into a sitting position.

Sal told me to eat, but I can't think about food.

Water, though. Water would be welcome.

I unshoulder the pack and let it fall to the step, hoping Sal packed water.

She did. It's there on top, two dented Thermoses that lighten the pack when I take them out. I want all of it, right now, every drop, and it's only extreme willpower that prevents me from taking greedy, thirsty gulps.

Water isn't the only thing Sal packed.

There's a paper wrapper of crusty bread, another of strong-smelling cheese, and one more of chicken. Christ. I can't think about chicken. Not now. I set the paper bundles on the step next to me and feel around the main cavity. My hand finds more paper.

The first letter is a torn sheet from a notebook, the kind with blue lines and a double red margin on the left, something that takes me back to my own childhood when everything was written in longhand. Emma's neat print fills the page.

Mom,

I'm not going to say I'm sorry because I'm not. But I guess I can explain.

It started with those men. Maybe it started with Jason, when he said all those things about it being impossible to get pregnant, but I really think it was the men on the highway. They changed me, but you changed me more.

See, you weren't the one lying there in that ditch. You weren't the one whose clothes were being torn off, who could smell their foul breath, whose face felt drops of their sweat and spit.

But you kicked him anyway. I wish I could tell you what that felt like, to have you come crashing into my party like you were the one in the ditch with the torn clothes and the bad breath in your face and the spit and sweat in your eyes. It felt like a robbery, Mom. Like you were taking what belonged to me.

And then you did it again. You tried to tell me how I should feel and how I should act. There's a term for that, for people who pretend like they know how a person feels, but I don't know what to call it. So I'll just say it's not fair.

Mother Win and Mother Jen said the women who came to this place came here because they were damaged. I don't think I could have understood that before the day it happened to me. And I don't think you'll ever be able to understand it.

I don't hate you. But right now, I need to be with people like me. Mother Jen says it's for the best.

Emma

Mother Win. Mother Jen. Motherfuckers.

They've stolen my own baby from me.

When Emma was young, I made the mistake of reading a book I should have left on the shelf. A slice of history, Nick called it. And it was all of that. Several histories, an anthology of cults. For almost a year I sat up at night, shivering even in the summer heat, wondering if my daughter would ever fall prey to the kind of monsters I'd read about.

They were all men, those monsters. There was Reverend Jones and his Guyana nightmare, Koresh and his Branch Davidians — whatever that stood for. There was Manson and Applewhite and Jeffs, all peddling their own brand of utopia. I kept Emma at home as much as possible after I read that book, always making sure to reach the school pickup line early, always watching her as she walked through the double doors into safety. And I was always, always, looking for men who didn't seem to belong.

It never crossed my mind that the pathology of narcissism, the preoccupation with fantasies of savior status, could dwell just as easily in women.

The second letter is from Sal, and it confirms my fears.

> Dear Miranda,
>
> You may think you know the situation here. I need to tell you how much worse it is than you think.
>
> For almost as long as I've been in Femlandia, I've been living in a culture of terror. And I'm not the only one.

The gates and the fences and the security — they serve more than one purpose. Yes, they keep the unwanted out. They also keep us from leaving. This is a one-way system, Miranda. You need to know that. You need to know that only two people control the system. I suspect you can guess who they are.

I had a chance to leave with Ingrid, years ago. Believe me, I wanted to go. I thought if I stayed, I could make things better here. I was wrong.

I'll leave Kate out of this for now, as I believe she is as much a victim as the others. Everything starts and ends with your mother and Jen Jones. Everything. They created the rules. They created the breaking down and the building up of psyches through a kind of pseudo-therapy I can only call monstrous and ill guided. The women who came to Femlandia came with wounds. Instead of healing those wounds, Jen and Win applied salt. They keep them raw and burning, and they allow no room for questions. Your daughter is their current project.

You are not the only woman to have spent a month in isolation. If Femlandia continues along its dark path, you will not be the last.

Come tonight, late. I've given you everything I can offer, and I'll be there to help. I'll also make sure Jen comes alone after you pull the bell.

I hope one day you can forgive me,

Sal

I read the letter twice and feel my heart sinking. Sal's forgotten what I am, what I've become: a housewife with a part-time job. An erstwhile part-time job. I'm not fucking Rambo. Not by a long stretch. But I'm supposed to show up at the gates of Femlandia at midnight. And I'm supposed to take it down.

A fluttering sound to my left makes me jump. It's only a single chicken, a leftover from the recent raid, clucking contentedly and scouring the earth for sustenance. Chickens, in laying season, produce an egg a day. I could survive on eggs. And farms like this one will have root cellars, dark and cool places where last year's harvest has been processed and put up, where potatoes are ready to plant. There will be a generator, a store of oil, homemade candles for light and hand-chopped wood for winter fires.

After all these weeks, I've finally found my

farm. What the hell, I can do it. I can self-partner, like all those celebrities do. Although my best guess is that self-partnering celebrities don't have five acres of land to plow and till.

Oliver's and Walter's drawings end the fantasy. As much as I cleaned and scrubbed, as long as I worked ridding the parlor and kitchen of the violence that happened here, I would never be able to erase those drawings. I would see them in my sleep and I would see them in the scars of dirt the last chicken makes on her daily foraging rounds. I would see them on the backs of my eyelids, like permanent tattoos.

I would hate myself every time I saw them.

I shift the backpack between my legs, ready to repack it. A dull clunk sounds as it hits the wood of the porch steps. I could swear I emptied it. Water. Lunch. Letters. Nothing else. Until I unzip the outer compartment and plunge one hand inside.

Sal packed more than she let on.

She packed Nick's gun.

SEVENTY

With nearly twelve hours to wait until my rendezvous with Sal, I fill the time in the only way that makes sense. My first stop is the barn, and the single tool I'm looking for is there, hanging between two hammered-in pegs on the wall. Its metal edge is straight and sharp, cleaned after its last use. Nearby, I find a pair of gloves. They aren't essential, but the work I have ahead of me may take all day, perhaps into the evening.

I start digging her grave around back, close enough to an old apple tree to lend some shade, far enough away to avoid its roots. Within thirty minutes, I've stripped down to a tank top and rolled-up camp pants, but the work is good. Cathartic, in some way. I don't remember ever doing real work before. That was Nick's job.

By seven in the evening, I've unearthed a hole three feet deep and barely long and wide enough for her body. Leaning on the spade, I contemplate my work. It isn't deep enough, not nearly deep enough, but I'll build a cairn of sorts, some fortress of rocks to frustrate whatever nocturnal predators might come along, attracted by the scent.

When I step into the kitchen, I realize the hardest work is yet to come.

She's been here for weeks, maybe five, maybe more than that. Long enough, at any rate, for the insect and maggot activity to have subsided. I saw an animal at the zoo once, a forgotten little creature who had become trapped in a maintenance shed. One of the handlers estimated he'd been there a few weeks. Thank the gods I found Ms. Morris later than I found that ferret.

Once I find a comforter from the upstairs bedroom, it takes a strength I didn't know I had in me to pull her body from the kitchen, out the back door, and past what I suppose might have been a healthy kitchen garden not very long ago. It takes more strength to roll her into the grave, and still more to cover her with loose earth. By the time I find and pile a few dozen rocks, my bones are crying in pain.

It's the most difficult thing I've ever done, and if I were thinking straight, I'd know that something far more taxing is about to come.

Seventy-One

A waning gibbous moon hangs in the night sky while I wait outside the gates that will take me back inside Femlandia. It's just enough light to make out the glint of the double Xs decorating an otherwise nondescript metal barrier. In other words, too much light.

My watch is now the kind that's right only twice a day — I don't know when the battery failed — but I know I've been in the dark for at least two hours. In mid-August, that means it's ten o'clock.

So I wait. While I wait, I huddle low to the ground and walk through everything I know. This doesn't take two hours; it takes two minutes. Because I don't know how I'm supposed to reverse a quarter century of conditioning, not with a half-assed bachelor's in anthropology. Win once called it an M.R.S. degree with a minor in manicures. Hell, maybe my mother was right.

I saw things, though, over the years at the zoo. I saw a gang of chimpanzees kill one of their kind, and I saw them stockpile ammunition to hurl at humans. But that wasn't all. I saw Bunny share his rewards with one of the young bonobos. I saw three female chimps drown in a moat trying to save a young female who had fallen. I saw the essence of fairness and the most primitive type of relationship repair after a fight.

I saw complexity in beings that are thought to be far less complex than we are, and I think maybe there's some hope for us after all.

When the moon has moved through a narrow section of sky and hidden its face behind a tree, I face the gates, once more thinking of Bluebeard, that old devil who killed his wives and locked them up.

Pull bell?

Yes.

It rings its midnight song, and I wait.

But not for long.

I hear Sal's voice first, calming and convincing. "It could be another woman in trouble, Jen. Someone else who found us. Someone who needs us."

"Oh, all right," Jen says. Little in her voice matches her words.

My left hand, buried in the pocket of my

trousers, wraps itself around the butt of Nick's gun. The metal, cold at first, begins to warm as I start to slide the weapon out.

I don't have killing in mind. I've seen enough of that, and I've done more than my share. Mutiny is what I'm after, a modern Christian-versus-Bligh game of wills. All I need to do is force Jen Jones out, exile her, and start over again.

She stops short when she sees me, a half smile on her lips. "You're not coming back in here, Miranda. Sorry." But the smile fades when she notices the glint of metal, shining in the light of the moon. Jen turns, a second too late. Sal, taller and broader than Jen, has already taken hold of the woman by an arm, wrestling her closer to the gate that divides us.

My hand trembles, maybe from the weight of the gun, more likely from terror and fatigue, but I hold my target in sight.

Jen calls out. "Kate! Kate!" She reaches forward with her free hand toward the inside bell.

And then everything I don't want to happen starts happening.

SEVENTY-TWO

It's too fast, too much of a jumble of sights and sounds to process. First Win comes flying through the inner gate, followed by Kate and Emma. Sal releases her hold on Jen and darts backward to lock the door, trapping them all, leaving no outlet, before opening the outer gate and allowing me in. There's a click, and bright lights flood the area. Filtered through the leaves overhead, they make hellish patterns around me, as if the ground were on fire. My mother plants herself in front of Jen, in between us. She seems somehow younger and more agile than her sixty-some years should allow. There's no pleading and no tears, nothing more than a look of utter disgust on her face. No, not even that. It's more a weary disappointment.

I think back to Emma's letter and her words.

I don't think you'll ever be able to understand it.

Maybe not. Probably not. But how much does my own mother not understand?

"Those boys," I say. "Those boys tried to save their mother. Those goddamned little boys went against three grown men."

"They'll grow into the same thing," Win says. "It's in their nature. They can't help it."

"Is that what you're preaching, Mom? Really?"

"It's a fact. Look at your own husband."

And I do. I picture Nick, not the strongest soul I've known, and in the end far weaker than I ever could have predicted. The world went to shit and what did Nick do? He abandoned us. But I can't think of him as evil, and I can't believe his actions had anything at all to do with an arrangement of chromosomes. Nick was just Nick, a mix of the good and the imperfect, rather like all of us.

I can't do this. I can't hold my own mother at gunpoint, no matter what she's done. Slowly, I lower the weapon.

Kate, it seems, has other plans.

It would be comical under other circumstances. Kate wresting the gun from my hand with the same ease a mother might snatch a sharp knife from a child. Emma running to throw her arms around Win, shielding her with her own slim body. Jen glaring at me and then charging forward, fists raised in fury. A hundred faces peering through the inner gates at the showdown, waiting to see how this five-character tragedy will play out.

Something tells me it won't end well.

SEVENTY-THREE

Kate's breakdown happens the way I imagine a heart attack might happen, preceded by the most subtle of last-minute warnings, a confused terror, and a sudden realization that all is about to be irrevocably lost. She's no longer the tower of strength she was on that first day. Physically, yes, she's the same, but her eyes dart and flicker with a certain kind of madness as she keeps the gun trained on first Win, then Jen, then Win.

Emma stands, lost, in the middle of all of it, but I'm not sure Kate registers this. I don't believe she can see clearly through the veil of tears clouding her eyes.

"Kate," I say, my voice unsteady. "Please don't. Please. Give me the gun." I manage one, two, then three steps forward, and stop the instant Kate's trigger finger begins to curl. How many more foot-pounds of pressure can that trigger take? Surely not many. Surely not any more than it already bears.

"Kate. Please."

"Did they tell you?" she says. "Did they tell you how many times they brought me to the edge? How many hours they spent working me over and breaking me down before they fixed me the way they wanted to? Did they tell you any of that?"

I can't find my voice, so I answer with nothing more than a slow shake of the head.

She seems to be talking to someone else, not to me.

"They did it. Both of them." As she speaks, the barrel of Nick's gun sways a few inches to the right, then to the left. With each arc, it briefly captures Emma in its deadly sights.

I saw what this gun did to the man on the highway. What it did — what I did — to Mr. Howard Joseph Tebbetts of Vienna, Virginia.

So I know.

Now Kate's tears fall freely. "They're doing it to her," she says, gesturing at Emma with the weapon. "They've done it to all of us. You come here with a problem, and they don't solve that problem. They pick at it, like worrying a wound. They pick and pick and pick until it's infected, and then they open it up and drown it with acid so it burns, so the only cure is more hate. If they see you getting better, getting on your feet, they open that wound up again, all the way. No one gets well here."

"That isn't true!" Win cries. "She's unstable."

Kate keeps the gun trained on my mother, but when she speaks next, it isn't to Win. It's to Sal, to Nell, to Emma. To all the women crowding the inner gate. "Nell? How many times did they remind you of that shithead ex-husband of yours while you were pregnant?" She doesn't wait for an answer. "Luca? What did Jen tell you when the ultrasound showed twins? Or maybe I should ask what she showed you."

Luca's head dips low, chin almost to her chest. Beside her, Nell has gone the color of bleached cotton, and one of the other women lets out a low, choked sob.

"They took pictures when we arrived," Kate says to me. "Some physical, some were psych evaluations, pictures of the nonphysical damage. You want to hear about your mother's brand of therapy, her brand of healing? Go on. Ask her. Ask any of them. Ask them about the days and weeks we spent in isolation until we told them what they wanted to hear."

A murmur ripples through the group of women, the sort of tentative sound you might hear as an orchestra pauses before it builds to a final crescendo. Still, Kate is the only one who speaks.

"A man — some man — some husband or father or uncle made us victims." She looks around at the others, eyes landing quickly on the women behind the locked gate before returning their aim to Win. "Anyone can do that. But it takes a special kind of talent to keep us victims. They fed off of us, see? They fed off of our pain, and they fed it back to us and they poisoned us. They poisoned me."

Emma screams, a deep and dark feral sound, and presses her body against her grandmother once more. She spreads her arms, making herself larger. "They didn't. They helped you. They're helping me."

"You silly girl," Kate says. The words come out like a sigh, soft and sympathetic. "Move away from her."

"No."

"Please."

Emma stands silent and shakes her head. The gun in Kate's hand wavers and begins to shake.

"Emma," I say quietly. "Come away. Please come away." I want to tell her we'll work something out, we'll talk and cry and hug. We'll fix everything that's broken. The only thing I see broken is my daughter, split apart by a bullet. I lunge forward, only to feel two strong hands on my arms holding me back.

"Don't, Miranda," Sal says. "Don't make this worse."

"She's my daughter," I say. "My baby."

Kate goes still now, a tall statue alone in the little clearing. "I've done things I'll never be able to undo. To those children." She looks straight at me as she speaks. "They're only children. Some of them are so small. Emma, you need to move away." Her tears shine in the moonlight, silvery tracks on her cheeks as her voice trails off.

I think about the other night, about the plaintive wails of what I thought were animals.

Emma still refuses to let go, and Kate does the most peculiar thing.

She twists her hand so slowly I can count each frame of motion as if it were disconnected. The barrel of Nick's gun pointing at Win. The barrel turned to one side. Kate's muscled and tattooed arm folded at the elbow. A quiet mumbling before the shine of silvery steel slipped between her lips.

And finally, the still shot I know I'll never be able to unsee, accompanied by the deafening report in the night, the punctuation of one last sentence.

"I'm so sorry," is what she had said.

Then she said no more.

Seventy-Four

Rachael came to Win on a late summer evening one week after her baby was delivered and pronounced stillborn. She was in pieces, understandably, when she arrived, but after an hour Win had succeeded in calming her.

"He was breathing when I saw him," Rachael said, spitting her words, each sound coming in an explosion of rage and confusion. "He was breathing. Sal took him away and he was still breathing!"

"Have a cup of tea, dear," Win said, for the moment steering away from the topic at hand. "Everything's better with a cup of tea." Win could have offered the drink iced, or she could have poured lemonade. But no. Hot tea, boiling hot, was the right choice, even for an August night.

You had to calculate these things, gauge their effect, engineer the desired trigger for each custom target.

For Rachael, that trigger was heat.

Win watched the woman's face, the puckered flesh that ran from just below Rachael's left eye along the line of her cheek and jaw. She watched it twitch with a memory as she offered the steaming cup, keeping the handle away from Rachael, making her touch the hot porcelain with her bare hand.

"Do you remember what he did to you?" Win asked.

The twitch intensified, and the entire left side of Rachael's once pretty face, a face that should have been as unlined and unmarred as all twenty-year-old faces deserve to be, seemed as if it were now playing host to legions of subcutaneous, restless parasites. The skin rippled and squirmed. Rachael was remembering.

And Win thought this was good. A step in the right direction.

The remembering caused them pain, and Win would have given much of herself to take away the pain, or to bear a portion of it — the whole of it, even — if transferring the women's burdens onto her own shoulders would help.

"Good and hot," Win said, as Rachael sipped the tea. "But not as hot as the iron he held to you. No. Not as hot as that."

Rachael screwed her face into a grimace,

and Win kept silent, distant. In another minute, after another series of well-placed words, after only one or two more precisely articulated triggers, the tears would come. Rachael would break, and Win would put her back together. She had seen the process of tearing apart and of reconstructing when Jen worked with Kate.

"You'll have a daughter soon," Win said, now holding the shuddering woman in her arms, stroking her hair, occasionally allowing a finger to stray over the scarred skin of Rachael's cheek. Just a bit more reinforcement. "And your daughter will be safe, won't she?" She didn't wait for a response. At this point, Rachael was too fucked-up to respond. But the woman was receptive. Win continued. "She'll be beautiful, like you are, won't she? Safe and beautiful and free." With her free hand, Win grasped the woman's chin and gently tipped her head up and down.

"Okay."

"Because we know it's for the best," Win coaxed.

This time, Rachael nodded on her own.

"You need to say it, dear."

"It's all for the best."

Win nodded. "Once more."

Rachael choked down a final sob. "It's all

for the best."

"That's a good girl. Now, here's what I want you to do. Think of it as a favor to me."

Rachael's eyes widened with their question.

"I want you to go home and lie down. Close your eyes. And keep saying those words. Say them until you sleep. If you find your mind wandering — and our minds do wander, dear — I want to you put your hand to your face. Like this." Carefully, oh so carefully, Win took hold of Rachael's left hand and placed it on the puckered skin. At first, Rachael resisted, but Win added a slight pressure, keeping the contact.

"What about my boy?" Rachael asked. "What did Sal do to him?"

These questions did not surprise Win. She knew that eventually the other women would ask the same. Curiosity was a natural part of the human makeup, inevitable. They would ask if they could visit, if they could have them back, if they might be allowed a last look. When this happened, Win would need to start the process over from the beginning. Only when the questions stopped would she let the women go.

Rachael, all things considered, had been easy. Win told Jen of the meeting when they retired to bed later that evening, and Jen smiled.

The two of them had become good at their job. After all, they had practiced and perfected the process on Kate quite a few years ago.

Seventy-Five

Behind the inner gate, a hundred faces go wide-eyed and wide-mouthed as Kate's body falls to the earth. It isn't difficult to understand their shock. This was Kate, not the soft-spoken Luca or the sparrowlike Nell, but Kate. Kate, who would kick ass in a swimming race, who would walk around the grounds with a confident swagger, bare-breasted, head held high. The woman lying on the dry, cracked soil with half of her head gone was supposed to be the invincible one.

No more.

Someone lets out a scream of rage. Someone — I can't tell who — raises her fists to the iron bars and wails, actually wails, with all the stridence and fury of a siren. Little Maya, nestled in Luca's arms, extends her small hands through the gate toward Kate's still body.

In the lull, which may only be a matter of seconds but seems to stretch to hours, I think of Jonestown again, of the people who, once the veil of blindness was lifted from their eyes, wanted to leave with that congressman. I think of the shootings and the poisonings and the rantings of their leader, of the Reverend Jim Jones as he convinced more than nine hundred men and women to embrace the glory of death. It was, I remember, an unparalleled human disaster.

Of course, it wasn't much of a choice, not with armed guards standing ready to dispatch anyone who might be having second thoughts about drinking the Kool-Aid or the Flavor-Aid or whatever the delivery mechanism of death really was.

My eyes follow the arc of Kate's arm, the trajectory of the single gun as its recoil forced it away from her. There's only one weapon here, not enough to do large-scale damage. Or maybe it is. Maybe it's already done its horrid little job.

We all move at once. Jen, Win, Sal, and me. We forget about Kate and have only a single focus. There's nothing feminine about us anymore, nothing human. Jen's kaftan is no longer pristine white, but smudged with haphazard patterns of brown and red and gray, like badly painted camouflage. My mother's face, already worried with age, is a grimace, her skin pulled tight enough over her bones to show the skull underneath. My own hands seem to be detached from my body. They've turned into claws.

Sal reaches the gun before any of us, picks it up, contemplates its heft. And then, the strangest thing happens.

One of the women behind the inner gate draws in her breath sharply. She points to a spot beyond our struggling, panting group. The gun momentarily forgotten, we all turn toward the outer gate.

Five pairs of eyes, yellow, almost glowing, peer in from the darkness of the road. They seem to float, detached from the bodies that contain them. At once, they begin to chatter and sing.

Emma draws in a sharp breath and now everyone is fixed on the pack of coyotes, just as the pack fixes its stare on us. We stay this way for a long time, studying one another, and I wonder which of us is civilized and which is wild.

At last, perhaps out of boredom, perhaps out of disgust, the coyotes turn from the gate in a graceful choreographed movement. And they walk on.

Seventy-Six

The hush ends with two words.

"Shoot them."

It's Nell's voice, and hers is quickly joined by the voices of others, first Luca, then Maria, then Rachael. The words, commingled and muddy at first, synchronize and become a rhythmic chant.

shoot them shoot them shoot them shoot them shoot them

Sal stands with the gun cocked and raised to a ready position.

Every child has a moment when they hate their parents. Emma has had her moment, and I've had mine. They often pass, maybe after days, maybe after years. What I feel toward Win right now will not pass. It's a hatred that has penetrated to my bones, buried itself in the marrow and reproduced, spread out through my body. A part of me, maybe all of me, says I don't care whether Win Somers lives or dies.

But Emma's words still ring in my ears.

I don't think I could have understood that before the day it happened to me.

And my mother's:

You're the kind of woman who thinks that because a pile of shit didn't fall on you, there was no pile of shit.

"Sal," I say, finding a resonance and a steadiness in my voice. "Sal, don't do it."

"Then what? Keep them here? Let them plan and plot and conspire until they turn it around on us and we all end up like we were before?"

"We'll give the boys back!" Jen cries. "All of them. They can go back and live with you." She looks questioningly at Win, who nods.

Sal keeps her sights on Win but throws her own voice over her shoulder toward the women crowding the gate. "Do you hear that? They'll *give* your sons back? Isn't that nice? Rachael, how long has it been since you've seen your boy? Fourteen years?" She laughs, almost cackles, and the muscles in her wrist tense as she applies more pressure to the trigger. "Fourteen years too late, ladies."

At once, the image of two boys, older boys, squatting and staring at me with wide, frightened eyes, becomes clear.

They don't talk, Oliver said. *It's like no one's ever taught 'em about sounds.*

My veins turn to ice. Fourteen years old without language is a long time, an eternity. Even if Rachael were reunited with her son now, I can't see it being a happy reunion.

And yet.

When I began working with Bunny, they said it was impossible. People with degrees and credentials and a hundred journal articles tucked under their belts laughed at me. People who knew about critical periods and feral children laughed at me. But I pressed on. I wrote the grant proposals and I worked my ass off, and eventually, Bunny proved I wasn't the lunatic they all thought I was.

The chanting continues. I interrupt it with a raised hand, a sign.

"They can stay," I say. "We have to let them stay." I'm one voice out of dozens. The others drown me out.

shoot them shoot them shoot them shoot them shoot them

Unlike Kate's, Sal's gun hand doesn't waver. The barrel stays true in its aim, pointed at the stronger of the two women. I see the tactic here — she'll take out Jen first, then my mother. There's a sense now that death would be kinder than what I'm about to propose. The coyotes have moved on, but their voices continue to carry a song through the night air. They'll be back. And they'll be hungry.

"Sal," I say, and move quietly toward the outer gate, my hand on the bolt. I peer out into the rough darkness and find nothing. "We aren't killers. Pack them a few days' worth of food and clothing, and let them both go. Maybe they'll make it to another Femlandia. Banish them." The word rings in my head long after I say it.

Outside, a lone coyote sings as if it has heard me.

For a moment that stretches into what feels like hours, the chanting stops. Nell speaks first, followed by another voice, then another. *They'll never make it. Are there still other Femlandias? I thought the last one was in trouble a year ago. It'll take weeks, anyway.* In the end, all speculation dies down and is replaced by a funereal kind of silence.

The decision made, Sal lowers the gun and sends Nell back to the main compound to pack two knapsacks with provisions.

Jen and Win, huddled together, stare at me with wide, frightened eyes. Their answer isn't rehearsed; it can't be. Still, both speak at the same time. A single word: "No."

Maybe it's at this moment, this precise

second, that I understand the depth of their fear and the extent of their love. Maybe it's when Jen reaches forward to an unsuspecting Sal and captures Nick's gun. Maybe it's when the first explosion happens and my mother crumples to the ground, the shot having stopped her heart. Maybe it's when Jen turns the gun on herself, and Sal rushes to knock it away, and the second explosion cracks the night's silence like a hammer through glass, and Jen's body slumps, almost gracefully, landing next to Win's own.

"Oh, Win. Oh, my poor, beautiful darling," Jen whispers in a childish voice as she covers my mother with caresses, her hands moving furiously over the dead woman's skin. She lifts her face, now streaked with dirt and tears, toward me. "I loved her, you know." Her eyes drift away, toward the outer gates, and she looks beyond them into the nothingness of the world. "I couldn't let it happen. Not out there. Not the way it was or the way it is now."

She doesn't plead to stay when Nell returns with the two knapsacks, passing them through the inner gate before locking it again. Jen stands, dusts herself off, and shoulders both of the packs. "Bury her well," she says as she opens the last barrier dividing Femlandia from the world.

"We will," I tell her. No one contradicts me. The women only look out through iron bars. In the quiet, I sense a collective sigh of relief, a hundred and fifty souls being freed.

"One thing I can say about Win is that she tried," Jen says when Sal and I slide the bolt back into its home. "Be careful, Miranda, that what you try doesn't put everything back the way it was."

There are no goodbyes, no final words, only the lonely cry of a coyote in the distance as the women of Femlandia turn, one by one, back to the compound. Once again, I think of Captain Bligh, sent off to sea by his own crew. What we're doing to Jen Jones is no more or less than sentencing her to death. Or perhaps not. Perhaps, like Bligh, she's a survivor.

I don't know, and I can't say I care.

Seventy-Seven

The night they decided, they decided together. It wasn't a one-woman show, but a two-woman show, a meeting of minds and of hearts.

"I don't want to go back," Win said after she and Jen had made love. "I don't ever want us to go back."

"We won't have to. If it comes to that, we have another choice." Jen stood then, leaving Win in the wide double bed, and disappeared for a moment into the main room of the bungalow. When she returned, she was carrying a small cloisonné box. "I brought this back from Mexico," she said. "For us."

Win reached out a hand and took the box, fingering the craftsmanship, running a hand over the colorful enamel.

"Open it," Jen said.

Inside the box was a vial of clear liquid and two syringes. "Fast?"

"Very."

Win closed the box and handed it over. "Put it someplace where it won't be found."

Seventy-Eight

Emma took time to come around, to get over the shock of that life-changing night. I have Sal to thank for that, also Nell and Luca. The women were able to explain better than I ever could what my mother had done, how both she and Jen had worked on the women of Femlandia, breaking them down and putting them back together the way they wanted.

There were burials and there were reunions, grief followed by joy, even if that joy was bittersweet when Rachael understood that her son, Jason, was not quite right.

"He isn't human," she said after the first day. "He stares at me like a wild thing. When I try to dress him, he rips off the clothes and hurls them at me. And if I get too close, he bites." Rachael held out one arm and showed me the marks. The worst, of course, was Jason's habit of masturbating on a schedule. Every morning after breakfast, and every evening after dinner, he would simply reach down and get to business. When Rachael failed to provide him with a receptacle, he would find one on his own. A paper sack. A tea cup. A dustrag.

The other women, Nell, Luca, a younger girl named Tess, have had better luck. Their babies have adapted, started cooing or laughing or babbling, depending on their age. Maya's twin brother, now with a name instead of a number, has said his first word.

As for me, I have a job again, one that keeps me busy during the days and keeps me awake at night.

Emma assists me when she isn't in school. She even persuaded Leila to join our little tribe of teachers. The girls have made up sets of picture cards, but it was Oliver who had the idea of rewards. A grape from the vineyard, a slice of apple or pear when the weather started to turn.

"Like that Russian dude used," Oliver says. "Only this time, it'll be good stuff instead of bad."

I smile at his enthusiasm, but the smile hides my worst fears. Jason, the oldest of the boys, has passed by a window, one that was wide open to him only a few years ago and has now begun to close. It closed without him even knowing, without realizing that window was a one-shot deal, a use-it-or-lose-it opportunity.

"Do you think he'll ever talk?" Oliver asks one day after we've finished our work. "I mean, like me and Walter do."

Oliver's a bright kid, but he's still a kid. Part of me wants to hide the truth from him, let him believe that Jason will turn the corner and begin putting words together into strings that make sense. I remind myself that Oliver has already seen more than any other boy of his age, so I decide to be honest with him. "I don't think so, Ollie."

His throat works, Adam's apple bobbing up and down, as if he's trying to keep a sob in check. "Why not?"

"It's too late," I say. "Think about it like the rooms of a house. When you're young, the doors to the rooms are all wide open. There's a room that makes your eyes work the way they're supposed to, a room that tells your ears how to function, even rooms that help you sing a song at the right pitch or train you to play chess. And there's a language room, too. But you have to visit each of these rooms before the doors close. Jason didn't make it in time."

I tell him we can help, that we can teach Jason sounds and words. I tell him I'll do my best, even though I know Jason's sounds will be strange ones and his words will never connect in the right ways.

This is what haunts my dreams and invades my sleep.

This, and mourning my mother.

Now that I live in a home that was once hers, I feel the ghost of Win. I sense her in each corner. Sometimes, I see her reflection in a mirror and I think back to what she told me, to the horror story of her younger life. Emma's right. I can't understand it. I can only understand the words of the story, but not its sense.

On the nights when sleep comes, it comes because we've reached a kind of equilibrium here, living together as we do. I've no books to offer Leila, but I have stories in my head, stories of Kipling and Steinbeck, of Shakespeare and Sam Shepard. They were men with their own flaws, like all of us, but even flawed, they left us with gifts. I try to pass them on.

Epilogue

Granny Emma died yesterday, and we buried her in the afternoon. No one cried.

Not that we didn't love her — we did. At a hundred and three, Granny Emma was the oldest woman here, and she still knew how to tell a good joke, make us laugh until our bellies ached. Also, she said she was ready.

I asked her once if she minded being old.

"Not a bit," she said, letting Harold and me help her from the bed to the chair and wheel her out into her garden. "Not one bit. I always thought I had my first child too young, but if I hadn't, I guess I never would have known you." She looked at us with narrowed eyes then. "And don't you two be getting any ideas about that. Just because I don't have regrets doesn't mean you're ready to start a family at your age. Got it?"

We said we did.

"I must be the only great-great-grandma in the world now," she said. "Even outlasted my own babies." She looked past us, asked Harold to bring her a rose from the arbor. By the time he got back with a single red flower, she was already dead.

I thought we could have waited a day, and so did my mother, but the Eldermen won the argument in the end. They said August was no time to dicker around with bodies, what with the flies and the humidity and something about not wanting another breakout of hepatitis like we had in 2098. They say it was pretty bad, but I don't know. I was just learning to walk.

I talked to Harold right before the burial.

"You gotta see it their way, Miranda. They've been studying up on this, on diseases and shit. They know."

So we watched a few of the men dig a hole, we made a wreath from roses and herbs, and we put Granny Emma in the ground next to Grandpa Oliver.

After, the men went one way, and the women went another. Everyone had chores.

Granny Emma said it didn't used to be this way; everyone did everything. She and Grandpa Oliver would spend a day in the slaughterhouse, the next day they would weave, and the day after that they might put up applesauce or squash, depending on the season.

"It was pretty goddamned egalitarian," she told me once. "None of that 'women wash the clothes and men mow the lawns' nonsense. If a job needed to get done, you did it. Now . . ." Granny Emma trailed off, collected her thoughts, and decided I was old enough to hear. "Now we're back in a rut. Like it was wired into us. You got a penis, you handle machinery. You don't, you pull weeds." She bent her head close to mine. "Between you and me and the walls, I don't care for it. I liked our way better." She got that faraway look in her eyes again, the one I'd seen many times, usually when a breeze rustled through the woods at the north end of the compound. "Well. I liked some of our ways better."

I asked her what she meant.

"Never you mind, girlie."

And that's the way our conversations would go, every day after I came home from school, sometimes after supper when we'd sit on the bungalow's porch if the weather was kind. She'd talk about the new ways and the old ways and then she'd get that look, that distant look, and sometimes she'd shake her head and start talking about Grandpa Oliver, about what a fine man he turned out to be. About irony.

"Never would've met him if I stayed outside. Not that my dear mother and I had much choice."

Granny Emma told me stories about what happened, how everything fell apart, almost overnight. She said once the crash of '22 made the Great Depression look like nothing. She said people were killing themselves, and the ones who didn't kill themselves either got sick or went crazy, so they ended up dead anyway.

Outside is better now. Stuff works again, and some of us go to the movies in Middleburg on Friday nights. A few families have left, a trickle here and a trickle there. They say the last people to move to Landia came before my mother was born. They didn't stay very long.

Harold wants to leave once we finish up school, but I don't know. There are ties here, long and straggled roots that go back nearly a century. My mother and grandmother are Elderwomen, and I'll be one, too.

The only problem is that the men try to run everything, and they usually get their way. Like with Granny Emma's burial.

So I don't know. Perhaps I will stay, let Harold go out into the world and do his thing, either make that outside place better or screw it up. I could have a baby on my own, if I want. That's what they all did back in the old days. Everybody helped out, arguments were settled without a fight, and the people here seemed happy.

Today I went to see her, my old granny, the oldest woman in Landia until yesterday. I put August roses on her grave and told her about my plans, told her I'd stick around for a while. Maybe find a way to make Landia like it used to be.

ACKNOWLEDGMENTS

I wrote this novel in the same metaphorical closet where most authors do their work. Only after emerging from said closet did all the other people — readers, editors, agents, graphic designers, publicists, booksellers, and so forth — descend on *Femlandia* to work their magic. And magic it is, whether we're talking about agent Laura Bradford, first readers Sophie van Llewyn and Stephanie Hutton, editors Cindy Hwang and Cicely Aspinall, and countless others to whom I owe thanks.

But what about inside the closet? Were there ghostly helpers standing at the ready? Of course there were, and of course I need to thank them, too.

Charlotte Perkins Gilman was sitting in the dark with me, toting a copy of her 1915 feminist utopia *Herland*. (If you think I cut the title *Femlandia* out of whole cloth, you are very much mistaken.) I don't know what

Charlotte would think of my turning her novel on its head and putting a dystopian spin on it, but I like to imagine she would be proud — at least of the macabre ingenuity on my part. So, thank you, Charlotte, for giving me heroes I could morph into villains of the most despicable sort.

Stephen King made a few appearances in between cranking out his own work. I can't say he influenced my writing, because the fact is he's awesome and I'm not. But his voice reminded me to not hold back on the violence, to write for myself and not for anyone else, and to always — if appropriate — insert a reference to that most frightening of folktales, "Bluebeard." Thank you, Mr. King.

And then there were the women, angry and patriarchy hating after having read *Vox*. Their loathing of toxic masculinity was palpable, and I think more than one scribbled misandric death threats on the walls of my closet. (It was dark, so hard to say.) I don't agree with them, but I'm grateful all the same. They wanted something, and I gave them what they wanted. A world without men. A utopia. I thank them for the inspiration.

As always, I remain indebted to my husband, Bruce Dalcher, without whom this world would be a very bleak place indeed.

ABOUT THE AUTHOR

Christina Dalcher earned her doctorate in theoretical linguistics from Georgetown University. She specializes in the phonetics of sound change in Italian and British dialects and has taught at several universities.

Her short stories and flash fiction appear in more than one hundred journals worldwide. Recognition includes the Bath Flash Award short list, nominations for the Pushcart Prize, and multiple other awards. She lives in Norfolk, Virginia, with her husband.

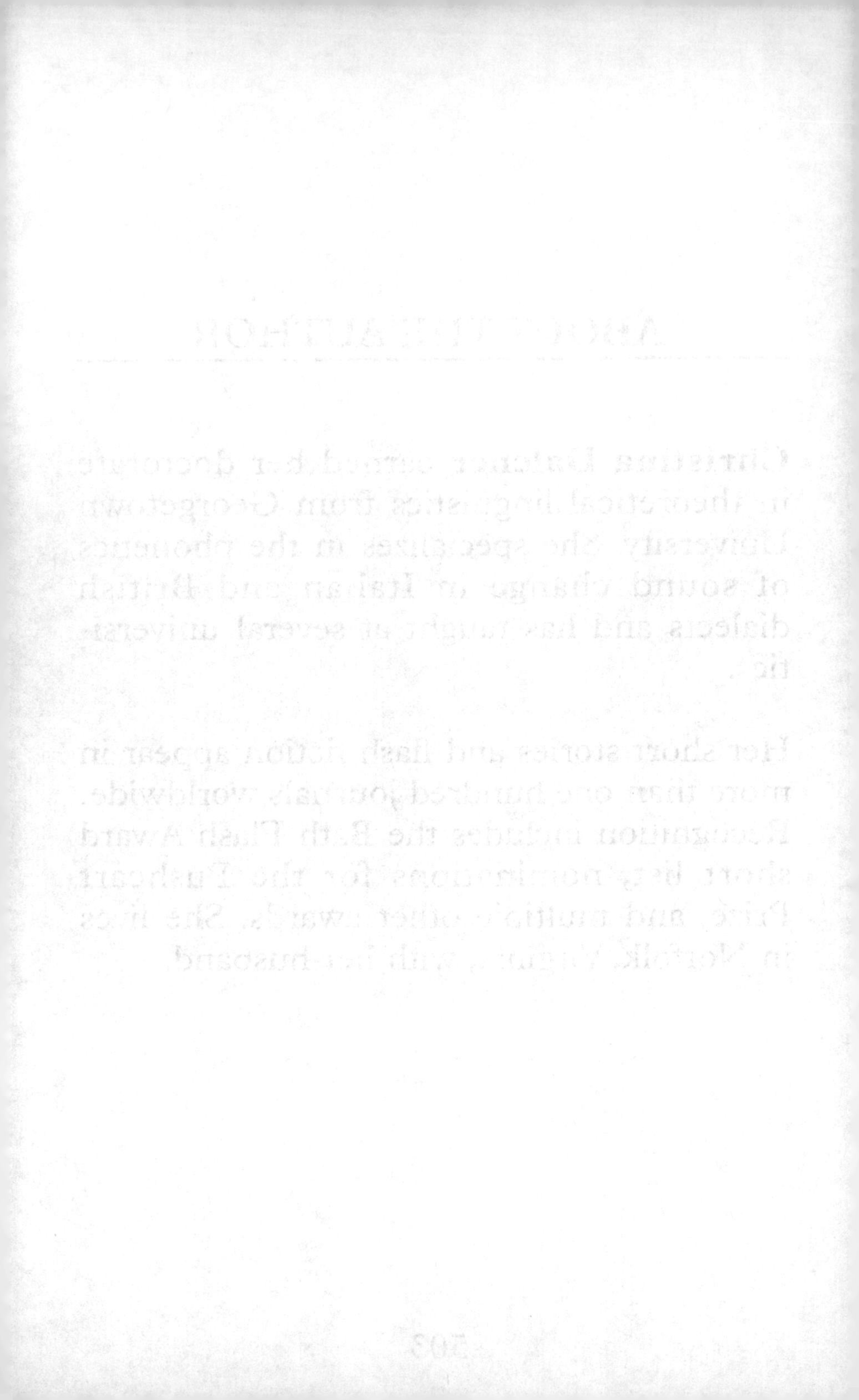

The employees of Thorndike Press hope you have enjoyed this Large Print book. All our Thorndike, Wheeler, and Kennebec Large Print titles are designed for easy reading, and all our books are made to last. Other Thorndike Press Large Print books are available at your library, through selected bookstores, or directly from us.

For information about titles, please call:
(800) 223-1244

or visit our website at:
gale.com/thorndike

To share your comments, please write:
Publisher
Thorndike Press
10 Water St., Suite 310
Waterville, ME 04901